C0-ADX-493

The Philistines

Arlo Bates

LITERATURE HOUSE / GREGG PRESS
Upper Saddle River, N. J.

Republished in 1970 by
LITERATURE HOUSE
an imprint of The Gregg Press
121 Pleasant Avenue
Upper Saddle River, N. J. 07458

Standard Book Number—8398-0154-8
Library of Congress Card—74-104412

Printed in United States of America

THE PHILISTINES.

THE PHILISTINES

BY

ARLO BATES

The web of our life is of a mingled yarn, good and ill together.

All's Well that Ends Well; iv. — 3

BOSTON

TICKNOR AND COMPANY

211 Tremont Street

1889

Electrotyped by
C. J. Peters & Son, Boston,
U. S. A.

DEDICATION.

To my three friends who, by generously acting as amanuenses, have made it possible that the book should be finished, I take pleasure in gratefully dedicating

THE PHILISTINES.

"This is no square temple to the gate of which thou canst arrive precipitately; this is no mosque to which thou canst come with tumult but without knowledge."

Persian Religious Hymn.

CONTENTS.

THE PHILISTINES.

I

IN PLACE AND IN ACCOUNT NOTHING.

1 Henry IV.; v. — 1.

WHEN Arthur Fenton, the most outspoken of all that band of protesting spirits who had been so well known in artistic Boston as the Pagans, married Edith Caldwell, there had been in his mind a purpose, secret but well defined, to turn to his own account his wife's connection with the Philistine art patrons of the town. Miss Caldwell was a niece of Peter Calvin, a wealthy and well-meaning man against whom but two grave charges could be made, — that he supposed the growth of art in this country to depend largely upon his patronage, and that he could never be persuaded not to take himself seriously. Mr. Calvin was regarded by Philistine circles in Boston as a sort of re-incarnation of Apollo, clothed upon with modern enlightenment, and properly arrayed in respectable raiment. Had it been pointed out that to make this theory probable it was necessary to conceive of the god as having undergone mentally much the same metamorphosis as that which had transformed his flowing vestments into trousers, his admirers would have received the remark as highly complimentary to Mr. Peter Calvin. To assume identity between their idol and Apollo would be immensely flattering to the son of Latona.

Fenton understood perfectly the weight and extent of Calvin's influence, yet, in determining to profit by it, he did not in the least deceive himself as to the nature of his own course.

"Honesty," he afterward confessed to his friend Helen Greyson, who scorned him for the admission, "is doubtless a charming thing for digestive purposes, but it is a luxury too expensive for me. The gods in this country bid for shams, and shams I purpose giving them."

So well did he carry out his intention, that in a few years he came to be the fashionable portrait-painter of the town; the artist to whom people went who rated the worth of a picture by the amount they were required to pay for it, and the reputation of the painter in conventional circles; the man to whom a Boston society woman inevitably turned when she wished the likeness of her charms preserved on canvas, and when no foreigner was for the moment in vogue and on hand.

The steps by which Fenton attained to this proud eminence were obvious enough. In the first place, he persuaded Mr. Calvin to sit to him. Mr. Calvin always sat to the portrait painters whom he endorsed. This was a sort of official recognition, and the results, as seen in the needlessly numerous likenesses of the gentleman which adorned his Beacon Hill mansion, would have afforded a cynic some amusement, and not a little food for reflection. Once launched under distinguished patronage, Fenton was clever enough to make his way. He really was able to paint well when he chose, a fact which was, on the whole, of less importance in his artistic career than were the adroitness of his address, and his ready and persuasive sympathy. The qualifications of a fashionable doctor, a fashionable clergyman, and a fashionable portrait-painter are much the same ; it is only in the man-milliner that skill is demanded in addition to the art of pleasing.

As usually happens in such a case, Fenton's old friends avoided him, or found themselves left in the distance by his rapid strides toward fame and fortune. Then such of them as still came in contact with him made his acquaintance in a new character, and learned to accept him as a wholly different man from the one they had supposed themselves to know in the days when he was never weary of pouring forth tirades against the Philistinism he had now embraced. They admired the skill with which he painted stuffs and gowns, but among themselves they agreed that the old-time vigor and sincerity were painfully lacking in his work ; and if they grumbled sometimes at the prices he got, it is only just to believe that it was seldom with any real willingness to pay, in the sacrifice of convictions and ideals, the equivalent which he had given for his popularity.

Fenton was one morning painting, in his luxuriously appointed studio, the portrait of a man who was in the prime of life, and over whom vulgar prosperity had, in forming him, left everywhere her finger marks plainly to be seen. He was tall and robust, with light eyes and blonde whiskers, and a general air of insisting upon his immense superiority to all the world. That he secretly felt some doubts of the perfection of his social knowledge, there were indications in his manner, but on the whole the complacency of a portly bank account overcame all misgivings of this sort. His character might have been easily inferred from the manner in which he now set his broad shoulders expansively back in the armchair in which he was posing, and regarded the artist with a patronizing air of condescending to be wonderfully entertained by his conversation.

"You are the frankest fellow I ever saw," he said, smiling broadly.

"Oh, frank," Fenton responded; "I am too frank. It will be the ruin of me sooner or later. It all comes of being born with a habit of being too honest with myself."

"Honesty with yourself is generally held up as a cardinal virtue."

"Nonsense. A man is a fool who is too frank with himself; he is always sure to end by being too frank with everybody else, just from mere habit."

Mr. Irons smiled more broadly still. He by no means followed all Fenton's vagaries of thought, but they tickled his mental cuticle agreeably. The artist had the name of being a clever talker, and with such a listener this was more than half the battle. The men who can distinguish the real quality of talk are few and far to seek; most people receive what is said as wit and wisdom, or the reverse, simply because they are assured it is the one or the other; and Alfred Irons was of the majority in this.

Fenton painted in silence a moment, inwardly possessed of a desire to caricature, or even to paint in all its ugliness, the vulgar mouth upon which he was working. The desire, however, was not sufficiently strong to restrain him from the judicious flattery of cleverly softening and refining the coarse lips, and he was conscious of a faint amusement at the incongruity between his thought and his action.

"And there is the added disadvantage," he continued the conversation as he glanced up and saw that his sitter's face was quickly, in the silence, falling into a heavy repose, "that frankness begets frankness. My sitters are always telling me things which I do not want to know, just because I am so beastly outspoken and sympathetic."

"You must have an excellent chance to get pointers," responded the sitter, his pale eyes kindling with animation. "You've painted two or three men this winter that could have put you up to a good thing."

"That isn't the sort of line chat takes in a studio," Fenton returned, with a slight shrug. "It isn't business that men talk in a studio. That would be too incongruous."

Irons sneered and laughed, with an air of consequence and superiority.

"I don't suppose many of you artist fellows would make much of a fist at business," he observed.

"Modern business," laughed the other, amused by his own epigram, "is chiefly the art of transposing one's debts. The thing to learn is how to pass the burden of your obligations from one man's shoulders to those of another often enough so that nobody who has them gets tired out, and drops them with a crash."

His sitter grinned appreciatively.

"And they don't tell you how to do this?"

"Oh, no. The things my sitters tell me about are of a very different sort. They make to me confidences they want to get rid of; things you'd rather not hear. Heavens! I have all I can do to keep some men from treating me like a priest and confessing all their sins to me."

Mr. Irons regarded the artist closely, with a curious narrowing of the eyes.

"That must give you a hold over a good many of them," he said. "I shall be careful what I say."

Fenton laughed, with a delightful sense of superiority. It amused him that his sitter should be betraying his nature at the very moment when he fancied himself particularly on his guard.

"You certainly have no crimes on your conscience that interfere with your digestion," was his reply; "but in any case, you may make yourself easy; I am not a blackmailer by profession."

"Oh, I didn't mean that," Mr. Irons answered, easily; "only of course you are a man who has his living to make. Every painter has to depend on his wits, and when you come in contact with men of another class professionally it would be natural enough to suppose you would take advantage of it."

The "lady's finger" in Fenton's cheek stood out white amid the sudden red, and his eyes flashed.

"Of course a sitter," he said in an even voice, which had somehow lost all its smooth sweetness, "is in a manner my guest, and the fact that his class was not up to mine, or that he wasn't a gentleman even, wouldn't excuse my taking advantage of him."

The other flushed in his turn. He felt the

keenness of the retort, but he was not dexterous enough to parry it, and he took refuge in coarse bullying.

"Come, now, Fenton," he cried with a short, explosive laugh, "you talk like a gentleman."

But the artist, knowing himself to have the better of the other, and not unmindful, moreover, of the fact that to offend Alfred Irons might mean a serious loss to his own pocket, declined to take offence.

"Of course," he answered lightly, and with the air of one who appreciates an intended jest so subtile that only cleverness would have comprehended it, "that is one of the advantages I have always found in being one. I think I needn't keep you tied down to that chair any longer to-day. Come here and see how you think we are getting on."

And the sitter forgot quickly that he had been on the very verge of a quarrel.

II

SOME SPEECH OF MARRIAGE.

Measure for Measure; v.—I.

WHEN dinner was announced that night, Mrs. Arthur Fenton had not appeared, but presently she came into the room with that guilty and anxious look which marks the consciousness of social misdemeanors. She was dressed in a gown of warm primrose plush, softened by draperies of silver-gray net. It was a costume which her husband had designed for her, and which set off beautifully her brown hair and creamy white skin.

"I hope I have not kept you waiting long," she said, "but I wanted to dress for Mrs. Frostwinch's before dinner, and I was late about getting home."

There was a certain wistfulness in her manner which betrayed her anxiety lest he should be vexed at the trifling delay. Arthur Fenton was too well bred to be often openly unkind to anybody, but none the less was his wife afraid of his displeasure. He was one of those men who have the power of making their disapproval felt from the simple fact that they feel it so strongly themselves. The most oppressive of domestic tyrants are by no means those who vent their ill-nature in open words.

The man who strenuously insists to himself upon his will, and cherishes in silence his dislike of whatever is contrary to it, is oftener a harder man to live with than one who is violently outspoken. Fenton was hardly conscious of the absolute despotism with which he ruled his home, but his wife was too susceptible to his moods not to feel keenly the unspoken protest with which he met any infringement upon his wishes or his pleasure. To-night he was in good humor, and his sense of beauty was touched by the loveliness of her appearance.

"Oh, it is no matter," he answered lightly. "How stunning you look. That topaz," he continued, walking toward her, and laying his finger upon the single jewel she wore fastened at the edge of the square-cut corsage of her gown, "is exactly right. It is so deep in color that it gives the one touch you need. It was uncommonly nice of your Uncle Peter to give it to you."

"And of you to design a dress to set it off," returned she, smiling with pleasure. "I am glad you like me in it."

"You are stunning," her husband repeated, kissing her with a faint shade of patronage in his manner. "Now come on before the dinner is as cold as a stone. A cold dinner is like a warmed-over love affair ; you accept it from a sense of duty, but there is no enjoyment in it."

Mrs. Fenton smiled, more from pleasure at his

evident good nature than from any especial amusement, and they went together into the pretty dining-room.

Fenton acknowledged himself fond of the refinements of life, and his sensitive, sensuous nature lost none of the delights of a well-appointed home. He lived in a quiet and elegant luxury which would have been beyond the attainment of most artists, and which indeed not infrequently taxed his resources to the utmost.

The table at which the pair sat down was laid with exquisite damask and china, the dinner admirable and well served. The dishes came in hot, the maid was deft and comely in appearance, and the master of the house, who always kept watch, in a sort of involuntary self-consciousness, of all that went on about him, was pleasantly aware that the most fastidious of his friends could have found nothing amiss in the appointment or the service of his table. How much the perfect arrangement of domestic affairs demanded from his wife, Fenton found it more easy and comfortable not to inquire, but he at least appreciated the results of her management. He never came to accept the smallest trifles of life without emotion. His pleasure or annoyance depended upon minute details, and things which people in general passed without notice were to him the most important facts of daily life. The responsibility for the comfort of so highly organized a creature, Edith had found to be anything but a light burden. Only a wife could have appreciated the pleasure she had in having the most delicate shades in her domestic management noted and enjoyed ; or the discomfort which arose from the same source. It was delightful to have her husband pleased by the smallest pains she took for his comfort ; to know that his eye never failed to discover the little refinements of dress or cookery or household adornment ; but wearing was the burden of understanding, too, that no flaw was too small to escape his sight. Mrs. Fenton's friends rallied her upon being a slave to her housekeeping ; few of them were astute enough to understand that, kind as was always his manner toward her, she was instead the slave of her husband.

The room in which they were dining was one in which the artist took especial pleasure. He had panelled it with stamped leather, which he had picked up somewhere in Spain ; while the ceiling was covered with a novel and artistic arrangement of gilded matting. Among Edith's wedding gifts had been some exquisite jars of Moorish pottery, and these, with a few pieces of Algerian armor, were the only ornaments which the artist had admitted to the room. The simplicity and richness of the whole made an admirable setting for the dinner table, and as the host when he entertained was willing to take the trouble of overlooking his wife's arrangements, the Fentons' dinner parties were among the most picturesquely effective in Boston.

"I have two big pieces of news for you," Mrs. Fenton said, when the soup had been removed. "I have been to call on Mrs. Stewart Hubbard this afternoon, and Mr. Hubbard is going to have you paint him. Isn't that good?"

Her husband looked up in evident pleasure.

"That isn't so bad," was his reply. "He'll make a stunning picture, and the Hubbards are precisely the sort of people one likes to have dealings with. Is he going at it soon?"

"He is coming to see you to-morrow, Mrs. Hubbard said. The picture is to be her birthday present. I told her you were so busy I didn't know when you could begin."

"I would stretch a point to please Mr. Hubbard. I am almost done with Irons, vulgar old cad. I wish I dared paint him as bad as he really looks."

"But your artistic conscience won't let you?" she queried, smiling. "He is a dreadful old creature; but he means well."

"People who mean well are always worse than those who don't mean anything; but I can make it up with Hubbard. He looks like Rubens' St. Simeon. I wish he wore the same sort of clothes."

"You might persuade him to, for the picture.

But my second piece of news is almost as good. Helen is coming home."

"Helen Greyson?"

"Helen Greyson. I had a letter from her to-day, written in Paris. She had already got so far, and she ought to be here very soon."

"How long has she been in Rome?" Fenton asked.

He had suddenly become graver. He had been intimate with Mrs. Greyson, a sculptor of no mean talent, in the days when he had been a fervid opponent of people and of principles with whom he had later joined alliance, and the idea of her return brought up vividly his parting from her, when she had scornfully upbraided him for his apostasy from convictions which he had again and again declared to be dearer to him than life.

"It is six years," Mrs. Fenton answered. "Caldwell was born the March after she went, and he will be six in three weeks. Time goes fast. We are getting to be old people."

Fenton stared at his plate absently, his thoughts busy with the past.

"Has Grant Herman been married six years?" he asked, after a moment.

"Grant Herman? Yes; he was married just before she sailed; but what of it?"

Fenton laid down the fork with which he had been poking the bits of fish about on his plate. He folded his arms on the edge of the table, and regarded his wife.

"It is astonishing, Edith," he observed, "how well one may know a woman and yet be mistaken in her. For six years I have supposed you to be religiously avoiding any allusion to Helen's love for Grant Herman, and it seems you never knew it at all."

It was Mrs. Fenton's turn to look up in surprise.

"What do you mean?" she asked.

Her husband laughed lightly, yet not very joyously.

"Nothing, if you will. Nobody ever told me they were in love with each other, but I am as sure that Helen made Herman marry Ninitta as if I had been on hand to see the operation."

"Made him marry her? Why should he marry her if he didn't want to?"

"Oh, well, I don't know anything about it. I know Ninitta followed Herman to America, for she told me so; and I am sure he had no idea of marrying her when she got here. Anybody can put two and two together, I suppose, especially if you know what infernally Puritanical notions Helen had."

"Puritanical?"

The artist leaned back in his chair and smiled at his wife in his superior and tantalizing fashion.

"She thought she'd outgrown Puritanism," he returned, "but really she was, in her way, as much of a Puritan as you are. The country is full of people who don't understand that the essence of Puritanism is a slavish adherence to what they call principle, and who think because they have got rid of a certain set of dogmas they are free from their theologic heritage. There never was greater rubbish than such an idea."

Mrs. Fenton was silent. She had long ago learned the futility of attempting any argument in ethics with Arthur, and she received in silence whatever flings at her beliefs he chose to indulge in. She had even come hardly to heed words which in the early days of her married life would have wounded her to the quick. She had readjusted her conception of her husband's character, and if she still cherished illusions in regard to him, she no longer believed in the possibility of changing his opinions by opposing them.

Her thoughts were now, moreover, occupied with the personal problem which would in any case have appealed more strongly to the feminine mind than abstract theories, and she was considering what he had told her of Mrs. Greyson and Grant Herman, a sculptor for whom she had a warm admiration, and a no less strong liking.

However we busy ourselves with high aims, with learning, or art, or wisdom, or ethics, personal human interests appeal to us more strongly than anything else. Human emotions respond instinctively and quickly to any hint of the emotional life of others. Nothing more strikingly shows the essential unity of the race than the readiness with which all minds lay aside all concerns and ideas which they are accustomed to consider higher, to give attention to the trifling details of the intimate history of their fellows. Quite unconsciously, Edith had gathered up many facts, insignificant in themselves, concerning the relations of Mrs. Greyson and Herman, and she now found herself suddenly called upon to reconsider whatever conclusions they had led her to in the light of this new development. The sculptor's marriage with an ex-model had always been a mystery to her, and she now endeavored to decide in her mind whether it were possible that her husband could be right in putting the responsibility upon Helen Greyson. The form of his remark seemed to her to hint that the Italian's claim upon Herman had been of so grave a nature as to imply serious complications in their former relations; but she strenuously rejected any suspicion of evil in the sculptor's conduct.

"I am sure, Arthur," she said, hesitatingly, "there can have been nothing wrong between Mr. Herman and Ninitta. I have too much faith in him."

"To put faith in man," was his answer, "is only less foolish than to believe in woman. I didn't, however, mean to imply anything very dreadful. The facts are enough, without speculating on what is nobody's business but theirs. I wonder how he and Helen will get on together, now she is coming home? Mrs. Herman is a jealous little thing, and could easily be roused up to do mischief."

"I do not believe Helen had anything to do with their marriage," Edith said, with conviction. "It was a mistake from the outset."

"Granted. That is what makes it so probable that Helen did it. Grant isn't the man to make a fool of himself without outside pressure, and in the end a sacrifice to principle is always some ridiculous tomfoolery that can't be come at in any other way. However, we shall see what we shall see. What time are you going to Mrs. Frostwinch's?"

"I am going to the Browning Club at Mrs. Gore's first. Will you come?"

"Thank you, no. I have too much respect for Browning to assist at his dismemberment. I'll meet you at Mrs. Frostwinch's about ten."

III

IN WAY OF TASTE.

Troilus and Cressida; iii. — 3.

ONE of the most curious of modern whims in Boston has been the study of the poems of Robert Browning. All at once there sprang up on every hand strange societies called Browning Clubs, and the libraries were ransacked for Browning's works, and for the books of whoever has had the conceit or the hardihood to write about the great poet. Lovely girls at afternoon receptions propounded to each other abstruse conundrums concerning what they were pleased to regard as obscure passages, while little coteries gathered, with airs of supernatural gravity, to read and discuss whatever bore his signature.

A genuine, serious Boston Browning Club is as deliciously droll as any form of entertainment ever devised, provided one's sense of the ludicrous be strong enough to overcome the natural indignation aroused by seeing genuine poetry, the high gift of the gods, thus abused. The clubs meet in richly furnished parlors, of which the chief fault is usually an over-abundance of bric-a-brac. The house of Mrs. Gore, for instance, where

Edith was going this evening, was all that money could make it; and in passing it may be noted that Boston clubs are seldom of constitutions sufficiently vigorous to endure unpleasant surroundings. The fair sex predominates at all these gatherings, and over them hangs an air of expectant solemnity, as if the celebration of some sacred mystery were forward. Conversation is carried on in subdued tones; even the laughter is softened, and when the reader takes his seat, there falls upon the little company a hush so deep as to render distinctly audible the frou-frou of silken folds, and the tinkle of jet fringes, stirred by the swelling of ardent and aspiring bosoms.

The reading is not infrequently a little dull, especially to the uninitiated, and there have not been wanting certain sinister suggestions that now and then, during the monotonous delivery of some of the longer poems, elderly and corpulent devotees listen only with the spiritual ear, the physical sense being obscured by an abstraction not to be distinguished by an ordinary observer from slumber. The reader, however, is bound to assume that all are listening, and if some sleep and others consider their worldly concerns or speculate upon the affairs of their neighbors, it interrupts not at all the steady flow of the reading.

Once this is finished, there is an end also of inattention, for the discussion begins. The central and vital principle of all these clubs is that a poem by Robert Browning is a sort of prize enigma, of which the solution is to be reached rather by wild and daring guessing than by any commonplace process of reasoning. Although to an ordinary and uninspired intellect it may appear perfectly obvious that a lyric means simply and clearly what it says, the true Browningite is better informed. He is deeply aware that if the poet seems to say one thing, this is proof indisputable that another is intended. To take a work in straightforward fashion would at once rob the Browning Club of all excuse for existence, and while parlor chairs are easy, the air warm and perfumed, and it is the fashion for idle minds to concern themselves with that rococo humbug Philistines call culture, societies of this sort must continue.

Once it is agreed that a poem means something not apparent, it is easy to make it mean anything and everything, especially if the discussion, as is usually the case, be interspersed with discursions of which the chief use is to give some clever person or other a chance to say smart things. When all else fails, moreover, the club can always fall back upon allegory. Commentators on the poets have always found much field for ingenious quibbling and sounding speculation in the line of allegory. Let a poem be but considered an allegory, and there is no limit to the changes which may be rung upon it, not even Mrs. Malaprop's banks of the Nile restraining the creature's headstrong ranging. Only a failure of the fancy of the interpreter can afford a check, and as everybody reads fiction nowadays, few people are without a goodly supply of fancies, either original or acquired.

Although Fenton had declined to go to Mrs. Gore's with his wife, he had finished his cigar when the carriage was announced, and decided to accompany her, after all. The parlors were filling when they arrived, and Arthur, who knew how to select good company, managed to secure a seat between Miss Elsie Dimmont, a young and rather gay society girl, and Mrs. Frederick Staggchase, a descendant of an old Boston family, who was called one of the cleverest women of her set.

"Is Mr. Fenwick going to read?" he asked of the latter, glancing about to see who was present.

"Yes," Mrs. Staggchase answered, turning toward him with her distinguished motion of the head and high-bred smile. "Don't you like him?"

"I never had the misfortune to hear him. I know he detests me, but then I fear, that like olives and caviare, I have to be an acquired taste."

"Acquired tastes," she responded, with that air of being amused by herself which always entertained Fenton, "are always the strongest."

"And generally least to a man's credit," he

retorted quickly. "What is he going to inflict upon us ?"

"Really, I don't know. I seldom come to this sort of thing. I don't think it pays."

"Oh, nothing pays, of course," was Fenton's reply, "but it is more or less amusing to see people make fools of themselves."

The president of the club, at this moment, called the assembly to order, and announced that Mr. Fenwick had kindly consented — "Readers always kindly consent," muttered Fenton aside to Mrs. Staggchase — to read, *Bishop Blougram's Apology*, to which they would now listen. There was a rustle of people settling back into their chairs ; the reader brushed a lank black lock from his sallow brow, and with a tone of sepulchral earnestness began :

"'No more wine ? then we'll push back chairs, and talk.'"

For something over an hour, the monotonous voice of the reader went dully on. Fenton drew out his tablets and amused himself and Miss Dimmont by drawing caricatures of the company, ending with a sketch of a handsome old dowager, who went so soundly to sleep that her jaw fell. Over this his companion laughed so heartily that Mrs. Staggchase leaned forward smilingly, and took his tablets away from him ; whereat he produced an envelope from his pocket and was about to begin another sketch, when suddenly, and apparently somewhat to the surprise of the reader, the poem came to an end.

There was a joyful stir. The dowager awoke, and there was a perfunctory clapping of hands when Mr. Fenwick laid down his volume, and people were assured that there was no mistake about his being really quite through. A few murmurs of admiration were heard, and then there was an awful pause, while the president, as usual, waited in the never-fulfilled hope that the discussion would start itself without help on his part.

"How cleverly you do sketch," Miss Dimmont said, under her breath; "but it was horrid of you to make me laugh."

"You are grateful," Fenton returned, in the same tone. "You know I kept you from being bored to death."

"I have a cousin, Miss Wainwright," pursued Miss Dimmont, "whose picture we want you to paint."

"If she is as good a subject as *her* cousin," Fenton answered, "I shall be delighted to do it."

The president had, meantime, got somewhat ponderously upon his feet, half a century of good living not having tended to increase his natural agility, and remarked that the company were, he was sure, extremely grateful to Mr. Fenwick, for his very intelligent interpretation of the poem read.

"Did he interpret it?" Fenton whispered to Mrs. Staggchase. "Why wasn't I told?"

"Hush!" she answered, "I will never let you sit by me again if you do not behave better."

"Sitting isn't my *metier*, you know," he retorted.

The president went on to say that the lines of thought opened by the poem were so various and so wide that they could scarcely hope to explore them all in one evening, but that he was sure there must be many who had thoughts or questions they wished to express, and to start the discussion he would call upon a gentleman whom he had observed taking notes during the reading, Mr. Fenton.

"The old scaramouch!" Fenton muttered, under his breath. "I'll paint his portrait and send it to *Punch*."

Then with perfect coolness he got upon his feet and looked about the parlor.

"I am so seldom able to come to these meetings," he said, "that I am not at all familiar with your methods, and I certainly had no idea of saying anything; I was merely jotting down a few things to think over at home, and not making notes for a speech, as you would see if you examined the paper."

At this point Miss Dimmont gave a cough which had a sound strangely like a laugh strangled at its birth.

"The poem is one so subtile," Fenton continued, unmoved; "it is so clever in its knowledge of human nature, that I always have to take a certain time after reading it to get myself out of the mood of merely admiring its technique, before I can think of it critically at all. Of course the bit about 'an artist whose religion is his art' touches me keenly, for I have long held to the heresy that art is the highest thing in the world, and, as a matter of fact, the only thing one can depend upon. The clever sophistry of Bishop Blougram shows well enough how one can juggle with theology; and, after all, theology is chiefly some one man's insistence that everybody else shall make the same mistakes that he does."

Fenton felt that he was not taking the right direction in his talk, and that in his anxiety to extricate himself from a slight awkwardness he was rapidly getting himself into a worse one. It was one of those odd whimsicalities which always came as a surprise when committed by a man who usually displayed so much mental dexterity, that now, instead of endeavoring to get upon the right track, he simply broke off abruptly and sat down.

His words had, however, the effect of calling out instantly a protest from the Rev. De Lancy Candish. Mr. Candish was the rector of the Church of the Nativity, the exceedingly ritualistic organization with which Mrs. Fenton was connected. He was a tall and bony young man, with abundant auburn hair and freckles, the most ungainly feet and hands, and eyes of eager enthusiasm, which showed how the result of New England Puritanism had been to implant in his soul the true martyr spirit. Fenton was never weary of jeering at Mr. Candish's uncouthness, his jests serving as an outlet, not only for the irritation physical ugliness always begot in him, but for his feeling of opposition to his wife's orthodoxy, in which he regarded the clergyman as upholding her. The rector's self-sacrificing devotion to truth, moreover, awakened in the artist a certain inner discomfort. To the keenly sensitive mind there is no rebuke more galling than the unconscious reproof of a character which holds steadfastly to ideals which it has basely forsaken. Arthur said to himself that he hated Candish for his ungainly person. "He is so out of drawing," he once told his wife, "that I always have a strong inclination to rub him out and make him over again." In that inmost chamber of his consciousness where he allowed himself the luxury of absolute frankness, however, the artist confessed that his animosity to the young rector had other causes.

As Fenton sank into his seat, Mrs. Staggchase leaned over to quote from the poem, —

"'For Blougram, he believed, say, half he spoke.'"

The artist turned upon her a glance of comprehension and amusement, but before he could reply, the rough, rather loud voice of Mr. Candish arrested his attention.

"If the poem teaches anything," Mr. Candish said, speaking according to his custom, somewhat too warmly, "it seems to me it is the sophistry of the sort of talk which puts art above religion. The thing that offends an honest man in Bishop Blougram is the fact that he looks at religion as if it were an art, and not a vital and eternal necessity, — a living truth that cannot be trifled with."

"Ah," Fenton's smooth and beautiful voice rejoined, "that is to confound art with the artificial, which is an obvious error. Art is a passion, an utter devotion to an ideal, an absolute lifting of man out of himself into that essential truth which is the only lasting bond by which mankind is united."

Fenton's coolness always had a confusing and irritating effect upon Mr. Candish, who was too thoroughly honest and earnest to quibble, and far from possessing the dexterity needed to fence with the artist. He began confusedly to speak, but with the first word became aware that Mrs. Fenton had come to the rescue. Edith never saw a contest between her husband and the clergyman without interfering if she could, and now she instinctively spoke, without stopping to consider where she was.

"It is precisely for that reason," she said, "that art seems to me to fall below religion. Art can make man contented with life only by keeping his attention fixed upon an ideal, while religion reconciles us to life as it really is."

A murmur of assent showed Arthur how much against the feeling of those around him were the views he was advancing.

"Oh, well," he said, in a droll *sotto voce*, "if it is coming down to a family difference we will continue it in private."

And he abandoned the discussion.

"It seems to me," pursued Mr. Candish, only half conscious that Mrs. Fenton had come to his aid, "that Bishop Blougram represents the most dangerous spirit of the age. His paltering with truth is a form of casuistry of which we see altogether too much nowadays."

"Do you think," asked a timid feminine voice, "that Blougram was *quite* serious? That he really meant all he said, I mean?"

The president looked at the speaker with despair in his glance; but she was adorably pretty and of excellent social position, so that snubbing was not to be thought of. Moreover, he was thoroughly well trained in keeping his temper under the severest provocation, so he expressed his feelings merely by a deprecatory smile.

"We have the poet's authority," he responded, in a softly patient voice, "for saying that he believed only half."

There was a little rustle of leaves, as if people were looking over their books, in order to find the passage to which he alluded. Then a young girl in the front row of chairs, a pretty creature, just on the edge of womanhood, looked up earnestly, her finger at a line on the page before her.

"I can't make out what this means," she announced, knitting her girlish brow, —

> "'Here, we've got callous to the Virgin's winks
> That used to puzzle people wholesomely.'

Of course he can't mean that the Madonna winks; that would be too irreverent."

There were little murmurs of satisfaction that the question had been asked, confusing explanations which evidently puzzled some who had not thought of being confused before; and then another girl, ignoring the fact that the first difficulty had not been disposed of, propounded another.

"Isn't the phrase rather bold," she asked, "where he speaks of 'blessed evil?'"

"Where is that?" some one asked.

"On page 106, in my edition," was the reply; and a couple of moments were given to finding the place in the various books.

"Oh, I see the line," said an old lady, at last. "It's one — two — three — five lines from the bottom of the page:

> "'And that's what all the blessed evil's for.'"

"You don't think," queried the first speaker, appealing personally to the president, "that Mr.

Browning can really have meant that evil is blessed, do you?"

The president regarded her with an affectionate and fatherly smile.

"I think," he said, with an air of settling everything, "that the explanation of his meaning is to be found in the line which follows, —

"'It's use in Time is to environ us.'"

"Heavens!" whispered Fenton to Mrs. Staggchase; "fancy that incarnate respectability environed by 'blessed evil!'"

"For my part," she returned, in the same tone, "I feel as if I were visiting a lunatic asylum."

"Yes, that line does make it beautifully clear," observed the voice of Miss Catherine Penwick; "and I think that's so beautiful about the exposed brain, and lidless eyes, and disemprisoned heart. The image is so exquisite when he speaks of their withering up at once."

Fenton made a droll grimace for the benefit of his neighbor, and then observed with great apparent seriousness, —

"The poem is most remarkable for the intimate knowledge it shows of human nature. Take a line like

'Men have outgrown the shame of being fools;'

We can see such striking instances of its truth all about us."

"How can you?" exclaimed Elsie Dimmont, under her breath.

Fenton had not been able wholly to keep out of his tone the mockery which he intended, and several people looked at him askance. Fortunately for him, a nice old gentleman who, being rather hard of hearing, had not caught what was said, now broke in with the inevitable question, which, sooner or later, was sure to come into every discussion of the club:

"Isn't this poem to be most satisfactorily understood when it is regarded as an allegory?"

The members, however, did not take kindly to this suggestion in the present instance. The question passed unnoticed, while a severe-faced woman inquired, with an air of vast superiority, —

"I have understood that Bishop Blougram is intended as a portrait of Cardinal Wiseman; can any one tell me if Gigadibs is also a portrait?"

"Oh, Lord!" muttered Fenton, half audibly. "I can't stand any more of this."

And at that moment a servant came to tell him that his carriage was waiting.

IV

NOW HE IS FOR THE NUMBERS.

Romeo and Juliet; ii.—4.

WHEN Mr. and Mrs. Fenton were in the carriage, driving from Mrs. Gore's to Mrs Frostwinch's, Arthur broke into a pleasant little laugh, as if a sudden thought had amused him.

"Why in the world, Edith," he asked, "couldn't you let that moon-calf Candish fight his own battle to-night? He would have tied himself all up in two moments, with a little judicious help I should have been glad to give him."

"I knew it," was her answer, "and that is precisely why I wanted to stop things. What possible amusement it can be to you to get the better of a man who is so little a match for you in argument, I don't understand."

"I never begin," Fenton responded. "Of course if he starts it I have to defend myself."

The stopping of the carriage prevented further discussion, and the pair were soon involved in the crowd of people struggling toward the hostess across Mrs. Denton Frostwinch's handsome drawing-room. Mrs. Frostwinch belonged, beyond the possibility of any cavilling doubt, to the most exclusive circle of fashionable Boston society.

Boston society is a complex and enigmatical thing, full of anomalies, bounded by wavering and uncertain lines, governed by no fixed standards, whether of wealth, birth, or culture, but at times apparently leaning a little toward each of these three great factors of American social standing.

It is seldom wise to be sure that at any given Boston house whatever, one will not find a more or less strong dash of democratic flavor in general company, and there are those who discover in this fact evidences of an agreeable and lofty republicanism. At Mrs. Frostwinch's one was less likely than in most houses to encounter socially doubtful characters, a fact which Arthur Fenton, who was secretly flattered to be invited here, had once remarked to his wife was an explanation of the dulness of these entertainments.

For Mrs. Frostwinch's parties were apt to be anything but lively. One was morally elevated by being able to look on the comely and high-bred face of Mrs. Bodewin Ranger, but that fine old lady had a sort of religious scruple against saying anything in particular in company, a relic of the days of her girlhood, when cleverness was not the fashion in her sex and when she had been obliged to suppress herself lest she outshine the high-minded and courtly but dreadfully dull gentleman she married.

One had here the pleasure of shaking one of the white fingers of Mr. Plant, the most exquisite *gourmet* in Boston, whose only daughter had made herself ridiculous by a romantic marriage with a country farmer. The Stewart Hubbards, who were the finest and fiercest aristocrats in town, and whose ancestors had been possessed not only of influence but of wealth ever since early colonial days, were old and dear friends of Mrs. Frostwinch and always decorated her parlors on gala nights with their benign presence. Mr. Peter Calvin, the leader of art fashions, high priest of Boston conservatism, and author of numerous laboriously worthless books, seldom failed to diffuse the aroma of his patronizing personality through the handsome parlors of this hospitable mansion when there was any reasonable chance of his securing an audience to admire him; and in general terms the company was what the newspapers call select and distinguished.

For Mrs. Frostwinch was entitled to a leading place in society upon whichever of the three great principles it was based. She was descended from one of the best of American families, while her good-tempered if somewhat shadowy husband was of lineage quite as unexceptional as her own. She was possessed of abundant wealth, while in cleverness and culture she was the peer of any of the brilliant people who frequented her house. She was moderately pretty, dressed beautifully, was sweet tempered, and possessed all good gifts and graces except repose and simplicity. She perhaps worked too hard to keep abreast of the times in too many currents, and her mental weariness instead of showing itself by an irritable temper found a less disagreeable outlet in a certain nervous manner apt to seem artificial to those who did not know her well. She was a clever, even a brilliant woman, who assembled clever and brilliant people about her, although as has been intimated, the result was by no means what might have been expected from such material and such opportunities. The truth is that there seems to be a fatal connection between exclusiveness and dulness. The people who assembled in Mrs. Frostwinch's handsome parlors usually seemed to be unconsciously laboring under the burden of their own respectability. They apparently felt that they had fulfilled their whole duty by simply being there ; and while the list of people present at one of Mrs. Frostwinch's evenings made those who were not there sigh with envy at thought of the delights they had missed, the reality was far from being as charming as their fancy.

" I wish somebody would bring Amanda Welsh Sampson here," murmured Arthur in his wife's ear, as the Fentons made their way toward their hostess. " It would be too delicious to see how she'd stir things up, and how shocked the old tabby dowagers would be."

But there were some social topics which were too serious to Edith to be jested upon.

"Mrs. Sampson!" she returned, with an expression of being really shocked. "That dreadful creature!"

The rooms were well filled; the clatter of innumerable tongues speaking English with that resonant dryness which reminds one of nothing else so much as of the clack of a negro minstrel's clappers indefinitely reduplicated, rang in the ears with confusing steadiness. An hour was spent in fragmentary conversations, which somehow were always interrupted at the instant the interesting point was reached. The men bestirred themselves with more or less alacrity, making their way about the room with a conscientious determination to speak to everybody whom duty called upon them to address, or more selfishly devoting themselves to finding out and chatting with the pretty girls. Fenton found time for the latter method while being far too politic to neglect the former. He was chatting in a corner with Ethel Mott, when Fred Rangely, whose successful novel had made him vastly the fashion that winter, joined them.

"When wit and beauty get into a corner together," was Rangely's salutation, "there is sure to be mischief brewing."

"It isn't at all kind," Miss Mott retorted, "for you to emphasize the fact that Mr. Fenton has all the wit and I not any."

"It is as kind," Fenton said, "as his touching upon the plainness of my personal appearance."

"Your mutual modesty in appropriating wit and beauty," Rangely returned, "goes well toward balancing the account."

"One has to be modest when you appear, Mr. Rangely," Miss Mott declared, saucily, "simply to keep up the average."

"Come," Fenton said, "this will serve as an excellent beginning for a quarrel. I will leave you to carry it on by yourselves. I have got too old for that sort of amusement."

Rangely looked after the artist as the latter took himself off to join Mrs. Staggchase, who was holding court not far away.

"You may follow if you want to," Ethel said, intercepting the glance.

Rangely laughed, a trifle uneasily.

"I don't want to," he replied, "if you will be good natured."

"Good natured? I like that! I am always good natured. You had better go than to stay and abuse me. But then, as you have been at Mrs. Staggchase's all the afternoon, you ought to be pretty well talked out."

The young man turned toward her with an air of mingled surprise and impatience.

"Who said I had been there?" he demanded.

"It was in the evening papers," she returned, teasingly. "All your movements are chronicled now you have become a great man."

"Humph! I am glad you were interested in my whereabouts."

"But I wasn't in the least."

"Are you sparring as usual, Miss Mott?" asked Mr. Stewart Hubbard, joining them. "Good evening, Mr. Rangely."

"Oh, Mr. Hubbard," Miss Mott said, ignoring the question, "I want to know who is to make the statue of *America*. It is going to stand opposite our house, so that it will be the first thing I shall see when I look out of the window in the morning, and naturally I am interested."

"Mr. Herman is making a study, and Mr. Irons has been put up to asking this new woman for a model. What is her name? The one whose *Galatea* made a stir last year."

"Mrs. Greyson," Rangely answered. "I used to know her before she went to Rome."

"Is she clever?" demanded Miss Mott, with a sort of girlish imperiousness which became her very well. "I can't have a statue put up unless it is very good indeed."

"She might take Miss Mott as a model," Mr. Hubbard suggested, smiling.

"For America? Oh, I am too little, and altogether too civilized. I'd do better for a model of Monaco, thank you."

"There is always a good deal of chance about you," Rangely said in her ear, as Mr. Staggchase spoke to Mr. Hubbard and drew his attention away.

Mr. Staggchase was a thin, wintry man, looking,

as Fenton once said, like the typical Yankee spoiled by civilization. He had always in a scene of this sort the air of being somewhat out of place, but of having brought his business with him, so that he was neither idle nor bored. It was upon business that he now spoke to Hubbard.

"Did you see Lincoln to-day?" he asked. "He has got an ultimatum from those parties. They will sell all their rights for $70,000."

"For $70,000," repeated Mr. Hubbard, thoughtfully. "We can afford to give that if we are sure about the road; but I don't know that we are. If Irons gets hold of any hint of what we are doing he can upset the whole thing."

"But he won't. There is no fear of that."

A movement in the crowd brought Edith Fenton at this moment to the side of Mr. Hubbard. She was radiant to-night in her primrose gown, and the gentleman, with whom she was always a favorite, turned toward her with evident pleasure.

"Isn't it a jam," she said. "I have ceased to have any control over my movements."

"That is unkind, when I fancied you allowed yourself to give me the pleasure of seeing you," returned he with elaborate courtesy. "Let me take you in to the supper-room."

"Thank you," Edith replied, taking his arm. "I do not object to an ice, and I want to ask a favor. Haven't you some copying you can give a *protégée* of mine? She's a lovely girl, and she really writes very nicely. I assure you she needs the work, or I wouldn't bother you."

They made their way into the hall before he answered. Then he asked, with some seriousness, —

"Are you sure she is absolutely to be trusted?"

"Trusted? Why, of course. I'd trust her as absolutely as I would myself."

"I asked because I do happen to have some copying I want done; but it is of the most serious importance that it be kept secret. It is the prospectus of a big business scheme, and if a hint of it got on the air it would all be ruined."

Edith looked up into his face and smiled.

"Her name," she said, "is Melissa Blake, and you will find her —— Or, wait; what time shall I send her to your office to-morrow?"

Her companion smiled in turn. They had reached the door of the supper-room, where the clatter of dishes, the popping of champagne corks, and the rattle of silver were added to the babble of conversation which filled the whole house. About the tables was going on a struggle which, however well-bred, was at least sufficiently vigorous.

"You take a good deal for granted," he said. "However, it will do no harm for me to see the young woman. She may come at eleven. What shall I bring you?"

V

'TWAS WONDROUS PITIFUL.

Othello; i. — 3.

"DEAR JOHN, I will give it up any day you say, and go back to Feltonville and live on the farm; but you know" —

Melissa Blake broke off and left her chair to take a seat on the corner of that on which her betrothed, John Stanton, was sitting, a proceeding which made it necessary for him to put his arm about her trig waist to support her.

"Don't think I don't understand, dear," she said, nestling up to him, "how hard it is, and what a long drag it has been, but we should neither of us ever feel quite satisfied to give it up. We can hold on, can't we, as long as we are together."

He kissed her fondly, but with a certain air of distraction which showed how full was his mind of the matter which troubled him. Two years before, he had come to Boston, and obtained work as a carpenter, determined to pay the debts left by his dead father, before he would marry and settle down on the small farm which belonged to his betrothed, and which, while it might be made to yield a living, could by no means be looked to for more. For the sake of being near him, Melissa had given up the school teaching of which she was fond, and come to the city also, and although she had found the difficulty of earning the means of support far greater than she had anticipated, she had still clung to the fortunes of her lover, to whom her steadfastness and unfailing cheer were of a value such as men realize only when it is lost.

"I got a letter to-day," John went on, while Melissa stroked his fingers fondly, "about the meadows. The time for redeeming them is up this month, and if I try to do it I can't pay anything on the debts this winter. The truth is"—

Melissa sat up suddenly.

"John!" she exclaimed.

"Why, what — what is the matter?"

She looked at him with wide open eyes, drawing in her under lip beneath her white teeth, with the air of profound meditation. Then she freed herself abruptly from his arms and went hastily to the table upon which were her writing materials. She had been at work copying when her lover came in, and her papers lay still open, with ink scarcely dry, where she had stopped to welcome him. She took one sheet up and studied it eagerly, and then turned toward him with shining eyes, her whole face aglow.

"Oh, John!" she exclaimed.

He regarded her in puzzled silence. Then in an instant the glad light faded from her eyes, and her lips lost their smile. An expression of pain and almost of terror replaced the look of joy. There had suddenly come to Melissa a sense of what she was doing. In the paper she held was written the plan of the formation of a syndicate to purchase the very range of meadows along the river in Feltonville of which those mentioned by John formed a part. At Mrs. Fenton's direction, Melissa had gone to see Mr. Hubbard, and had by him been employed to copy these papers for use at a meeting of the proposed stockholders, which was to take place in a few days.

"Mrs. Fenton tells me," he had said, "that you are to be trusted. It is absolutely essential that you do not mention these plans to any living being. Perfect secrecy is expected from you, and it is only because Mrs. Fenton is your guarantee that I run the risk of putting them into your hands."

"I think you can trust me," she had answered; "even if," she had added, with the ghost of a smile, "there were anybody that I know who would be at all likely to be interested."

And now the temptation had come to her in a way of which she had never dreamed. She had gone on with her copying, smiling to herself at the coincidence which put into the hands of a Feltonville girl this plan for the metamorphosis of the sleepy old village into a bustling manufacturing town, but she had not considered that this scheme might have important bearing upon the fortunes of her lover. She knew that Stanton's father had owned meadows along the river where the new factories were to lie, and she knew also that when old Mr. Stanton died these had been sold with a condition of redemption, but until this moment she had not connected the facts. She did not understand business, and had been puzzling her brain as she wrote, to understand what was meant by the statement that a certain company would sell a "six months' option at seventy thousand dollars" on a water-power for two thousand dollars. She did understand now, however, that were John in possession of the secret of the syndicate's plans, he could redeem his father's meadows with the money he had saved toward the payment of the debts which had forced the old man into the bankruptcy that broke his heart, and once he owned these lands lying in the midst of the desirable tract, John could command his own price for them. She held in her hand the secret which would free her lover from the heavy burden of years, and bring quickly the wedding-day for which they had both waited and longed so patiently.

The blood bounded so hotly in Melissa's veins as she realized all this, that she could scarcely breathe; but like a lightning flash a thought followed which sent the tide surging back to her heart, and left her cold and faint. She remembered that this knowledge was a trust. That she had given her word not to betray it. With instant recoil, she leaped to the thought that advising her lover to redeem these meadows was not betraying the secret. Like a swift shuttle flew her mind between argument and defence, between temptation and resistance, between love and duty.

"Why, what is it, Milly?" John demanded, starting up and coming to her. "What in the world makes you act so funny? Are you sick? Why don't you speak?"

It is not easy to express the force of the struggle which went on in poor Milly's mind. It seemed to her at that moment as if all the hopes of her life were set against her honesty. The material issues in any conflict between principle and inclination are of less importance than the desire which they represent. The few thousand dollars involved in the redemption of the Stanton meadows was little when compared to the magnificent scheme of which this would be a mere trifling accident, but the sum represented all the desires of Milly Blake's life, while over against it stood all her faith, her honesty, and her religion.

For an instant she wavered, standing as if by some spell suddenly arrested, with arms half extended. Then she flung down the paper and threw herself upon her lover's breast with a burst of tears.

"Why, Milly," he said, soothingly. "Milly, Milly."

He was unused to feminine vagaries. His betrothed was of the outwardly quiet order of women, and an outburst like this was incomprehensible to him. He could only hold the weeping girl in his strong embrace, soothing her in helpless masculine fashion, awkward, but exactly what she needed.

"There, John," she cried at last, giving him a tumultuous hug, and looking up into his face through her tears, "I always told you you were engaged to a fool, and this is a new proof of it."

"But what in the world," Stanton asked, looking down into her eyes with mingled fondness and bewilderment, "is it all about? What is the matter?"

"It is nothing but my foolishness," she answered, leading him back to the chair from which he had risen. "I was going to show you something in a paper I am copying, and just in time I remembered that I had particularly promised not to show it to anybody."

He regarded her curiously.

"But why," he asked, with a certain deliberateness which somehow made her uneasy, "did you want to show it to me."

"Because — because — "

She could not equivocate, and her innocent soul had had little training in the arts of evasion.

"Because what?"

Stanton leaned back in his chair, holding her by the shoulders as she sat upon his knee, and searching her face with his strong brown eyes. Milly's glance drooped.

"Don't ask me, John," she responded, putting her hand against his cheek, wistfully. "Don't you see I couldn't tell you without letting you know what is in the paper, and that is precisely the thing I promised not to do."

There are few men in whom a woman's open refusal to yield a point, no matter how trifling, does not arouse a tyrannous masculine impulse to compel obedience. Stanton had really no great curiosity about the secret, whatever it might be, but he instinctively felt that it was right to demand the telling because his betrothed refused to speak. His face grew more grave. The hands upon Milly's shoulders unconsciously tightened their hold. The girl intuitively felt that a struggle was coming, although even yet the signs were hardly tangible. She grew a little paler, putting her hand beneath her lover's bearded chin, and holding his face up so that she could look straight into his fearless, honest eyes.

"Dear John," she said, wistfully, "you know I never have a secret of my own that I keep from you in all the world."

"But why," demanded he, "can it do any harm for you to give me some reason why you ever thought of telling me this ; and just at a time, too, when we were talking of business."

" Because," she answered, thoughtlessly, " it was about business."

A new light came into Stanton's face. His lips subtly changed their expression.

" It must have been a chance to make some money," he said.

She grew deadly pale, but she did not answer him. He searched her face an instant, and then he lifted her in his strong arms, rising from the chair, and seating her in his place. He took a step forward, and stretched out his hand to take the paper she had thrown upon the table. With a cry of terror she sprang up and caught his arm.

" John ! " she exclaimed. " Oh, for pity's sake, don't look at it."

He turned and regarded her with a more unkind glance than she had ever seen upon his face.

" Will you tell me ? " he asked.

" I can't, I can't ! " she answered, half sobbing.

He looked at the paper, and then at his sweetheart. Then with a rough motion he shook off her fingers from his arm, and without a word went abruptly from the room.

Milly looked toward the door which had closed after him as if she could not believe that he had really gone ; then she sank down to the floor, and, leaning her head upon a chair, she sobbed as if her heart were broken.

VI

THE INLY TOUCH OF LOVE.

Two Gentlemen of Verona; ii.—7.

GRANT HERMAN looked across the breakfast table at his Italian wife thoughtfully a moment, considering, as he often did, what was likely to be the effect of something he was about to say. In six years of married life he had not learned how to adapt himself to the narrower mind and more personal views of his wife. He perhaps fell into the error, so common to strong natures, of being unable to comprehend that by far the larger part of the principles which influence broad minds do not for narrow ones exist at all. He continually tried to discover what process of reasoning led Ninitta to given results, but he was never able to appreciate the fact that often it was by no chain of logic whatever that certain conclusions had been arrived at. A mental habit of catching up opinions at haphazard, of acting simply from emotions, however transient, instead of from convictions, was wholly outside his mental experience, and equally unrealized in his comprehension.

He regarded Ninitta, whose foreign face and

beautiful figure looked as much out of place behind the coffee urn as would the faun of Praxiteles at an afternoon reception, and a smothered sigh rose to his lips with the thought how utterly he was at a loss to comprehend her. It happened in the present case, as it often did, that his failure to understand arose chiefly from the fact that there was nothing in particular to understand, and, when he spoke, Ninitta received his remark quite simply.

"Mrs. Greyson is at home again," he said.

"Mrs. Greyson," she echoed, her dark eyes lighting up with genuine pleasure. "Oh, that is indeed good. Where is she? Have you seen her?"

There shot through Herman's mind the reflection that since his wife could not know that he married her out of love not for herself but for Helen Greyson, it was absurd to have fancied that Ninitta would be jealously displeased at Helen's return; and the inevitable twinge of conscience at his wife's trusting ignorance followed.

"I haven't seen her," he answered; "she only arrived yesterday. Mrs. Fenton told me when I met her at the Paint and Clay Exhibition last night."

Ninitta folded her hands on the edge of the table, with a gesture of childish pleasure.

"I wonder what she will say to Nino," she said musingly, her voice taking a new softness.

A sudden spasm contracted the sculptor's throat. His whole being was shaken by the return of the woman to whom all the passionate devotion of his manhood was given, and he never heard that soft, maternal note with which his wife spoke of his boy without emotion.

"She may say that the young rascal ought to be out of his bed in time for breakfast," he retorted with affected brusqueness. "He has all the Italian laziness in him."

He pushed back his chair as he spoke, and rose from the table. He hesitated a moment, as if some sudden thought absorbed him, then he went to his wife and kissed her forehead.

"Good-by," he said. "I sha'n't come up for lunch. Don't coddle the boy too much."

"But when," his wife persisted, as he turned away, "shall I see Mrs. Greyson? I want to show her the *bambino*."

She always spoke in Italian to her husband and her child, and indeed her English had never been of the most fluent.

"The *bambino*," the father repeated, smiling. "He will be a *bambino* to you when he is as big as I am, I suppose. I do not know about Mrs. Greyson, but I will find out, if I can."

He left the room and went to the chamber where his swarthy boy of five lay still luxuriously in his crib, although he was fully awake. Nino gave a soft cry of joy at the sight of his father, and greeted him rapturously.

"Papa," he asked in Italian, "does the kitty

know how much she hurts when she scratches? she made a long place on my arm, and it hurt like fire."

"Do you know how much you hurt her to make her do it?" his father returned, smiling fondly.

"Oh, but she is so soft and so little, of course I don't hurt her," Nino answered, with boyish logic. "Anyway, she ought not to hurt me. I don't like to be hurt."

The foolish, childish words came back to Herman's mind a couple of hours later, as he waited in the boarding-house parlor for Helen Greyson. He smiled with bitterness to think how perfectly they represented his own state of mind. He said to himself that he was tired of being hurt, and rose at the moment to take in both his hands the hands of a beautiful woman, to his eyes no older and no less fair than when he had said good-by to her on his wedding morning, six years before. He tried to speak, but tears came instead of words; choked and blinded, he turned away abruptly, struggling to regain his composure.

The meeting after long years of those who have loved and been separated, may, for the moment, carry them back to the time of their parting so completely that all that lies between seems annihilated. The old emotion reasserts itself so strongly, the past lives again so vividly, that there seems to have been no break in feeling, and they stand in relation to one another as if the parting were yet to come. When they had been together a little, the time which lay between them would once more become a reality; but at the first touch of their hands those bitter days of loneliness ceased to exist, and they seemed to stand together again, as when they were saying good-by six years before.

With her old time self-control, it was Helen who spoke first, and her words recalled him from the past and its passion, to the present and its duty.

"Tell me how Ninitta is," she said, "and the boy. I do so want to see that wonderful boy."

The sculptor commanded his voice by a powerful effort.

"They are both well," he answered. "The boy is a wonderful little fellow, although perhaps I am not an unprejudiced judge. Ninitta is crazy to show him to you. She has pretty nearly effaced herself since he came, and only lives for his benefit."

"She is a happy woman," Helen said, assuming that air of cheerfulness which is one of the first accomplishments that women are forced by life to learn. "I should know she would be devoted to her children."

There were a few moments of silence. Both cast down their eyes, and then each raised them to study whatever changes time might have made in the years that lay between them. Helen's heart was beating painfully, but she was determined not to lose her self-control. She knew of old how completely she could rule the mood of her companion, and she felt that upon her calmness depended his. She had been schooling herself for this interview from the moment she began to consider whether she might return to America, and she was therefore less unprepared than was Herman for the trying situation in which she now found herself ; yet it required all her strength of mind and of will not to give way to the tide of love and emotion which surged within her breast.

Herman fixed his eyes resolutely on an ungainly group in pinkish clay which represented an American commercial sculptor's idea of Romeo and Juliet at the moment when the Nurse separates them with a message from Lady Capulet. With artistic instinct he noted the stupidity of the composition, the vulgarity of the lines, the cheap ugliness of the group. In that singular abstraction which comes so frequently in moments of high emotion, he let his glance wander to the pictures on the wall, the enormities in embroidery which adorned the chair backs, the garish hues of the rug lying before the open grate. Then it occurred to him, with a vague sense of amusement, how great was the incongruity between such a setting as this vulgar boarding-house reception-room, and the woman before him. The idea brought to his mind the contrast between the life to which Helen had come, and the life at Rome, artistic, rich, and full of possibilities, which she had left.

The thought of Rome recalled instantly the old days there, almost a score of years ago, when he had first known Ninitta. So vivid were the memories which awakened, that he seemed to see again the Roman studio, the fat old aunt, voluble and sharp eyed, who always accompanied her niece when the girl posed; and most clearly of all did his inner vision perceive the fresh, silent maiden whose exquisite figure was at once the admiration and the despair of all the young artists in Rome. He remembered how Hoffmeir had discovered the girl drawing water from an old broken fountain he had gone out to sketch; and the difficulties that had to be overcome before she could be persuaded to pose. The Capri maidens are brought up to be averse to posing, and Ninitta had not long enough breathed the air of Rome to have overcome the prejudices of her youth. He reflected, with a bitterness rendered vague by a certain strange impersonality of his mood, how different would have been his life had Hoffmeir been unable to overcome the girl's scruples. He wondered whether the fat old aunt, and the greasy, good-natured little priest with whom she had taken counsel, would have urged Ninitta to take up the life of a model, could they have foreseen all the results to which this course was to lead in the end.

Then, with a sudden stinging consciousness, the

thought came of all that her decision had meant to his life. The old question whether he had done right in marrying Ninitta forced itself upon him as if it were some enemy springing up from ambush. He raised his eyes, and his glance met that of Mrs. Greyson.

"It is no use, Helen," he broke out, impulsively, "we must talk frankly. It is idle to suppose that we can go on in an artificial pretence that we have nothing to say."

She put up her hand appealingly.

"Only do not drive me away again," she pleaded. "Don't say things that I have no right to hear!"

A dark red stained Herman's cheek, and the tears came into his eyes.

"No," he returned. "if any one is to be driven away it shall not be you."

"But why need we trouble the things that are past," she went on, with wistful eagerness. "Why cannot we accept it all in silence, and be friends."

He looked at her with a passionate, penetrating glance. She felt a wild and foolish longing to fling herself upon the floor and embrace his feet; but the old Puritan training, the resistant fibre inherited from sturdy ancestors, still did not fail her.

"You have your wife," she hurried on, "your home, your boy. That is enough. That" —

"That is not enough," he interrupted, with an emphasis, which seemed stern. "Helen, I shall not talk love to you. I am another woman's husband. I made a ghastly mistake when I married Ninitta, but it is done. She loves me; she is happy, and I love" — his voice faltered into a wonderful softness more eloquent than words, — "I love Nino."

She would not let him go on. She sprang up and ran to him, taking his hands in hers with a touch that made his blood rush tingling through his veins.

"Yes," she cried, "you love Nino! Think of that! Think most of all that whatever you are, good or bad, you are for your son, for Nino! Come! There is safety for us in that. We will go and talk with Nino between us. Then we shall say nothing of which we can be ashamed or regret."

There came to Herman a vision of his boy clasped in Helen's arms which made him feel as if suffocating with the excess of his emotion. He rose blindly, only half conscious of what he was doing; and without giving time for objections Helen hastened to dress herself for the street, and in a few moments they were walking together toward the sculptor's house.

To Herman's surprise, his wife was absent when he reached home. The maid did not know where she had gone. She often went out in the morning without saying where she was going, and of course the servant did not ask.

"That is odd," Herman said; "but she has probably gone shopping or something of the sort. It is too bad, she had so set her heart on showing you the *bambino*, as she calls him, herself."

But it proved that Nino also was out, having been taken for a walk; and so Helen, who returned home at once, saw neither of them.

VII

THIS DEED UNSHAPES ME.

Measure for Measure; iv. — 4.

NINITTA had not gone shopping. She was posing for Arthur Fenton, at his studio. Even the presence of her boy could not wholly make up to the Italian for the loss of all the old interest and excitement of her life as a model. The boy was with his nurse or at the kindergarten for long hours during which Ninitta, who had few of the resources with which an educated woman would have filled her time, mingled longings for her old life with blissful gloatings over Nino's beauty and cleverness. Her husband was always kind, but since his marriage delicacy of sentiment had made him shrink from having his wife pose even for himself, while naturally no thought of her doing so for another would have been entertained for a moment.

Ninitta had been so long in the life, to pose had been so large a part of her very existence, that she hardly knew how to do without the old-time flavor. Mrs. Fenton had perceived something of this without at all appreciating the strength of the feeling of the sculptor's wife, and she had at one time tried to interest Ninitta in what might perhaps be called missionary work among the models of Boston, a class of whose calling Edith held views which her husband was not wholly wrong in calling absurdly narrow. She was met at once by the difficulty that it was impossible to make Ninitta see that missionary work was needed among the models, and the effort resulted in nothing except to convince Mrs. Fenton that she could do little with the Italian.

Just how Arthur Fenton had persuaded her to pose without her husband's knowledge, Ninitta could not have told ; and the artist himself would have assured any investigator, even that speculative spirit which held the place left vacant by the dismissal of his conscience, that he had never deliberately tried to entice her. He had talked to her of the picture he was painting for a national competitive exhibition, it is true, and dwelt upon the difficulty of procuring a proper model ; he had met her on the street one day and taken her into his studio to see it ; he had regretted that it was impossible to ask her ; and of a hundred apparently blameless and trivial things, the result was that this morning, while Helen and Herman were walking across the Common to find her, Ninitta was lying amid a heap of gorgeous stuffs and cushions in Fenton's studio, while he painted and talked after his fashion.

It is as impossible to trace the beginnings of

any chain of events as it is to find the mystery of the growth of a seed. Whatever Arthur Fenton's faults, he certainly believed himself to be one who could not betray a friend. The ideal which he vaguely called honor, and which served him as that ultimate ethical standard which in one shape or another is necessary to every human being, forbade his taking advantage of any one whose friendship he admitted. His instinct of self-indulgence had, however, made him so expert a casuist that he was able to silence all inner misgivings by arguing that the demands of art were above all other laws. He reasoned that Ninitta's posing could do no possible harm to Grant Herman, while the success of his *Fatima* depended upon it; and since art was his religion, he came at last to feel as if he were nobly sacrificing his prejudices to his highest convictions in violating for the sake of art his principle which forbade his deceiving her husband.

Least of all, in asking the Italian to pose, had Fenton been actuated by any intention of tempting her to evil. He needed a model for the *Fatima* as he needed his canvas and brushes; and his satisfaction at having induced Ninitta to serve his purpose was in kind much the same as his pleasure that his brushes and canvas were exactly what he wanted.

But it is always difficult to tell to what an action may lead; and most of all is it hard to foresee the consequences which will follow from the violation of principle. Perhaps the air of secrecy with which Ninitta found it necessary to invest her coming, had an intoxicating effect upon the artist; perhaps it was simply that his persistent egotism moved him to test his power. Men often feel the keenest curiosity in regard to the extent of their ability to commit crimes into which they have yet not the remotest intention of being betrayed; and especially is this true in their relations to women. Men of a certain vanity are always eager to discover how great an influence for evil they could exercise over women, even when they have not the nerve or the wickedness to exert it. A man must be morally great to be above finding pleasure in the belief that he could be a Don Juan if he chose; and moral grandeur was not for Arthur Fenton.

From whatever cause, the fact was, that as he painted this morning and reflected, with a complacency of which he was too keen an analyst not to know he should have been ashamed, how he had secured the model he desired despite her husband, the speculation came into his mind how far he could push his influence over Ninitta. At first a mere impersonal idea, the thought was instantly, by his habit of mental definiteness, realized so clearly that his cheek flushed, partly, it is to be said to his credit, with genuine shame. He looked at the beautiful model, and turned away his eyes.

Then, hardly conscious of what he was doing, he laid down his palette, and took a step forward.

At that instant the studio bell rang sharply. He started with so terrible a sense of being discovered in a crime, that his jaw trembled and his knees almost failed under him.

Then instantly he recovered his self-possession, although his heart was beating painfully, and looked up at the clock.

"Heavens!" he exclaimed. "I had no idea how late it was! It is that beastly Irons for his last sitting. I'd forgotten all about him."

Ninitta rose from her position and hurried toward the screen behind which she dressed.

"Don't let him in," she said. "He knows me."

The bell rang again, as they stood looking at each other.

"I will try to send him off," Arthur said. "Dress as quickly as you can."

She retreated behind the screen while he went to the door and unlocked it. Instantly Irons stepped inside.

"You must excuse me," the artist said. "I'll be ready for you in fifteen minutes. I have a model here, and got to painting so busily that I forgot the time. Come back in a quarter of an hour."

"Oh, I don't mind," Irons said, advancing into the studio. "I'll look round until you are ready."

"But I never admit sitters when I have a

model," Fenton protested, standing before him. "I shall have to ask you to go."

The other stopped and looked at the artist with suspicion in his eyes.

"What a fuss you make," he commented coarsely. "No intrigue, I suppose?"

A hot flush sprang into Fenton's face. He tried to assume a haughty air, but the consciousness of being entrapped in a misdemeanor had not left him. The need of getting Mrs. Herman out of the studio unseen would have been awkward at any time; when to this was added the sense of guilt and shame which was begotten of the base impulse to which he had almost yielded, the situation became for him painfully embarrassing

"I am not in the habit of carrying on intrigues with my models," he replied, haughtily. "Or," he added, regaining self-possession, "of discussing my affairs with others."

Mr. Irons laughed in a significant way which made Arthur long to kill him on the spot, and, stepping past Fenton, he walked further into the studio.

"Don't put on airs with me," he said. "Your looks give you away. You've been up to some mischief."

He paused an instant before the unfinished picture on the easel, then when the artist coolly took the canvas and placed it with its face to the wall, he turned with deliberate rudeness and craned his neck so that he could look behind the screen. A leering smile came over his coarse features. Without a word he went over to the most distant corner of the studio, where he apparently became absorbed in studying a sketch hanging on the wall.

There was a dead silence of some moments. Fenton was literally speechless with rage, yet, too, his quick wit was busy devising some way of escape from the unpleasant predicament in which he found himself. He did not speak, nor did Mr. Irons turn until Ninitta had completed her toilet and slipped hastily out. As the door closed after her, Irons wheeled about and confronted the indignant artist with a smile of triumphant glee.

"Sly dog!" he said.

Fenton advanced a step toward his tormentor with his clenched hand half raised as if he would strike.

"What do you mean?" he demanded. "Do you call yourself a gentleman?"

"Oh, come, now," the other responded, with an easy wave of the hand, "no heroics, if you please. They won't go down with me. She's a devilish fine woman, and I don't blame you."

"I tell you," began Fenton, "you"—

"Oh, of course, of course. I know all that. But sit down while I say something to you."

As if under the constraining influence of a nightmare, Fenton obeyed when Mr. Irons, having seated himself in an easy chair, waved him into another with a commanding gesture. The artist felt himself to have lost his place as the stronger of the two, of which he had hitherto been proudly conscious, and he sat angrily gnawing his lip while his tormentor regarded him with smiling malice.

"Do you remember telling me one day," Irons asked, fixing his narrow eyes on the other's disturbed face, "that you could make your sitters tell you things?"

Fenton stared at his questioner in angry silence, but did not answer.

"Now, if," continued Irons; "I say if, you observe, — if Stewart Hubbard should chance to tell you where the new syndicate mean to locate their mills, it might be a mighty good thing for you."

Still Fenton said nothing, but his regard became each moment more wrathful.

"Of course," the sitter continued, with an assumption of airy lightness which grated on every nerve of the hearer, "you are not in a position to turn such knowledge to advantage; but I am, and I am always inclined to help a bright fellow like you when there is a good chance. So if you should come to me and say that the mills are to be so and so, I'd do all I could to make things pleasant for you. I happen to belong to a syndicate myself that has bought a mill privilege at Wachusett, and it is important to us to have the new railroad go our way, and we'd like to know how far the other fellows' plans are dangerous to our interests, don't you see."

Still Fenton did not speak. He had grown very pale, and his lips were set firmly together. His hands clasped the arms of his chair so strongly that the blood had settled under the middle of the nails. Mr. Irons looked at him with narrow, piercing eyes. He paused a moment and then went on.

"You are perfectly capable of keeping a secret," he said in a hard, deliberate tone, "so I don't in the least mind telling you what we should do. Your sitters always tell you things, you know; and you are to be trusted. The case is here; our syndicate stand in with the railroad corporation and ask the Railroad Commissioners for a certificate of exigency, to authorize laying the new branch out through Wachusett. Now we have information that Staggchase and Stewart Hubbard and that set, are planning to spring a petition asking for special legislation locating the road somewhere else. Of course, they'll have to get it in under a suspension of the rules, but they can work that easily enough. The Commissioners will have to hold on, then, until the Legislature finishes with that petition."

He paused again, with an air which convinced the artist that he was going on with this elaborate explanation to cover his awkwardness. Fenton did not speak, and his visitor continued, —

"The Commissioners might settle the matter now, but they won't, and we've got to have the fight, I suppose; so, of course, you can see how it is for our interest to know just what we are fighting."

He rose as he spoke, and with an air of deliberation, buttoned his overcoat, which he had not removed.

"I don't think you feel like painting this morning," he observed, "and I'll come in again. I'll leave you to think over what I have said."

Fenton rose also, regarding him with fierce, level eyes.

"And suppose," he said, "that I call you a damned scoundrel, and forbid you ever to set foot in my studio again?"

The other laughed, with the easy assurance of a bully who feels himself secure.

"Oh, you won't," he replied. "If you did, — well, I am on the committee for the new statue, and have to see Herman now and then you know, and I should, perhaps, ask him why his wife poses for you. Good morning."

And with a chuckling laugh, he took himself out.

VIII

A NECESSARY EVIL.

Julius Cæsar ; ii. — 2.

"OH, I assure you that my temper has been such for a week that my family have threatened to have me sent to a nervine asylum," Ethel Mott observed to Fred Rangely, who was calling on her, ostensibly to inquire after her health, some trifling indisposition having kept her housed for a few days. "What with my cold and my vexation at losing things I wanted to go to, I have been positively unendurable."

"That's your way of looking at it," he responded ; "but I hardly fancy that anybody else found it out. But what has there been to lose, except the Throgmorton ball ?"

"Well, first there was the concert Saturday night."

"Do you care so much about the Symphonies, then ? I thought you were the one girl in Boston who doesn't pretend to care for music."

"Oh, but we have lovely seats this year, and the nicest people all about us, you know. Thayer Kent and his mother are directly behind us."

"Where he can lean forward and talk to you," interrupted Rangely, jealously.

"Yes," she said, nodding with a gleam of mischievous laughter in her dark eyes. "And I do have a nice time at the Symphonies. Besides, I don't in the least object to the music, you know."

Fred fixed his gaze on a large old-fashioned oil painting on the opposite wall, a copy from some of the innumerable pastorals which have been made in imitation of Nicholas Poussin. It was of no particular value, but it was surrounded by a beautiful carved Venetian frame, and was one of those things which confer an air of distinction upon a Boston parlor, because they are plainly the art purchases of a bygone generation.

"But you have, of course, had no end of girls running in to see you," he observed.

"Yes; but, then, that didn't make up for the Throgmorton ball. You ask what else there was to lose; I should think that was enough. Why, Janet Graham says she never had such a lovely time in her life."

"Is Miss Graham engaged to Fred Gore?" Rangely asked.

Ethel's gesture of dissent showed how little she would have approved of such a consummation.

"No, indeed," she returned. "Fred Gore only wants Janet's money, anyway; and she can't abide him, any more than I can."

"Then, you have the correct horror of a marriage for money."

"I think a girl is a fool to let a man marry her

for her money. She'd much better give him her fortune and keep herself back. Then she'd at least save something. I don't approve of people's marrying for money anyway ; although, of course," she added, with a twinkle in her eye, "I think it is wicked to marry without it."

There shot through Rangely's mind the reflection that Thayer Kent had not an over-abundance of this world's goods ; and to this followed the less pleasant thought that he was himself in the same predicament.

"But Jack Gerrish hasn't anything," he said, aloud.

"But Janet has enough, so she can marry anybody she wants to," was the reply; "and Jack Gerrish is too perfectly lovely for anything."

The visitor laughed, but he was evidently not at his ease. He was always uncomfortably conscious that Ethel had not the slightest possible scruple against laughing at him, and he was not a little afraid of her well-known propensity to tease. Ethel regarded him with secret amusement. A woman is seldom displeased at seeing a man disconcerted by her presence, even when she pities him and would fain put him at his ease. It is a tribute to her powers too genuine to be disputed, and while she may labor to overcome the man's feeling, her vanity cannot but be gratified that he has it.

"Did you ever know anything like the way Elsie

Dimmont is going on with Dr. Wilson ? " Ethel said, presently, by way of continuing the conversation. " I can't see what she finds to like in him. He's as coarse as Fred Gore, only, of course, he's cleverer, and he isn't dissipated."

" Wilson isn't a half bad fellow," Rangely replied, rather patronizingly. " Though, of course, I can understand that you wouldn't care for that kind of a man."

" Am I so particular, then ? "

" Yes, I think you are."

" Thank you for nothing."

" Oh, I meant to be complimentary, I assure you. Isn't it a compliment to be thought particular in your tastes ? "

" That depends upon how you are told. Your manner was not at all calculated to flatter me. It said too plainly that you thought me captious."

" But I don't."

" Of course you wouldn't own it," Ethel retorted, playing with a tortoise-shell paper-cutter she had picked up from the table by which she sat ; " but your manner was not to be mistaken. It betrayed you in spite of yourself."

Rangely knew how foolish he was to be affected by light banter like this, but for his life he could not have helped it. The fact that Ethel knew how easily she could tease him lent a tantalizing sparkle to her eyes. She smiled mockingly as he vainly tried to keep the flush from rising in his cheeks.

"You are singularly fond of teasing," he observed, in a manner he endeavored to make cool and philosophical.

"Now you are calling me singular as well as captious."

"The girl who is singular," returned he, in an endeavor to turn the talk by means of an epigram which only made matters worse for him, "the girl who is singular runs great risk of never becoming plural."

Ethel laughed merrily, her glee arising chiefly from a sense of the chance he was giving her to work up one of those playful mock quarrels which amused her and so thoroughly teased her admirer.

"Upon my word, Mr. Rangely," she said, assuming an air of indignant surprise, "is it your idea of making yourself agreeable to tell an unfortunate girl that she is destined to be an old maid? I could stand being one well enough, but to be told that I've got to be is by no means pleasant."

He knew she was playing with him, but he could not on that account meet her on her own ground. He endeavored to protest.

"You are trying to make me quarrel."

"Make you quarrel?" she echoed. "I like that! Of course, though, to be so full of faults that you can't help abusing me is one way of making you quarrel."

"How you do twist things around!" exclaimed he, beginning to be thoroughly vexed.

She pursed up her lips and regarded him with an expression more aggravating than words could have been. She had been for several days deprived of the pleasure of teasing anybody, and her delight in vexing Rangely made his presence a temptation which she was seldom able to resist. She was unrestrained by any regard for the young author which should make her especially concerned how seriously she offended him; and when she now changed the conversation abruptly, it was with a forbearing air which was anything but soothing to his nerves.

"Don't you think," she asked, "that Mr. Berry was absurd in the way he acted about playing at Mrs. West's?"

"No, I can't say that I do," the caller retorted savagely. "Mrs. West gives out that she is going to give the neglected native musicians at last a chance to be heard, and then she invites them to play their compositions in her parlor. Westbrooke Berry isn't the man to be patronized in any such way. Just think of her having the cheek to give to a man whose work has been brought out in Berlin an invitation which is equivalent to saying that he can't get a public hearing, but she'll help him out by asking her guests to listen to him. Heavens! Mrs. West is a perfectly incredible woman."

Ethel smiled sweetly. In her secret heart she agreed with him ; but it did not suit her mood to show that she did so.

"You seem bound to take the opposite view of everything to-day," she said, in tones as sweet as her smile ; "or perhaps it is only that my temper has been ruined by my cold. I told you it had been bad."

He rose abruptly.

"If everything is to put us more at odds," he said, rather stiffly, "the sooner I withdraw, the better. I am sorry I have fallen under your displeasure ; it is generally my ill luck to annoy you."

And in a few moments he was going down the street in a frame of mind not unusual to him after a call upon Miss Mott, from whose house he was apt to come away so ruffled and irritated that nothing short of a counteracting feminine influence could restore his self-complacency.

This office of comforter usually fell to the lot of Mrs. Frederick Staggchase. Indeed, his fondness for this lady was so marked as to give rise to some question among his intimates whether he were not more attached to her than to the avowed object of his affection.

An hour after he had made his precipitate retreat from Ethel's, he found himself sitting in the library at Mrs. Staggchase's, with his hostess comfortably enthroned in a great chair of carved oak on the opposite side of the fire. The conversation had somehow turned upon marriage. There is always a certain fascination, a piquant if faint sense of being upon the borderland of the forbidden, which makes such a discussion attractive to a man and woman who are playing at making love when marriage stands between them.

"But, of course," Rangely had said, "two married people can't live at peace when one of them is in love with somebody else."

Mrs. Staggchase clasped with her slender hand the ball at the end of the carved arm of the chair in which she was sitting, looking absently at the rings which adorned her fingers. She possessed to perfection the art of being serious, and the air with which she now spoke was admirably calculated to imply a deep interest in the subject under discussion.

"I do not understand," she observed, thoughtfully, "why a man and woman need quarrel because they happen to be married to each other, when they had rather be married to somebody else. It wouldn't be considered good business policy to pull against a partner because one might do better with some other arrangement; and it does seem as if people might be as sensible about their marriage relations as in their business."

Her companion glanced at her, and then quickly resumed his intent regard of the fire beside which he sat.

"But people are so unreasonable," he remarked.

Mrs. Staggchase assented, with a characteristic bend of the head, and a movement of her flexible neck. She looked up with a smile.

"I think Fred and I are a model couple," she said. "Fred came into my room this noon, just as I had finished my morning letters. 'Good-morning,' he said, 'I hope you weren't frightened.' — 'Frightened?' I said, 'what at?' — 'Do you mean to say you didn't know I was out all night?' — 'I hadn't an idea of it,' said I. He'd been playing cards at the club all night, and had just come in. He says that the next time, he shan't take the trouble to expose himself."

Rangely laughed in a somewhat perfunctory way.

"But if that is a model fashion of living, what becomes of the old notions of kindred souls, and all that sort of thing?" he asked. "I shouldn't want my wife" —

He paused, rather awkwardly, and Mrs. Staggchase took up the sentence with a smile of amusement, in which there was no trace of annoyance. She was too well aware how completely she was mistress of the situation, in dealing with Rangely, to be either vexed or embarrassed in talking with him.

"To be as frank with another man as I am with you?" she finished for him. "Oh, very likely not. You have all the masculine jealousy which is aroused in an instant by the idea that a woman should be at liberty to like more than one man. You are half a century behind us. Marriage as you conceive it is the old-fashioned article, for the use of families in narrow circumstances intellectually as well as pecuniarily. Love in a cottage is necessary, because people under those conditions can't live unless they are extravagantly devoted to each other. Marriage with us is just what it ought to be, an arrangement of mutual convenience. Fred and I suit each other perfectly, and are sufficiently fond of each other; but there are sides of his nature to which I do not answer, and of mine that he does not touch. He finds somebody who does; I find somebody on my part. You, for instance."

Rangely leaned back in his chair, and clasped his plump white fingers, regarding Mrs. Staggchase with a smile of amusement and admiration.

"You are so awfully clever," was his response, "that you could really never be uncommonly fond of anybody. You'd analyze the whole business too closely."

She laughed slightly, and went on with what she was saying, without heeding his interruption.

"Fred and I make good backgrounds for each other, and, after all, that is what is required. You answer to my need of companionship in another direction, and since that side of my nature is unintelligible to my husband, he is not defrauded, while I should be if I starved my desire for such friendship, to please an idea like yours, that a wife should find her all in her husband. Fortunately, Mr. Staggchase is a broader man than you are."

"Thank you," Rangely retorted, with a faint tinge of annoyance visible, despite his air of jocularity. "Arthur Fenton says a broad man is one who can appreciate his own wife. If Mr. Staggchase does that" —

"Come," interrupted Mrs. Staggchase, smiling with the air of one who has had quite enough of the topic, "don't you think the subject is getting to be unfortunately personal? I have a favor to ask of you."

Rangely was too well aware of the uselessness of trying to direct the conversation to make any attempt to continue the talk, which, moreover, had taken a turn not at all to his liking. He settled himself in his chair, in an attitude of easy attention.

"I am always delighted to do you a favor," he said. "It isn't often I get a chance."

The relations between these two were not easy to understand, unless one accepted the simplest possible theory of their friendship. It was, on the part of Mrs. Staggchase, only one of a succession of platonic intimacies with which her married life had been enriched. She found it necessary to her enjoyment that some man should be her devoted admirer, always quite outside the bounds of any possible love-making, albeit often enough she permitted matters to go to the exciting verge of a flirtation which might merit a name somewhat warmer than friendship. She was a brilliant and clever woman who allowed herself the luxury of gratifying her vanity by encouraging the ardent attentions of some man, which, if they ever became too pressing, she knew how to check, or, if necessary, to stop altogether. She was fond of talking, and she frankly avowed her conviction that women were not worth talking to. She liked an appreciative masculine listener with whom she could converse, now in a strain of bewildering frankness, now in a purely impersonal and intellectual vein, and who, however he might at times delude himself by misconstruing her confidences into expressions of personal regard, was clever enough to comprehend the little corrective hints by which, when necessary, she chose to undeceive him.

Analyzed to its last elements, her feeling, it must be confessed, was pretty nearly pure selfishness; but she was able, without effort, and by half-unconscious art, to throw over it the air of being disinterested friendship. Such a nature is essentially false, but chiefly in that it gives to a passing mood the appearance of a permanent sentiment, and, while seeking only self-gratification, seems actuated by genuine desire to give pleasure to another.

The attitude of Rangely toward Mrs. Staggchase was, perhaps, no more unselfish, and was certainly no more noble, but his sentiment was at least more genuine. He was flattered by her preference, and he was bewildered by her cleverness. He liked to believe himself capable of interesting her, and without in the most remote degree desiring or anticipating an intrigue, he was ready to go as far as she would allow in his devotion. He was constantly tormented by a vague phantom of conquest, which danced with will-o'-the-wisp fantasy before him, and from day to day he endeavored to discover how deeply in love she was willing he should fall. He was really fond of her, a fact that did not prevent his entertaining a half-hearted passion for Ethel Mott, the result of this mixture of emotion being that he was the slave, albeit with a difference, of either lady with whom he chanced to be. That he was the plaything of Mrs. Staggchase's fancy he was far from realizing, although from the nature of things he naturally regarded his fondness for Miss Mott as the permanent factor in the case. He even felt a certain compunction for the regret he supposed Mrs. Staggchase would feel when he should decide formally to transfer his allegiance to her rival; a misgiving he might have spared himself had he been wise enough to appreciate the situation in all its bearings. The lady understood perfectly how matters stood, but Rangely was her junior, and, besides, no man in such a case ever comprehends that he is being played with.

"It is in regard to the statue of *America* that I want you to be useful," Mrs. Staggchase said, replying to her visitor's proffer of service with a smile. "Do you know what the chances are in regard to the choice of a sculptor?"

"Why, I suppose Grant Herman will have the commission."

"But I think not."

"You think not? Who will then?"

"That is just it. Mr. Hubbard has been backing Mr. Herman; and Mr. Irons, who never will agree to anything that Mr. Hubbard wants, is putting up the claims of this new woman, just to be contrary."

"What new woman? Mrs. Greyson?"

"Yes. Mrs. Frostwinch told me all about it yesterday. Now there is a young man that we are interested in" —

"Who is 'we'?" interrupted Rangely.

"Oh, Mrs. Frostwinch, and Mrs. Bodewin Ranger, and a number of us."

"But whom have you got on the committee?"

"Mr. Calvin; and don't you see that Mr. Calvin's name in a matter of art is worth a dozen of the other two."

"Yes," Rangely assented, rather doubtfully, "in the matter of giving commissions it certainly is."

Mrs. Staggchase smiled indulgently, playing

with the ring in which blazed a splendid ruby, and which she was putting on and off her finger.

"If you think," she said, "that you are going to entrap me into a discussion of the merits of art and Philistinism, you are mistaken. I told you long ago that I was a Philistine of the Philistines, deliberately and avowedly. The true artistic soul which you delight to call Pagan is only the servant of Philistinism, and I own that I prefer to stand with the ruling party. As, indeed," she added, with a mischievous gleam in her eye, "do many who will not confess it."

Rangely flushed. The thrust too closely resembled reproaches which in his more sensitive moments he received at the hand of his own inner consciousness, so to speak, not to make him wince. He felt himself, besides, becoming involved in a painful position. He had long been the intimate friend of Grant Herman, and felt that the sculptor had a right to expect whatever aid he could give him in a matter like this.

"But who," he asked, "is your *protégé?*"

"His name," Mrs. Staggchase replied, "is Orin Stanton. He is a fellow of the greatest talent, and he has worked his way"—

Rangely put up his hand in a gesture of impatience.

"I know the fellow," he said. "He made a thing he called *Hop Scotch,* of which Fenton said the title was far too modest, since he'd not only scotched the subject but killed it."

"One never knew Mr. Fenton to waste the chance of saying a good thing simply for the sake of justice," Mrs. Staggchase observed, with unabated good humor. "But you are to help us in the *Daily Observer*, and there is to be no discussion about it. Since you know you are too good-natured not to oblige me in the end, why should you not do it gracefully and get the credit of being willing."

And then, being a wise woman, she disregarded Rangely's muttered remonstrance and turned the conversation into a new channel.

IX

THIS IS NOT A BOON.

Othello; iii. — 3.

IF the old-time opinion that a woman whose name is a jest with men has lost her claims to respect, Mrs. Amanda Welsh Sampson might be supposed to have little ground for the inner anger she felt at the scantness of the courtesy with which she was treated by Mr. Irons. That gentleman was calling upon her in her tiny suite of rooms at the top of one of those apartment hotels which stand upon the debatable ground between the select regions of Back Bay and the scorned precincts of the South End, and he was apparently as much at home as if the sofa upon which he lounged were in his own dwelling.

The apartment of Mrs. Amanda Welsh Sampson gave to the experienced eye evidences of a pathetic struggle to make scanty resources furnish at least an appearance of luxury. The walls were adorned with amateur china painting in the shape of dreadful placques and plates in livid hues; there was abundance of embroidery that should have been impossible, in garish tints and uneven stitches; much shift had been made to produce an imposing appearance by means of cheap Japanese fans and the inexpensive wares of which the potteries at Kioto, corrupted by foreign influence, turn out such vast quantities for the foreign market. Against the wall stood an upright piano — if a piano could be called upright which habitually destroyed the peace of the entire neighborhood — and over it was placed a scarf upon which apparently some boarding-school miss had taken her first lesson in painting wild flowers.

The room was small, and so well filled with furniture that there seemed little space for the long limbs of Alfred Irons, who, however, had contrived to make himself comfortable by the aid of various cushions covered with bright-colored sateens. He had lighted a cigar without thinking it necessary to ask leave, and had even made himself more easy by putting one leg across a low chair.

Mrs. Sampson was fully aware that in her struggles with life she had sometimes provoked laughter, often disapproval, and now and then given rise to positive scandal, yet she was still accustomed to at least a fair semblance of respect from the men who came to see her; women, it is to be noted, being not often seen within her walls, since those who were willing to come she did not care to receive, and those whom she invited seldom set her name down on their calling lists. Among themselves, at the clubs or elsewhere, the men speculated more or less coarsely and unfeelingly upon the foundations of the numerous scandals which had from time to time blossomed like brilliant and life-sapping parasites upon the tree of Mrs. Sampson's reputation. Her name, either spoken boldly or too broadly hinted at to be misunderstood, adorned many a racy tale told in smoking-rooms after good dinners, or when the hours had grown small in more senses than one; and her career was made to point more than one moral drawn for the benefit of the sisters and daughters of the men who joked and sneered concerning her.

Mrs. Amanda Welsh Sampson was born of a good old Boston family, to which she clung with a desperate clutch which her relatives ignored so far as with dignity they were able. Her father had been a lawyer of reputation, and his portrait was still displayed prominently in the daughter's parlor, a circumstance which had given Chauncy Wilson opportunity for a jest rather clever than elegant concerning Judge Welsh's well-known fondness in life for watching the progress of criminal cases. Of her husband, the late Mr. Sampson, there was very little said, and not much was known beyond the fact that having run away from school to marry him, Amanda had shared a shady and it was whispered rather disreputable existence for three years, at the end of which she was fortunately relieved from the matrimonial net by his timely decease; an event of which she sometimes spoke to her more intimate male friends with undisguised satisfaction.

It might not have been easy to tell how far Mrs. Sampson's subsequent career was forced upon her by circumstances, and how far it was the result of her own choice. She always represented herself as the victim of a hard fate: but her relatives, one of whom was Mr. Staggchase, declared that Amanda had no capabilities of respectability in her composition. Mrs. Staggchase, upon whom marriage had conferred the privilege of expressing her mind with the freedom of one of the family, while it happily spared her from the responsibility of an actual relative, declared that everything had been done to keep Mrs. Sampson within the bounds of propriety, but all in vain. The income from the estate of the late Judge Welsh was not large, and as Mrs. Sampson's tastes, especially in dress, were somewhat expensive, it followed that she was often reduced to devices for increasing her bank account which were generally adroit and curious, but often not of a character to be openly boasted of. She had had some business transactions already with Irons, who was at this moment laying out the plan of work in a fresh operation where she might make herself useful.

"Of course," he said, "all the men from Wachusett way are on our side, and the men from the other part of the county will be against us."

"What other part of the county?" Mrs. Sampson inquired.

She had laid down her sewing and was listening intently, with a look of keen intelligence, the tips of her long and rather large fingers pressed closely together. She hated Irons devoutly, but his scheme meant financial profit to her, and various bills were troublesomely overdue.

"That's what we have to discover. When we find out, I'll let you know. The other syndicate have been deucedly close-mouthed about their plans, but of course they can't keep dark a great while longer; and in any case I am on the track of the information."

"And what," Mrs. Sampson asked, with an air of innocence too obviously artificial, "am I expected to do?"

Irons glanced at her with a wink, taking in her plain, vivacious face with its sparkling eyes, her fine figure, and stylish, if somewhat too pronounced, presence.

"The old game," he said. "Show a tender and sisterly interest in a few of the country members. There are one or two men from the western part of the state that we want to capture at once before the thing is started. Do you know anybody in that region?"

"My father, Judge Welsh," she answered with

an amusing touch amid her frankness of the air with which she always mentioned her ancestors in society, "had numerous connections there."

"Ah, that is good," the visitor responded, with evident satisfaction.

He knocked the ashes from his cigar into a tiny bronze which Mrs. Sampson had put within his reach when he showed signs of throwing them upon the carpet, and then plunged into a discussion of the members of the State Legislature with whom it was possible for Mrs. Sampson to establish an acquaintance, and whom she was likely to be able to influence. He drew from his pocket a list of men, and with quite as business-like an air his hostess produced a similar document from her desk; the pair being soon deep in consultation over the schedules.

Lobbying in Massachusetts is not by the public recognized as a well-organized business, and yet any one who desires to secure personal influence to aid or to hinder legislation is seldom at a loss to find people well experienced in such work. The lobby to the eyes of the public, moreover, consists entirely of men, if one excepts the group of foolish intriguers in favor of the vagaries of proposed law-making by which it is supposed the distinctions of sex may be abolished. There are in the city, however, women who by no means lack experience in manipulating the votes of country members, and who are but too willing to sell their services to whoever can make it to their pecuniary interest to favor a bill.

Mrs. Amanda Welsh Sampson was extremely adroit and careful in concealing her connection with the law-making of the State. She was in evidence in most public places ; at the theatres, the concert halls, the County Club races, and at every fashionable entertainment to which her cleverness could procure her admission, her conspicuous figure, made more prominent by a certain indefinable loudness of style, a marked dash of manner, and gowns in a taste rather daring than refined, was too conspicuous to be overlooked. Yet it is doubtful if she had ever been up the steps leading to the gilded-domed capitol in her life. She went about much ; and the unchaperoned life which in virtue of her widowhood and her love of freedom she chose to lead, the width of the circle over which her acquaintance extended, allowed her to carry on her work unobserved ; so that while a great variety of stories of one sort of queerness or another were told of Mrs. Sampson, this particular side of her career was almost unknown.

"There is Mr. Greenfield," Mrs. Sampson observed, tapping her teeth with her pencil. "His wife was a cousin of my husband. I don't know them at all, but I could easily ask him to come and see me. It would be only proper to offer him the hospitality of the town, you know."

"Good!" cried Mr. Irons, slapping his open palm down on his knee. "Greenfield's the hardest nut we've got to crack in the whole business. He's the sort of man you can't talk to on a square business basis. You've got to mince things damned fine with him, and he's chairman of the Railroad Committee, you know. He'd have a tremendous amount of influence, anyway."

"He's a little tin god at Fentonville, I've heard," Mrs. Sampson responded, laughing in the mechanical way which was her habit. "When he's at home they say the sun doesn't rise there till he's given his permission."

Irons in his excitement took his leg down from its supporting chair and sat up straight, dropping his list of members to the floor and clasping his knees with his heavy hands.

"Now look here, old lady," he said, "here's a chance to show your mettle. If you'll manage Greenfield, I'll run the rest of the hayseed crowd, and I'll make it something handsomer than you ever had in your life."

The woman smiled a smile of greed and cunning.

"I'll take care of him," she said. "And he shall never know he has been taken care of either."

Irons laughed with coarse jocoseness.

"A man has very little chance that falls into your clutches," he observed, "but in this particular case you've got a heavy contract on hand. Greenfield's got his price, of course, like everybody else, but I'm hanged if I know what it is. If you offered him tin he'd simply fly out on the whole thing and nobody could hold him. There isn't any particular pull in politics on him. This new-fashioned independence has knocked all that to pieces; and Greenfield is an Independent from the word go. I don't know what you're to bait your hook with, unless it's your lovely self."

Mrs. Sampson began a laugh, and then recovering herself, she frowned.

"Don't be personal," she said. "I won't stand it."

She began to feel that the circumstances were such as to make her important to her caller's schemes, and her air by insensible degrees became more assured and less subservient. She knew her man, and she was prepared for his becoming proportionately more respectful. He dusted a little heap of ashes from the small table beside him and scattered them with his foot, in a well-meant attempt to cover the traces of his previous untidiness. She watched him with a covert sneer.

"Even so difficult a problem as that," she said, with a slight toss of the head, a bit of antique coquetry which impressed him with a new sense of her thorough self-possession, and imposed itself upon his untrained mind as the air of a true woman of the world; "I fancy I can solve. Leave him to me. I'll find out what can be done with him."

"If he can be got hold of," Irons remarked, reflectively, "he will carry the whole thing through. They'd believe him up at Feltonville if he told them it was right to walk backward and vote to give their incomes to the temperance cranks."

He rose to go as he spoke, unconsciously assuming with the overcoat he put on that air of stiffness and immaculate propriety which he wore always in public. He seldom allowed himself the undignified freedom which marked his intercourse with Mrs. Sampson, and he liked the rest he found in being for a time his vulgar, ill-bred self with no restraints of artificial manner.

"Well, good afternoon," he said, extending his large hand, into which she laid hers with a certain faint air of condescension. "I've got to go to a meeting of the committee on the new statue. They've got a new fellow they are trying to push in, a young unlicked cub that Peter Calvin's running. I'll let you know anything that's for our advantage."

When he was gone, Mrs. Sampson produced a brush and a dustpan from behind the books on a whatnot and carefully collected the scattered ashes of his cigar.

"Vulgar old brute!" she muttered. "To think

of my having to clean up after him; his mother was my grandmother's laundress."

Then she smiled contemptuously, and added by way of self-consolation,—

"But it will all count in the bill, Al Irons."

X

THE BITTER PAST.

All's Well That Ends Well; v. — 3.

"DO you see much of Mrs. Herman?" Helen Greyson asked of Edith Fenton, as they sat at luncheon together in the latter's pretty dining-room.

"Why, no," was the somewhat hesitating answer. "I really see very little of her. The fact is we have so little common ground to meet on. — You know Arthur says I am dreadfully narrow, and I am sometimes afraid he is right. I have tried to know her, but of course I couldn't take her into society. She wouldn't enjoy it, and she wouldn't feel at home, even if she'd go with me."

Helen smiled with mingled amusement and wistfulness.

"No," she responded. "I can't exactly fancy Ninitta in society. She'd be quite out of her element. My master in Rome, Flammenti, had a way of saying a thing was like the pope at a dancing-party, and I fancy Ninitta at an afternoon tea would be hardly less out of place."

"But she must be very lonely," Edith said, stirring her coffee meditatively. "She used to have a few Italians come to see her; people she met that time she ran away, you remember, and we brought her home, but they don't come now."

"Why not?"

Edith smiled and raised her eyebrows.

"A question of caste, I believe."

"Of caste?" echoed Helen. "What do you mean?"

"When her son was born," Edith responded, "she told them that the *bambino* was born a gentleman, and couldn't associate with them."

Helen laughed lightly; then her face clouded, and she sighed.

"Poor Ninitta!" she said. "There is something infinitely pitiful in her devotion and faithfulness to her youthful love."

Edith's face assumed an expression of mingled perplexity and disquiet. With eyes downcast she seemed for a moment to be seeking a phrase in which properly to express some thought which troubled her. Then she looked up quickly.

"I don't know that I ought to say it," she remarked, "but I can't help feeling that Ninitta is not so fond of her husband as she used to be. Of course I may be mistaken, but either I overestimated her devotion before they were married, or she cares less for him now."

An expression of pain contracted Helen's brow.

"Isn't it possible," she suggested, "that her

being more demonstrative in her love for the boy makes her seem cold toward her husband?"

"No," returned Edith, shaking her head, "it is more than that. I fancy sometimes that she unconsciously expected to be somehow transformed into his equal by marrying him; and that the disappointment of being no more on a level with him when she became his wife than before, has made her somehow give him up, as if she concluded that she could never really belong to his life. Of course I don't mean," she added, "that Ninitta would reason this out, and very likely I am all wrong, anyway, but certainly something of this kind has happened."

"Poor Ninitta," repeated Helen, "fate hasn't been kind to her."

"But Mr. Herman?" Edith returned. "What do you say of him? I think his case is far harder. What a mistake his marriage was. I cannot conceive how he was ever betrayed into such a *més-alliance.* She cannot be a companion to him; she does not understand him: she is only a child who has to be borne with, and who tries his patience and his endurance."

Edith had forgotten her husband's suggestion that her companion was responsible for Grant Herman's marriage; but Helen, who for six years had been questioning with herself whether she had done well in urging the sculptor to marry his model, heard this outburst with beating heart and flushing cheek. Had Helen allowed Herman to break his early pledge to Ninitta, and marry his later love, it is probable that all her life would have been shadowed by a consciousness of guilt. The conscience bequeathed to her, as Fenton rightly said, by Puritan ancestors, would ever have reproached her with having come to happiness over the ruins of another woman's heart and hopes. Having in the supreme hour of temptation, however, overcome herself and given him up, it was not perhaps strange that Helen unconsciously fell somewhat into the attitude of assuming that this sacrifice gave her not only the right to sit in judgment upon Ninitta, but also that of having done somewhat more than might justly have been demanded of her. She had often found herself wondering whether she had been wise; whether her devotion to an ideal had not been overstrained; and if she ought not to have considered rather the happiness of the man she loved than devotion to an abstract principle.

It was also undoubtedly true, although Helen had not herself reflected upon this phase of the matter, that her half a dozen years' residence in Europe had softened and broadened her views. In the present age of the world there is no method possible by which one can resist the whole tendency of modern thought and prevent himself from moving forward with it, unless it be active and violent controversy. No man can be a fanatic without opposition, either real or vividly fancied, upon which to stay his resolution, and it is equally difficult to maintain a stand at any given point of faith unless one has steadily to fight with vigor for the right to possess it.

It is probable that to-day Helen might have found it more difficult than six years before to urge Herman to marry Ninitta, since besides the self-sacrifice then involved would now be a doubtfulness of purpose. She sat silent some moments, reflecting deeply, while her hostess watched her with a loving admiration which was growing very strongly upon her.

"But what is to be done now," Helen asked slowly. "You would not have him cast her off?"

"Oh, no," returned Edith, in genuine consternation. "Now, it is six years too late."

"I am afraid I do not wholly agree with your point of view," answered Mrs. Greyson, roused by the doubt in her own mind to a need to combat the assumption that the marriage was a mistake. "I certainly do not feel that the mere ceremony is the great point. See!" she continued, becoming more animated, and half involuntarily saying aloud what she had so often said in her own mind; "a man makes a woman love him. As time goes on, he outgrows her. It is no fault of hers. Why should the fact that he has or has not come into the marriage relations affect her claims on him? Isn't he in honor bound to marry her?"

"But suppose," Edith returned, "that he has not only outgrown her but made some other woman love him too?"

It was merely a chance shot of argument, but it smote Helen so that she trembled as she sat.

"Is not that woman to be considered?" Edith continued. "Is the good of the man to count for nothing? Mr. Herman is sacrificed to an old mistake. Perhaps it is right that he should pay the price of his error; and that in the end it will be overruled for his good, we may hope. But it is hard to have patience now with the state of things."

Helen tapped her teaspoon nervously against her cup.

"But what can be done?"

"Nothing," Mrs. Fenton said, without the slightest hesitation. "You and I may think these things, but it would be a crime for Mr. Herman to think them."

"It might be cowardice to yield to them," responded Helen; "but how crime? And how can one help the thoughts from turning whithersoever they will?"

Edith pushed back her plate, leaned forward with folded arms resting upon the edge of the table. She flushed a little, as she did sometimes when she felt it her duty to say something to her husband which it was hard to utter.

"I do not think you and I agree in this," she

said, in a voice which her earnestness made somewhat lower than before. "Marriage is to me a sacrament, and this very fact gives it a nature different from ordinary promises. We promise to love until death do us part. To me that is as imperative as any vow I can make to God and man."

"But love," Helen urged, with a somewhat perplexed air, "is not a thing to be coerced."

"It must be," Edith returned, inflexibly. "Even if my husband ceased to love me, that does not absolve me. I must fulfil my promise and my duty."

"But," Helen responded, doubtfully and slowly, "it seems to me a sacrilege to live with a man after one has ceased to love him."

"But I would love him," Edith broke in almost fiercely. "That is just the point. One must refuse to cease to love him."

"But if he ceased to love her?"

A flush came into Edith's clear cheek, and her eyes shone. Half unconsciously to herself, she was fighting with the doubts which would now and then rise in her own mind of her husband's affection.

"Then," she said, in a low voice, "one must still be worthy of his love; one must do one's duty. Besides," she added, looking up with a gleam of hope, "when one has made a solemn vow, as a wife vows to love her husband until death part them, I firmly believe that strength to keep that vow will not be withheld."

Helen was silent a moment. She by no means agreed to the position Edith took. She had no belief in those promises in virtue of which the sacraments of the church took on a peculiar sanctity; she did not at all trust to any special help bestowed by higher powers. She did not, however, care to argue upon these points, and she said more lightly, —

"You task womanhood pretty heavily."

"A little woman who is a *protégée* of mine," Edith returned, in the same manner, "said rather quaintly the other day, that women were made so there should be somebody to be patient with men. She's having trouble with her lover, I suspect, and takes it hardly."

"But," Helen persisted more gravely, "it seems to me that you set before the unloved wife a task to which humanity is absolutely unequal."

"You remember St. Theresa and her two sous," Edith replied, her eyes shining with deep inner feeling; "how she said, 'St. Theresa and two sous are nothing, but St. Theresa and two sous and God are everything.' I can't argue, but for myself, I could not live if I should give up my ideal of duty."

As often it had happened before, Helen found herself so deeply moved by the fervor and the genuineness of Edith's faith, that she felt it impossible to go on with an argument which could convince only at the expense of weakening this rare trust. She brought the conversation back to its starting point.

"But about Ninitta," she said. "I saw her yesterday, and she acted as if she had something on her mind. She somehow seemed to be trying to tell me something. I told her that the *bambino*, as she calls Nino, must keep her occupied most of the time, and she said the nurse stole him away half of the day; she has the peasant instinct to take entire charge of her own child."

"If that is a peasant instinct," Edith rejoined laughing, "I am afraid I am a peasant."

"Oh, but you are reasonable about it, and know that it is better for the boy to have change and so on. She acts as if she felt it to be a conspiracy between the nurse and her husband to steal the child's affections from her. Really, I felt as if she was coming to love Nino so fiercely that she had fits of almost hating her husband."

The ringing of the door bell and the entrance of the servant with a card interrupted the conversation, and Helen had only time to say, —

"Of course on general principles you know I do not agree with you. Indeed, I should find it hard to justify what I consider the most meritorious acts of my life if I did. But I do want to say that, given your creed, your view of marriage seems to me the noble — indeed, the only one."

As Helen walked home in the gray afternoon, sombre with a winter mist, she thought over the conversation and measured her life by its principles.

"If one accepts Edith's standard," she reflected, "it is impossible not to accept her conclusions. She is a St. Theresa, with her strict adherence to forms and her loyalty to her convictions. But surely one's own self has some claims. My first duty to whatever the highest power is, — the All, perhaps, — must be to do the best I can with myself. It could not be my duty to go on living with Will" —

She stopped, with a faint shudder, raising her eyes and looking about upon the wet and dreary landscape with an almost furtive glance, as if she were oppressed by the fear that the eyes of the husband with whom she had found it impossible to live, and who for six years had been under the sod, dead by his own hand, might be watching her unawares. It was one of those moments when a bygone emotion is so vividly revived, as if some long hidden landscape were revealed by a sudden lightning flash. The years had brought her immunity from the poignancy of the pain of old sorrows, but for one brief and bitter instant she cowed with the old fear, she trembled with the old-time agony.

Then she smiled at the unreasonableness of her feeling, and dropping her eyes, walked on with slightly quickened steps.

"It cannot be a woman's duty to go on living with a man who is dragging her down, or even who prevents her from realizing her best; and yet, there is the influence. That is a trick of my old Puritan training, of course, but after all it is right to consider. One must count influence as a factor if one believes in civilization, and I do believe in civilization; certainly, I would not go back to barbarism. But is a woman to be tied down — oh! how a woman is always tied down! limitation — limitation — limitation; that is the whole story of a woman's life; and the harder she struggles to get away from her bonds the more she proves to herself by the pain of the wrist cut by the fetters how impossible it is to break them. Women contrive to deceive men sometimes into believing that they have overcome the limitations of their sex; and they even deceive themselves; but they never deceive each other. A woman may believe that she herself has accomplished the impossible, but she knows no one of her sisters has."

She smiled sadly and yet humorously, pausing a moment on the curbstone before crossing the wet and icy street. Then as she went on and a coachman pulled up his horses almost upon their haunches to let her pass, she took up the thread of her reflections once more, —

"Yet surely women must not rebel against civilization. Civilization is after all quite as largely as anything else a determined ignoring and combatting on the part of mankind of the cruel disadvantages under which nature has put women. No; we must look at it in the large; we must hold to the conventional even, rather than fight against civilization, however wrong and illogical and heartless civilization may be. It is the best we have and we go to the wall without it."

She had reached her boarding-house and fitted her latch-key into the lock. As she opened the door she looked back into the gathering dusk of the misty afternoon, and her thought was almost as if it were a last word flung to some presence to be left behind and shut out, a personality with whom she had argued, and who had logically defeated but not convinced her.

"And yet," she said inwardly, with a sudden swelling of defiance and conviction, "not for all the universe could I have done it. I could not go on living with Will, — though," she added, a sudden compunction seizing her, "I was fond of him in a way, poor fellow."

And the door closed.

XI

THE GREAT ASSAY OF ART.

Macbeth ; iv. — 3.

THE inner history of the effigies which in Boston do duty as statues would be most interesting reading, amusing or depressing as one felt obliged to take it. To know what causes led to the production and then to the erection of these monstrosities could hardly fail to be instructive, although the knowledge might be rather dreary.

The subject has been too much discussed to make it easy to touch it, but all this examination has by no means resulted in general enlightenment, as was sufficiently evident at the meeting of the committee in charge of the new statue of *America* about to be erected in a properly select Back Bay location. The committee consisted of Stewart Hubbard, Alfred Irons, and Peter Calvin, three names which were seldom long absent from the columns of the leading Boston daily newspapers. Mr. Irons had been strongly objected to by both his associates, neither of whom felt quite disposed to assume even such equality as might seem to follow from joint membership of the committee. That gentleman had, however, sufficient influence at City Hall to secure appointment, a whim which had seized him to pose as a patron of art being his obvious motive; and neither Mr. Hubbard nor Mr. Calvin was prepared to go quite to the length of declining to serve with the obnoxious parvenu.

Stewart Hubbard was a most admirable example of the best type of an American gentleman. Arthur Fenton once described him as "a genuine old Beacon street, purple window-glass swell;" a description expressive, if not especially elegant. Tall and well-built, with the patrician written in every line of his handsome face, his finely shaped head covered with short hair, snowy white although he had hardly passed middle age, his clear dark eyes straightforward and frank in their glances, he was a striking and pleasing figure in any company. He had graduated, like his ancestors for three or four generations, at Harvard; and if he knew less about art than his place on the committee made desirable, he at least had a pretty fair idea of what authorities could be trusted.

Peter Calvin's place in Boston art matters has already been spoken of. He took himself very seriously, moving through life with a sunny-faced self-complacency so inoffensive and sincere as to be positively delightful. He was too good-natured and in all respects of character too little virile to meet Irons with anything but kindness, but as he was a trifle less sure of his social standing than

Hubbard, he was naturally more annoyed at the choice of the third member of the committee. He made not a few protests to his friends, and gently represented himself as a martyr to his devotion to the cause of art from having accepted the place he held.

When one considered, however, the way in which committees upon art matters are made up at City Hall, it becomes evident that the wonder was not that the present body was no better, but that it should be so good. The truth was that the choice of Hubbard and Calvin had been considered a great concession to the unreasonable prejudices of the self-appointed arbitrators of art affairs in town. A short time before, a committee consisting of a butcher, a furniture dealer and a North End ward politician, had been sent to New York on a matter connected with a public monument, and their action had been so egregiously absurd as to bring down upon their heads and upon the heads of those who appointed them such a torrent of ridicule that even the tough hide of City Hall could not withstand it. It was felt that the public was more alive on art matters than had been suspected ; and when a South Boston liquor-dealer manifested a singular but unmistakable desire to be appointed on the *America* committee, he had been promptly suppressed with the information that this was to be "a regular bang-up, silver-top committee," and was forced to soothe his disappointed ambition with such consolation as lay in the promise that next time he should be counted in.

When the committee had been named, a hint was dropped in one or two newspaper offices that the powers which work darkly at City Hall expected due credit for the self-sacrifice involved in putting on two men at least from whom no reward was to be expected. The journals improved the opportunity, and praised highly the choice of all three of the members. When this called out a protest from the artists, because no artist had been appointed, City Hall had no words adequate to the expression of its disgust.

"That's what comes of trying to satisfy them fellows," one City Father observed, in an indignant and unstilted speech to his colleagues. "They want the earth, and nothing else will satisfy them. What if they ain't got no artist on the committee; everybody knows that Peter Calvin's a man who's published a lot of books about art, and it stands to reason he's a bigger gun than a feller that just paints."

The committee paid no attention to the discussion concerning their fitness, of which indeed they did not know a great deal, but came together in a matter-of-fact way, precisely as they would have assembled to transact any other business.

"I don't know what you think," Mr. Irons observed, as the three gentlemen settled themselves in the easy-chairs of Mr. Hubbard's private office and lighted their cigars, "but it seems to me we had better try to come to some reasonably definite idea of what we want this monument to be before we go any farther. It will be time enough to talk about who's to get the order when we've made up our minds what the order is to be."

Both the words and the manner rasped the nerves of Mr. Calvin almost beyond endurance. He was accustomed to phrasing his views with elegance, and although in truth his ideas in the matter on hand were not widely different from those of Mr. Irons, the latter had stated the proposition with a boldness which made it impossible for him to agree with it. By birth, by instinct, and by lifelong training a faithful servant of the god Dagon, he yet seldom professed his allegiance frankly. He sheltered his slavish adherence to conventions under a decent show of following convictions; so that the pure and straightforward Philistinism which Mr. Irons professed from simple lack of a knowledge of the secrets of what might perhaps be called the priestly cult of Philistia, appeared to Peter Calvin shockingly crude and offensive.

"Perhaps," he said, with a smile which was hardly less sweet than usual, so well trained were the muscles of his face in producing it, "it can hardly be said that we can decide. The artist after all cannot be expected to accept too many limitations if he is to produce a work of art. His genius must have full play."

Secretly, Irons had a most profound respect for the other's art knowledge, and he was too anxious to appear well in his capacity as a member of the statue committee to be willing to run any risks by attempting to controvert any æsthetic proposition laid down by Mr. Calvin. He was by no means fond of the man, however, and to his dislike his envy of Calvin's reputation, socially and æsthetically, added venom. He hastened now, with quite unnecessary vigor, to defend himself from the mildly implied attack.

"I suppose we have got to give an order — or a commission, if the word suits you better — of some sort; and whatever it is to be it needs to be defined."

His manner was so evidently belligerent that Mr. Hubbard hastened to interpose.

"That is pretty well defined for us, isn't it?" he said. "We were directed to give a commission for a single figure representing America, to be executed in bronze and not to exceed a fixed sum in cost. That does not leave much latitude, so far as I can see, beyond the right of selecting or rejecting models shown us. For my own part, I may as well say at once, I am in favor of giving Mr. Herman whatever terms he wants to make a model, and trusting everything to him. Of course we should still have the right to veto the arrangement if the figure he made should not prove satisfactory."

Mr. Hubbard spoke with a certain elegant deliberation and precision which Irons supposed himself to regard as affected, while secretly he thoroughly envied it.

"Oh, we all know what Herman would do," Irons retorted. "He'd make one of those things that nobody could understand, and then say it was artistic. We want something to please folks."

Irons was more concerned about his popularity than even in regard to the reputation as an art patron he was laboriously striving to build up. He was an inordinately vain man, but he was an exceedingly shrewd one. His self-esteem was gratified by seeing his name among those of men influential in art matters; he bought pictures largely for the pleasure of being talked of as a man who patronized the proper painters, and he was looked upon as likely at no distant day to become president of a club which Fenton dubbed the Discourager of Art; but he realized that for a man who still had some political aspirations there was a substantial value in popular favor not to be found in any reputation for culture, however delightful the latter might be. He distinctly intended to please the public by his action in regard to the statue, a resolution which was rendered the more firm by the fact that he vastly over-estimated the interest which the public was likely to take in the matter. He trimmed the ashes from his cigar as he spoke, with an air which was intended to convey the idea that he would stand no nonsense.

"Won't Mr. Herman enter a competitive trial?" Calvin asked. "We might ask two or three others and then select the best model."

"He won't go into a competition. He says it's beneath an artist's dignity."

"Damned nonsense!" blustered Irons, sitting up in his chair in excitement over such an extraordinary proposition. "Don't we all go into competitions whenever we send in sealed proposals? Beneath his dignity! Great Scott! The cockiness of artists is enough to take away a man's breath."

Mr. Hubbard, who was a lawyer chiefly occupied, as far as business went, in managing his own large property and certain trust funds, and Mr. Calvin, who had never in his life soiled his aristocratic hands with any business whatever, smiled in the mutual consciousness that "sealed proposals" were as much outside their experience as competitions were foreign to that of Grant Herman. The thought, passing and trivial as it was, moved their sympathy a little toward the sculptor's view of the matter, although since secretly Mr. Calvin was determined that the commission should be given to Orin Stanton, the fact made little difference.

"You evidently don't want to undergo the general condemnation that has fallen on whoever has had a share in the Boston statues thus far," Mr.

Calvin observed, glancing at Irons with a genial smile. "If you are going to set yourself to hit the popular taste and keep yourself clear of the claws of the critics at the same time, I fear you've a heavy task laid out."

"The critics always pitch into everything," Irons responded with a growl. "It's the taste of the people I want to please. I believe in art as a popular educator, and people can't be educated by things they won't look at."

"Oh, as to that," Stewart Hubbard rejoined, with a twinkle in his eye, "conventionality is after all the consensus of the taste of mankind."

Peter Calvin was at a loss to tell whether his friend was in earnest or was only quizzing Irons, so he contented himself with an appreciative look, and a smile of dazzling warmth. Irons, on the other hand, looked toward the speaker with suspicion.

"I haven't much sympathy with a good deal of the stuff artists talk," he continued, following his own train of thought. "It doesn't square very well with common sense and ain't much more than pure gassing, I think. The truth is, genius is mostly moonshine. The man I call a genius is the one that makes things work practically."

"In other words," said Calvin, spurred to emulate Hubbard's epigram, and involuntarily glancing toward the latter for approval, "you think a genius is a man who is able to harness Pegasus to the plough, and make him work without kicking things to pieces."

"That's about it," Irons assented; "and I think Herman is too toploftical and full of cranky theories. They say Mrs. Greyson has hit the nail exactly on the head in that statue she showed in Paris last year. That pleased the critics and the public both, and that's exactly what we are after. I think we ought to ask her to make a design."

Mr. Calvin saw and seized the opportunity easily to introduce his own especial candidate.

"If each of you have a sculptor," he said, lightly, "I can hardly do less than to have one, too. There's an exceedingly clever fellow just home from Rome, that I want to see given a chance. He's done some very promising work, and I look upon him as the coming man."

The two men regarded him with some interest, as one who has introduced a new element into a game. Mr. Hubbard leaned back in his chair, and sent a puff of cigar smoke floating upward, before he answered.

"I can't enter my man for the triangular contest," said he. "He won't go into a competition unless he's paid for making the design. He says, in so many words, that he doesn't want the commission to make the statue unless he can do it in his own way. He will be unhindered, or he will let the whole thing alone."

"For my part," Mr. Irons responded, settling himself in his chair, with a certain air of determination, "I don't take a great deal of stock in this letting an artist have his own way. He might put up a naked woman, or any rubbish he happened to think of. The amount of the matter is that it isn't such a devilish smart thing to make a figure as they try to make out. Any man can do it that has learned the trade, and I haven't any great amount of patience with the fuss these fellows make over their statues."

Neither of his companions felt inclined to enter into a general discussion of the principles underlying art work, and, although neither agreed with this broad statement, there was no direct response offered. Calvin and Hubbard looked at each other, and the latter asked, —

"Have you any notion what Mrs. Greyson would do?"

"No, I have never talked with her."

"Very likely she'd give us another figure like those that are stuck all over Boston, like pins in a pincushion," Hubbard objected. "Some carpet-knight, with a face spread over with a grin as inane as that of Henry Clay on a cigar-box cover."

Irons laughed contemptuously, and rose, throwing away his cigar stub.

"Well, I must go," he announced. "We don't seem to be getting ahead very fast. I'll try and find out if she'll go into a competition, and you two had better do the same with your folks. Then we shall at least have something to go upon. The *Daily Observer* has already begun to ask why something isn't done, and I'd like to get the thing finished up, myself."

The two others rose also, and it was thereby manifest that this unproductive sitting of the committee was at an end.

XII

WHOM THE FATES HAVE MARKED.

Comedy of Errors; i. — 1.

NEVER was a man more utterly wretched than was Arthur Fenton, after the luckless day when Mr. Irons had lighted upon the presence of Mrs. Herman at the studio. He raged against himself, against chance, most of all against the unmannerly and coarse-minded fellow who had forced himself into the studio, and then persisted in imagining evil which had never existed. He experienced all the acute anguish of finding himself in the toils, and of the added sting from wounded vanity, since he felt that he had been wanting in adroitness and presence of mind. It is to be doubted if he did not suffer more than would have been the case had the injurious suspicions of Irons been correct. To a vain man, it is often harder to be entrapped through stupidity or awkwardness than through crime.

Fenton realized well enough how impossible it was now to correct the evil that had been done. He might have explained away the fact that Ninitta had been his model, but his own bearing under the accusation had produced an impression not to be eradicated. The wavering before his eyes, for a single instant, of the will-o'-the-wisp fire of sudden temptation had blinded him, so that he had been guilty of a cursed piece of folly, which had put him at once in the power of Irons. He knew enough of the latter to be pretty sure that he was capable of keeping his threat to enlighten Herman concerning his wife's visit to the studio, and disgrace in the eyes of Herman meant more than Arthur dared to think. Sensitive to the last fibre of his being, the artist grew faint with exquisite pain at the thought of what he must endure from a scandal spread among his friends. An accusation without foundation would have been almost more than he could bear, but one supported by such circumstantial evidence as lay behind the story Irons would tell if he set himself to make trouble, — the bare idea drove Fenton wild.

Fenton had always prided himself upon his superiority to public opinion, but without public respect he could not but be supremely miserable. It is true that he valued his own good opinion above that of the world. It was his theory that the ultimate appeal in matters of conduct was always to the man's inner consciousness, and in this highest court only the man himself could be present, all the world being shut out. It followed that a person's own opinion of his acts was of infinitely more weight than that of any or all other people whosoever.

"All standards are arbitrary," he was accustomed to say, "and all terms are relative. Every man must make his own ethical code, and nobody but the man himself can tell how far he lives up to it. Why should I care whether people who do not even know what my rules of conduct are, consider my course correct or not? Very likely the things they condemn are the things it has cost me most struggle and self-denial to achieve. We have outgrown old ethical systems, because the world has become enlightened enough to perceive that every mind must make its own code; to realize that what a man is must be his religion."

This course of reasoning was one shared by many of Fenton's friends, and indeed by a goodly company of nineteenth century thinkers. Fenton was in reality only going with the majority of liberalists in regarding sincerity to personal conviction as the highest of ethical laws; and he was generally pretty logical in choosing the approval of his inward knowledge to that of the world outside. Yet his vanity was keenly sensitive to disapprobation, and when the censure of the world coincided with the condemnation of his own reason he suffered. To self-contempt was added a baffled sense of having been discovered; and as his imagination now ran forward to picture the effects of Irons's disclosure, the suffering he endured was really pitiful.

"Nobody will understand," he said to himself one day, half in bitter self-contempt and half in self-defence, "that I couldn't help doing as I did; no cruelty surpasses that of holding weak and sensitive natures accountable for shortcomings they are born incapable of avoiding."

And having accomplished an epigram at his own expense, he felt as if he had to some degree atoned for his fault, just as a flagellant looks upon his self-scourging as expiatory.

How to act in the position in which he had been placed by Irons's insulting proposal was a question which he found more difficult to answer than according to his theories, it should have been. When a man becomes his own highest law he is constantly exposed to the danger of finding his theories of conduct utterly confounded by a change in self-interest; and Fenton began to have a most painful sense of being ethically wholly at sea. He had not yielded to temptation, however. He had given Stewart Hubbard a couple of sittings, and so great had been his fear lest he should inadvertently gather from his sitter some hint of the knowledge he had been urged to obtain, that he had half unconsciously been reserved and silent. The picture was going badly, and the sitter wondered what had come over the witty and vivacious artist.

Besides these vexations the artist had, moreover, other causes for uneasiness at this time. His financial affairs were by no means in satisfactory condition. He had been filling a good many orders and getting excellent prices for his work, yet somehow he had been all the year running behindhand. He lived beyond his means, priding himself upon being the one Boston artist who had been born, bred, and educated a gentleman, as he chose to put it to himself, and who was able to live as a man of the world should. His summer had been passed at Newport, a place which Edith by no means liked, and where her ideas of propriety and religion were constantly offended, especially in regard to the sanctity of marriage. He entertained sumptuously, spent money freely at the clubs, and, in a word, tried to be no less a man of fashion than an artist.

The result was beginning to be disastrous. Living pretty closely up to his income, a few losses and a speculation or two which turned out unlucky, were sufficient to embarrass him seriously. It was the old trite and dreary story of extravagance and its inevitable consequence; and as Fenton had no talent for finance, his struggles rather made matters worse than bettered them, as the efforts of a fly to escape from the web, even although they may damage the net, are apt to end also in binding the victim more securely.

The truth was that the painter, like many another man endowed with imaginative gifts, had little practical knowledge of affairs beyond a talent for spending money; and it is amazing how stupid a clever man can contrive to be when he is taken out of his sphere. For such men there is no safety save in keeping out of debt, and once the balance was on the wrong side of his account, Fenton, self-poised as he was, lost his head. It troubled and worried him to be in debt even when he could see his way clear to paying everything, and now that matters began to get too complicated to be settled by plain and obvious arithmetic, he was miserable.

In the midst of these unhappy complications, he was one morning working upon the portrait of Miss Damaris Wainwright, whose cousin and aunts, the Dimmonts, had induced her to have it painted, although she was in deep mourning. He was interested in the lovely, melancholy girl, and he felt that he was doing some of the best work of his life in her portrait. He sometimes was proud of his skill, and at others he was unreasonably vexed that this picture should be so much better than that of Mr. Hubbard promised to be.

He had been talking this morning half-absently, and merely for the sake of keeping his sitter interested. He had not noticed that her whole being was keyed up to a pitch of intense feeling, and he had almost unconsciously accomplished the really difficult task of putting his sitter at her ease and making her ready to talk.

Suddenly, after a brief silence, she said, —

"You provoke confidences."

Some note in her voice and the closeness of

connection between her words and the thought in his own mind that he certainly must be able to do what Irons asked, arrested Fenton's attention.

"Yes," he returned, his air of sincerely meaning what he said being by no means wholly unreal; "that is because I am unworthy of them."

Miss Wainwright smiled. The self-detraction seemed delicate, and the unexpectedness of the reply amused her.

"That is perhaps a modest thing to say, Mr. Fenton," she responded, "but the truth must be — if you'll pardon my saying anything so personal — that you are very sympathetic."

The artist moved backward a step from his easel, regarding his work with that half-shutting of the eyes and turning of the head which seems to be an essential of professional inspection.

"Even so," persisted he, "a sympathetic person is one whose emotions are fickle enough to give place to whatever others any sudden accident brings up; and if one's feelings are so transient, how can he be worthy of confidence?"

"I can't argue with you," Damaris replied, smiling and shaking her head, "but all the same I don't agree with what you say."

"Oh, I hoped you wouldn't when I said it," Fenton threw back lightly.

He went on with his work, outwardly tranquil, as if he had no thought beyond the perfect shading of the cheek he was painting; but his mind was in a tumult. He thought how easy it is to deceive; how constantly, indeed, we do deceive whether we will or no; how foolish it is to rule our lives by standards which rest so largely on mere seeming; how — Bah! Why should he pretend to himself? He was not really concerned with generalities or great moral principles. He was trying to decide whether he should worm a secret out of Hubbard to throw as a sop to that vile cursed cad, Irons, to keep his foul mouth shut about Ninitta. Heavens! What a tangle he had got into simply because he wanted a decent model for his picture! The abominable prudery and hypocrisy of the time lay behind the whole matter. But this would never do. He must work now; not think of these exciting things. It was hardly a brief moment before to his last words he added aloud, —

"Did what you said mean that I was to be favored with a confidence?"

A painful, deep problem was weighing upon her heart, wearing away her reason and her life alike. She had almost been ready to ask advice of the artist, although she by no means knew him well enough to render so intimate a conversation other than strange.

"Not necessarily," was her reply to Fenton's question.

She found it after all impossible to utter anything definite upon the subject which lay so near her heart. She even felt a dim wonder whether she had really ever seriously contemplated speaking of it, even never so remotely.

"I was thinking," she continued, "of the point the conversation had reached this morning when I left my friend at the door downstairs."

"It was some great moral problem, I think you said," Fenton responded, trying to recall accurately what she had told him earlier in the sitting of a talk she had had with a friend on her way to the studio. "The object of life, or something of that sort. Well, the object of life is to endure life, I suppose, just as the object of time is to kill time."

"We had got so far in our talk as to decide," Miss Wainwright went on, too much absorbed in recalling the interview she was relating to notice the painter's words, "he decided, that is, not I — that the only thing to do is to enjoy the present and to let the future go; but I object that one cannot help dreading what might come."

She spoke, of course, solely with reference to her own inner experiences, but Fenton, with the egotism which is universal to humanity, received the words in their application to his own case. If he could but determine what would come, he might decide how to act in this hard present. Yet, whatever that future might be, he must at any cost extricate himself from this coil which pressed so cruelly upon him.

"Even so he would be right," he answered her words. "Happiness in this world consists, at best, in a choice of evils, and at least one may make of the present a sauce *piquante* to cover the flavor of the dread of the future."

"You take a more desperate view of the matter than my friend," Miss Wainwright said, sighing bitterly. "His only fear is that I shall lose everything by not making sure of whatever present happiness is possible."

Fenton glanced at her curiously, aware no less from her tone and manner than from her words that the conversation was touching her as well as himself through some keen personal experience. A feeling of sharp and irritating remorse stung him from the thought that he, whose whole sensuous nature strove for selfish joyousness in life, was discussing this question from his own standpoint, while the pale, lovely girl before him was regarding the whole problem from the high plane of duty. Instinctively he set himself to justify his position against hers; to demonstrate that his Pagan, selfish philosophy was the true guide.

"Oh," he cried out with sudden vehemence, waving his palette with a gesture of supreme impatience, "I do take a desperate view! Life is desperate, and the most absurd of all the multitudinous ways of making it worse is to waste the present in dreading the future. I've no patience with the notion that seems to be so many people's creed, that we can do nothing nobler than to be as miserable as possible. It is a dreadful remainder of that awful malady of Puritanism. Besides, where is the logic of supposing we shall be better prepared for any misfortune that may come if we can only contrive to dread it enough beforehand. Good heavens! We all need whatever strength we can get from happiness whenever it comes, as much as a plant needs the sunshine while it lasts. You wouldn't prepare a delicate plant for cloudy days by keeping it in the shadow; and I think one is simply an idiot who keeps in the shade to accustom himself to-day after to-morrow's storm."

His excitement increased as he went on. He was arguing against the coward sense that he had deserved the troubles which had come upon him. He was saying in as plain language as the conditions of the conversation would allow, that he had been right in gratifying his desires; in living as he wished without too closely considering the consequences which were likely to follow. He spoke with a bitter earnestness born of the intense strain under which he was laboring; and he did not consider how his words might or might not affect his hearer. The thought came into his mind how he had deliberately sacrificed his convictions in marrying Edith Caldwell and going over to Philistinism; and he reflected that this decision had shaped his life. Already his course was determined; it was idle to ignore the fact.

Why should he hesitate from squeamish scruples to do what Irons asked when to meet the consequences of the latter's anger would not only be supremely disagreeable but contrary to his whole theory of life?

It was one of Fenton's peculiarities that he never knowingly shrank from telling himself the truth about his thoughts and actions with the most brutal frankness. Indeed, it might not be too much to say that this self-honesty was a sort of fetish to which he made expiatory sacrifices in the shape of the most cruelly disagreeable admissions before his inner consciousness. He constantly settled his moral accounts by setting down on the credit side "Self-contempt to balance," a method of mental bookkeeping by no means rare, albeit seldom carried on in connection with such clear powers of moral discrimination as Fenton possessed when he chose to exercise them.

"If you chance on ill-luck," he ran on, arguing aloud with himself concerning the possible consequences of betraying Mr. Hubbard's trust, "you'll be glad you were happy while it was possible; and if the fates make you the one person in a million, by letting you get through life decently, you surely can't think it would be better to spend it moping until you are incapable of enjoying anything."

The form of his speech was still that of one talking simply from the point of view of his hearer. It did not for a moment occur to Damaris Wainwright that in all he had said there had been anything but a perfectly disinterested discussion of the principles involved in her own questions and in her own perplexities. Yet, as a matter of fact, his words were but the surface indications of the conflict going on in his own mind. He was arguing down his disinclination to accept the obvious and dishonorable means of escaping from an unpleasant position; he was fighting against the better instincts of his nature, and trying to convince himself that the easy course was the one to be chosen, the one logically following from the conclusions forced upon him by his study of life.

"But duty!" she interposed, rather timidly, as he paused.

She was confused by his persistent ignoring of all the standards by which she was accustomed to judge, and she threw out the question as one in desperation brings forward a last argument, half foreseeing that it will be useless.

"Duty!" he echoed, fiercely. "Life is an outrage, and what duty can take precedence of righting it as far as we can. That old fool of a Ruskin — I beg your pardon, Miss Wainwright, if you're fond of him — did manage to say a sensible thing when he told a boarding-school full of girls that their first duty was to want to dance. To allow that there is any duty above making the best of life is a species of moral suicide."

She looked at him with an expression of profoundest feeling. She was too little used to arguments of this sort to discern that the whole matter was involved in the definition one gave to the phrase "The best of life," and that to assume that this meant mere selfish or sensuous enjoyment, was to beg the whole question. She was carried away by the dramatic fashion in which he ended, dashing down his palette and throwing himself into a chair.

"There!" he exclaimed, with an air of whimsical impatience. "Now I've got so excited that I can't paint! That's what comes of having convictions."

The struggle was over. He brushed all doubts and questions aside. There was but one thing to do, and, disagreeable as it might be, he must accept the situation. The mention of the word "duty" reminded him that he had long ago settled in his own mind the folly of being bound down by superstitions masquerading under grand names as ethical principles. The duty of self-preservation was above all others. He must defend himself, no matter if he did violate the principles by which fools allowed their lives to be narrowed and hampered. He would set himself to work upon Hubbard to-morrow, and get this unpleasant thing over.

His sitter came down from the dais upon which she had been sitting, and held out her hand.

"You have decided my life for me," she said, in a low voice, "and I thank you."

Those who knew her perplexities had argued with her in vain; and this stranger, talking to his own inner self, had said the final word which had moved her to a conclusion they had not been able to force upon her.

He looked up with a smile, as he pressed her hand, but he said nothing; refraining from adding, as he might have done truthfully, —

"And I have decided my own."

XIII

THIS "WOULD" CHANGES.

Hamlet; iv. — 7.

MELISSA BLAKE was growing paler in these days, worn with the ache of a hurt love. Since the night on which he had parted from her in anger, John had been to see her only on brief errands which he could not well avoid, and while he had made no allusion to the difference which separated them, it was evident that he still brooded over his fancied grievance.

This phase of John's character, its least amiable characteristic, which marred it amid many excellent qualities, was not wholly unknown to Melissa. She was by far the more clear-headed of the two, and she understood her lover with much greater acuteness than he was able to bring to the task of comprehending her. It was from intelligent perception and not merely from the feminine instinct for making excuses, that she said to herself that John was worn out with the strain of burdens long and uncomplainingly borne; and she was, it might be added, near enough to the primitive savagery of the rustic New Englanders of the last generation, to find it perfectly a matter of course that a man should make of his womenfolk a sort of scapegoat upon whom to visit his wrath against the sins alike of fate and of his fellows.

She waited for John to relent from his unjust anger, but she did not protest, and when he chose once more to be gracious unto his handmaiden he would be met only with faithful affection and with no reproaches. From the abstract standpoint, nothing could be farther astray than the fulness and freedom of Milly's forgivenesses; practically, this illogical feminine weakness made life easier and happier, not alone for everybody about her, but for herself as well. Doubtless such a yielding disposition tempted her lover to injustices he would never have ventured with a more spirited woman, but after all her forgiveness was so divine as almost to turn the transgression into a virtue for causing it.

When the account of Milly's life was made up, there must be put into the record long, wordless stretches of uncomplaining and prayerful patience, hidden from the eyes of all mankind. The capabilities of women of this sort for quiet suffering are as infinitely pathetic as they are measureless; and, although she was silent, the dark rings under her eyes and the lagging step told how her sorrow was wearing upon her. She went on faithfully with her work; she held still to the faith that somehow help was sure to come; and as only such women can be, she was patient with the patience of a god.

Milly was surprised one afternoon by a visit from Orin Stanton, the half brother of John. The sculptor had never before come to see her, and, although Milly was little given to censoriousness, she could not avoid the too-obvious reflection that, in one known to be so consistently self-seeking as was Orin, the probability was that some selfish motive lay behind the call. Orin had never been especially fond of Milly, and since his return from Europe, where he had been maintained by the liberality of an old lady, who, in a summer visit to Feltonville, had been attracted by his talent for modelling in clay, he had avoided as far as possible all intercourse with his townspeople. The old lady, who took much innocent pleasure in imagining herself the patroness of a future Phidias, died suddenly one day, leaving the will by which provision was made for young Stanton's future unhappily without signature; a fact which ever after furnished him with definite grounds upon which to found his accusations against society and fate.

It was largely in virtue of this interesting and pathetic story that Mrs. Frostwinch and Mrs. Bodewin Ranger had taken it upon themselves to better the fortunes of Stanton. Large-hearted ladies in Boston, as elsewhere in the world, find no difficulty in discovering signs of genius in a work of art where they deliberately look for it; and being moved by the sculptor's history, — in which, to say sooth, there was nothing remarkable, and, save the disappointment in regard to the will, little that was even striking — his patronesses were not slow in coming to regard his productions with admiration curiously resembling momentary veneration. They in a mild way instituted a Stanton cult, as a minor interest in lives already richly full, and when more weighty matters did not interfere, Mrs. Frostwinch, in varying degrees of enthusiasm, could be charming in her praises of the sculptor, whom she designated as "adorably ursine," and of his work, which in turn, she termed "irresistibly insistent," whatever that might mean.

Bearish, Orin Stanton certainly was, whether one did or did not find the quality adorable. He was heavy in mould, with a face marked by none of the delicacy one expects in an artist and to which his small eyes and thick lips lent a sensual cast. Milly had always found his countenance repulsive, strongly as she strove not to be affected by mere outward appearances. He wore his hair long, its coarse, reddish masses showing conspicuously in a crowd, when he got to going about among such people as hunt lions in Boston.

Mrs. Bodewin Ranger patronized him from afar, and could not be brought to invite him to her house.

"Really, my dear," the beautiful old lady said to

her husband; "it seems to me that people are not wise in asking Mr. Stanton about so much. It only unsettles him, and he should be left to associate with persons in his own class."

"I quite agree with you," her husband replied, as he had replied to every proposition she had advanced for the half century of their married life.

Mrs. Frostwinch was less rigid. It is somewhat the fashion of the more exclusive of the younger circles of Boston to make a more or less marked display of a democracy which is far more apparent than real. Partly from the genuine and affected respect for culture and talent which is so characteristic of the town, and partly from some remnants of the foolish superstition that the persons who produce interesting works of art must themselves be interesting, the social leaders of the town are, as a rule, not unwilling to receive into a sort of lay-brotherhood those who are gifted with talent or genius. No fashion of place or hour, however, can change the essential facts of life; and it is perhaps quite as much the incompatibility of aim, of purpose in life, as any instinctive arrogance on either side, that makes any intimate union impossible. It is inevitable that members of any exclusive circle shall regard others concerning whose admission there has been question with some shade of more or less conscious patronage, and sensitive men of genius are very likely as conscious of "the pale spectrum of the salt" as was Mrs. Browning's poet Bertram, invited into company where he did not belong, because it was socially too high and intellectually and humanely too low. The members of what is awkwardly called fashionable society are too thoroughly trained in the knowledge of the principles of birth, wealth, and mutual recognition upon which their order is founded, to be likely to lose sight of the fact that artists and authors and actors, not possessing, however great their cleverness in other directions, these especial qualifications, can only be received into the charmed ring on sufferance; and nothing could be more absurd or illogical than to blame them for recognizing this fact.

Mrs. Frostwinch, at least, was in no danger of forgetting where she stood in relation to such lions as she invited to her house. She understood accurately how to be gracious and yet to keep them in their place. Indeed, she did this instinctively, so thoroughly was she imbued with the spirit of her class. She did not open her doors to many people on the score of their talent, and least of all did she encourage lions of appearance so coarse and uncouth as Orin Stanton. She found the role of lady patroness amusing, however, and, although she would not have put the sculptor's name on the lists of guests for a dinner or an evening reception, she did invite him to a Friday afternoon, when she knew Stewart Hubbard was likely to be present; and a glowing knowledge of this honor was in Orin's mind when he went to call on Melissa.

"I've no doubt you're surprised to see me," Orin said, brusquely, as he seated himself, still in his overcoat. "The truth is, I don't run round a great deal, and if I do, it's where it will do me some good."

Milly smiled to herself. She was not without a sense of humor.

"Naturally, I don't expect you to waste your time on me," she answered. "You must be very busy, and I suppose you have lots of engagements."

"Oh, of course," he returned, with an obvious thrill of self-satisfaction. "The Boston women are always interested in art, and I could keep going all the time, if I had a mind to. I'm going to Mrs. Frostwinch's to-morrow. She wants to introduce me to Mr. Hubbard, one of the committee on the new statue."

To Orin's disappointment this fact seemed to make little impression upon Milly, who was far too ignorant of Boston's social distinctions to realize that an invitation to one of Mrs. Frostwinch's Fridays was an honor greatly to be coveted.

"I am glad if people are interesting themselves in your work, Orin," she said, with a manner she tried not to make formal.

She had never been able to like Orin, and since the time when he had not only utterly refused to share with John the burden of their father's debts but had scoffed at what he called his brother's "idiocy" in paying them, Milly had found comfort in having a definite and legitimate excuse for disliking him. She regarded him as greatly gifted; in the eyes of Feltonville people, Orin's talents, since they had received the sanction of substantial patronage, had loomed into greatness somewhat absurdly disproportionate to their actual value. She was not insensible of the honor of being connected, as the betrothed of John, with so distinguished a man as she felt Orin to be; but she neither liked nor trusted him.

"Oh, there are some people in Boston who know a good thing when they see it," the young man responded, intuitively understanding that here he need not take the trouble to affect any artificial modesty. "It's about that that I came to talk to you."

"About — I don't think I understand."

"I want your help."

"My help? How can I help you?"

The sculptor tossed his hat into a chair, and leaned forward, tapping on one broad, thick palm with the fingers of the other hand.

"They tell me," he said, "that you know Mrs. Fenton pretty well; Arthur Fenton's wife, — he's an awful snob, I hate him."

"Mrs. Fenton has been very kind to me," Milly responded, involuntarily shrinking a little, and speaking guardedly.

"Well, put it any way you like. If she's interested in you, that's all I want," Stanton went on, in his rough way. "You'll have a pull on her through the church racket, I suppose."

Melissa looked at him with pain and disgust in her eyes. She always shrank from Orin's rough coarseness; and she always felt helpless before him. She made no reply, but played nervously with the pen she had laid down upon his entrance. He regarded her curiously.

"You see," he said, with a clumsy attempt at easy familiarity, "Mrs. Fenton's a niece of Mr. Calvin, who is on the statue committee. Mrs. Frostwinch says Mr. Calvin's the man who has most influence in the committee, and it occurred to me that it would be a good thing if you'd put Mrs. Fenton up to taking my part with Calvin. You see," he continued, in an offhand manner, "artists don't get any show nowadays unless they keep their eyes open, and I mean to be wide awake. I'm ready to do a good turn, too, for anybody that helps me. John told me the other day that you and he had had a row, and if you can do me a good turn in this, I may be able to pay you by smoothing John down."

Milly flushed painfully. Her delicacy was outraged, but, too, her combative instinct was roused to defend her lover.

"John and I haven't quarrelled," she said, in a voice a little raised; "he is worried about the debts and that makes him out of sorts, sometimes, that is all."

A look of shrewd cunning came into Orin's narrow eyes. He suspected the allusion to John's determination to clear his father's memory from dishonor to be a clever device to win a concession from him. He looked upon the remark as a statement from Milly of the price of her aid.

"If I get this commission," he said, watching the effect of his words, "I shall be in a position to help John pay off those debts, and I shall tell him he has you to thank for my helping him out in his foolishness,—for it is foolishness to waste money on dead debts."

A glad light sprang into Milly's face. She was too childlike to suspect the thought which led Orin to make this proffer, and the hope of having John aided at once and of being able to contribute to the bringing about of this result, made her heart beat joyfully.

"You know how glad I shall be if I can help you," she said quickly. "I will speak to Mrs. Fenton when I see her to-morrow; though I do not see what good I can do you," her honesty forced her to add, with sudden self-distrust.

"Oh, you just put in and do your level best," Orin responded, with the smile which Mrs. Frostwinch had once called his "deplorably Satanic grin," "and it is sure to come out all right. There are other wires being pulled."

XIV

THE SHOT OF ACCIDENT.

Othello ; iv. — 1.

IT was not often that Arthur Fenton permitted himself to be ill-tempered at home. He had too keen an appreciation of good taste to allow his dark humors to vent themselves upon the heads of those with whom he lived.

"A man is to be excused for being cross abroad," he was wont to observe, "but only a brute is peevish at home."

On the morning following his conversation with Damaris Wainwright, however, he was decidedly out of sorts, and proved but ill company for his wife at the breakfast table. She ventured some simple remark in relation to a plan which Mr. Candish had for the re-decoration of the Church of the Nativity, and her husband retorted with an open sneer.

"Oh, don't talk about Mr. Candish to me," he said. "He is that obsolete thing, a clergyman."

"I supposed," Edith responded good-naturedly, "that a question of artistic decoration would interest you, even if it was connected with a church."

"I hate anything connected with a religion,"

Fenton observed savagely. "A religion is simply an artificial scheme of life, to be followed at the expense of all harmony with nature."

It was evident to Edith that her husband was nervous and irritable, and with wifely protective instinct she attributed his condition to overwork. She did not take up the challenge which he in a manner flung down. She seldom argued with him now; she cast about in her mind for a safe topic of conversation, and, by ill-luck, hit upon the one least calculated to restore Arthur to good humor and a sane temper.

"Helen was in last evening," she said. "She is troubled about Ninitta; but I think it is because she isn't used to her ways."

Fenton started guiltily.

"What about Ninitta?" he demanded.

"Helen says she acts strangely, as if she had something on her mind; and that she complains bitterly that her husband doesn't care for her."

Arthur shrugged his shoulders. He was on his guard now, and perfectly self-possessed.

"No?" he said, inquiringly. "Why should he?"

"Why should he?" echoed his wife indignantly. Then she recovered herself, and let the question pass, saying simply: "That would lead us into one of our old discussions about right and wrong."

"Those struggles and quibbles between right and wrong," Fenton retorted contemptuously, "have ceased to amuse me. They were interesting when I was young enough for them to have novelty, but now I find grand passions and a strong will more entertaining than that form of amusement."

Edith raised her clear eyes to his with a calmness which she had learned by years of patient struggle.

"And yet," she answered, "the people whom I have found most true, most helpful, and even most comfortable, have been those who believed these questions of right and wrong the most vital things in the universe."

"Oh, certainly," was the reply. "A superstition is an admirable thing in its place."

He rose from the table as he spoke, and stood an instant with his hand upon the back of his chair, looking at her in apparent indecision. She saw that he was troubled, and she longed to help him, but she had learned that his will was definite and unmanageable, and she secretly feared that her inquiry would be fruitless when she asked, —

"What is it that troubles you this morning, Arthur? Has anything gone wrong?"

"Things are always wrong," replied he. Then, with seeming irrelevance, he added: "People are so illogical! They so insist that a man shall think in the beaten rut. They are angry because I don't like the taste of life. Good Heavens! Why haven't I the same right to dislike life that I have to hate sweet champagne? If other people want to live and to drink Perrier Jouet, I am perfectly willing that they should, but, for my own part, I don't want one any more than the other."

What he said sounded to Edith like one of the detached generalities he was fond of uttering, and if she had learned that beneath his seemingly irrelevant words always lay a connecting thread of thought, she had learned also that she could seldom hope to discover what this cord might be. To understand his words, now, it would have been necessary for her to be aware of the net spread for him by Irons, the struggle in his mind as he talked with Miss Wainwright, and the effort he was now making to bring himself up to the firmness needed for the important interview with Mr. Hubbard which lay before him. In the sleepless hours of the night, Fenton had gone over the ground again and again; he had painted to himself the baseness of the thing he meant to do, and all his instincts of loyalty, of taste, of good-breeding, rose against it; but none the less did he cling doggedly to his determination. His purpose never wavered. His decision had been made, and this summing up of the cost did not shake him; it only made him miserable by the keen appreciation it brought him of the bitter humiliation fate — for so he viewed it — was heaping upon his head.

The strength and weakness which are often mingled in one character, like the iron and clay in the image of the prophet's vision, make the most surprising of the many strange paradoxes of human life. Fenton was sensuous, selfish, yielding, yet he possessed a tenacity of purpose, a might of will, which nothing could shake. He looked across the table now, at his sweet-faced, clear-eyed wife, with a dreadful sense of her purity, her honor, her remoteness ; it cut him to the quick to think that the breach of trust he had in view would fill her mind with loathing ; yet the possibility of therefore abandoning his purpose did not occur to him. Indeed, such was his nature, that it might be said that the possibility of abandoning his deliberately formed intention, on this or on any other grounds, did not for him exist.

It was one of the peculiarities which he shared with many sensitive and sensuous natures, that his first thought in any unpleasant situation was always a reflection upon the bitterness of existence. He always thought of the laying down of life as the easiest method of escape from any disagreeable dilemma. He was infected with the distaste of life, that disease which is seldom fatal, yet which in time destroys all save life alone. He thought now how he hated living, and the inevitable reflection came after, how easy it were to get out of the coil of humanity. A faint smile of bitterness curled his lips as he recalled a remark which Helen Greyson had once quoted to him as having been made of him by her dead husband. "He'll want to kill himself, but he won't. He's too soft-hearted, and he'd never forget other people and their opinions." He had acknowledged to himself that this was true, and he wondered whether Mrs. Greyson appreciated its justice.

The thought of Helen brought up the old days when he had been so frankly her friend that he had told her everything that was in his heart except those things which vanity bade him conceal lest he fall in her estimation.

It was so long since he had known a friend on those intimate terms under which it makes no especial difference what is said, since even in silence the understanding is perfect, and the pleasure of talking depends chiefly on the exchange of the signs of complete mutual comprehension, that the old days appealed to him with wonderful power. There is an immeasurable and soothing restfulness in such intercourse, especially to a man like Fenton, in whom exists an inner necessity always to say something when he talks; and as he recalled them now, something almost a sob rose in Arthur's throat. Many men suppose themselves to be cultivating their intellect when they are only, by the gratification of their tastes, quickening their susceptibilities; and Fenton's whole self-indulged existence had resulted chiefly in rendering him more sensitive to the discomforts of a universe in the making of which other things had been considered besides his pleasure.

He looked across the breakfast table at his wife. He noted with appreciation the beautiful line of her cheek outlined against the dark leather of the wall behind her. He felt a twinge of remorse for coming so far short of her ideal of him. He knew how resolutely she refused to see his worst side, and he reflected with philosophy half bitter and half contemptuous, that no woman ever lived who could wholly outgrow the feeling that to believe or to disbelieve a thing must in some occult way affect its truth. At least she had fulfilled all the unspoken promises, so much more important than vows put into words could be, with which she had married him. A remorseful feeling came over his mind, and instantly followed the instinctive self-excuse that she could never suffer as keenly as he suffered, no matter how greatly he disappointed her.

"People are to be envied or pitied," he said aloud, "not for their circumstances, but for their temperaments."

Edith looked up inquiringly. He went round to where she was sitting, smiling to think how far she must be from divining his thought.

"I stayed at the club too late last night," he said, stooping to kiss her smooth white forehead in an unenthusiastic, habitual way which always stung her. "Some of the fellows insisted upon my playing poker, and I got so excited that I didn't sleep when I did get to bed."

Edith sighed, but she made no useless remonstrances.

Walking down to his studio, carefully dressed, faultlessly booted and gloved, and, as Tom Bently was accustomed to say, "too confoundedly well groomed for an artist," Fenton tried in vain to determine how he should manage the important conversation with Mr. Hubbard. He had racked his brains in the night in vain attempts to solve this problem, but in the end he was forced to leave everything for chance or circumstances to decide.

When Stewart Hubbard sat before him, Fenton was conscious of a tingling excitement in every vein, but outwardly he was only the more calm. A close observer might have noticed a nervous quickness in his movements, and a certain shrillness in his voice, but the sitter gave no heed to these tokens, which he would have regarded as of no importance had he seen them. The talk was at first rather rambling, and was not kept up with much briskness on either side. Fenton, indeed, was so absorbed in the task which lay before him that he hardly followed the other's remarks, and he suddenly became aware that he had lost the thread of conversation altogether, so that he could not possibly imagine what the connection was when Hubbard observed, —

"Yes, it is certainly the hardest thing in the world for one being to comprehend another."

Fenton rallied his wits quickly, and retorted with no apparent hesitation, —

"It is so. Probably a cat couldn't possibly understand how a human mother can properly bring up a child when she has no tail for her offspring to play with."

"That wasn't exactly what I meant," the other returned, laughing; "but what a fellow you are to give an unexpected turn to things."

"Do you think so?" the artist said. Then, with a painful feeling of tightness about the throat, and a soberness of tone which he could not prevent, he added, — "That is a reason why I have always felt that I was one of those comparatively rare persons whom wealth would adorn, if somebody would only show me an investment to get rich on."

"You are one of those still rarer persons who would adorn wealth," Mr. Hubbard retorted, ignoring the latter part of the artist's remark. "Only that you are so astonishingly outspoken, that you might cause a revolution if you had Vanderbilt's millions to add weight to your words. It doesn't do to be too honest."

The sigh which left Fenton's lips was almost one of relief, although he felt that this first attempt to turn the talk into financial channels had failed.

"No," he replied. "Civilized honesty consists largely in making the truth convey a false impression, so that one is saved a lie in words while telling one in effect."

"It is strange how we cling to that old idea that as long as the letter of what we say is true it is no matter if the spirit be false," was Mr. Hubbard's response. "I thought of it yesterday at the meeting of the committee on the statue, when we were all sitting there trying to get the better of each other by telling true falsehoods."

"How does the statue business come on?" Fenton asked.

"Not very fast. I am sure I wish I was out of it. America always was a trouble, and this time is no exception to the rule."

"I hope," Arthur said, speaking with more seriousness, "that Grant Herman will be given the commission. He's all and away the best man."

He had secretly a feeling that he was putting an item on the credit side of his account with the sculptor in urging his fitness for this work.

"It is hard to do anything with Calvin and Irons. I've always been for Herman, but I don't mind telling you in confidence that I stand alone on the committee."

"Isn't there any way of helping things on? Wouldn't a petition from the artists do some good?"

"It might. But if you get up one don't let me know. I'd rather be able to say that I had no knowledge of it if it came before us."

Fenton smiled and continued his painting. With a thrill half of triumph, half of rage, he became aware that he was this morning succeeding admirably in getting just the likeness he wanted in the sitter's portrait. He had feared lest his excitement should render him unfit for work, but it had, on the contrary, spurred him up to unusual effectiveness. The thought came into his mind of the price at which he was buying this skill, and it was characteristic that the reflection which followed was that at least, if he caused Hubbard to lose money by betraying the secret he hoped to get from him, he was, to a degree, repaying him by painting a portrait which could under no other circumstances be so good.

It was no less characteristic of Fenton's mental habits that he looked upon himself as having committed the crime against his sitter which had yet to be carried out. In his logic, the legitimate, however distorted, legacy from Puritan ancestors, the sin lay in the determination; and he would have held himself almost as guilty had circumstances at this moment freed him from the disagreeable necessity of going on with his attempt. Doubtless in this fact lay in part the explanation of the firmness of his purpose. He would still have suffered in self-respect, since abandonment of his plan, even if voluntary, would not alter the fact that he had in intention been guilty. He would have said that theoretically there was no difference between intention and commission, and however casuists might reason, he took a curious delight in being scrupulously exacting with himself in his moral requirements, the fact that he held himself in his actions practically above such considerations naturally making this less difficult than it otherwise would have been. Every man has his private ethical methods, and this was the way in which Arthur Fenton's mind held itself in regard to that right of which he often denied the existence.

"I suppose," he remarked at length, with deliberate intent of entrapping Hubbard into some inadvertent betrayal of his secret, "that you business men have no sort of an idea how ignorant a man of my profession can be in regard to business. I had a note this morning from a broker whom I've been having help me a little in a sort of infantile attempt at stock gambling, and he advises me to find a financial kindergarten and attend it."

"I dare say he is right," the other returned, smiling. "You had better beware of stock gambling, if you are not desirous of ending your days in a poorhouse."

"But what can one do? It is only the men of large experience and so much capital that they do not need it who have a chance at safe investments."

He felt that he was bungling horribly, but he

knew no other way of getting on in his attempt. He was terrified by the openness of his tactics. It seemed to him that any man must be able to perceive what he was driving at, but he desperately assured himself that after all Hubbard could not possibly have any reason to suspect him of a design of pumping him.

"Oh, there are plenty of safe investments," the sitter said, as if the matter were one of no great moment. Then, looking at his watch, he added, "I must go in fifteen minutes. I have an engagement."

Fenton dared not risk another direct trial, but he skirted about the subject on which his thoughts were fixed. His attempts, however, though ingenious, were fruitless; and he saw Hubbard step down from the dais where he posed, with a baffled sense of having failed utterly.

"The country is really beginning to look quite spring-like," he said, as he stood by while his sitter put on his overcoat.

He spoke in utter carelessness, simply to avoid a silence which would perhaps seem a little awkward; but the shot of accident hit the mark at which his careful aim had been vain.

"Yes, it is," the other responded. "I was out of town with Staggchase yesterday, looking at some meadows we talk of buying for a factory site, and I was surprised to see how forward things are."

Yesterday Mrs. Staggchase had casually mentioned to Fred Rangely that her husband had gone to Feltonville; and at the St. Filipe Club in the evening, as they were playing poker, Rangely had excused the absence of Mr. Staggchase, who was to be of the party, by telling this fact.

After Hubbard was gone, Fenton stood half dizzy with mingled exultation and shame. He exulted in his victory, but he felt as if he had committed murder.

And that evening Mrs. Amanda Welsh Sampson received a note from Mr. Irons, in which Feltonville was mentioned.

XV

LIKE COVERED FIRE.

Much Ado about Nothing; iii. — 2.

MRS. AMANDA WELSH SAMPSON was playing a somewhat difficult game, and she was playing it well. She was entertaining Mr. Greenfield, the Feltonville member, and she had also as a casual guest for the evening, Mr. Erastus Snaffle, and successfully to work the one off against the other was a task from which the cleverest of society women might be excused for shrinking, even had it been presented to her in terms of her own circle.

Greenfield was an honest, straightforward countryman; big, and rather burly, with a clear eye and a curling chestnut beard. He was a man at once of great force of character, and of singular simplicity. He exerted a vast influence in his country neighborhood in virtue of the respect inspired by his invincible integrity, a certain shrewdness which was the more effective at short range from the fact that it was really narrow in its spread, and perhaps most of all of his bluff, demonstrative kindliness. Tom Greenfield's hearty laugh and cordial handshake had won him more votes than many a more able man has been able to secure by the most thorough acquaintance with the questions and interests with which election would make it the duty of a man to be concerned; but it must be added that no man ever used his influence more disinterestedly and honestly, or more conscientiously fulfilled the duties of his position, as he understood them.

Such a man was peculiarly likely to become the victim of a woman like Mrs. Sampson. The plea of relationship on which she had sought his acquaintance disarmed suspicion at the outset. His country manners were familiar with family ties as a genuine bond, and he had no reason whatever to suppose that any ulterior motive was possible to this woman who affected to be so ignorant of politics and public business.

In the weeks which had elapsed since her interview with Alfred Irons, Mrs. Sampson had been making the most of the fraction of the season which remained to her. She had offered excuses which Greenfield's simple soul found satisfactory why she had not sought her cousin's acquaintance early in the winter, and the very irksomeness of the enforced absence from his country home which seized him as spring came on, made him the more susceptible to the blandishments of the mature siren who, with cunning art, was meshing her nets about him.

He had quite fallen into the habit of passing his

unoccupied evenings with the widow, and she in turn had denied herself to some of her familiar friends on occasions when she had reason to expect him. Had she known he was likely to come this evening, she would have taken care to guard against his meeting with Snaffle; but as that gentleman was first in the field, she had her choice between sending Greenfield away and seeing them together. Like the clever woman she was, she chose the latter alternative, and found, too, her account in so doing.

Erastus Snaffle was more familiarly than favorably known in financial circles of Boston, as the man who had put afloat more wild-cat stocks than any other speculator on the street. It might be supposed that his connection with any scheme would be enough to wreck its prospects, yet whatever he took hold of floated for a time. There was always a feeling among his victims that at length he had come to the place where he must connect himself with a respectable scheme for the sake of re-establishing his reputation; but this hope was never realized. Perhaps whatever he touched ceased from that moment to be either reliable or respectable. However, since Snaffle was possessed of so inexhaustible a fund of plausibility that he never failed to find investors who placed confidence in his wildest statements, it after all made very little difference to him what his reputation or his financial standing might be.

By one of those singular compensations in which nature seems now and then to make a struggle to adjust the average of human characteristics with something approaching fairness, Snaffle was hardly less gullible than he was skilful in ensnaring others. He was continually making a fortune by launching some bogus stock or other, but it seemed always to be fated that he should lose it again in some equally wild scheme started by a brother sharper. Perhaps between his professional strokes he was obliged to practise at raising credulity in himself merely to keep his hand in ; perhaps it was simply that the habit of believing financial absurdities had become a sort of second nature in him ; or yet again is it possible that he felt obliged to assume credulity in regard to the falsehoods of his fellow sharpers, as a sort of equivalent for the faith he so often demanded of them ; but, whatever may have been the reason, it was at least a fact that his money went in much the same way it came.

In person, Erastus Snaffle was not especially prepossessing. His face would have been more attractive had the first edition of his chin been larger and the succeeding ones smaller, while the days when he could still boast of a waist were so far in the irrevocable past that the imagination refused so long a flight as would be required to reach it. His eyes were small and heavy-lidded, but in them smouldered a dull gleam of cunning that at times kindled into a pointed flame. His dress was in keeping with his person, and his manner quite as vulgar as either.

He was sitting to-night in one corner of the sofa, his corpulent person heaped up in an unshapely mass, talking with a fluency that now and then died away entirely, while he paused to speculate what sort of a game his hostess might be playing with Mr. Greenfield.

"The fact is," Mrs. Sampson was saying, as Snaffle recalled his attention from one of these fits of abstraction, "that I don't know what I shall do this summer; and I don't like to believe that summer is so near that I must decide soon."

"You were at Ashmont last year, weren't you?" Snaffle asked. "Why don't you go there again."

Mrs. Sampson shot him a quick glance which Snaffle understood at once to mean that he was to second her in something she was attempting. He did not yet get his clew clearly enough to understand just how, but the look put him on the alert, as the hostess answered, —

"Oh, it is all spoiled. The railroad has been put through and all the summer visitors are giving it up. I'm sure I don't know what will become of all the poverty-stricken widows that made their living out of taking boarders. That railroad has been an expensive job for Ashmont in every way."

Greenfield smiled, his big, genial smile which had so much warmth in it.

"That isn't usually the way people look at the effect of a railroad on a town."

This time the look which Mrs. Sampson gave Snaffle told him so plainly what she wanted him to do that he spoke at once, her almost imperceptible nod showing him that he was on the right track.

"Oh, a railroad is always the ruin of a small town," he said, "unless it is its terminus. It sucks all the life out of the villages along the way. You go along any of the lines in Massachusetts, and you will find that while the towns have been helped by the road, the small villages have been knocked into a cocked hat. All the young people have left them; all the folks in the neighborhood go to some city to do their trading, and the stuffing is knocked out of things generally."

Mrs. Sampson looked at Snaffle with a thoroughly gratified expression.

"I don't know much about the business part of the question, of course," she said, "but I do know that a railroad takes all the young men out of a village. A woman I boarded with at Ashmont last year wrote to me the other day in the greatest distress because her only son had left her. She said it was all the railroad, and her letter was really pathetic."

"Oh, that's a woman's way of looking at it," rejoined Greenfield, the greatest struggle of whose life, as Mrs. Sampson was perfectly well aware, was to keep at home his only child, a youth just coming to manhood. "It is easy enough for boys to get away nowadays, and just having a railroad at the door wouldn't make any great difference."

"It does, though, make a mighty sight of difference," Snaffle said, rolling his head and putting his plump white hands together. "Somehow or other, the having that train scooting by day in and day out unsettles the young fellows. The whistle stirs them up, and keeps reminding them how easy it is to go out West or somewhere or other. I've seen it time and again."

"Well," Greenfield returned, a shadow over his genial face, "I have a youngster that's got the Western fever pretty bad without any railroads coming to Feltonville. But what you say is only one side of the question. When a railroad comes it always brings business in one way or another. The increase of transportation facilities is sure to build things up."

"Oh, yes, it builds them up," Snaffle chuckled, as if the idea afforded him infinite amusement, "but how does it work. There are two or three men in the town who start market gardens and make something out of it. They sell their produce in the city and they do their trading there; they hire Irish laborers from outside the village; and how much better off is the town, except that it can tax them a trifle more if it can get hold of the valuation of their property."

"Which it generally can't," interpolated Greenfield grimly, with an inward reminder of certain experiences as assessor.

"Or somebody starts a factory," Snaffle went on, "and then the town is made, ain't it? Outside capital is invested, outside operatives brought in to turn the place upside down and to bring in all the deviltries that have been invented, and all the town has to show in the long run is a little advance in real estate over the limited area where they want to build houses for the mill-hands. There's no end of rot talked about improving towns by putting up factories, but I can't see it myself."

Snaffle sometimes said that he believed in nothing but making money, and there was never any reason to suppose he held an opinion because he expressed it. He said what he felt to be politic, and a long and complicated experience enabled him to defend any view with more or less plausibility upon a moment's notice. He was clever enough to see that for some reason the widow wished him to pursue the line of talk he had taken, and he was ready enough to oblige her. He never took the trouble to inquire of himself what his opinions were, because that question was of so secondary importance; he merely exerted himself to make the most of any points that presented themselves to his mind in favor of the side it was for his advantage to support.

"'Pon my word," Greenfield said, with a laugh,

"you talk like an old fogy of the first water. I wouldn't have suspected you of looking at things that way."

"Mr. Snaffle is always surprising," Mrs. Sampson said, with her most dazzling smile, "but he is generally right."

"Thank you. I can't help at any rate seeing that there are two sides to this thing, and I am too old a bird to be caught with the common chaff that people talk."

Mr. Greenfield settled himself comfortably in his chair and laughed softly. The discussion was so purely theoretical that he could be amused without looking upon it seriously.

"For my part," he remarked, his big hand playing with a paper-knife on one of the little tables, which, to a practised eye, suggested cards, "I am of the progressive party, thank you. I believe in opening up the country and putting railroads where they will do the most good. A few people get their old prejudices run against, but on the whole it is for the interest of a town to have a railroad, and it is nonsense to talk any other way."

Mrs. Amanda Welsh Sampson leaned forward to lay her fingers upon the speaker's arm.

"That is just it, Cousin Tom," she said, with a languishing glance. "You always look at things in so large a way. You never let the matter of personal interest decide, but think of the public good."

The flattery was somewhat gross, but men will swallow a good deal in the way of praise from women. They are generally slow to suspect the fair sex of sarcasm, and allow themselves the luxury of enjoying the pleasure of indulging their vanity untroubled by unpleasant doubts concerning the sincerity of compliments which from masculine lips would offend them. Greenfield laughed with a perceptible shade of awkwardness, but he was evidently not ill pleased.

"Oh, well," he returned, "that is because thus far it has happened that my personal interests and my convictions have worked together so well. You might see a difference if they didn't pull in the same line."

Mrs. Sampson considered a moment, and then rose, bringing out a decanter of sherry with a supply of glasses and of biscuit from a convenient closet in the bottom of a secretary.

"That's business," Snaffle said, joyously. "Sherry ain't much for a man of my size, but it's better than nothing."

"It is a hint though," the hostess said, filling his glass.

"A hint!" he repeated.

"Yes; a hint that it is getting late, and that I am tired, and you must go home."

"Oh, ho!" he laughed uproariously; "now I won't let you in for that good thing on the Princeton Platinum stock. You'll wish you hadn't turned me out of the house when you see that stock quoted at fifty per cent above par."

"Ah, I know all about Princeton Platinum," she responded, showing her white teeth rather more than was absolutely demanded by the occasion; "besides, I've no money to put into anything."

"What about Princeton Platinum?" Greenfield asked, turning toward the other a shrewd glance. "I've heard a good deal of talk about it lately, but I didn't pay much attention to it."

"Princeton Platinum," the hostess put in before Snaffle could speak, "is Mr. Snaffle's latest fairy story. It is a dream that people buy pieces of for good hard samoleons, and" —

"Good *what?*" interrupted the country member.

"Shekels, dollars, for cash under whatever name you choose to give it; and then some fine morning they all wake up."

"Well?" demanded Snaffle, to whom the jest seemed not in the least distasteful. "And what then?"

"Oh, what is usually left of dreams when one wakes up in the morning?"

The fat person of the speculator shook with appreciation of the wit of this sally, which did not seem to Greenfield so funny as from the laughter of the others he supposed it must really be. The latter rose when Snaffle did and prepared to say good-night, but Mrs. Sampson detained him.

"I want to speak with you a moment," she said. "Good-night, Mr. Snaffle. Bear us in mind when Princeton Platinum has made your fortune, and don't look down on us."

"No fear," he returned. "When that happens, I shall come to you for advice how to spend it."

There was too much covetousness in her voice as she answered jocosely that she could tell him. The struggle of life made even a jesting supposition of wealth excite her cupidity. She sighed as she turned back into the parlor and motioned Greenfield to a seat. Placing herself in a low, velvet-covered chair, she stretched out her feet before her, displaying the black silk stocking upon a neat instep as she crossed them upon a low stool.

"I am sure I don't know how to say what I want to," she began, knitting her brows in a perplexity that was only part assumed. "Something has come to me in the strangest way, and I think I ought to tell you, although I haven't any interest in it, and it certainly isn't any of my business."

Her companion was too blunt to be likely to help her much. He simply asked, in the most straightforward manner, —

"What is it?"

"It's about public business," she said. "Why!"

she added, as if a sudden light had broken upon her. "I really believe I was going to be a lobbyist. Fancy me lobbying! What does a lobbyist do?"

"Nothing that you'd be likely to have any hand in," returned Greenfield, smiling at the absurdity of the proposition. "What is all this about?"

"I suppose I should not have thought of it but for the turn the talk took to-night," she returned with feminine indirectness. "It was odd, wasn't it, that we should get to talking of the harm railroads do, when it was about a railroad that I was going to talk."

"There's only one railroad scheme on foot this spring that I know anything about, and that's for a branch of the Massachusetts Outside Railroad through Wachusett. That isn't in the Legislature either."

"That's the one. It's going to be in the Legislature. There's going to be an attempt to change the route."

"Change the route?"

"Yes, so it will go through — but will you promise not to tell this to a living mortal?"

"Of course."

"I suppose," she said, regarding her slipper intently, "that I really ought not to tell you; but I can't help it somehow. Your name is to be used."

"My name?"

"Yes, the men who are planning the thing say that it will be so evident that you'd want the road to go this new way, that if you vote with the Wachusett interest they'll swear you are bought."

"Swear I'm bought? Pooh! Tom Greenfield is too well known for that sort of talk to hold water."

"But through your own town" —

Mrs. Sampson regarded her companion closely as she slowly pronounced these words. They roused him like an electric shock.

"Through Feltonville?"

She nodded, compressing her lips, but saying nothing.

"Phew! This is a tough nut to crack. But are you sure that is to be tried?"

"Yes; there is a scheme for a few monopolists to buy up mill privileges and run factories at Feltonville; and they mean to make the road serve them, instead of its being put where the public need it."

"So that's what Lincoln's been raking up in Boston," Greenfield said to himself. "I knew he was up to some deviltry. Wants to sell off those meadows he's been gathering in on mortgages."

"Of course you'll want to help your town," Mrs. Sampson said, regretfully. "The men that voted for you'll expect you to do it; but it's helping on a sly scheme at the expense of the state. I'm sorry you've got to be on that side."

"Got to be on that side?" he retorted, starting

up. "Who says I've got to be on that side? we'll see about that before we get through. The men that voted for me expect me to do what is right, and I don't think they'll be disappointed just yet."

And all things considered, Mrs. Amanda Welsh Sampson thought she had done a good evening's work.

XVI

WEIGHING DELIGHT AND DOLE.

Hamlet; i. — 2.

"OH, this is completely captivating," Mrs. Frostwinch said, as she sat down to luncheon in Edith Fenton's pretty dining-room, and looked at the large mound-like bouquet of richly tinted spring leaves which adorned the centre of the table. "That is the advantage of having brains. One always finds some delightful surprise or other at your house."

"Thank you," Edith returned, gayly; "but at your house one always has a delightful surprise in the hostess, so you are not forced to resort to makeshifts."

Helen Greyson, the third member of the party, smiled and shook her head.

"Really," she said, "is one expected to keep up to the level of elaborate compliment like that? I fear I can only sit by in admiring silence while you two go on."

"Oh, no," the hostess responded. "Mrs. Frostwinch is to talk to you. That is what you people are here for. I am only to listen."

Edith had invited Helen and Mrs. Frostwinch to take luncheon with her, and she had really done it to bring these two more closely together. She was fond of them both, and the effect of her life in the world into which her marriage had introduced her had been to render her capable of judging both these women broadly. She admired them both, and while her feeling of affection had by circumstances been more closely cemented with Helen, she felt that a strong friendship was possible between herself and Mrs. Frostwinch should the lines of their lives ever fall much together.

The modern woman, particularly if she be at all in society, has generally to accept the possibilities of friendship in place of that gracious boon itself. The busy round of life to-day gives ample opportunity for judging of character, so that it is well nigh impossible not to feel that some are worthy of friendship, some especially gifted by nature with the power of inspiring it, while, on the other hand, there are those who repel or with whom the bond would be impossible. But friendship, however much it be the result of eternal fitness and the inevitable consequence of the meeting of two harmonious natures, is a plant of slow growth, and few things which require time and tranquillity for their nourishment flourish greatly in this age of restlessness and intense mental activity. The radical and unfettered Bohemian, or such descendants of that famous race as may be supposed still to survive, attempts to leap over all obstacles, to create what must grow, and to turn comradeship into friendship simply because one naturally grows out of the other; the more conservative and logical Philistine recognizes the futility of this attitude, and in his too careful consistency sometimes needlessly brings about the very same failure by pursuing the opposite course.

Edith was not of the women who naturally analyze their own feelings toward others over keenly, but one cannot live in a world without sharing its mental peculiarities. The times are too introspective to allow any educated person to escape self-examination. The century which produced that most appalling instance of spiritual exposure, the "*Journal Intime*," which it is impossible to read without blushing that one thus looks upon the author's soul in its nakedness, leaves small chance for self-unconsciousness. Edith could not help examining her mental attitude toward her companions, and it was perhaps a proof of the sweetness of her nature that she found in her thought nothing of that shortcoming in them, or reason for lack of fervor in friendship other than such as must come from lack of intercourse.

Perhaps some train of thought not far removed from the foregoing made her say, as the luncheon progressed, —

"Really, it seems to me as if life proceeded at a pace so rapid nowadays that one had not time even to be fond of anybody."

"It goes too fast for one to have much chance to show it," Helen responded; "but one may surely be fond of one's friends, even without seeing them."

"If you will swear not to tell the disgraceful fact," Mrs. Frostwinch said, "I'll confess that I abhor Walt Whitman; but that one dreadful, disreputably slangy phrase of his, 'I loaf and invite my soul,' echoes through my brain like an invitation to Paradise."

Edith smiled.

"If Arthur were here," she returned, "he would probably say that you think you mean that, but that really you don't."

"My dear," Mrs. Frostwinch answered, with her beautiful smile and a characteristic undulation of the neck, "your husband, although he is clever to an extent which I consider positively immoral, is only a man, and he does not understand. Men do what they like; women, what they can. There may be moral free will for women, although I've ceased to be sure of that even; but socially no such thing exists. Do we wear the dreadful clothes we are tied up in because we want to? Do we order society, or our lives, or our manners, or our morals? Do we" —

"There, there," interrupted Helen, laughing and

putting up her hand. "I can't hear all this without a protest. If it is true I won't own it. I had rather concede that all women are fools" —

"As indeed they are," interpolated Mrs. Frostwinch.

"Than that they are helpless manikins," continued Helen. "In any other sense, that is," she added, "than men are."

"My dear Mrs. Greyson," the other said, leaning toward her, "you take the single question of the relation of the sexes, and where are we? I wouldn't own it to a man for the world, but the truth is that men are governed by their will, and women are governed by men; and, what is more, if it could all be changed to-morrow, we should be perfectly miserable until we got the old way back again; and that's the most horribly humiliating part of it."

"It is easy to see that you are not a woman suffragist," commented Edith.

"Woman suffrage," echoed the other, her voice never for an instant varied from its even and high-bred pitch; "woman suffrage must remain a practical impossibility until the idea can be eradicated from society that the initiative in passion is the province of man."

"Brava!" cried the hostess. "Mr. Herman ought to hear that epigram. He asked me last night if he ought to put an inscription in favor of woman suffrage on the hem of the *America* he is modelling."

Helen turned toward her quickly.

"Is Mr. Herman making a model of the *America?*" she asked. "Has he the commission?"

"He hasn't the commission, because nobody has it, but he has been asked by the committee to prepare a model."

"That is" — began Helen. "Strange," she was going to say, but fortunately caught herself in time and substituted "capital. It is good to think that Boston will have one really fine statue."

"Aren't you in that, Mrs. Greyson?" Mrs. Frostwinch asked.

"No," Helen answered. "I am really doing little since I came home. I am waiting until the time serves, I suppose."

She spoke without especial thought of what she was saying, desiring merely to cover any indications which might show the feeling aroused by what she had just heard and the decision she had just taken to have nothing to do with the contest for the statue of *America*, although she had begun a study for the figure.

"I admire you for being able to make time serve you instead of serving time like the rest of us," Mrs. Frostwinch said.

"I shouldn't hear another call you a time server without taking up the cudgels to defend you," responded Edith.

Mrs. Frostwinch smiled in reply to this. Then she turned again to Helen.

"To tell the truth, Mrs. Greyson," she observed, "I am glad you are not concerned in this statue, for I am myself one of a band of conspirators who are pushing the claims of a new man."

"Is there a new sculptor?" Helen asked, smiling. "That is wonderful news."

"Yes; we think he is the coming man. His name is Stanton; Orin Stanton."

"Oh," responded Helen, with involuntary frankness in her accent.

Mrs. Frostwinch laughed with perfect good nature.

"You don't admire him?" she commented. "Well, many don't. To say the truth, I do not think anybody alive, if you will pardon me, Mrs. Greyson, knows the truth about sculpture. Perhaps the Greeks did, but we don't, even when we are told. I know the Soldiers' Monument on the Common is hideous beyond words, because everybody says so; but they didn't when it was put up. Only a few artists objected then."

"And the fact that a few artists have brought everybody to their opinion," Edith asked, "doesn't make you feel that they must be right; must have the truth behind them?"

"No; frankly, I can't say that it does," Mrs. Frostwinch responded.

She leaned back in her chair, a soft flush on her thin, high-bred face. Her figure, in a beautiful gown of beryl plush embroidered with gold, seemed artistically designed for the carved, high-backed chair in which she sat, and both her companions were too appreciative to lose the grace of the picture she made.

"I cannot see that it is bad," she went on. "Mr. Fenton has proved it to me, and even Mr. Herman, who seems, so far as I have seen him, the most charitable of men, when I asked him how he liked it, spoke with positive loathing of it. I can't manage to make myself unhappy over it, that's all. And I believe I am as appreciative as the average."

To Helen there was something at once fascinating and repellent in this talk. She was attracted by Mrs. Frostwinch. The perfect breeding, the grace, the polish of the woman, won upon her strongly, while yet the subtile air of taking life conventionally, of lacking vital earnestness, was utterly at variance with the sculptor's temperament and methods of thought. She no sooner recognized this feeling than she rebuked herself for shallowness and a want of charity, yet even so the impression remained. To the artistic temperament, enthusiasm is the only excuse for existence.

"I think Mrs. Fenton is right," she said. "The few form the correct judgment, and the many adopt it in the end because it is based on truth. It seems to me," she continued, thoughtfully, "that the prime condition of effectiveness is constancy, and only that opinion can be constant that has truth for a foundation, because no other basis would remain to hold it up."

"That may be true," was the reply, "if you take matters in a sufficiently long range, but you seem to me to be viewing things from the standpoint of eternity."

The smile with which she said these last words was so charming that Helen warmed toward her, and she smiled also in replying, —

"Isn't that, after all, the only safe way to look at things?"

"What deep waters we are getting into," Edith commented. "And yet they say women are always frivolous."

"The Boston luncheon," returned Mrs. Frostwinch, "is a solemn assembly for the discussion of mighty themes. Yesterday, at Mrs. Bodewin Ranger's, we disposed of all the knotty problems relating to the lower classes."

"I didn't know but it might be something about my house. The last time Mrs. Greyson lunched here we solemnly debated what a wife should do whose husband did not appreciate her."

She spoke brightly, but there was in her tone, an undercurrent of feeling which touched Helen, and betrayed the fact that this return to the old theme was not wholly without a cause. Mrs. Greyson divined that Edith was not happy, and with the keenness of womanly instinct she divined also that there was not perfect harmony between

Mrs. Fenton and her husband. She looked up quickly, with an instinctive desire to turn the conversation, but found no words ready.

Edith had at the moment yielded to a woman's craving for sympathy. An incident which had happened that forenoon troubled and bewildered her. She had been down town, and remembering a matter of importance about which she had neglected to consult her husband in the morning, she had turned aside to visit his studio, a thing she seldom did in his working hours. She found him painting from a model, and she was kept waiting a moment while the latter retired from sight. She thought nothing of this, but as she stood talking with Arthur, her glance fell upon a wrap which she recognized as belonging to Mrs. Herman, and which had been carelessly left upon the back of a chair in sight. Even this might not have troubled her, had it not been that when she looked questioningly from the garment to her husband, she caught a look of consternation in his eyes. His glance met hers and turned aside with that almost imperceptible wavering which shows the avoidance to be intentional; and a pang of formless terror pierced her.

All the way home she was tormented by the wonder how that wrap could have come in her husband's studio, and what reason he could have for being disturbed by her seeing it there. She was not a woman given to petty or vulgar jealousy, and she had from the first left the artist perfectly free in his professional relations to be governed by the necessities or the conveniences of his profession. She could not to-day, however, rid herself of the feeling that some mystery lay behind the incident of the morning. She began to frame excuses. She speculated whether it were possible that Arthur were secretly painting the portrait of his friend's wife, to produce it as a surprise to them all. She said to herself that Ninitta naturally knew models, and might easily have enough of a feeling of comradeship remaining from the time when she had been a model herself, to lend or give them articles of dress. Unfortunately, she knew how Ninitta kept herself aloof from her old associates since the birth of her child, and the explanation did not satisfy her.

No faintest suspicion of positive evil entered Edith's mind. She was only vaguely troubled, the incident forming one more of the trifles which of late had made her very uneasy in regard to her husband. She told herself that she had confidence in Arthur ; but the woman who is forced to reflect that she has confidence in her husband has already begun, however unconsciously, to doubt him.

"The question is profound enough," Mrs. Frostwinch answered Edith's words in her even tones, which somehow seemed to reduce everything to a well-bred abstraction. "Of course the thing for a woman to do is to remain determinedly ignorant until it would be too palpably absurd to pretend any longer; and then she must get away from him as quietly as possible. The evil in these things is, after all, the stir and the talk, and all the unpleasant and vulgar gossip which inevitably attends them."

Poor Edith cringed as if she had received a blow, and to cover her emotion she gave the signal for rising from the table. But as she did so, her eyes met those of Helen, and the truth leaped from one to the other in one of those glances in which the heart, taken unaware, reveals its joy or its woe with irresistible frankness. Whatever words Edith and Helen might or might not exchange thereafter, the story of Mrs. Fenton's married life and of the anguish of her soul was told in that look; and her friend understood it fully.

XVII

THE HEAVY MIDDLE OF THE NIGHT.

Measure for Measure ; iv. — 10.

THE temper of clubs, like that of individuals, changes from time to time, however constant remains its temperament. Those who reflected upon such matters noticed that at the St. Filipe Club, where a few years back there had been much talk of art and literature, and abstract principles, there had come to be a more worldly, perhaps a Philistine would say a more mature, flavor to the conversation. There were a good many stories told about its wide fireplaces, and there was much running comment on current topics, political and otherwise. There was, perhaps, a more cosmopolitan air to the talk.

That the old-time flavor could sometimes reappear, however, was evident from the talk going on about nine o'clock on the evening of the day of Edith's luncheon. The approach of the time set for an exhibition of paintings in the gallery of the club turned the conversation toward art, and as several of the quondam Pagans were present, the old habits of speech reasserted themselves somewhat.

"I understand Fenton's going to let us see his new picture," somebody said.

"He is if he gets it done," Tom Bently answered. "He's painting so many portraits nowadays that he didn't get it finished for the New York exhibition."

"He must be making a lot of money," Fred Rangely observed.

"He needs to to keep his poker playing up," commented Ainsworth.

"He's lucky if he makes money in these days when it's the swell thing to have some foreign duffer paint all the portraits," Bently said. "It makes me sick to see the way Englishmen rake in the dollars over here."

"How would you feel," asked Rangely, "if you tried to get a living by writing novels, and found the market glutted with pirated English reprints?"

"Oh, novels," retorted Tom, "they are of no account any way. Modern novels are like modern investments; they are all principle and no interest."

"I like that," put in Ainsworth, "when most of them haven't any principle at all."

"Neither have investments in the end," Bently returned. "At least I know mine haven't."

"If you were a writer you'd be spared that pain," was Rangely's reply, "for want of anything to start an investment with."

"I've about come to the conclusion," another

member said, "that a man may be excused for making literature his practice, but that he is a fool to make it his profession. It does very well as an amusement, but it's no good as a business."

"The idea is correct," Rangely replied, ringing the bell and ordering from the servant who responded, "although it does not strike me as being either very fresh or very original."

There was a digression for a moment or two while they waited for their drinks and imbibed them. And then Fred, with the air of one who utters a profound truth, and answers questions both spoken and unspoken, observed as he set down his glass, —

"There's one thing of which I am sure; American literature will never advance much until women are prevented from writing book reviews."

"Meaning," said Arthur Fenton, entering and with his usual quickness seizing the thread of conversation at once, "that some woman critic or other hit the weak spot in Fred's last book."

"Hallo, Fenton," called Bently, in his usual explosive fashion. "I haven't seen you this long time. I did not know whether you were dead or alive."

"Oh, as usual, occupying a middle ground between the two. Are you coming upstairs, Fred?"

A smile ran around the circle.

"At it again, Fenton?" Ainsworth asked.

"You'll have to go West and be made a senator if you keep on playing poker every night."

"If I don't have better luck than I've been having lately," Fenton rejoined, as he and Rangely left the room, "I should have to have a subscription taken up to pay my travelling expenses."

The card-rooms were upstairs, and Fenton and Rangely went to them without speaking. The artist was speculating whether a ruse he had just executed would be successful; his companion was thinking of the news he had just had from New York, that a girl with whom he had flirted at the mountains last summer was about to visit Boston.

Around a baize-covered table in the card-room sat three or four men, in one of whom Rangely recognized the corpulent and vulgar person of Mr. Erastus Snaffle. He nodded to him with an air of qualifying his recognition with certain mental reservations, while Fenton said as he took his place beside Chauncy Wilson, who moved to make room for him, —

"Good evening, Mr. Snaffle. Have you come up to clean the club out again?"

Mr. Snaffle looked up as if he did not fully comprehend, but he chuckled as he answered, —

"I should think it was time. I was never inside this club that I didn't get bled."

The men laughed in a somewhat perfunctory way, and the cards having been dealt, the game went on. They were all members of the club except Snaffle, and they all knew that this rather doubtful individual had no business there at all. There had of late been a good deal of feeling in the club because the rule that forbade the bringing of strangers into the house had been so often violated. The St. Filipe was engaged in the perfectly fruitless endeavor to enforce the regulation that visitors might be admitted provided the same person was not brought into the rooms twice within a fixed period. Some of the members violated the rule unconsciously, since it was awkward to invite a friend into the club and to qualify the courtesy with the condition that he had not been asked by anybody else within the prescribed period, and it was easy to forget this ungracious preliminary. Some few of the members — since in every club there will be men who are gentlemen but by brevet, — deliberately took advantage of the uncertainty which always arises from so anomalous a regulation, and the result of deliberate and of involuntary breaches of the rule had been that the club house was made free with by outsiders to a most unpleasant extent.

Not yet ready to do away with the by-law, since many members found it convenient and pleasant to take their friends into the club-house, the managers of the affairs of the St. Filipe were making a desperate effort to discover all offenders who were intentionally guilty of violating the regulation. They had their eye on several outsiders who made free with the house, and it was understood that certain men were in danger of being requested not to continue their visits to a place where they had no right. Snaffle, who had been first brought to the club by Dr. Wilson to play poker, was one of these, and the men who sat playing with him to-night were secretly curious to know how he happened to be there on this particular occasion. He had come into the card-room alone, with the easy air of familiarity which usually distinguished him, and appearances seemed to point to his having taken the liberty of walking into the house in the same way. The men liked well enough to have him in the game, because he played recklessly and always left money at the table, but not one of them, even Dr. Wilson, who was more recklessly democratic in his habits and instincts than any of the rest, would have cared to be seen walking with Erastus Snaffle on the streets by daylight.

When Snaffle entered the club house, the servant whose duty it was to wait at the outer door, had gone for a moment to the coat-room adjoining the hall. Here Snaffle met him and offered him his coat and hat. The servant extended his hand mechanically, but he looked at the new-comer so pointedly that the latter muttered, by way of credentials, —

"I came with Mr. Fenton."

The servant made no comment, but as Mr. Snaffle went upstairs, he reported to the steward that the intruder was again in the house and had been introduced by Mr. Fenton. The steward in turn reported this to the Secretary, and before Arthur himself came in, a rod was already preparing for him in the shape of a complaint to be made before the Executive Committee.

It was thus that precisely the thing happened which Fenton had with his usual cleverness endeavored to guard against. Impudent as Mr. Snaffle was capable of being, he would never have ventured uninvited into the precincts of the St. Filipe Club, where even when introduced he found himself somewhat overpowered by the social standing and the lofty manners of those around him. This feeling of awe showed itself in two ways, had any one been clever enough to appreciate the fact. It rendered him unusually silent, and it induced him to play high, as if he felt under obligations to pay for his admission into company where he did not belong.

It was to this last fact that he owed his invitation to be present on this particular evening. Arthur Fenton was going to the club to play poker, urged partly by the love of excitement and perhaps even more by the hope of raising a part or the whole of the fifty dollars of which he had pressing need, when he encountered Snaffle standing on a street corner. Fenton's acquaintance with the man had been confined to their meetings in the card-room of the St. Filipe, but he had once or twice carried home in his pocket very substantial tokens of Snaffle's reckless play. Almost without being conscious of what he did, Fenton stopped and extended his hand.

"Good evening," he said. "What is up? Are you ready for your revenge?"

"Oh, I'm always ready for a good game," Snaffle answered. "I was going to see my best girl, but I don't mind taking a hand instead."

Fenton smiled as the other turned and walked with him toward the club, but inwardly he loathed the fat, vulgar man at his side. His sense of the fitness of things was outraged by his being obliged to associate with such a creature, and that the obligation arose entirely from his own will, only showed to his mind how helpless he was in the hands of fate. He was outwardly gracious enough, but inwardly he nourished a bitter hatred against Erastus Snaffle for constraining him to go through this humiliation before he could win his money.

As they neared the club, Fenton recalled the fact that there had been some talk about visitors, and that the presence of this very man had been especially objected to, and reflected that in any case he had no desire to be seen going in with him. As they entered the vestibule the door was not opened for them, and Fenton's quick wit appreciated the fact that the servant who should be sitting just inside, was not in his place. With an inward ejaculation of satisfaction at this good fortune, he put his hand to his breast pocket.

"Oh, pshaw!" he exclaimed. "There are those confounded letters I promised to post. You go in, Mr. Snaffle, and I'll go back to the letter box on the corner. You know the way, and you'll find the fellows in the first card-room."

He opened the door as he spoke, and as Snaffle entered and closed it after him, Fenton ran down the steps and walked to the next corner. He had no letters to mail, but it was characteristic of his dramatic way of doing things that he walked to the letter-box, raised the drop and went through the motion of slipping in an envelope. He was accustomed to say that when one played a part it could not be done too carefully, and it amused him to reflect that if he were watched his action would appear consistent with his words, while if he were timed he would be found to have been gone from the club house exactly long enough. Not that he supposed anybody was likely to take the trouble to do either of these things, but Fenton was an imaginative man and he found a humorous pleasure in finishing even his trickery in an artistic manner.

It was Saturday night, and just before midnight a servant opened the card-room door. The room was full of smoke, empty glasses stood beside the players, and piles of red and blue and white "chips" were heaped in uneven distribution along the edges of the table.

"It is ten minutes of twelve, gentlemen," the servant said, and retired.

"Jack-pots round," said Rangely, dealing rapidly. "Look lively now."

He and Fenton had been winning, the pile of blue counters beside the latter representing nearly thirty dollars, with enough red and white ones to cover his original investments. The first jack-pot and the second were played, Dr. Wilson wining one and Snaffle the other on the first hand. On the third, Fenton bet for a while, holding three aces against a full hand held by the fifth man.

"It's all right," Fenton remarked, as Rangely chaffed him. "I am waiting for the 'kittie-pot.' See what a pile there is to go into that. I always expect to gather in the 'kittie.'"

The fourth pot was quickly passed, and then Wilson, who had been managing the "kittie," put upon the table the surplus, which to-night chanced to be unusually large. The cards were dealt and dealt three times again before the pot could be opened, and then Rangely started it. Arthur looked at his hand in disgust. He held the nine of hearts, the five, six, eight, and nine of spades, and as he said to himself he never had luck in drawing to either straight or flush. Still the stake was good, and he came in, discarding his heart. He drew the seven of spades. Rangely was betting on three aces, and Wilson on a full hand, so that the betting ran rather high.

"Twelve o'clock, gentlemen," the servant said at the door.

And when Fenton began his Sunday by winning the pot on his straight flush, he found himself more than sixty dollars to the good on his evening's work.

"You've regularly bled me, Fenton," Snaffle observed with much jocularity, as the players came out of the club house. "I've hardly got a car fare left to take me home. I'm afraid the St. Filipe is a den of thieves."

"I don't mind lending you a car fare, Mr. Snaffle," the artist returned, endeavoring to speak as pleasantly as if he did not object to the familiarity of the other's address. "But don't abuse the club."

"I think I'll go to church," Dr. Wilson said with a yawn. "It must be most time."

"Church-going," Fenton returned, sententiously, "is small beer for small souls."

"There, Fenton," retorted Rangely, as at this minute they came to the corner where they separated, "don't feel obliged to try to be clever. You can't do it at this time of night."

Snaffle continued his walk with the artist almost to Fenton's door, although the latter suspected that it was out of his companion's way. Arthur was willing, however, to give the loser the compensation of his society as a return for the greenbacks in his pocket, and his natural acuteness was so far from being as active as usual that when he found Mr. Snaffle speaking of Princeton Platinum stock he did not suspect that he was being angled for in turn, and that the gambling for the evening was not yet completed. He listened at first without much attention, but the man to whom he listened was wily and clever, and after he was in bed that night the artist's brain was busy planning how to raise money to invest in Princeton Platinum.

"I never saw such luck as yours," Snaffle observed admiringly. "The way you filled that spade flush on that last hand was a miracle. It is just that sort of luck that runs State street and Wall street."

Fenton smiled to himself in the darkness, the proposition was so manifestly absurd, but he was already bitten by the mania for speculation, and when once this madness infects a man's brain the most improbable causes will increase the disease. Snaffle, of course, was too shrewd to ask his companion to buy Princeton Platinum stock, and indeed declared that although he had charge of putting it upon the market, he was reluctant to part with a single share of it. He added with magnanimous frankness, that all mining stock was dangerous, especially for one who did not thoroughly understand it.

But his negatives, as he intended, were more

effective than affirmatives would have been, and the bait had been safely swallowed by the unlucky fish for whom the astute speculator angled. Fenton had invited him to the club to be eaten, but the wily visitor secretly regarded the money he lost at the poker table as a paying investment, believing that in the end it was not the bones of plump Erastus Snaffle which were destined to be picked.

XVIII

HE SPEAKS THE MERE CONTRARY.

Love's Labor's Lost; i. — 1.

MRS. AMANDA WELSH SAMPSON sat in her bower, enveloped in an unaccustomed air of respectability, and in a frame of mind exceedingly self-satisfied and serene. She had secured a visit from a New York relative, a distant cousin whose acquaintance she had made in the mountains the summer before, and she hoped from this circumstance to secure much social advantage. For at home Miss Frances Merrivale moved in circles such as her present hostess could only gaze at from afar with burning envy. In her own city, Miss Merrivale would certainly never have consented to know Mrs. Sampson, relationship or no relationship; but she chanced to wish to get away from home for a week or two, she thought somewhat wistfully of the devotion of Fred Rangely at the mountains last summer, and she was not without a hope that if she once appeared in Boston, the Staggchases, who should have invited her to visit them long ago, she being as nearly related to Mr. Staggchase as to Mrs. Sampson, might be moved to ask her to come to stay with them.

It cannot be said that Mrs. Amanda Welsh Sampson, dashing, vulgar social adventurer that she was, had much in common with her guest. Miss Merrivale, it is true, had the incurable disease of social ambition as thoroughly as her hostess; but the girl had, at least, a recognized and very comfortable footing under her feet, while the unfortunate widow kept herself above the surface only by nimble but most tiresome leaps from one precarious floating bit to another. In these matters, moreover, a few degrees make really an immense difference. There is all the inequality which exists between the soldier who wields his sword in a disastrous hollow, and one who strikes triumphant blows from the hillock above. The elevation is to be measured in inches, perhaps, but that range reaches from failure to success. Whether social ambition is proper pride or vulgar presumption depends not upon the feeling itself so much as upon the grade from which it is exercised, and Miss Merrivale very quickly understood that while she was placed upon one side of the dividing line between the two, her hostess was unhappily to be found upon the other.

Indeed Miss Frances had hardly recognized what Mrs. Sampson's surroundings were until she found herself established in the little apartment as a guest of that lady. Her newly found cousin had at the mountains spoken of her father, the late judge, and of her own acquaintances among the great and well known of Boston, with an air which carried conviction to one who had not known her too long. She spoke with playful pathos of her poverty, it is true, but when a woman's gowns will pass muster, talk of poverty is not likely to be taken too seriously. Miss Merrivale knew, moreover, that the widow, like herself, could boast a connection with the Staggchase family.

Now she found herself at the top of an apartment house in a street of Nottingham lace curtains carefully draped back to show the Rogers' groups on neat marble stands behind their precise folds. The awful gulf which yawned between this South End location and the region where abode those whom she counted her own kind socially, was apparent to her the moment she arrived and looked about her. Fred Rangely had called, but Mrs. Sampson had regaled her guest with such tales of his devotion to Mrs. Staggchase that Miss Merrivale received him with much coldness, and his call was not a success. Now she was impatiently waiting for the appearance of Mrs. Staggchase, who, it did not occur to her to doubt, would of course call. She was curious to see her relative, and her fondness for Rangely, such as it was, was marvellously quickened by the presence of a rival in the field. Instead of the appearance of Mrs. Staggchase, however, came a note asking Miss Merrivale to dine, whereat that young woman was angry, and her hostess, although she was too clever to show it, was secretly furious.

This invitation was the result of a conversation between Mr. and Mrs. Richard Staggchase, which had begun by that gentleman's asking his wife at dinner when she was going to call upon Miss Merrivale.

"Not at all, my dear," Mrs. Staggchase answered, "as long as she is visiting that dreadful Mrs. Sampson. I'm not sure, Fred, but that if I had known that creature could claim a cousinship to you, I should have refused to marry you."

"She is a dose," Mr. Staggchase admitted. "I wonder where she lives now. Didn't Frances Merrivale send her address?"

"She lives on Catawba Street, at the top of a speaking tube in one of those dreadful apartment houses where you shout up the tube and they open the door for you by electricity. I wonder how soon it will be, Fred, before you'll drop in a nickel at the door of an apartment house and the person you want to see will be slid out to you on a platform."

"Gad! That wouldn't be a bad scheme," her husband returned, with an appreciative grin. "But, really now, what are you going to do about this girl. She's a sort of cousin, you know, and she's a great friend of the Livingstons."

"We might ask her to come here after she gets through with that woman. I'll write her if you like."

"Without calling?" Mr. Staggchase asked, lifting his eyebrows a little.

"My dear," his wife responded, "I try to do my duty in that estate in life to which I have been appointed, and I am willing to made all possible exceptions to all known rules in favor of your family; but Mrs. Sampson is an impossible exception. I will do nothing that shows her that I am conscious of her existence."

"But it will be awfully rude not to call."

"One can't be rude to such creatures as Mrs. Sampson," returned Mrs. Staggchase, with unmoved decision. "She is one of those dreadful women who watch for a recognition as a cat watches for a mouse. I've seen her at the theatre. She'd pick out one person and run him down with her great bold eyes until he had to bow to her, and then she'd stalk another in the same way. Call on her, indeed! Why, Fred, she'd invite you to a dinner *tête-à-tête* to-day, if she thought you'd go."

Mr. Staggchase laughed rather significantly.

"Gad! that might be amusing. She is of the kittle cattle, my dear, but you must own that she's a well-built craft."

"Oh, certainly," replied his better half, who was too canny by far to show annoyance, if indeed she felt any, when her husband praised another woman. "If everybody isn't aware of her good points, it isn't that she is averse to advertising them. She has taken up with young Stanton, the sculptor, just because some of us have been interested in him."

"Is he going to make the *America* statue?"

"That is still uncertain, but for my part I half hope he won't, if that Sampson woman is his kind."

Mr. Staggchase dipped his long fingers into his finger bowl, wiped them with great deliberation and then pushed his chair back from the table. It was very seldom that his wife denied a request he made her, but when she did he knew better than to contend in the matter.

"Very well," he said, "you may do whatever you please. Whether you women are so devilish hard on each other because you know your own sex is more than I should undertake to say."

"Are you going out?"

"Yes," he answered, "I have got to go to a meeting of the Executive Committee of the St. Filipe. There is some sort of a row; I don't know what. How are you going to amuse yourself."

"By doing my duty."

"Do you find duty amusing then; I shouldn't have suspected it."

"Oh, duty's only another name for necessity. I'm going to the theatre with Fred Rangely. He wrote an article for the *Observer* in favor of that great booby Stanton's having the statue. It was a very lukewarm plea, but I asked him to do it, and as a reward"—

"He is allowed the inestimable boon of taking you to the theatre," finished her husband. "I must say, Dian, that you are, on the whole, the shrewdest woman I know."

"Thank you. I must be just, you know," she returned smiling as brilliantly as if her husband were to be won again.

It was not without reason that Mrs Staggchase had spoken of herself and her husband as a model couple. Given her theory of married life, nothing could be more satisfactory and consistent than the way in which she lived up to it. Her ideal of matrimony was a sort of mutual *laisser faire*, conducted with the utmost propriety and politeness. She made an especial point of being as attractive to her husband as to any other man; and she had the immense advantage of never having been in love with anybody but herself and of being philosophical enough not to consider the good things of conversation wasted if they were said for his exclusive benefit. She had no children, and had once remarked in answer to the question whether she regretted this, "There must be some pleasure in having sons old enough to flirt with you; but I don't know of anything else I have lost that I have reason to regret."

Her husband, thorough man of the world as he was, and indeed perhaps for that very reason, never outgrew a pleased surprise that he found his wife so perennially entertaining. He was not unwilling that she should exercise her fascinations on others when she chose, since he had no feeling toward her sufficiently warm to engender anything like jealousy ; but he appreciated her to the full.

He rose from his seat and walked to the sideboard, where he selected a cigar.

"I must say," he observed, between the puffs as he lighted it, "that you are justice incarnate. You have always kept accounts squared with me most beautifully."

Mrs. Staggchase laughed softly, toying with the tiny spoon of Swiss carved silver with which she had stirred her coffee. Her husband had expressed perfectly her theory of marital relations. She balanced accounts in her mind with the most scrupulous exactness, and was an admirable debtor if a somewhat unrelenting creditor. She had a definite standard by which she measured her obligations to Mr. Staggchase, and she never allowed herself to fall short in the measure she gave him. She was fond of him in a conveniently mild and reasonable fashion, and a marriage founded upon mutual tolerance, if it is likely never to be intensely happy, is also likely to be a pretty comfortable one. Mrs. Staggchase paid to her husband all her tithes of mint and anise and cumin, and she even sometimes presented him with a propitiatory offering in excess of her strict debt;

only such a gift was always set down in her mental record as a gift and not as a tribute.

"This Stanton is an awful lout, Fred," she observed. "Perhaps he can make a good statue of *America*, but if he can it will be because he is so thoroughly the embodiment of the vulgar and pushing side of American character."

"Then why in the world are you pushing him?"

"Oh, because Mrs. Ranger and Anna Frostwinch want him pushed. I don't know but they may believe in him. Mrs. Ranger does, of course, but the dear old soul knows no more about art than I do about Choctaw. As to the statues, I don't think it makes much difference, they are always laughed at, and I don't think anybody could make one in this age that wouldn't be found fault with."

"Nobody nowadays knows enough about sculpture to criticise it intelligently," Staggchase remarked, somewhat oracularly, "and the only safe thing left is to find fault."

"That is just about it, and so it may as well be this booby as anybody else that gets the commission. It isn't respectable for the town not to have statues, of course."

Mr. Staggchase moved toward the door.

"Well," he said, "I don't know who's in the fight, but I'll bet on your side. Good night. I hope virtue will be its own reward."

"Oh, it always is," retorted his wife. "I especially make it a point that it shall be."

XIX

HOW CHANCES MOCK.

II Henry IV.; iii. — 1.

A MAN often creates his own strongest temptations by dwelling upon possibilities of evil; and it is equally true that nothing else renders a man so likely to break moral laws as the consciousness of having broken them already. The experience of Arthur Fenton was in these days affording a melancholy illustration of both of these propositions. The humiliating inner consciousness of having violated all the principles of honor of his fealty to which he had been secretly proud begot in him an unreasonable and unreasoning impulse still further to transgress. When arraigned by his inner self for his betrayal of Hubbard, it was his instinct to defend himself by showing his superiority to all moral canons whatever. He felt a certain desperate inclination to trample all principles underfoot, as if by so doing he could destroy the standards by which he was being tried.

Fenton was not of a mental fibre sufficiently robust to make this impulse likely to result in any violent outbreak, and, indeed, but for circumstances it would doubtless have vapored itself away in words and vagrant fancies. He had once remarked, embodying a truth in one of his frequent whimsically perverse statements, that the worst thing which could be said of him was that he was incapable of a great crime, and only the constant pressure of an annoyance, such as the threats of Irons in regard to Ninitta, or the presence of an equally constant temptation, such as that to which he was now succumbing in allowing his relations with Mrs. Herman to become more and more intimate, would have brought him to any marked transgression.

In a nature such as that of Fenton there is, with the exception of vanity and the instinct of self-preservation, no trait stronger than curiosity. The artist was devoured by an eager, intellectual greed to know all things, to experience all sensations, to taste all savors of life. He made no distinction between good and bad ; his zeal for knowledge was too keen to allow of his being deterred by the line ordinarily drawn between pain and pleasure. His affections, his passions, his morals were all subordinate to this burning curiosity, and only his instinct of self-preservation subtly making itself felt in the guise of expediency, and his vanity prettily disguised as taste, held the thirst for knowledge in check.

It was by far more the desire to learn whether he could bend Ninitta to his will than it was passion which carried Fenton forward in the dangerous path upon which he was now well advanced; and it was perhaps more than either a half-unconscious eagerness to taste a new experience. Even the double wickedness of betraying the wife of a friend and of enticing a woman to her fall had for Fenton, in his present mood, an unholy fascination. He was too self-analytical to deceive himself into a supposition that he was in love with Ninitta, and even his passion was so much under the dominion of his head that he could have blown it out like a rushlight, had he really desired to be done with it. He looked at himself with mingled approbation, amusement, and horror, as he might have regarded a favorite and skilful actor in a vicious *rôle*; and the man whose mind is to him merely an amphitheatre, where games are played for his amusement, is always dangerous.

As for Ninitta, the processes of her mind were probably quite as complex as those of his, although they appeared more simple, in virtue of their being more remote. She had, in the first place, a curious jealousy of her husband because of his passionate fondness for Nino, and a dull resentment at the secret conviction that the father had the gifts and powers which were sure to win more love than the child would bestow upon her. She could better bear the thought that the boy should die, than that he should live to love anybody more than he loved her.

It was also true that Grant Herman, large-hearted and generous as he was, did not know how to make his wife happy. He was patient and chivalrous and tender; but he was hardly able to go to her level, and as she could not come to his, the pair had little in common. He felt that somehow this must be his fault; he told himself that, as the larger nature, it should be his place to make concessions, to master the situation, and to secure Ninitta's happiness, whatever came to him. He had even come to feel so much tenderness toward the mother of his child, the woman in whose behalf he had made the great sacrifice of his life, that a pale but steadfast glow of affection shone always in his heart for his wife. But his patience, his delicacy, his steadfastness counted for little with Ninitta. She had been separated from him for long years of betrothal, during which he had developed and changed utterly. She had clung to her love and faith, but her love and faith were given to an ardent youth glowing with a passion of which it was hardly possible to rekindle the faint embers in the bosom of the man she married. Even Ninitta, little given to analysis, could not fail to recognize that her husband was a very different being from the lover she had known ten years before. One fervid blaze of the old love would have appealed more strongly to her peasant soul than all the patience and tender forbearance of years.

Indeed, it is doubtful whether Ninitta might not have been better and happier had Herman been less kind. Had he made a slave of her, she would have accepted her lot as uncomplainingly as the women of her race had acquiesced in such a fate for stolid generations. She could have understood that. As it was, she felt always the strain of being tried by standards which she did not and could not comprehend; the misery of being in a place for which she was unfitted and which she could not fill, and the fact that no definite demands were made upon her increased her trouble by the double stress of putting her upon her own responsibility, and of leaving her ignorant in what her failures lay.

There was, too, who knows what trace of heredity in the readiness with which Ninitta tacitly adopted the idea that infidelity to a husband was rather a matter of discretion and secrecy; whereas faithfulness to her lover had been a point of the most rigorous honor. And Ninitta found Arthur Fenton's silken sympathy so insinuating, so soothing; the tempter, merely from his marvellous adaptability and faultless tact, so satisfied her womanly craving, and fostered her vanity; she was so completely made to feel that she was understood; she was tempted with a cunning the more infernal because Fenton kept himself always up to the level of sincerity by never admitting to himself that he intended any evil, that it was small wonder that the time came when her ardent Italian nature was so kindled that she became involuntarily the tempter in her turn.

It was one of the singular features of Fenton's present attitude that even he, with all his clear-sightedness, failed to see the error of supposing that his departure from the paths of rectitude was nothing but a temporary episode. He fully expected to take up again his former attitude toward life when he would have scorned such a contemptible action as the betrayal of Hubbard, or the more trifling, but perhaps even more humiliating act of smuggling Snaffle into the club that he might win his money. He even had a certain vague feeling that if he had any viciousness to get through he must do it at once, lest the resumption of his former respectability should deprive him of the opportunity. He maintained before the world, indeed, a perfect propriety of deportment, partly from the force of habit and partly from the instinctive cunning which always tried to preserve for him the means of retreat ; but so complete was his abandonment, for the time being, to the enjoyment of evil, that he was constantly assailed with the temptation to make some public demonstration of his state of feeling. He secretly longed to shock poeple with blasphemous or imprudent expressions ; to outrage all honor by stealing his host's spoons when he dined out ; his fancy rioted in whimsical evil of which, of course, he gave no outward sign.

He had a scene with Alfred Irons, one morning, at his studio. Irons came in with a look on his face which secretly enraged the artist, who was almost rude in the coldness of his greeting, although the caller only grinned at this evidence of his host's irritation

"Well, Fenton," he said, with bluff abruptness, "I suppose it is time for us to square accounts, isn't it?"

"I was not aware that we had any accounts to square," the other returned, with his most icy manner.

Irons laughed, and looked about the studio.

"That's your new picture, I suppose" he observed, settling himself back in his chair, with the determined mien of a man who recognizes the fact that he has a battle to fight, but is perfectly willing to join the fray.

The significance of his air, as he nodded toward the big canvas on the easel, so plainly brought up the unfortunate hold which the *Fatima* had given Irons over the artist, that Fenton flushed in spite of himself.

"It is a picture," he returned; "and it is unfinished."

Irons chuckled.

"Very well," he said. "We won't fence. I thought you might be interested to know that we've got our railroad business into first-rate shape; and there's no doubt that the Wachusett route will carry the day. I tell you we had a hot time in the Senate yesterday," he went on, warming with the excitement of his subject. "We made a pretty stiff fight in the Railroad Committee to get them to report 'not expedient' on the Feltonville petition. I tell you Staggchase fought like a bull tiger at the hearing, and those fellows must have put in a pot of money. But we beat 'em. Then the fight came to get the report accepted in the Senate. Everybody said that Tom Greenfield would settle the thing with a big broadside in favor of his own town; and I'll own that I was scared blue myself. But we haven't been cooking Tom Greenfield all this time for nothing. I don't mind telling you that your help in the matter was of the greatest value; and when Greenfield got up in the Senate yesterday, and put in his best licks for the Wachusett route, you'd have thought they'd been struck by a cyclone. We got a vote to sustain that report that buries the Feltonville project out of sight; and now there's no doubt that the Railroad Commissioners will give us our certificate without any more trouble."

During this rather long and not wholly coherent speech, Fenton sat with his eyes coldly fixed upon his visitor, without giving the slightest sign of interest.

"I am glad," he said, in a manner as distant as he could make it, "that your business is likely to succeed to your mind."

"Oh, it must succeed. The Commissioners only suspended operations till the Legislature disposed of the question of special legislation. Now they're all ready to give us what we want."

"And all this," Fenton said, "is of what interest to me?"

Irons flushed angrily.

"You were good enough," he returned, drawing his lips down savagely, "to give us a bit of information which we found of value. Very likely we might have hit upon it somewhere else, but that's no matter, as long as we did get it through you. We've no inclination to shirk our debt. Now what's your price?"

Fenton rose from his chair, with an impulsive movement; then he controlled himself and sat down again. He looked at his visitor with eyes of fire.

"I am not aware," he returned, "that I have ever been in the market, so that I have not been obliged to consider that question."

Alfred Irons was silent for a moment. He felt somewhat as if he had received a dash of ice-water in the face. He wrinkled up his narrow eyes and studied the man before him. He could not understand what the other was driving at. He was little likely to be able to follow the subtile changes of Fenton's imaginative mind, and he could at present see no explanation of the way in which his advances were met, except the theory that the artist was fencing to insure a larger reward for his treachery than might be given him if he accepted the first offer in silence.

Fenton, on his part, was so filled with rage that it was with difficulty that he restrained himself. The length to which his intimacy with Ninitta had now gone, however, made it absolutely necessary that he should avoid a quarrel in which her name might be brought up; and he had, moreover, put himself into the hands of Irons, by giving him the information in regard to the plans for Feltonville.

"Oh, well," Irons said at length, rising with the air of one who cannot waste his time puzzling over trifles; "have it your own way. It's only a matter of words."

He took out his pocket-book, and with deliberation turned over the papers it contained. He selected one, read it carefully, and then held it out to Fenton.

"Our manufacturing corporation is practically on its legs now," he said, "and the stock will be issued at once. That entitles you to ten shares. They will be issued at sixty, and ought to go to par by fall. Indeed, in a year's time, we'll make them worth double the buying price, or I am mistaken."

Fenton looked at the paper as if he were reading it, but its letters swam before his eyes. He needed money sorely, and had this gift come in a shape more readily convertible into cash, he might have found it impossible to resist it. As it was, he allowed himself to be fiercely angry. He was furious, but he was consciously so. He raised his eyes, flashing and distended, and fixed them upon the mean, hateful face before him. He paused an instant to let his gaze have its effect.

"And I understand," he said, with a slow, careful enunciation, "that in consideration of the service I have done you, you give me your promise never to mention the fact that you saw a lady in my studio."

"Certainly," Irons returned.

Fenton's look made him uncomfortable. The artist was reasserting the old superiority over him which the visitor had found so irritating, and it was Iron's instinct to meet this by an air of bluster.

"Very well," Arthur said. "We may then consider what you are pleased to call our account as closed."

He walked forward deliberately and laid the paper he held on the heap of glowing coals in the grate. It curled and shrivelled, and before Irons could even compress his thick lips to whistle, nothing remained of the document but a quivering film.

"Well," Irons commented, "you are a damned fool ; but then that's your own business."

The artist bowed gravely.

"Naturally," he replied.

He stood waiting as if he expected his caller to go, and, despite himself, Irons felt that he was being bowed out of the studio. He took his leave awkwardly, feeling that he had somehow been beaten with trumps in his hand, and hating Fenton ten times more heartily than ever.

"The confounded snob!" he muttered under his breath, as he went down the stairs of Studio Building. "He puts on damned high-headed airs; but I'm not done with him yet."

And Fenton meanwhile stood looking at that thin fluttering film on the red coals with despair in his heart. He had taken the money which he imperatively needed to pay notes soon due, and invested in Princeton Platinum, with which the obliging Erastus Snaffle had supplied him out of pure generosity, if one could credit the seller's statements; and he had been secretly depending for relief upon this very gift from Irons which he had destroyed. His affairs were every day becoming more inextricably involved, and Fenton, it has already been said, with all his cleverness, had no skill as a financier.

"Well," he commented to himself, shrugging his shoulders, "that is the end of that; but I did make good play."

The satisfaction of having well acted his part, and of having got the better of Irons, did much toward restoring the artist's naturally buoyant spirits. He fell to reckoning his resources, and by dint of introducing into the account several pleasing but most improbable possibilities, he succeeded in building up between himself and ruin a fanciful barrier which for the moment satisfied him ; and beyond the moment he refused to look.

XX

VOLUBLE AND SHARP DISCOURSE.

Comedy of Errors; ii. — I.

MRS AMANDA WELSH SAMPSON had in the course of a varied, if not always dignified career, learned many things. There are people who seem compelled by circumstances to waste much of their mental energy in attending to the trivial and sordid details of life, and the widow often repined that she was one of these unfortunates. She secretly fretted not a little, for instance, over the fact that she was compelled to be gracious to servants, to butcher and baker and candlestick maker, from unmixed reasons of policy. To be gracious in the *rôle* of a *grande dame* would have pleased her, but she resented the necessity; and she avenged herself upon fate by gloating upon the stupidity of that power in wasting her energies in these petty things, when results so brilliant might have been attained by a more wise utilization of her cleverness.

This morning, for instance, when Mrs. Sampson chatted affably with the carpenter who had come to do an odd job in the china closet of her tiny dining-room, she really enjoyed the talk. She was one of those women who cannot help liking to chat with a man, and John Stanton was both good looking enough and intelligent enough to make her willing to exert herself for his entertainment. This did not, however, prevent her being inwardly indignant that she felt herself compelled to converse with Stanton because experience had taught her that a little amiability properly exhibited was sure to increase the work and lessen the bill at the same time. She did not forego the pleasure of pitying herself because she chanced to find the task imposed upon her an agreeable one. There are few people in this world who are sufficiently just and sufficiently sane to deny themselves the luxury of self pity merely because the occasion does not justify that feeling.

Stanton, with his coat off and his strong arms bare to the elbow, was planing down a shelf to make it fit into its place, and as he paused to shake the long creamy shavings out of his plane, he looked up to say apologetically, —

"I'm making an awful litter, ma'am, but I don't see how I can help it."

Mrs. Sampson laughed.

"Oh, it isn't of the least consequence," she answered. "If I was inclined to complain it would be because after keeping me waiting for six weeks for this work, you come just when I have company staying with me, and gentlemen coming to dine."

She had walked into the room with a not illy simulated air of having come with the intention of going out again immediately, and stood well posed, so that her fine figure came out in relief against a crimson Japanese screen.

"I haven't anything to do with that, ma'am," Stanton replied. "The boss makes out the orders, and we go where we are sent."

"Well," the widow said, smiling brilliantly, and moving across the room to the table where the dishes taken from the closet were piled, "it can't be helped, I suppose; but I hope you will let me get things cleared up in time for dinner."

"Oh, I'll surely get through by eleven or half past."

"And I don't have dinner till half past six."

The carpenter looked up questioningly. Then he went on with his work.

"I never can get used to city ways," he observed. "I don't see how folks can get along without having dinner in the middle of the day when it's dinner time."

Mrs. Sampson busied herself with the plates, arranging things on the sideboard ready for evening. Her guest, Miss Merrivale, was out driving with Fred Rangely, and the widow's resources in the way of servants were so limited that it was necessary that the hands of the mistress should attend to many of the details of the housekeeping. She enjoyed talking to this stalwart, vigorous fellow. She was alive to the last fibre of her being to the influence of masculine perfections, and Stanton was a splendidly built type of manhood. She utilized the moments and secured an excuse for lingering by going on with her work while the carpenter continued his, carrying out her theory of getting the most out of a laborer by personal supervision, and withal gratifying her intense and instinctive fondness for the presence of a magnificent man.

"You are not city bred, perhaps," she answered his last remark, for the sake of saying something.

"Oh, no, ma'am," John answered. "I was raised at Feltonville."

The widow became alert at once.

"Feltonville?" she repeated. "Why, I have a cousin living there, the Hon. Thomas Greenfield."

"Oh, Tom Greenfield. Everybody knows Tom Greenfield," John said, his face lighting up. "We call him 'Honest Tom' up our way. He's here in the Legislature now."

"Yes, I know he is. He's coming here to dinner to-night."

"Is he? He's an awful smart man, and he's a good one, too, as ever walked. He's awful interested in Orin's getting the job to make the new statue of *America*. Orin," he added in explanation, "Orin Stanton, he's the sculptor and he's my brother; my half-brother, that is. You've heard of him?"

"Oh, of course," she answered, warmly.

Mrs. Sampson knew little of Orin Stanton, but she did know that Alfred Irons was on the committee having in charge the commission for the new statue, and the fact that Mr. Greenfield had an interest, however indirect, in the same matter, was a hint too valuable not to be acted upon.

Despite the confidence with which he had spoken to Fenton, the railroad business was by no means settled. The Staggchase syndicate had rallied to raise objections to prevent the Railroad Commissioners from authorizing the other route. A hearing had been granted, and for it elaborate preparations were being made. The Irons syndicate were extremely anxious that Greenfield should speak at this hearing, but there had been so much feeling aroused at Feltonville by his action in the Senate that he was not inclined to do so; and Mrs. Sampson, who had already proved so successful in influencing her relative, had been requested to continue her efforts.

The widow had pondered deeply upon the tactics she should use, and it is to be noted that she set down the amount of the obligation incurred by Irons as the greater because she had really become in a way fond of Greenfield, and she was too clever not to understand the fact, to which the senator with singular perversity remained obstinately blind, that he could not but injure his political prestige by the course he was taking.

She had aroused his combativeness by telling him that if his convictions forced him to vote against the Feltonville interest, people would say he was bought. She knew that now this was said, and that openly; — indeed, despite all her shrewdness and knowledge of human nature, she had moments when she wondered whether the charge might not be true, so incomprehensible did it seem that a man should throw away his own advantage. She had no sentiment strong enough to make her hesitate about going on to sacrifice Greenfield to her own interests, but she distinctly disliked the fact that Irons should also profit by the senator's loss.

All day the widow pondered deeply on the situation, and the result of the chance disclosure of John Stanton was that when her guests arrived she made an opportunity to take Irons aside for a moment's confidential talk.

The widow's dinner-party was a somewhat singular one to give in compliment to a young girl, there being no one of the guests near Miss Merrivale's own age except Fred Rangely. The widow's acquaintance among women whom she could ask to meet the New Yorker was limited, and having decided upon inviting Greenfield, Irons, and Rangely to dinner, the hostess sat gnawing her stylographic pen in despair a good half hour before she could decide upon a fourth guest. A woman she must have, and few women whom she wished to ask would come to her house even to call. When she now and then gathered at an afternoon tea a handful of people whose names she was proud to have reported in the society papers, she did it by securing a lion of literary or of theatrical fame, whose unwary feet she entangled in her cunningly laid snares before he knew anything about social conditions in Boston. There were many people, moreover, who would go to see a celebrity at a house like that of Mrs. Sampson much as they would have gone to the theatre, when they would have received neither the guest of honor nor the hostess, the latter of whom, to their thinking, stood for the time being much in the position of stage manager.

Mrs. Sampson never set herself to a problem like this without a feeling of bitterness. To consider what woman of any standing could be induced to eat her salt brought her true social position before her with painful vividness. She could not, in face of the facts which then forced themselves upon her, shut her eyes to the truth that her painful struggles for position had been pretty nearly fruitless. She did now and then get an invitation to a crush in a desirable house, some over-sensitive woman who had been to stare at one of Mrs. Sampson's captures thus discharging her debt, and at the same time virtually wiping her hands of all intercourse with the dashing widow. As for asking her to their tables or going to hers, everybody understood that that was not to be thought of.

With the cleverness born of desperation, Mrs. Sampson solved her difficulty by asking Miss Catherine Penwick to fill the vacant place. Miss Catherine Penwick was the last forlorn and fluttering leaf on the bare branches of a lofty but expiring family tree. The Penwicks had come over in the Mayflower, or at a period yet more remote, and the acme of the prosperity and social distinction of the name was coincident with the second administration of President Washington. Since that time its decadence had been steady ; at first slow, but later with the accelerating motion common to falling bodies, until nothing remained of the family revenues, little but a tradition of the family greatness, and none of the race but this frostbitten old lady, poor and forsaken in her desolate old age.

Miss Penwick was one of the learned ladies of her generation, a fact which counted for less in the erudite day into which it was her misfortune to linger than in those of her far-away youth. She struggled against the tide with pathetic bravery, endeavoring to eke out some sort of a livelihood by giving feeble lectures on Greek art, which no living being wished to hear, or could possibly be supposed to be any better for hearing, but to which the charitably disposed subscribed with spasmodic benevolence. The poor creature, with her antique curls quivering about her face, yellow and wrinkled now, its high-bred expression sadly marred by the look of anxious eagerness which comes of watching, like the prophet, for the ravens to bring one's dinner, was but too glad to be invited to sit at any table where she could get a comfortable meal and be allowed to play for the moment at being the grand lady her ancestresses had been in reality.

"I hope you don't mind my asking Miss Penwick as the only lady," Mrs. Sampson said to her guest; "but she is such a dear old creature, and our family and hers have been intimate for centuries. She is getting old, poor dear, and she hasn't any money any more, just as I haven't. But you know she is wiser than Minerva's owl, and quite the fashion in Boston. One really is nobody who doesn't know Miss Penwick; and she is *so* well bred."

Miss Penwick, dear old soul, had a feeling that Mrs. Amanda Welsh Sampson was somehow too hopelessly modern for one of her generation ever to be really in sympathy with the widow; but Mrs. Sampson had been born a Welsh, and Miss Catherine was too unworldly to be aware of all the gossip and even scandal which had made the name of the dashing adventuress of so evil savor in the nostrils of people like Mrs. Frederick Staggchase.

And it must be confessed also, that to such petty economies was the last of the Penwicks reduced by poverty that a dinner was an object to her. She could not afford to lose an opportunity of dining at the price of two horse-car tickets, and so promptly at the moment she presented herself in the dainty elegance of bits of real old lace, with family miniatures and locks of hair from the illustrious heads of great-great-grandmothers and grandfathers decorously framed in split pearls, the lustre of the jewels, like that of their wearer, tarnished by time.

Miss Merrivale did feel that the company assembled was an odd one, although she lived too far away to appreciate the fact that none of the guests, with the possible exception of Rangely, were exactly what she would have been asked to dine with at home. A country member, a self-made vulgarian, an antiquated spinster, and a literateur who, after all, was received rather upon sufferance into such exclusive houses as he entered at all, made up a group of which Miss Merrivale, with feminine instinct, felt the inferiority, despite the fact that she had no means of placing the guests. Miss Penwick appreciated the social standing of her fellow-diners, but she had by a long course of social humiliations come to accept unpleasant conditions where getting a dinner was concerned; and she was, moreover, somewhat relieved that at Mrs. Sampson's she was not obliged to meet anybody worse. Her instincts were keen enough, after all her melancholy experiences, to enable her to recognize the fact that Tom Greenfield was the most truly a gentleman of the three men, and she was pleased that he should take her in to dinner.

Mrs. Sampson, as she went in on the arm of Irons, contrived to let him know what she had heard that morning from young Stanton of Greenfield's interest in the young sculptor; adding a hint or two of the use to be made of this information. Rangely, just behind her, was chatting with Miss Frances in that half amorous badinage which some girls always provoke, perhaps because they expect and keenly relish it.

"Oh, no," he observed, just as Mrs. Sampson was able to give an ear to what was being said by the young people. "I am not fickle. I am constancy itself, but when you are in New York and I am in Boston, you really can't expect me to sigh loud enough to be heard all that distance."

"I know you too well to suppose you will sigh at all," she returned, with a coquettish air. "Especially with the consolations I am given to understand that you have near at hand."

"What consolations?" he asked, visibly disconcerted.

"What has that confounded widow been telling her?" he wondered inwardly. "Is it Mrs. Staggchase or Ethel Mott she's aiming at?"

Miss Merrivale tossed her head, as they paused in the doorway of the tiny dining-room a moment to give Mr. Irons opportunity to convey his ungainly length into its proper niche. Her shot had been purely a random one and, unless one believes in telepathy, so was the question by which she abruptly changed the subject.

"Do you know my cousin, Mrs. Frederick Staggchase?"

He held himself in hand wonderfully.

"Oh, yes," was his reply. "I know Mrs. Staggchase very well, but I didn't know she was your cousin. All the good gifts of life seem to fall to her lot."

"Thanks for nothing. She has not been to see me. She invited me to dine and I declined, and then she wrote and asked me to visit there when I finished my stay here."

"Shall you do it?"

The thought with which Rangely askėd this question was one oddly mingled of regret and of hope. He had flirted too seriously with Miss Merrivale to wish to meet her at Mrs. Staggchase's, although he had never seriously cared for her; and he reflected with a humorous sense of relief that if the pretty New Yorker should really visit her cousin, he was likely to be put in a position to give his undivided attention to wooing Miss Mott, a consummation for which he wished without having the strength of mind to bring it about. As she let his question pass in silence, he smiled to himself at the ignominious manner in which he must retreat from his attitude as the devoted admirer of Mrs. Staggchase and of Miss Merrivale, feeling that to set about the earnest attempt to win Ethel would be quite consolation enough to enable him to reconcile himself to even this. The comfort of having circumstances make for him a decision which he should make for himself, is often to a self-indulgent man of far more importance than the decision itself.

As the dinner progressed, Miss Penwick, warming with the good cheer — for Mrs. Sampson was too thoroughly a man's woman not to appreciate the value of palatable viands — become decidedly loquacious; and at last, by a happy coincidence for which her hostess could have hugged her on the spot, she introduced the name of Orin Stanton.

"I hear you are on the *America* committee, Mr. Irons," she said. "We ladies are so much interested in that just now. I called on Mrs. Bodewin Ranger yesterday, and she is really enthusiastic over this young Stanton that's going to make it. He is going to make it, isn't he?"

Irons laughed his vulgar laugh, which Fenton once said was the laugh of a swineherd counting his pigs.

"It has not been decided," he answered. "Stanton seems to have a good many friends."

"Oh, he has, indeed," responded Miss Penwick eagerly. "He is a young man of extraordinary genius. I saw a beautiful notice of him in the *Daily Observer* the other morning, Mr. Rangely," she continued, turning to Fred, "and Mrs. Frostwinch said she thought you wrote it. It was very appreciative."

"Yes, I wrote it," he responded, not very warmly. "Mr. Stanton is endorsed by Mr. Calvin, you know, Mr. Irons; and Mr. Calvin is our highest authority, I suppose."

Of those present no one except the hostess was surprised at this admission, which marked the great change in Rangely's position since the days when, like Arthur Fenton, he was a pronounced Pagan and denounced Peter Calvin as the incarnation of Philistinism in art. On one occasion Rangely had boldly reproached his friend with having gone over to the camp of the Philistines; and he had been met with the retort, —

"We have found it pleasant in the camp of Philistia, have we not?"

"We?" Rangely had echoed, with an accent of indignation.

"Yes," Arthur had replied, with cool scorn. "You Pagans pitched into me because I made my way over; but I am not so stupid as not to see that there has been considerable sneaking after me."

"But at least," Fred had urged, "we fellows preserved the decency of a respect for the principles we had professed."

"Ah, bah! The principles we had professed were the impossible dreams of extreme youth.

Honesty is a weakness that is outgrown by any man who has brains enough to do his own thinking. You still profess the principles, and betray them, while I boldly disavow them at the start."

"At least," Rangely had said, driven to his last defences, "if we have fallen off, we have done it unconsciously, and you" —

"I," Fenton had flamed out in interruption, "have, at least, made it a point to be honest with myself, whether I was with anybody else or not. I find it easier to be mistaken than to be vague, and I had far rather be."

The thought of Fenton floated through Fred's mind as he endorsed Peter Calvin, and with no especial thought of what he was saying, he observed, —

"Arthur Fenton wants Grant Herman to have the commission, and I must say Herman would be sure to do it well."

"If Fenton wants Herman," Irons returned, with an attempt at lightness which only served to emphasize the genuine bitterness which underlaid his words, "that settles my voting for him."

"Don't you and Mr. Fenton agree?" the hostess asked. "I supposed you were one of his admirers or you wouldn't have had him paint your portrait."

"I admire his works more than I do him," Irons answered, adding with clumsy jocularity "I am waiting for offers from the friends of candidates."

"I am interested in young Stanton," Mr. Greenfield said; "I might make you an offer."

"Oh, to oblige you," the other responded, "I will consent to support him without money and without price."

The talk meant little to any one save the hostess and Irons, but they both felt that this move in their game, slight as it seemed, was both well made and important. Later in the evening Irons took occasion to assure Greenfield that he would really support Stanton in the committee, adding that with the vote of Calvin this would settle the matter. When a few days later Irons asked the decision of Greenfield in regard to the railroad matter, he found that the attitude of the chairman of the committee was satisfactory. And honest Tom Greenfield had the satisfaction of believing that he had been instrumental in furthering the interests of Orin Stanton, in whose success he felt the pride common to people in a country district when a genius has appeared among them and secured recognition from the outside world sufficient to assure them that they are not mistaken in their admiration. Nor was the mind of the country member disturbed by any suspicion that he had been managed and deceived, and that he had really played into the hands of that most unscrupulous corporation, the Wachusett Syndicate.

XXI

A MINT OF PHRASES IN HIS BRAIN.

Love's Labor's Lost; i. — 1.

IT was a peculiarity which the St. Filipe shared with most other clubs the world over, that the doings of its committees in private session were always known within twenty-four hours and discussed by the knot of habitues of the house who kept close watch upon its affairs. It did not long remain a secret therefore, that the Executive Committee had taken a firm stand in regard to the troublesome matter of introducing strangers illegally, and that Fenton had been summoned to appear before them to answer to the charge of introducing Snaffle.

The excitement was intense. Fenton was a man whose affairs always provoked comment, and while there was much discussion in regard to what would be done, there was quite as much as to how he would take it. The men who had been in the card-room on the night in question chanced not to be on hand to say that Snaffle had appeared alone, and the word of the servant was accepted as conclusive.

"Fenton's a queer fellow anyway," one man observed reflectively. "He's a damned arrogant cuss."

"He has not only the courage of his convictions," Ainsworth responded, "but he has also the courage of his dislikes."

"He will never give up the assumption that he is above all rules," the first speaker continued. "He feels that he is being bullied if he is ever asked to submit to a law of any kind."

"The committee are bound to put things through this time. They've been waiting for a chance to jump on somebody for a long time, and Fenton put a rod in pickle for himself when he tried to run Rangely in for secretary last election."

"One thing is certain," Ainsworth said, rising and buttoning his coat; "Fenton isn't an easy man to tackle, and if we don't have some music out of this before we are done, I shall be surprised."

There was a general feeling that something unusual would come of this action on the part of the Executive Committee. Fenton was a man of so much audacity, so fertile in resource, and so persistent in his efforts, that while nobody knew what he would do, it was generally supposed that he would make a fight; and expectation was alive to see it.

As to Fenton, he was at first completely overwhelmed by the summons from the committee. Disgrace, reproof, — even examination was a horrible and unspeakable humiliation, which it seemed to him impossible to bear. He hated life and was so thoroughly wretched as to be physically almost prostrated, although his strong will kept him upon his feet still.

As he reflected, however, the hopeful side of the situation presented itself to his mind. He had been confident that his tracks were so well hidden that his share in introducing Snaffle into the Club would not be suspected, unless the guest had himself mentioned it. He made the Princeton Platinum stock a pretext for calling upon the speculator, and endeavored to discover whether the latter had spoken, but he learned nothing. He was not quite ready to ask frankly whether Snaffle had betrayed him, and short of doing so he could not discover. Still Fenton told himself that the only thing he had to fear was some hearsay that might have reached the ears of the Executive Committee, and he trusted to his cleverness to answer this.

He presented himself at the meeting of the committee with a bold front and an air of restrained indignation, which became him very well. All his histrionic instincts were aroused by such an occasion as this. He delighted to act a part, and the fact that real issues were the stake of his success, added a zest which he could not have found on the boards. He spoke to the gentlemen present or replied to their greeting with a manner of dignity which was effective because it was not in the least overdone, and then sat down very quietly to await what might be said.

He had not long to wait. The Secretary of the St. Filipe heartily disliked Fenton, chiefly because Fenton openly disliked him. He was a man who was petty enough to take advantage of his office to gratify his personal spite, and shallow enough not to perceive that he had done so. His whole fat person quivered with indignant gratification as he saw Fenton in the *rôle* of a culprit, and he bent his look upon the notes spread out before him because he was aware that his eyes showed more satisfaction than was by any means decorous.

The meeting partook of that awkward unofficial nature which makes matters of discipline so hard in a social club. The men present were Fenton's companions and associates, and the dignity with which their position invested them was hardly sufficient to put them at their ease. They heartily wished to be done with the disagreeable business, and were not without a feeling of personal vexation against the culprit for forcing upon them anything so unpleasant as sitting in judgment upon him.

The chairman, Mr. Staggchase, opened the case by saying in an offhand manner, that they were all very sorry for the turn things had taken, but that the evil of having strangers introduced into the club had grown to proportions which made it impossible longer to overlook it, and that this was especially true of the bringing into the house men who not only were there in violation of the rules, but who were of a character which made it more than a violation of good taste to introduce them into the club at all. He added that he was convinced that the present case was the result of a misunderstanding, and he hoped the gentleman who had been asked to meet the committee would comprehend that he was there rather to assist the government of the club in maintaining discipline, than for any other reason.

He looked at Fenton and smiled as he concluded, and the artist bowed to him with a glance of answering friendliness. Thus far all had been pleasant, so pleasant indeed that the corpulent Secretary had ceased smiling. The remarks of Mr. Staggchase had been conciliatory and gracious, and showed so distinct a leaning toward the accused, that the Secretary felt himself to be personally attacked in this slighting way of holding charges which he had given. He drew his thin lips together and cleared his throat in a preparatory cough, rustling his papers as if to call attention to them.

"If the Secretary is ready," Mr. Staggchase said, "he may read the memorandum of the matter about which we wished to consult Mr. Fenton."

"The charge against Mr. Fenton," the Secretary responded, with deliberate insolence, "is that on the evening of March 13th he brought Mr.

Erastus Snaffle into the club house, knowing that that individual had already been several times in the club within the time specified by the by-laws, and knowing him to be a man unfit to be introduced into a gentleman's club at any time."

"I have the honor of Mr. Erastus Snaffle's acquaintance," Fenton interpolated, in a perfectly cool, self-controlled voice, "in virtue of having had him presented to me by the Secretary of this club in the pool-room upstairs."

The members of the committee smiled, but the Secretary flushed with anger. The statement was literally true, and he could not at the moment go into the rather lengthy explanation which would have made it evident that his thus standing sponsor for Mr. Snaffle was entirely the result of a provoking accident rather than of his choice. He hurried on to cover the awkward interruption.

"Mr. Fenton further broke a rule of the club in neglecting, or I should say omitting to register his guest, and his share in the matter might not have been known had not Mr. Snaffle told the servant at the door that he came at Mr. Fenton's invitation."

Arthur had settled himself in an attitude of placid attention, secretly enjoying the clever thrust he had given his adversary. At these last words he sat upright.

"Mr. Staggchase," he said, turning toward the chairman, and speaking with sudden gravity, "do

I understand that I have been summoned before this committee in consequence of the report of a servant."

"I think such is the fact, Mr. Fenton," was the reply, "but of course your simple word will be received as ample exoneration."

"Exoneration!" echoed Fenton, starting to his feet, his face pale with excitement which easily passed for virtuous indignation. "Do you fancy I would stoop to exonerate myself from such a charge? Since when has the testimony of servants been received in a club of gentlemen?"

He had his cue, and he felt perfectly safe in letting himself go. He was frightened at the possible consequences of the coil in which he had become involved, since he foresaw easily enough that while his only course was to carry things through with a high hand, his words had already bitterly incensed the Secretary and might in the end set the committee also against him. He experienced a wild delight, however, in giving vent to his excitement in any form, and this simulation of burning indignation served to relieve his pent-up nervousness. He did believe the principle upon which with so much quickness he had hit as his best defence, and could with all his force sustain it. He looked about the room in silence a moment, but nobody was quick enough to pin him down to facts and insist upon his denying or allowing the charge brought against him. The indisputable correctness of his position that a servant's testimony could not be taken against a member in a club of gentlemen confounded them, and before any one thought of the right thing to say, Fenton continued, with growing indignation, —

"Why I personally should be chosen for insult by this committee I will not attempt to decide, although the source of the malice is to be guessed from the manner in which the evidence was brought to their notice. When the Secretary has a charge to bring against me that a gentleman would bring, I shall be ready to answer it. A charge like this it is an insult to expect me to notice."

He walked toward the door, as he finished, and turned to bow as he put his hand on the latch.

"Oh, come now, Fenton," Mr. Staggchase said confusedly, "don't go off that way. Of course" —

He hesitated, not knowing how to continue, and another member took up the word.

"All that is nonsense, of course. If the servant was mistaken, why can't you say so, and put yourself right with the committee?"

"Because," Fenton answered, throwing up his head, "I prefer retaining my self-respect even to putting myself right with this or any other committee. Good morning."

He went out quickly. He felt that this was a

good point for an exit, and he wished to get away lest he should be unable to keep up to the level of the scene as he had played it. So thoroughly was his whole attitude consciously theatrical, that he smiled to himself outside the door as the whimsisical reflection crossed his mind that he really deserved a call before the curtain. Then he remembered how awkward he should find it to be called back; and with a smile he ran down stairs to get his hat and coat, and hurried out of the house into the darkening spring afternoon.

When Fenton had gone, the members of the committee sat looking at each other in that condition of bewilderment which could easily turn to either indignation or contrition as the direction might be determined by the first impulse. Unfortunately for Fenton, it was his enemy the Secretary who spoke first.

"Heroics are all very well," he sneered, "but they don't change facts. He's evidently played poker enough to know how to bluff in good shape."

There was a rustle of impatience in the room. The men seemed to be reminded that a very high tone had been taken with them, and that they had all come in for a share of the rebuke which Fenton had administered. They were irritated by the mingling of a secret concurrence with the artist's position that a member of the club should not be impeached on the testimony of a servant, and the conviction that Fenton was really guilty of the charge brought against him, so that it was contrary to both justice and common sense to allow him to escape on a mere technicality.

"Fenton is so hot-headed," Mr. Staggchase began; and then he added: "I can't say that I blame him so very much, though. I don't fancy I should be very amiable myself if I were brought up on the word of one of the servants."

"But it was the duty of the servant to inform me," the Secretary returned doggedly, "and why shouldn't the committee take action on information which comes to it that way as well as any other. We didn't set the servant to spy on the members, and I can't for the life of me follow anything so fine spun as Fenton's theory. He only set it up, in my opinion, to get himself out of a bad box."

"He might at least have had the grace to deny it, if he could," another man said. "It leaves us in a devilish awkward fix as it is. We can't drop the matter, and if he shouldn't be guilty" —

"Oh, he's guilty, fast enough," the Secretary interrupted, his little green eyes shining under their fat lids. "He's one of the set that have been playing poker in the club until it's begun to be talked about outside, and I saw him go out with Snaffle that night myself."

There was some deliberation, some doubting, and some hesitation in regard to the proper course in such a case. The committee felt that their own dignity had suffered, that their authority should be asserted, and their majesty avenged. Mr. Staggchase was the most lenient in his views of the situation, and even he admitted that whether Fenton were innocent of the offence with which he was charged or not, he had at least treated the committee most cavalierly, and against the ground taken by most of the members, that if Fenton had been able to deny the charge he would have done so, he could only reply, —

"I don't think that at all follows. In the first place he wasn't asked. He is just the man to feel that a summons before this committee is in itself a pretty severe reprimand, as plenty of men would. He's high spirited and sensitive as the devil, and there was nothing in what he said to-day that wasn't compatible to my mind with his being perfectly innocent. Indeed, I don't believe he has cheek enough to carry it off so, if he were not sure of his position."

"Oh, as to cheek," retorted the Secretary, venomously, "Arthur Fenton has enough of that for anything. And, as for that matter, almost any man will fight when he is cornered."

In the end the Secretary prevailed, and the committee, albeit somewhat doubtingly, passed a vote of censure upon Fenton. The Secretary was directed to communicate this fact to the artist, and he took it upon himself also to include the information in the printed notices of the monthly meeting which were sent out a few days later, an innovation which stirred the club to its very depths and became town talk within twenty-four hours.

XXII

HIS PURE HEART'S TRUTH.

Two Gentlemen of Verona; iv. — 2.

HELEN GREYSON was at work in her studio modelling the hand of a statue. The pretty hand of Melissa Blake lay before her, so near that Milly's face came close to her own as she sat beside the modelling stand. It was one of those anomalies of which nature is fond the world over, and in which she displays nowhere more whimsical wilfulness than in New England, that Melissa, born of a race of plain country farmers, should have the hand of a princess. It was slender and beautiful, with exquisite taper fingers which had not as yet been spoiled by hard work, although were the present generation of New England maidens called upon to labor as vigorously as did their grandmothers the girl's hands would hardly have retained their comeliness so long.

Helen was working silently, absorbed in thought, and going on with her modelling mechanically. She was pondering the old question, whether she had done well in coming back to America, or whether she should have still kept the ocean between herself and Grant Herman. While she was in Europe, the longing to see him, to feel that he was near, to breathe the same air, had become ever more strenuous, until at last it could not be resisted. The sense of safety she had while so far away prevented her from appreciating that she was returning to the same danger from which she had fled. She told herself that time had so softened and changed her feelings, that Herman with wife and son was so different from the lonely man who had sought her love, and whom she had bravely renounced from a stern sense of duty, whether wise or not, that there could be no danger. She was a woman, and she had kept temptation at a distance until the nerve of resistance was worn out; then she had come home.

Now she asked herself what she had gained. She had renounced the passive acquiescence which she had won by years of hard struggle, and she had in exchange only a fierce unrest which was well-nigh unendurable. To be near Herman and yet to be as far removed from him as if the universe were between was a torture such as she had not dreamed of. All the old love awoke, and something of the old conviction which had made renunciation possible had failed her with time.

Nothing is more common than for the conscience half unconsciously to assume that a heroic self-sacrifice has been of so great efficacy that even the conditions which made it right are thereby altered. Without realizing it, Helen's mental attitude was that in giving up Herman's love and bringing about his marriage to Ninitta that his honor might be unstained, she had accomplished a self-denial so tremendous that even the need of making it was thereby destroyed. The idea was paradoxical, but that a proposition is paradoxical is no obstacle to its being held firmly by the feminine mind.

But by coming home Helen had also been put in a position where she could not avoid seeing something of Herman's married life, and it was at once impossible for her to help perceiving that it was a failure, or to evade the conclusion that if it were a failure she was to blame for the part she had taken in bringing it about. It is always dangerous to judge of actions by their results, since by so doing one refers them to the code of expediency rather than to that of ethics. Helen was not prepared to pronounce her old decision wrong; but the feeling that her renunciation had been vain forced itself more and more strongly upon her.

She was losing sight of her conviction that the need of doing what one felt to be right was in itself so imperative that no course of action could be wrong which was based upon this principle. The truth is that all mortals, and perhaps women especially, feel that a virtuous resolution, a noble self-denial, must bring with it a spiritual uplifting which will render it possible to hold to it. The hour of self-conquest is one of inner exaltation which is so vivid that it is impossible to realize that it can be otherwise than perpetual; a life of self-conquest is a continuous struggle against the double doubt which is the ghost of the short-lived exaltation that promised to be immortal.

From her reverie, Helen was aroused by a question of Melissa which almost seemed as if suggested by thought transference.

"Do you know," Melissa asked, "why the commission was not given to Mr. Herman?"

"The commission?" Helen repeated, so startled by the mention of the name which had been in her mind that for the moment she did not comprehend the question.

"Why, for the *America*," returned Melissa. "I thought you knew Mr. Herman, and Orin said that you had withdrawn."

Helen looked at her with a puzzled air.

"I did withdraw," she said, "but I did not know the matter had been decided. Who is Orin? Orin Stanton?"

"Yes, he is to make the statue."

"Did he tell you so?"

"Yes, he thinks I helped him by speaking to Mrs. Fenton; but she said Mr. Calvin already wanted Orin, so it made no difference."

"How long has it been decided?" asked Helen.

"He showed me the letter from Mr. Calvin day before yesterday. The committee hadn't met, but Mr. Irons had promised his vote, and he and Mr.

Calvin make a majority. Orin had been afraid Mr. Irons would vote for Mr. Herman, and I did not know but what you could tell. We are all so much interested in the statue."

Helen laid down her tools with an air of sudden determination.

"Why are you?" she asked, rather absently. "When Mrs. Fenton told me she had asked you to let me model your hands, she didn't mention your being interested in my art."

"Oh, I don't know anything about it," returned the other, with the utmost frankness, "only that Orin's a sculptor."

Helen smiled at the girl's *naîveté*.

"And am I to congratulate you on Orin's success?"

Melissa blushed.

"Of course I am pleased," she answered, "especially for John's sake."

"And John?" Helen pursued, finishing her preparations for leaving her work.

"John is Orin's half-brother," Milly replied, in a voice and with a manner which made it unnecessary for Mrs. Greyson to question farther.

"I shall not work any more this morning," she said. "I have to go out."

She dressed herself for the street, and, for the first time in six years, took the well-remembered way toward Herman's studio down among the warehouses and wharves. She was indignant at the action of the committee, of which she felt that Herman should be told. As, however, she neared the place, old associations and feelings made her heart beat quickly. When she put aside the great Oran rug and entered the studio, she felt a choking sensation in her throat, and the tears sprang to her eyes. She remembered so vividly the day when she had stood in this very spot and parted from her lover, that it almost seemed to her for the moment as if she had come to enact that scene again.

The place was more bare than of old. The pictures from the walls and many of the ornaments had been removed to the house which Herman had fitted up on his marriage with Ninitta; but in his usual place stood the sculptor, at work by his modelling stand, and over the rail of the gallery above, toward which her eyes instinctively turned as the old memories wakened, she saw the sculptured edge of a marble Grecian altar. The recollections were too poignant, and she started forward quickly, as if to escape an actual presence.

The studio was so large that Herman had fallen into the way of saving himself the trouble of answering the bell by putting up the sign "Come in" upon the door, and he was not aware of Helen's presence until he saw her standing with her hand upon the portière, as he had seen her six years before when she had renounced him, placing his honor before their love. With an exclamation that was almost a cry, he dropped his modelling tool and started forward to meet her.

"Helen!" he cried, and the intensity of his feelings made it impossible for him to say more.

Yet, however strong the emotions which were aroused by this meeting, — and for both of them the moment was one of keenest feeling, — they were schooled to self-control, and after that first exclamation the sculptor was outwardly calm as he went to greet his visitor. Even for those who are not guided by principle, self-restraint comes as the result of habit, and none of us in this age of the world assert the right of emotion to vent itself in utterance. The Philoctetes of Sophocles might shriek to high heaven, and Mars vent the anguish of his wounds in cries and sobs, but we have changed all that. Even the muse of tragedy is self-possessed in modern days; good breeding has conquered even the fierce impulse of passion to find outlet in words.

Both Herman and Helen were alive to the danger of the situation, and their meeting was one of perfect outward calm.

"Good morning," she said, "it seemed so natural to walk in, that I should almost have done it if your card hadn't been on the door."

She held out her hand as she spoke.

"I cannot shake hands," he said, "I am at work, you see."

She answered by a little conventional laugh

which might mean anything. Both of them hesitated a moment, their real feeling being too deep for it to be easy quickly to call to mind conventionalities of talk. Then the sculptor turned to lead the way up the studio, waving his hand as he did so toward the place where he had been working.

"You couldn't have come more opportunely," remarked he. "You are just in time to criticise my model for *America*. I was just looking it over for the last touches."

"It was that I came to talk about," Helen returned, moving forward toward the modelling stand on which was a figure in clay. "I have just learned that the commission has already been awarded ; and I thought you ought to know how the committee is acting."

"I do know," he answered. "Mr. Hubbard came and told me, although the committee meant to keep the decision quiet until after the models were in."

"But you are finishing yours."

"Yes, I declined to enter a competition and was hired to make a model. Of course I finish that, whatever the decision of the committee. Mr. Hubbard told me because he had before assured me of his support, and he wished to avoid even the suspicion of double dealing."

"The action of the committee is outrageous!" Helen protested, indignantly. "They might as well put up a tobacconist's sign as the thing Orin Stanton will make. It shows that you are right in refusing to enter a competition, since they have decided without even seeing the models they asked for."

"Yes," was Herman's reply. He paused a moment, and added, "Was that the reason you withdrew?"

Helen flushed slightly, and turned her face aside.

"It hardly seemed worth while," she began; but he interrupted her.

"I would not have gone in," he said, "even as I did, if I had known there was a chance of your competing."

She turned toward him, and her eyes unconsciously said what she had been careful not to put into words.

"Ah!" he exclaimed, with sudden comprehension. "You knew I was in it and that is why you withdrew."

"Well," she said, trying to laugh lightly, "it would not have been modest for me to compete against my master."

She moved away as she spoke. She had a tingling sense of his nearness, a passionate yearning to turn toward him and to break down all barriers which made her afraid. She felt that she had been rash in coming to the studio, and had overestimated her own strength. She glanced around quickly, as if in search of something which would help to bring the conversation to conventional levels; but her eye fell upon a terra-cotta figure which sent the blood surging into her head so fiercely that a rushing sound seemed to fill her ears. It was the nude figure of a soldier lying dead upon a trampled mound, with broken poppies about him, while across the pedestal ran the inscription, —

> "I strew these opiate flowers
> Round thy restless pillow."

It was the figure beside the clay mòdel of which, yet wet from his hand, the sculptor had told her, that day long ago, of her husband's death. In the years since, she had believed herself to have worn her love into friendship, to have beaten her passion into affection; but every woman, even the most clear-headed, deceives herself in matters of the heart, and now Helen knew what pitiful self-deception her belief had been.

Over and over and over again has it been noted how great a part in human life and action is played by trifles, and despite this constant reiteration the fact remains both true and unappreciated. And yet it is, after all, more exact to consider that the thing is simply our habit of noticing the obvious trifles rather than the underlying causes, as it is the straws on the surface of the current that catch our eye rather than the black flood which sweeps them along. It was the chance sight of the figure of the dead soldier which now broke down Helen's self-control, but the true explanation of her outburst lay in long pent up and well-nigh resistless emotions.

She turned toward her companion with a passionate gesture.

"It is no use," she broke forth, "I did wrong to come home. I should have kept the ocean between us. I must go back."

Herman grasped the edge of the modelling stand strongly.

"Helen," he said, in a voice of intensest feeling; "We may as well face the truth. We were wrong six years ago."

"Stop!" she interrupted piteously, putting up her hand. "You must not say it. Don't tell me that all this misery has been for nothing, and that we have sacrificed our lives to an error. And, besides," she went on, as he regarded her without speaking, "however it was then, surely now Ninitta has claims on you which cannot be gainsaid."

"Yes," he said bitterly, "and of whose making?"

She looked at him, pale as death, and with all the anguish of years of passionate sorrow in her eyes. He faltered before the reproach of her glance, but he would not yield. The disappointment of his married life, his sorrow in the years of separation, the selfish masculine instinct which makes all suffering seem injustice, asserted themselves now. The effect of the fact that he was forbidden to love this woman was to make him half consciously feel as if he had now the right to consider only himself. He almost seemed absolved from any claims for pity which she might once have had upon him. Even the noblest of men, except the two or three in the history of the race who have shown themselves to be possessed of a certain divine effeminacy, instinctively feel that a disappointment in passion is an absolution from moral obligation.

"See," he said, with a force that was almost brutal; "we loved each other and we have made that love simply a means of torture. My God! Helen, the besotted idiots that fling themselves under the wheels of Juggernaut are no more mad than we were."

She hurried to him and clasped both her hands upon his arm.

"Stop!" she begged, her voice broken with sobs, "for pity's sake, stop! It is all true. I have said it to myself a hundred times; but I will not believe it. Don't you see," she went on, the tears on her cheek, "that to say this is to give up everything, that if there is no truth and no right, there is nothing for which we can respect each other, and our love has no dignity, no quality we should be willing to name."

He looked at her with fierce, unrelenting eyes.

"Ah," he retorted cruelly, "my love is too strong for me to argue about it."

She loosed her hold upon his arm and stepped backward a little, regarding him despairingly. She did not mind the taunt, but the moral fibre of her nature always responded to opposition. She broke out excitedly into irrelevant inconsistency.

"It is right," she cried. "We were right six years ago, and you shall not break my ideal now. I must respect you, Grant. Out of the wreck of my life I will save that, that I can honor where I love."

She stopped to choke back the sobs which shook her voice, and to wipe away the tears which blinded her. The sculptor stood immovable; but his face was softened and full of yearning.

"And, oh," Helen said, the memory of sorrowful years surging upon her, "you would not try to shake my conviction if you realized how absolutely it has been my only support. It is so bitter to doubt whether the thing that wrings the heart is really right after all."

Herman made a sudden movement as if he would start forward, then he restrained himself.

"Forgive me," he said, in a strangely softened voice. "You have forgiven me for being cruel before. To have done a thing because you believe it is right is of more consequence than anything else can be. The truth is in the heart, not the thing."

She tried to smile. She felt as if she were acting again an old scene, the trick of taking refuge from too dangerous personal feeling in the expression of general truths carrying her back to the time when the expedient had served them both before.

"But people who have faith," she said, "who believe creeds and doctrines, can have little conception how much harder it is for us than for them to do what we think is the right."

He did not answer her, and a moment they stood in silence with downcast looks. Then she moved slowly down the great studio toward the door, and he followed by her side.

As she put her hand upon the Oran rug to lift it, she raised her eyes and met his glance. The blood rushed into their faces. They remembered their parting embrace and the burning kisses of long ago.

"Good-by," she said, and even before he could answer her she had gone out swiftly.

XXIII

AS FALSE AS STAIRS OF SAND.

Merchant of Venice; v. — 2.

THE fact that her mother was a Beauchester Mrs. Staggchase never forgot, although she seldom spoke of it. It formed what she would have called a background to her life, and gave her the liberty of doing many things which would have been unallowable to persons of less distinguished ancestry. It was, perhaps, in virtue of her Beauchester blood, for instance, that she made the somewhat singular selection of guests brought together at a luncheon which she gave in honor of Miss Frances Merrivale when that young lady came to pay her a visit, at the conclusion of her stay with Mrs. Amanda Welsh Sampson.

Miss Merrivale had been in doubt whether she could properly accept this invitation, in view of the fact that her cousin's wife had neglected to call upon her since her arrival in Boston. The reflection, however, that this visit to the Staggchase's was the chief object of her becoming Mrs. Sampson's guest at all had decided the young lady upon overlooking considerations of etiquette, and from the flat of the widow she had removed to the more aristocratic region of Back Bay.

Miss Frances had been shrewd enough to forestall all possible objections by accepting the invitation before mentioning it to Mrs. Sampson; and however deep the chagrin of that enterprising individual, she was too astute to protest against the inevitable. Mrs. Sampson even, in her secret heart, considered the advisability of calling upon her late guest in her new quarters, but reluctantly abandoned the idea as being likely, on the whole, to be productive of no good results socially. That Miss Merrivale would probably forget her as quickly as possible she was but too well assured, and it pretty exactly indicates the position of the widow toward society that this prospective ingratitude moved her to no indignation. It was so exactly the course which in similar circumstances she herself would have pursued, that no question of its propriety presented itself to her mind. Even the faint air of conscious guilt with which the girl announced her intention did not arouse in Mrs. Sampson any feeling of surprise or bitterness. Society to her mind was a ladder, and being so, to climb it was but to follow the use for which it was designed.

Miss Merrivale was of better stuff, and if not well bred enough to live up to the obligations she had assumed by becoming Mrs. Sampson's guest, she was at least conscious of them; and she said good-by with an air of apologetic cordiality, quieting her conscience by the secret determination some time to repay the widow's kindness in one way or another, although she should be obliged to repudiate her socially. Had she known Mrs. Staggchase better, and been aware how much she fell in that lady's estimation by throwing Mrs. Sampson overboard, her decision might have been different.

"She is coming, my dear," Mrs. Staggchase had said to her husband, on receiving Miss Merrivale's acceptance of her invitation. "I shouldn't have expected it of one of your family."

"You know we can't all be born Beauchesters," he had returned, with good-natured sarcasm.

Once at Mrs. Staggchase's, Miss Merrivale began to see Boston society under very different auspices. She had been at a luncheon at Ethel Mott's, given in compliment to herself, where she had sat nearly speechless for an hour and a half while half a dozen young ladies had discussed the origin of evil with great volubility, and what seemed to her, however it might have impressed metaphysicians, astounding erudition and profundity. She had assisted at that sacred rite of musical devotees, the Saturday night Symphony concert, where a handful of people gathered to hear the music, and all the rest of the world crowded for the sake of having been there. She had been taken by Miss Mott to a select sewing-circle — that peculiar institution by means of which exclusive Boston society keeps tally of the standing of all its young women. She was somewhat bewildered, but enjoyed what might be called a hallowed consciousness that she was doing exactly the right thing; and it was, perhaps, only a delicate consciousness of the fitness of things that made her answer all questions as to the time of her arrival in Boston with the date of her coming to Mrs. Staggchase, ignoring her previous visit to a woman of whose existence it was only proper to assume her new acquaintances to be entirely unaware.

Fred Rangely was shrewdly and humorously appreciative of her attitude, being the more keenly conscious of the exact situation because he himself made a point of ignoring his acquaintance with Mrs. Sampson. He had debated in his mind what change in his conduct was advisable now that Miss Merrivale was visiting Mrs. Staggchase. He had astutely decided that the latter, at least, would make no remarks about him to her guest; and, in view of the fact that it was scarcely possible to conceal his flirtation with the New Yorker from the penetration of her hostess, he decided to content himself with hiding from the stranger his devotion to his older friend. He still assured himself that his serious intentions were directed toward Miss Mott, and he secretly smiled to himself with the foolish over-confidence of a vain man, when, from time to time, he heard allusions to the devotion of Thayer Kent to Ethel. Kent had been in the field before Rangely presented himself as a rival candidate for the damsel's good graces; and the novelist might have been less confident had not personal interest blinded him to a state of things which he would have apprehended easily enough where another was concerned. The easy familiarity, born of long friendship and perfect understanding, which Ethel showed toward Kent, Fred mistook for indifference. His own sudden popularity had somewhat turned his head, so that he failed to distinguish between the attentions shown to the author and those bestowed upon the man, and constantly felt himself to be making personal conquests when he was simply being lionized.

Mrs. Staggchase invited the guests for her luncheon before she spoke of them to Miss Merrivale.

"I have asked Mrs. Bodewin Ranger," she explained, "although she is old enough to be your grandmother, because she is the nicest old lady in Boston, and it is a liberal education to meet her."

The other guests were Mrs. Frostwinch, Ethel Mott, and Elsie Dimmont.

"Elsie Dimmont," Mrs. Staggchase observed, "needs to be looked after. She is either going to make a fool of herself by marrying that odious

Dr. Wilson or she is allowing herself to be made a fool of by him, which is quite as bad."

Secretly Mrs. Staggchase, for all her Beauchester blood, had a good deal of sympathy for the girl who was defying her family in receiving the attentions of a man of no antecedents, although, having done the same thing herself, she was the more strongly bound outwardly to discountenance any such insubordination.

Guests may be selected on the principle of harmony of taste and feeling, or simply with an eye to variety; in the present instance it was distinctly the latter method which had obtained; and it was perhaps to be regarded as no mean triumph of social civilization that a harmony apparently so perfect resulted from the strange combination which the hostess had brought about. Whether from a secret intention of rebuking Miss Dimmont for her associations with one socially so impossible as Chauncy Wilson, or with the less amiable design of disciplining Miss Merrivale for her friendship with Mrs. Sampson, the hostess adroitly and deliberately turned the conversation to social themes, and thence on to what perhaps were best described as the proprieties of caste.

She was too clever a woman to do this crudely, and indeed would have seemed to any but the most acute observer to follow the conversation rather than to lead it. Ethel and Elsie chatted briskly of the current gossip of the day, and it was

Mrs. Bodewin Ranger who was skilfully led on to strike the keynote of the talk by saying, —

"Doesn't it seem to you that the modern fashion of admitting artists into society is mixing up things terribly? Nowadays one is always meeting queer people everywhere, and being told that they are writers or painters."

The fine old lady smiled so genially that one seeing her benign countenance framed in its beautiful snowy curls, must know her well to realize that in truth she meant exactly what she said. Mrs. Frostwinch's answering smile was not without a tinge of sarcasm, —

"It is worse than that," she said. "You even meet actors in quite respectable houses."

"Oh, actors!" threw in Ethel Mott, briskly; "nowadays they even go below the level of humanity and invite those things called elocutionists."

"But of course," ventured Miss Merrivale, wishing to put herself on record and striking a false note, as usually happens in such cases, "one doesn't really know these people. They are only brought in to amuse."

"One never knows undesirable people, my dear," Mrs. Staggchase responded, without the faintest shadow of the sarcastic intent which her guest yet secretly felt in her words.

"Bless me!" broke in Elsie Dimmont, with characteristic explosiveness. "What an abandoned creature I must be! I am actually going to the Fenton's to dine to-night."

"Mr. Fenton," Mrs. Bodewin Ranger responded, in her soft voice, "is a gentleman by birth, and his wife was a Caldwell; her mother was a Calvin, you know."

Ethel Mott laughed.

"And so he passes," she said, "in spite of his being an artist. How pleased he would be if he knew it."

"It would be worth while to tell him," Mrs. Frostwinch interpolated, "just to hear his comments."

"We owe Arthur Fenton more scores than we can ever settle," observed the hostess, "for the things he says about women. He said to me the other day that the society of lovely woman is always a delight except when a man was in earnest about something."

"I said to him, one night," added Elsie Dimmont, "that Kate West wasn't in her first youth. 'Oh, no!' he said, 'her third or fourth at least.'"

The others smiled, except Mrs. Ranger.

"Poor Kate!" she said; "all you girls seem to dislike her somehow. Mrs. West was a somebody from Washington," she added, reflectively, as if she unconsciously sought in the girl's pedigree some explanation of her unpopularity.

"Is it so dreadful to come from Washington?" asked Miss Merrivale; and then wondered if she ought to have said it.

"It is not the coming from Washington," was

Mrs. Frostwinch's reply, delivered in the same faintly satirical manner which she had maintained throughout the discussion; "it is the being merely a somebody instead of having a definite family name behind her."

"It is all very well for you to make fun of my old-fashioned notions, Anna," Mrs. Ranger returned, good-naturedly. "You think just as I do."

"I should be sorry not to think as you do about everything," was the answer. "And, to be perfectly honest, I can't help being a little ashamed that a cousin of mine has gone on to the stage. She was always dreadfully headstrong."

"Has she talent?" asked Mrs. Staggchase.

"Yes, she has talent; but is anything short of genius an excuse for taking to the boards?"

"I wish I could act," put in Miss Dimmont, emphatically. "I'd go on to the stage in a minute."

Mrs. Ranger looked shocked and grieved as well.

"My dear," she said, "you can't realize what you are saying. The stage has always been a hotbed of immorality from the very beginning of theatrical art, and nothing can reform it."

"Reform it," echoed Mrs. Staggchase, suavely; "we don't want to reform it. Nothing would so surely ruin the actor's art as the reformation of his morals."

"Oh, my dear!" remonstrated Mrs. Ranger.

"Really, Diana," Mrs. Frostwinch said, good-naturedly, "your sentiments are too shocking for belief."

"But she doesn't mean them," added Mrs. Ranger.

"I am sorry to shock anybody," the hostess responded, "but I really do mean what I say. Not that I can see," she added, "that society can afford to be too squeamish on the question of morals."

A look of genuine distress began to shadow Mrs. Ranger's face, and it deepened as Miss Merrivale said, flippantly, —

"Is Boston such an abandoned place?"

"Really, Diana," the old gentlewoman remarked, with a manner in which playfulness and earnestness were pretty equally mingled, "I don't think you ought to talk so before these girls. When I was your age, half a century ago, it wouldn't have been considered at all proper."

Mrs. Staggchase laughed softly.

"But, nowadays," she returned, "the girls are so sophisticated that what we say makes no difference."

There was a moment of silence while the servant changed the plates, and then Miss Dimmont broke out, saying, with unnecessary force, —

"I don't care who people are if they only amuse me, and I'll know anybody I like, whether they had any grandfathers or not."

"Since when?." Ethel whispered significantly into her ear.

Elsie crimsoned, but she gave no other sign that she had heard or understood the thrust.

"Then there is Fred Rangely," Mrs. Staggchase remarked, in a tone so even that it showed she meant mischief. "He comes here to see Frances, and you can't think, Mrs. Ranger, that it's my duty to be rude to him just because he writes for the newspapers."

"It is impossible to imagine Mrs. Staggchase being rude to anybody," quickly interpolated Ethel, with smiling malice; "and I supposed Mr. Rangely had won at least a brevet right to be considered in the swim from his long intimacy with social leaders."

The hostess was too old a hand not to be pleased with a clever stroke, even at her own expense, and she took refuge in an irrelevant generality which might mean anything or nothing.

"One learns so much in life," she said, "and of it appreciates so little."

And Frances Merrivale looked from Miss Mott to Mrs. Staggchase with an uncomfortable wonder what allusions to Fred Rangely lay behind this talk, which she could not understand.

XXIV

THERE BEGINS CONFUSION.

I Henry VI.; iv. — I.

FRED RANGELY began to find himself in the condition of being controlled by circumstances, instead of himself controlling them. Nor with all his astuteness could he decide how far he was being managed by Mrs. Staggchase, or led on by Miss Merrivale. He went about in a state of continual astonishment at the extent to which he had committed himself with the latter, and fell into that dangerous mental condition where one seems passively to regard his own actions rather than to direct them.

Rangely had been so long settled in the conviction that he was to marry Ethel Mott, even the not infrequent rebuffs of that lady producing in his mind only temporary misgiving, that his present doubts bewildered him. He was less of a coxcomb than might seem to follow from this statement, albeit there was no timidity and little burning passion in his feeling toward her. His was simply the cool masculine assurance of a man selfish enough to regard even love in a cold-blooded manner. He approved of his own choice socially, financially, and æsthetically; and since he loved himself rather more for having selected Ethel, he fell into the not unnatural error of supposing himself to be in love with her.

His entanglement with Miss Merrivale, on the other hand, was largely a matter of vanity. What had begun as an idle flirtation, designed to kill the leisure of summer days in the mountains, was continued from a half-conscious fear that he should appear at a disadvantage by breaking it off. It so keenly wounded Rangely's self-love to be thought ill of by a woman, that he was often forced to play at devotion which he not only did not feel but of which the simulation was almost wearisome to him. Nevertheless he was not, in this instance, without a shrewd appreciation of all the possibilities of the situation. He said to himself philosophically, that if worst came to worst and the fates had really decided to marry him to Miss Merrivale, she had money, good looks, and a fair position, and might on the whole prove more manageable as a wife than one so clever and so high spirited as Ethel.

Miss Merrivale, on her part, was foolishly and fondly in love with the broad-shouldered egotist. She had made up her mind from a variety of causes that she should, on the whole, prefer to marry in Boston, although in reality this meant simply that she wanted to marry Fred Rangely. She pored over his books in secret, talked to him of them with a want of comprehension only made tolerable by the fervor of her admiration, and took pains to show him that she regarded him as the literary hope of his generation of novelists. In vulgar parlance, she flung herself at his head ; and in such a case a girl's success may be said to depend almost wholly on opportunity and the extent of her lover's vanity.

Rangely had vanity enough and Mrs. Staggchase supplied the opportunity. If a feminine mind could ever properly be called spherical, that epithet should be applied to Mrs. Staggchase's inner consciousness. She was so sufficient unto herself, she so absolutely scored success or failure simply as a matter of her own sensations that her self-poise was perfect. She had even the quality, rare in a woman, of being almost indifferent whether others shared her opinions or not. She was content with the knowledge that she had succeeded in doing what she wished, while often the results and effects were so subtile and remote as to be imperceptible to others. Life was to her a toy with which she amused herself, and she found her chief enjoyment in trying experiments upon it of which the results were intangible to all but herself.

In the present case it amused Mrs. Staggchase and gave her some feminine satisfaction as well, to think that Rangely should marry Frances Merrivale. By promoting this marriage into which she was aware that he had no intention of being drawn, she avenged herself upon him for having presumed to show attentions to another while she honored him with her intimate friendship. It was not so much the nature of the punishment which pleased her as the fact that she was able to constrain him to her will. She found an ungenerous satisfaction in proving to herself that it lay within her power to do with him what she would ; and if this conclusion did not inevitably follow from the premises, her logic was at least satisfactory to herself, and that was sufficient to determine her course of action. She found some pleasure, too, in feeling that she was taking away a lover from Ethel Mott, for whom she had a dislike which in another woman would have been petty but which in Mrs. Staggchase was merely intellectual, since she was not a woman without understanding that one of her sex must feel the loss of even an admirer for whom she has no love. She did not share Rangely's mistake of supposing that Ethel would marry him, yet it was distinctly her intention that Miss Mott should not have the satisfaction of undeceiving him, but that Fred should carry through life the regretful and tantalizing conviction that he had thrown away this chance. It required only a little cleverness in bringing together the young man and Miss Merrivale, with a little skill in dropping now and then a word assuming his devotion to her guest, and Mrs.

Staggchase's plan was evidently in a fair way of accomplishment.

On the morning of the day of her luncheon, for instance, she had managed that Rangely should take Frances to some of the studios. The girl had little acquaintance with artistic life, but it attracted her by that romantic flavor which it is so apt to have for the uninitiated.

"I should think," she observed, as they walked along in the bright sunny morning, "that you would want to go to the studios all the time, if you know so many artists. I'm sure I should."

"Oh, it very soon gets to be an old story," was his answer. "One studio is very like another."

"But their work? That must be awfully interesting."

"Yes, to a novice, but that soon gets to be an old story too. An artist is only a man who puts paint or charcoal on cardboard or canvas with more or less cleverness, just as an author is a man who has more or less skill in getting ink on to paper."

Miss Merrivale laughed, with more glee than comprehension.

"You are always so witty," she said. "I don't wonder your books sell. I think that girl who couldn't tell which man she liked best was just too funny for anything. I can't for the life of me see how you think of such things, anyway."

"The trouble isn't to think what to say, but to tell what not to say."

"I'm sure I don't know what you mean. Now of course an artist just sees things, and all he has to do is to make pictures of them; but you have to make up things."

"But we see things too," the novelist responded, smiling upon her, and reflecting that she was looking uncommonly pretty that morning.

"Oh, but that's different. Now you never knew a girl who was hesitating which of two lovers to choose, and she wouldn't tell you how she felt if you did; but there it is all in your book so natural that every girl says to herself that's just the way she should feel."

The flattery was too evidently sincere not to be pleasing. So long as praise is genuine, few men are so exacting as to insist that it be also intelligent.

"Thank you," he said; "you at least understand the art of saying nice things. Though that," he added, with his warmest smile, "is perhaps only natural in one who must have had so many nice things said to her."

She laughed, her ready, girlish laugh, which always seemed to him so young; and they climbed the crooked stairs of Studio Building, their breath hardly being any longer sufficient for much speech.

"I'm going to take you to Arthur Fenton's first," Rangely observed, as they paused to rest on one of the landings. "These stairs are awful. I wonder how he gets his elderly sitters up here."

Miss Merrivale seated herself upon a bench benevolently placed on the landing.

"They sit down here, of course," she responded.

"This is a sort of life-saving station," he remarked, seating himself beside her.

"Oh, Mr. Rangely, how awfully funny you are."

"It's my trade; I have to be to earn my living. Now you and I are the only survivors from a wreck."

"Alone on a desert island?"

"Life-saving stations are not generally on desert islands; but I hope you wouldn't mind so very much if it were."

She looked at him with bright eyes, and then let her glance fall.

"That would depend," she responded demurely.

"Upon what? How I behaved?"

"Oh, of course you'd behave well."

"Of course; but how would I have to behave to make you contented on a desert island?"

She shot him a keen quick glance from beneath her bent brows.

"I never said I should be contented."

"But you implied it."

She whirled her muff over and over upon her two hands like the wheel of a squirrel cage, regarding it intently with her pretty head on one side.

"No, I didn't imply it either. I don't believe I could be contented."

"Not even with me?"

She flushed, but evidently not with displeasure.

"Why with you more than anybody else?" she softly inquired, with great apparent artlessness.

"Because," he began, "I should" — He was going to add, "be so fond of you," but reflected that this was perhaps going a little too fast and too far, and concluded instead — "take such good care of you."

Perhaps it was because approaching footsteps sounded on the stairs below them; perhaps it was because her subtile feminine sense appreciated the fact that he was on his guard; but for some reason or for no reason she tossed her head and rose to her feet.

"I am fortunately not obliged to go so far as a desert island to get taken care of," she said.

Her companion was not unwilling that the talk should be broken in upon. He smiled to himself as he followed her lead, and in a moment more he was knocking at the door of Fenton's studio, which was well up toward the roof. There was no response, and, as Fred rapped the second time, a carpenter who was at work on the casing of a door near by looked up, and said, —

"Mr. Fenton has a sitter, sir."

"He is in then?" said Rangely.

"Yes," answered John Stanton, straightening

himself up, with his plane in his hand, "but since Mrs. Herman went in half an hour ago, he hasn't opened the door to anybody."

"Mrs. Herman?" echoed Rangely, in astonishment.

"Yes, sir."

It was a capricious fate which brought John Stanton to tangle the web of Fenton's life. His brother Orin's relations with artists had given John a sort of acquaintanceship with them at second-hand, a kind of vicarious proprietorship in the privileges of art circles. He had long known Fenton by sight, while that he recognized Mrs. Herman also was the result of accident. He had been standing with Orin a few days before on a street corner, when the sculptor had lifted his hat to Mrs. Herman and named her in answer to John's question. There had not been in his honest mind the faintest tinge of suspicion when he saw her enter the studio, and he never had any intimation of the mischief he had done in mentioning her name to Rangely.

Fred and Miss Merrivale went on to Tom Bentley's curio-crowded rooms, while the sound of their knock still lingered in the double ears of the two people who sat confronting each other within the studio, with looks on the one hand sullen; on the other, pleading. Fenton's picture of *Fatima* was finished, yet Ninitta continued to come to the studio. His brief passion, which had been more than half mere intellectual curiosity how far his power over the Italian could go, had ended with that curiosity. In its place was a gradually increasing hatred for this woman, who seemed to assert a claim upon him, this model whom he never had loved, and whom he could now scarcely tolerate, since he had ceased to respect her. He cursed himself vehemently after the fashion of such offenders, when eager, vibrating passion has given place to a sense of irksome obligations, but more vigorously still did he upbraid fate, to whose score he set down all annoyance.

As for Ninitta, she, perhaps, no more truly loved Fenton than he had cared for her, but she clung to him as a frightened child might clutch the arm of one with whom it has wandered into the darkness of some vault beset with pitfalls. Ninitta's moral sense was of the most rudimentary character. She was, perhaps, incapable of appreciating an ethical principle, and her spiritual life never soared beyond the crudest emotions and the simplest questions of personal feeling. She had come to live without the guidance of a priest, and this fact, in itself, had left her without moral support. She had now no particular consciousness of having done wrong, although she was moved by the fear of the consequences of the discovery of her transgression.

It has been said that Ninitta's affection for her husband might have been more enduring had he been less gentle with her. She came of a race of peasants whose women understood masculine superiority in the old brutal, physical sense, and whenever Herman bore patiently with his wife's caprices he lessened a respect which he could have retained only at the expense of a blow. With all Arthur Fenton's soft and caressing ways toward Ninitta, there was always an instinctive masterfulness in his attitude toward any woman and especially since he had tired of her did he keep Mrs. Herman figuratively at his feet. The more strongly her appealing attitude seemed to press upon him claims which he could not satisfy and had no mind to acknowledge, the more harsh he became, and the more she bent before him. The language of brutality was one which she understood by inherited instinct.

"But why," Fenton was saying impatiently, when Rangely's knock startled them, "do you come here, when I haven't sent for you? There's somebody at the door, now, and we haven't even the shadow of an excuse, since the picture is done."

"I wanted to see you," Ninitta answered humbly, her plain face working with her effort to keep back the tears. "It is so lonely at home, and they take even Nino away from me."

The artist started up impatiently, and took his wet palette from the stand beside him.

"Well!" he said, answering as she had spoken,

in Italian, "you must be anxious that your husband shall know of your coming here, or you would not take such pains to have him find it out."

He began painting sullenly, putting in the last touches upon the background of the portrait of a beautiful girl. The lovely face of Damaris Wainwright, so pathetic, so pure, and so noble, looking at him from the canvas stung him inwardly into an impotent fury. His fine sense of the fitness of things was outraged by the presence of Ninitta beside the spiritual personality which shone upon him from the portrait. He could even feel the incongruity between himself and his work, though this appealed to his sense of humor as the other aroused his anger.

Ninitta watched in silence a moment; then she rose from her seat, her wrap falling away from her shoulders. Her tears were done, and a white look of intense feeling showed the despair that she felt. All the isolation which tortured her, that pain which souls like hers, blind, groping, and helpless, are least able to bear, had left its stamp upon her. Perhaps even her sin had been a desperate and only half-conscious attempt once more to draw in sympathy really near a human heart. She had learned little from the changed conditions into which the fates of her life had brought her, but she had been separated, in mind no less than in body, from her own kind without being fitted for other companionship. She was utterly and fatally alone, and a terrible sense of her remoteness from all human fellowship smote her now at Arthur's cruelty. She hesitated an instant, supporting herself by the arms of the big carved chair in which she had been sitting; then, with an impulsive gesture, she threw her arms above her head, wringing her hands together.

"Oh, my God!" she cried, "what shall I do?"

Fenton turned quickly toward her.

"Oh, *mon Dieu!*" was his inward comment; "what a divine pose! What a glorious figure! But ah, how tiresome she is!" Then, aloud, he said: "Come, come, don't be foolish, Ninitta! You know as well as I do that there is no danger, if you are only careful."

And putting aside his palette again, he soothed her with soft words until she was calm enough to be sent home.

When she was gone, he shrugged his shoulders, and spread out his hands with a deprecatory gesture.

"After all," he soliloquized aloud, "it is difficult for civilization to get on without the sultan's sack and bowstring."

XXV

AFTER SUCH A PAGAN CUT.

Henry VIII.; i. — 3.

THE announcement by the Secretary of the St. Filipe Club that a vote of censure had been passed upon Fenton had not only caused a tempest of excitement, but had brought about the unexpected result of eliciting testimony to prove that the charge against him was without foundation. Men came forward to testify that Snaffle entered the club alone on the evening when Fenton was said to have brought him there, while Tom Bently, Ainsworth, and others had seen the artist come in afterward, and had spoken with him before he went upstairs with Fred Rangely to the card-room. The Executive Committee found itself in a most awkward predicament, and its members took what comfort they could in pitching upon the Secretary, who had, without authorization, announced the vote of censure on the call for the monthly meeting. He was now directed to write to Mr. Fenton a letter of apology, which he did with such small grace as he could command, taking the precaution to mark the note "confidential."

The artist experienced more than a feeling of

conscious virtue at being thus exonerated from a fault which he had committed; and it was with mingled glee and a certain dare-devil desperation that he resolved upon his own course of action.

The monthly meeting of the St. Filipe came on the evening of the day when Mrs. Staggchase gave her luncheon. By a misunderstanding of Fenton's wishes, his wife had invited friends to dine that night. He meant to excuse himself after dinner and go to the club for a short time, returning to his guests after he had said a few words upon which he had determined.

The guests were Mr. and Mrs. Stewart Hubbard, Helen Greyson, Ethel Mott, Miss Catherine Penwick, Thayer Kent, the Rev. De Lancy Candish, and Fred Rangely. It was wholly by chance, and without malicious intent that Edith assigned Ethel to Mr. Kent, while Rangely took Mrs. Greyson in to dinner. Mrs. Fenton, of course, knew that gossip had sometimes connected the names of Ethel and Rangely in a speculative way, but she partly suspected and partly knew by feminine intuition that Fred was practically out of the running, and that Ethel's heart was given to Thayer Kent. It was hardly to be expected that Rangely should be pleased at the sight of his rival's advantage; but having passed the morning in squiring Miss Merrivale, his conscience was hardly case-hardened enough to have made him at his ease had he been able to exchange places with Kent.

To Mr. Candish was given the care of Miss Penwick, since with her Edith knew that his sensitive awkwardness would be as comfortable as was possible with any one; and the guests were so arranged that the clergyman sat upon his hostess's left hand, being thus in a manner intrenched between her and Miss Penwick against the raillery which Mrs. Fenton knew her husband would press as far as his position as host would allow. Edith always made it a point to do all that she could for Mr. Candish's comfort, and it was largely on his account that she had included Miss Penwick in the list of guests. She had a certain tenderness for the forlorn old lady, but it might not have found active expression had not the rector's pleasure come into the question. Arthur had laughed when the proposed arrangement was submitted to him.

"Does your care for your pastor's spiritual welfare go so far," he asked jocosely, "that you don't dare trust him with a young woman? Really, it looks as if you were jealous of the red-haired angel."

"Mr. Candish is not a young woman's man," had been Edith's answer; whereat her husband laughed again.

The talk at dinner was less animated than was usual at Fenton's table. The host was preoccupied, despite his efforts not to appear so, and the company was somehow not fully in touch. No conversation could be wholly dull, however, which

Arthur led; and while the "lady's finger" in his cheek told his wife and Helen that he was laboring under some intense excitement, he held himself pluckily in hand.

The conversation at first was between neighbors, but soon the host, according to his fashion, began to answer any remark that his quick ears caught, no matter from whose lips.

"You talk about marriage like a Pagan," he heard Helen say to Rangely.

"Oh, no," Fenton broke in, "he doesn't go half far enough for a Pagan. The Pagan position is that matrimony is a matter of temperament and convenience; it is essentially Philistine to consider that a marriage ceremony imposes eternal obligations."

"There, Mr. Fenton," Mrs. Hubbard rejoined, "I haven't heard you say anything so heathenish for half a dozen years. I hoped your wife had reformed you."

"Or that he had come to years of discretion," suggested Mr. Hubbard, with his charming smile.

"Oh, but I find years of indiscretion so much more interesting," Fenton retorted.

A moment later Helen said something about the truth, and Rangely retorted, —

"Truth is generally what one wishes to believe."

"Except in Puritanism," broke in Arthur, "there it was whatever one didn't wish to believe."

"Don't you think," questioned Mr. Hubbard, "that you are always a little hard on the Puritans? You must admire their conviction and their bravery."

"Oh, yes," was Fenton's reply; "there is something superb in the earnestness of the Puritans, and their absorption in one idea; but that idea has left its birthmark of gloom on all their descendants, and one cannot forget that Puritanism was the soil from which sprang the unbelief of to-day."

"Bless us!" cried Rangely, "is Saul also among the prophets? Are you also condemning unbelief?"

"Not at all," said Fenton, coolly, "I only want those who defend Puritanism to accept its legitimate results."

"It seems to me," protested Mr. Candish, who had become very red according to his unfortunate wont; "that if you argue in that way, you must always condemn good, because evil may come after it."

"Oh, I do," retorted Fenton, airily.

Everybody except the clergyman laughed at the unexpectedness of this reply; but Mr. Candish was wounded by the most faint suspicion of anything like trifling with sacred things.

"My husband is utterly abandoned, as you see, Mr. Candish," said Edith, coming to the rescue, as she always did when Arthur showed signs of baiting the rector. "Is the decision made in regard to the *America?*" she continued, turning to Mr. Hubbard, by way of changing the subject.

"Yes," he answered, "the commission is to be given to Orin Stanton."

"Orin Stanton?" asked Kent. "Who is he?"

"Oh, he," returned Fenton, "is a man that had the misfortune to be born with a wooden toothpick in his mouth instead of a silver spoon."

"Is he Irish?"

"No, but he ought to be to have won favor in the sight of a committee appointed by the Boston City Government."

"Come," said Helen; "that is rather severe when Mr. Hubbard is on the committee."

"Oh, I don't mind," returned Hubbard. "I know Fenton wouldn't lose a chance of having his fling at the Irish."

"Well," Fenton explained, defensively, "I am always irritated at the pity of the United States having expended so much blood and treasure to free itself from the dominion of the whole of Great Britain simply to sink into dependence upon so insignificant a part of that kingdom as Ireland."

"Mercy!" exclaimed Miss Penwick. "What extreme sentiments!"

They smiled at the old lady's words, and then Edith went back to the statue.

"I fancy young Stanton hasn't been above some wire-pulling," she remarked. "He sent his prospective sister-in-law, Melissa Blake, to ask me to use my influence with Uncle Peter in his behalf."

"He needn't have troubled," Mr. Hubbard returned. "Mr. Calvin supported him from the first."

"Oh, yes," Ethel said; "Mrs. Frostwinch and Mrs. Bodewin Ranger chose Stanton long ago and persuaded Mr. Calvin to help them."

"I can't fancy Mr. Calvin as anybody's tool," commented Kent, who would have regarded his companion's words as a trifle too frank to be spoken at the table of Mr. Calvin's niece, had his mind been in a condition to take exception to anything that she said.

"Isn't that Melissa Blake," asked Mr. Hubbard of Edith, "the one you recommended to me as a copyist?"

"Yes, I hope you found her satisfactory."

Mr. Hubbard smiled somewhat grimly.

"Indeed he did not," broke in Mrs. Hubbard speaking for him. "She broke confidence."

"Broke confidence!" echoed Edith, in astonishment. "Melissa Blake?"

"Yes," Hubbard returned. "I really didn't mean to tell you, but my wife, you see, has all the indignation of a woman against a woman."

"But how did she break confidence?" demanded Edith. "I would trust her as implicitly as I would myself."

"The papers she copied," was the reply, "were

the plans for a syndicate to put up mills at Fentonville. We kept the scheme quiet until the route of the new railroad should be decided, and when we came before the Committee of the House, the whole thing had been given away, and the Wachusett men had even secured the chairman, Tom Greenfield. He lives in Fentonville himself, and we had counted him at least as sure."

"That must have been the thing," placidly observed Miss Penwick to Rangely, "that Mr. Irons was talking to Mrs. Sampson about, the night we dined there to meet Miss Merrivale."

Rangely glanced up in vexation, to see if Miss Mott were listening, and caught a gleam of mischievous intelligence from her eyes.

"I don't remember it," he answered ambiguously.

"But how do you know," persisted Edith, "that the information came from Miss Blake?"

"Because Mr. Staggchase found out at Fentonville afterward that she came from there, and that a young man she is engaged to had just forfeited on a mortgage some of the meadows our company was to buy."

"The evidence doesn't seem to me conclusive," remarked Fenton, "and simply as a matter of family unity I am bound to believe in my wife's *protégés*."

Even the faint sense of humor which he felt at the situation could not prevent him from experiencing the sting of self-shame. Had it been an equal who was unjustly accused of a fault he had committed he would have felt less humiliated. To the degradation of having betrayed Hubbard, the addition of this last touch of having also unconsciously injured an inferior came to him like the exquisite irony of fate. He wondered in an abstract and dispassionate way whether the ghost of all his misdeeds were continually to rise before him. "Really," he said to himself with a smile that curled his lips "in that case I shall become a perfect Macbeth." And at that instant the ghost most dreadful of all rose at the feast like that of Banquo as Rangely said, —

"I knocked at your studio this morning but couldn't get in."

There flashed through Fenton's mind all the possibilities of discovery and disaster that might lie behind this remark, and his one strong feeling was that it would be unsafe to venture on a definite statement; he took refuge in the vaguest of general remarks.

"I am sorry not to have seen you," he said.

He tried to reflect, while Edith said something further in defence of Melissa. He joked with Ethel about the probable appearance of the statue young Stanton would make, which was to be set up directly opposite her father's house. He noticed that Helen was very silent, and he even reflected how handsome a man was Thayer Kent;

but through it all he seemed to hear the echo of that knock upon his studio door and a foreboding which he could not shake off made him reflect gloomily how utterly defenceless he should be in case of discovery.

A brief silence suddenly recalled him to his duties as host, and he caught quickly at the first topic which presented itself to his mind, going back to the question of the *America*, which had been much discussed because the funds to pay for it had been bequeathed to the city by a woman of prominent social position.

"I suppose," he observed, turning to Hubbard, "that with two such lights of the art world as Peter Calvin and Alfred Irons on the committee, the new statue will be regarded as the flower of Boston culture. Of all droll things," he added, "nothing could be funnier than coupling those two men. It is more striking than the lion and the lamb of Scriptural prophecy."

"Who is the lion and who the lamb?" asked Candish.

"It is your place to apply Scripture, not mine," retorted Fenton.

"I represent the minority of the committee," was Hubbard's reply to his host's question. "There is no other position so safe in matters of art as that of an objector."

"That is because art appeals to the most sensitive of human characteristics," Arthur retorted smiling, — "human vanity."

"Vanity?" echoed Mrs. Hubbard.

"That from you?" exclaimed Miss Mott.

"Really, Mr. Fenton," protested Miss Penwick, in accents of real concern, "you shouldn't say such a thing; there are so many people who would suppose you meant it."

The simple old creature knew no more of the real meaning of art than she did of that of the hieroglyphics on an Egyptian obelisk, but she had lectured on it, and she felt for it the deep reverence common to those who label their superstition with the name "culture."

"But I do mean it," returned Fenton, becoming more animated from the pleasure of defending an extravagant position. "What is the object of art but to perpetuate and idealize the emotions of the race; and how does it touch men, except by flattering their vanity with the assumption that they individually share the grand passions of mankind."

A chorus of protests arose; but Arthur went on, laughingly over-riding it.

"Really," he said, "we all care for the Apollo Belvidere and the Venus of Milo because it tickles our vanity to view the physical perfection of the race to which we belong; it is our own possibilities of anguish that we pity in the Laocöon and the Niobe; it is" —

"Oh, come, Fenton," interrupted Rangely; "we all know that you can be more deliciously wrongheaded than any other live man, but you can't expect us to sit quietly by while you abuse art."

"That is more absolute Philistinism," put in Hubbard, "than anything I have heard from Mr. Irons even."

"Oh; Philistinism," was Fenton's rejoinder, "is not nearly so bad as the inanities that are talked about it."

"That sounds like a personal thrust at Mr. Hubbard," Kent observed; and as Arthur disclaimed any intention of making it so, Mrs. Fenton gave the signal for rising.

XXVI

O, WICKED WIT AND GIFT.

Hamlet; i. — 5.

IT was fortunate for Fenton's plans that most of his guests had early engagements that evening, and by nine o'clock he was able to leave the house with Rangely to take his way to the meeting of the Club. As they came out of the house, Thayer Kent was just saying good-by to Miss Mott after putting her into her carriage. Fenton's fear lest he should be too late for the business meeting had made him follow rather closely in the steps of his departing guests, and he and Rangely were just in time to hear Ethel say, —

"But I am going that way and I will drop you at the club."

Kent hesitated an instant, and then followed her into the carriage. Fenton laughed as they drove away.

"With Ethel Mott," he said, "that is equivalent to announcing an engagement."

"Nonsense!" protested Fred, incredulously.

Fenton laughed again, a little maliciously.

"Oh, I've been looking for it all winter," he

said. "Ever since you devoted yourself to Mrs. Staggchase, and gave Thayer his innings. Well, since you didn't want her, I don't know that she could have done better."

Fenton pretty well understood the truth of the matter in regard to Rangely's relations to Ethel, and this little thrust was simply an instalment toward the paying of sundry old scores. He had never forgiven Fred for having taunted him, long ago, with going over to Philistinism; especially, as he inwardly assured himself, that the difference between their cases was that he had had the frankness openly to renounce Paganism, while his companion would not acknowledge his apostasy even to himself. In Fenton's creed, self-deception was put down as the greatest of crimes, and he had fallen into the way of half unconsciously regarding his inner frankness as a sort of expiation for whatever faults he might commit.

He chuckled inwardly at the discomfort which he knew his remark brought to Fred, humorously acknowledging himself to be a brute for thus taking advantage of circumstances with a man who had just eaten his salt. The excitement of the thing he was about to do had mounted into his head like wine, and he hastened toward the club with a feeling of buoyancy and exhilaration such as he had not known for months. He laughed and joked, ignoring Rangely's unresponsiveness; and when he entered the club parlors his cheeks were flushed and his eyes shone as in the old Pagan days.

He was just in season. The monthly business meeting was about being completed, and Fenton had scarcely time to recover his breath before the President said, —

"If there is no other business to come before this meeting we will now adjourn."

Then Fenton stepped forward.

"Mr. President," he said, in his smooth, clear voice, only a trifle heightened in pitch by excitement.

The President put up his eyeglasses and recognized him.

"Mr. Fenton."

There was an instant hush in the room. Every member of the club knew of the vote of censure, which had excited much talk, and of which the propriety had been violently discussed. A few were aware that the censure had been withdrawn, and all were sufficiently well acquainted with Fenton's high-spirited temperament to feel that something exciting was coming.

Fenton was too keenly alive to what he would have called the stage effect to fail of appreciating to the utmost the striking situation. He threw up his head with a delicious sense of excitement, the pleasing consciousness of a vain man who is producing a strong and satisfactory impression, and who feels in himself the ability to carry through the thing he has undertaken. With a sort of tingling double consciousness he felt at once the enthusiasm of injured virtue at last triumphant, and the mocking scorn of a Mephistopheles who bejuggles dupes too dull to withstand him. He looked around the meeting, and in a swift instant noted who of friends or foes were present ; and even tried to calculate in that brief instant what would be the effect upon one and another of what he was going to say.

"Mr. President," he began, deliberately, "if I may be pardoned a word of personal explanation, I wish to say that the motion I am about to make is not presented from personal motives. I might make this motion as one who has the right, having suffered ; but I do make it as one who believes in justice so strongly that I should still speak had my own case been that of my worst enemy. I move you, sir, that the St. Filipe Club pass a vote of unqualified censure upon its Executive Committee for admitting in the investigation of an alleged violation of its rules the testimony of a servant, thereby assuming that the word of a gentleman could not be taken in answer to any question the committee had a right to ask."

He had grown pale with excitement as he went on, and his voice gained in force until the last words were clear and ringing to the farthest corners of the room.

A universal stir succeeded the silence with

which he had been heard. Half a dozen men were on their feet at once amid a babble of comment, protestation, and approval. The Secretary managed to get the floor.

"Mr. President," he said, his round face flushed with anger, and his fat hands so shaking with excitement that the papers on the table before him rustled audibly, "since it must be evident that the gentleman's remarks are instigated by anger at the committee's treatment of himself, it is only justice to the committee to state what many of the members may not know, that a letter of ample apology has been sent by them to Mr. Fenton."

The men who had been eager to speak paused at this, and everybody looked at the artist.

"Mr. President," he said, with a delightful sense of having himself perfectly in hand, and of being in an unassailable position, "I have been insulted by the committee under cover of a charge which they now acknowledge to be false; and, contrary to the usage of the club, a printed notice of this has been sent to every member. I have received a note of apology from the Secretary."

He paused just long enough to let those who were taking sides against him emphasize their satisfaction at this acknowledgment by half-suppressed exclamations; then, in a voice of cutting smoothness, he continued, —

"At the head of that note was the word 'confidential,' which forbade me, as a gentleman, to show it. This was evidently the committee's idea of reparation for the outrage of that printed circular."

He paused again, and the impression that he was making was evident from the fact that nobody attempted to deprive him of the floor; then he went on again, —

"I have already said that my motion was not a personal matter; if my case serves as an illustration, so much the better, as long as the principle is enforced."

"The motion," interposed the President, gathering his wits together, "has not been seconded, and is therefore not debatable."

"I second it," roared Tom Bently in his big voice, adding *sotto voce:* "We won't let the fun be spoiled for a little thing like that."

The half laugh that followed this sally seemed to recall men from the state of astonishment into which they had been thrown by the audacity of Fenton's attack. There were plenty of men to speak now; — men who thought Fenton's position absurd; — men who believed in upholding the dignity of the Executive Committee; — men, more revolutionary, who were always pleased to see the existing order of things attacked; — men who wanted explanations, and men who offered them; — men who rose to points of order, and men who proposed amendments; with the inevitable men who are always in a state of oratorical effervescence, and who speak upon every occasion, quite without reference to having anything to say.

Fenton was keenly alive to everything that was said, and in his excitement fell into the mood not uncommon with people of his temperament of regarding the whole debate from an almost impersonal standpoint. His sense of humor was constantly appealed to, and he laughed softly to himself with a feeling of amusement scarcely tinged by concern for the result of the contest when Mr. Ranger, stately and ponderous, got upon his feet. He could have told with reasonable precision the inconsequent remarks which were to come; and the interruption which they made appealed to his sense of the ludicrous as strongly as it irritated many impatient members.

"I am confident," began Mr. Ranger with dignified deliberation, "that all the excitement which seems to be manifest in many of the remarks that have been made is wholly uncalled for. I am sure no member of this club can suppose for an instant that its Executive Committee can have intentionally been guilty of any discourtesy, and far less of any wrong to a member. And we all have too much confidence in their ability to suppose that they could fall into error in so important a thing as a matter of discipline. And I need not add," he went on, not even the real respect in which he was held being able wholly to suppress the movement of impatience with which he was heard, "that we all must hold Mr. Fenton not only as blameless but as painfully aggrieved."

"Mr. Facing-both-ways," said Fenton to himself as the speaker paused, apparently to consider what could be added to his lucid exposition of the situation.

One or two men had the hardihood to rise, but the President had too much respect for Mr. Ranger's hoary locks to deprive him of the floor.

"It seems to me," the speaker continued, placidly, "that this is a matter which is better adjusted in private. The discipline of the club must be maintained, and individual feeling should be respected; but where we all have the welfare of the club at heart, it seems to me that members would find no difficulty in amicably adjusting their differences with the club officials in private conference."

He gazed earnestly at the opposite wall a moment, as if seeking for further inspiration. Then as no handwriting appeared thereon, he resumed his seat with the same deliberate dignity that had marked his rising.

Mr. Staggchase, alert and business-like as usual, next obtained the floor.

"As chairman of the Executive Committee," he said, "perhaps I am too much in the position of a prisoner at the bar for it to be in good taste for me to speak on this motion. Naturally I do know something, however, about the circumstances of this case, and I am willing to say frankly that I cannot blame Mr. Fenton for feeling aggrieved at the painful position in which he has been placed entirely without fault on his part. It is only just to the committee, however, to state that the charge as presented to them in the first place was supported by evidence which appeared to them convincing; that Mr. Fenton never denied it; and that I and, I presume, every member of the committee supposed until this evening that the letter of apology sent him had been ample and satisfactory. That it was marked 'confidential' was certainly not the fault of the committee, who now learn this fact for the first time."

This statement evidently produced a strong impression. Fenton felt that it told against him, yet he was more irritated at what he considered the stupidity of the members in not seeing that Mr. Staggchase had not touched upon the point at issue at all, than he was by the injury done to his cause. In the midst of the excitement raging about him he sat, outwardly perfectly calm and collected. He refused to admit to himself that after all there was little probability of his motion's being carried; although in truth at the outset he had intended nothing more than to take this striking method of stating his grievance against the committee. He was amused and delighted at the commotion he had caused. He likened himself to the man who had sown the dragon's teeth, and while listening keenly to what was being said, he rummaged about in his memory for the name of that doughty classic hero.

It was with a shock that it came upon him all at once that the tide was turning against him. There had been warm expressions of sympathy with himself and of disapprobation at the course of the committee; and Grant Herman had announced his intention of offering another motion, when this should have been disposed of, to the effect that a printed notice of the removal of the vote of censure be sent to each member of the club; but it was evident that there was a general feeling that Fenton's attitude was too extreme. The club was evidently willing to exonerate him and to offer such reparation as lay in its power, but it was not prepared formally to rebuke its committee. The debate had continued nearly an hour, and speakers were beginning to say the same things over and over. At the farther end of the room some men began to call "question." The word brought Fenton to his feet like the lash of a whip; he put his hands upon his chest as if he were panting for breath, his eyes were fairly blazing with excitement, and when he spoke his voice shook with the intensity of his emotion.

"Mr. President," he began, "it seems to me that the honor of this club is in question. It had not occurred to me to regard this so much a personal affront as an insult to the club which has elected me to its membership. It is forced upon me by the remarks that have been made to look at the personal side of the matter. Gentlemen have been insisting that I am seeking reparation for an insult which they acknowledge has been offered me; which they acknowledge has been gratuitous, and to which all the publicity has been given which lay within the power of the officers of this club. Very well, then, far as it was from my original intention, I present my personal grievance and I claim redress. The vote of censure which the committee has passed upon me I regard as merely a stupid and offensive blunder; the implication conveyed by listening to a servant in relation to a charge against a member is an insult to him as a gentleman, which, to me personally, seems too intolerable to be endured. I came into this club as to a body of gentlemen, and I have a right to claim at your hands that I shall be treated as such by its officers."

Fenton had many enemies in the St. Filipe, but the splendid dash and audacity of his manner, even more than his words, produced a tremendous effect. There was an instant's hush as he ended, and then the voice of Tom Bently, big and vibrating, rang through the room in defiance of all rules of order and of all the proprieties as well.

"By God! He is right!" said Tom, and a burst of applause answered him.

The day was won, and although there were a few protests, they were silenced by cries of "Question! Question!" and the motion was carried by a majority which, if not overwhelming, was large enough to be without question.

"The motion is carried," announced the president.

Fenton rose to his feet again.

"Gentlemen," he said, "I cannot resist the temptation personally to thank you. Mr. President, I have now the honor to tender you my resignation from the St. Filipe Club."

He bowed and turned to walk from the room. He was full of a wild exultation over his success, and he reasoned quickly with himself that even if his resignation were accepted, he retired in good order. He had, too, a half-defined feeling that in thus tempting fate still further, he made a sort of expiatory offering for his actual guilt. He said to himself, with that lightning-like quickness which thought possesses in a crisis, that since the principle for which he contended stood above the question of his individual transgression, it was but just that the motion should have been carried, and that now he was ready to take his punishment by losing his membership in the St. Filipe.

But before he had gone half a dozen steps, two or three men had called out impulsively, —

"Mr. President! I move this resignation be not accepted."

There were plenty of men there who would gladly have seen Fenton leave the club; the members of the Executive Committee were smarting under the rebuke he had brought upon them; but the excitement of the moment, the admiration which courage and dash always excite, carried all before them. The motion was voted with noise enough to make it at least seem hearty, and with no outspoken negatives to prevent its appearing unanimous. His friends dragged him back and insisted upon drinking with him, the formalities of adjournment being swallowed up in the uproar. His triumph could not have been more complete, and its celebration, with much discussion, much congratulation and not a little wine, lasted until midnight.

And all the while, as he talked and jested and argued and laughed and drank, his brain was playing with the question of right and wrong as a child with a shuttlecock. Without a hearty conviction of the absolute justice of the principle for which he contended, it is doubtful if Fenton could have acted the lie of assumed innocence. He had entangled the question of his guilt with that of the propriety of the action of the committee so inextricably that one could scarcely be taken up without the other. He admired himself as an actor, he approved of himself as a logician, and he despised himself — without any heart-burning bitterness — as a liar. He was too clear-headed to be able to bejuggle himself with the reasoning that he had not been guilty of falsehood because he had never specifically and in word denied the charge of the committee. Yet with all his pride in his self-comprehension, he really deceived himself. He supposed himself to have been animated by the desire to establish a principle in which he really believed, to conquer and humiliate the Secretary, and to please himself by acting an amusing *rôle*; while in truth he had been instigated by his dominant selfish instinct of self-preservation. But he thoroughly enjoyed his triumph, and by the time he left the house he seemed to have established himself on quite a new footing of friendship with even the members of the Executive Committee.

As he went down the steps of the club, starting for home, Chauncy Wilson said to him, with his usual rough jocularity, —

"I'll bet you a quarter, Fenton, you did bring Snaffle in that night, after all. By the way, did you know that Princeton Platinum had gone all to flinders?"

XXVII

UPON A CHURCH BENCH.

Much Ado about Nothing; iii. — 3.

WHEN Fenton went to the club that night he left Helen Greyson and Mr. Candish, both of whom were sufficiently familiar to excuse the informality. The combination of the clergyman and the sculptor might seem likely to be incongruous, but the two had much more in common than at first sight appeared. Fenton had been right in declaring that Helen was by instinct a Puritan. It was true that she had shaken herself free from all the fetters of old creeds and that her religious beliefs were of the most liberal. The essence of Puritanism, however, was not its dogmas, but its strenuous earnestness, its exaltation of self-denial, and its distrust of the guidance of the senses.

The original Puritans made their religion satisfy their æsthetic sense, even while they were insisting upon the virtue of starving that part of their nature. To believe literally and with a realizing sense of its meaning the creed of Calvin, would have been impossible without madness to any nature short of the incarnate inhumanity of a Jonathan Edwards. The æsthetic sense of humanity demands that the imagination shall be nourished ; and the imagination is fed by receiving things as only ideally true. The Puritans were right in declaring that art was hostile to religion as they conceived it ; but they failed to perceive that this hostility arose from the fact that the acceptance of their theology was only possible in virtue of the very faculties to which art appealed. They were obliged to deprive the imagination of its natural food, in order that it should be forced to feed upon that the assimilation of which they conceived to be a moral obligation. It may, at first sight, seem a bold assertion that our Puritan ancestors believed their creed, however unconsciously, simply in the sense in which we believe in the bravery of the heroes of Homer or in the loves and sorrows of the heroines of Shakespeare. It is to be reflected, however, that those unhappy creatures who attempted to receive Calvinism literally and absolutely paid for their mistake with madness ; and that it did not enter into the minds of generations of Puritans, who lived and died in the error that they believed with their understanding what they really received only with the imagination, to take this view, in no way affects its truth.

Helen's position differed from that of her Puritan grandmothers from the fact of her having turned her imagination back to art; but she shared with them the temperament which made Puritanism possible. The æsthetic sense, which is as universal in mankind as the passions, clung in her case to sensuous beauty, while that of Mr. Candish clung to what he considered beauty moral and spiritual; but the controlling force in the life of both was the stinging inspiration of a fixed idea of duty. They were thus able, although rather as a matter of unconscious sympathy than of deliberate understanding, to comprehend each other; and if Helen had the broader sight, Mr. Candish possessed the greater power of ignoring self.

Edith stood on a middle ground between the two. At the time of her marriage she had been much nearer to the position occupied by the clergyman; and she would have been startled and shocked had she realized how much her views had been modified during the six years of her life with Fenton. She had certainly been led into no toleration of moral laxity, and indeed the effect of her husband's cynical Paganism had been to make her dread more acutely any infringement upon moral laws. She had been constantly learning, however, the enjoyment and appreciation of beauty, not merely in a conventional and Philistine sense, but as a pure Pagan æstheticism. The change showed itself chiefly in her increased tolerance of views less rigid than her own, which made possible the perfecting of the intimacy with Helen, which had begun simply from her sense of pity for the sadness of the other's life.

"Isn't it charming," Edith said to-night, as the three sat before the fire after Arthur had gone out, "to see Mr. and Mrs. Hubbard together. It's not only that they are so fond of each other, but they are so perfectly in accord. It seems to me an ideal marriage."

Helen looked at her with an inward sigh.

"It is much the fashion, nowadays," she said, "to insist that the ideal marriage is no marriage at all."

Mr. Candish looked at her inquiringly.

"Or, in other words," she explained, with a passing thought of his want of quickness of apprehension, "that no marriage can be ideal."

"Or anything else, for that matter," put in Edith quickly. "The iconoclasts of this generation will spare absolutely nothing."

"These objectors don't take into account," observed Mr. Candish, "that if we once begin to give up things because their possibilities are not realized, we shall soon end by having nothing left. Plenty of people do not live up to the possibilities of marriage, but the fact is that the trouble is with themselves. The blame that they lay on the institution really belongs on their own shoulders."

"Yes," agreed Edith; "like everything else it comes back to a question of egotism."

"And egotism," added Helen, smiling, yet wistfully, "is the supreme evil."

Mr. Candish nodded approvingly.

"I don't know," he said, "that a bachelor like myself has any right to discuss marriage, except on general principles; but certainly, even without taking the religious view of it, one can see that the very objections brought against wedlock are reasons in its favor."

"Yes," Edith returned, but she moved uneasily in her chair, and Helen divined that the subject was painful to her.

"The difficulty is," she said, with an air of dismissing the whole subject, "that most people marry for the honeymoon and very few for the whole life."

She fell to thinking in an absorbed mood which was not wholly free from irritation, how constantly this question of marriage met one at every turn, as if the whole fabric of life, social and ethical, depended entirely upon this institution. She sighed a little impatiently, looking into the fire with mournful eyes. She thought of the marriages with which her destiny had been most intimately connected, her own ill-starred mating, the union of Herman and Ninitta, that of Fenton and Edith. She had long ago settled in her own mind that wedlock was not only the mainstay of society, but that it was largely a concession to the weakness of her sex; and yet instinctively she protested;

that revolt against being a woman which few of her sex have failed at one time or another to experience taking the form of a revolt against matrimony.

"Indeed," she broke out, half humorously and half pathetically, "the most joyful promise for the Christians hereafter is that they shall neither marry nor be given in marriage."

Mr. Candish looked a little shocked; but Edith said softly, —

"That is only possible when they become as the Sons of God."

Helen spread out her hands in a deprecatory gesture.

"Come, Edith," she said, "that isn't fair, to take the discussion into regions where I can't follow you."

Edith smiled, but made no rejoinder in words. Turning to Mr. Candish she remarked, with an abrupt change of subject, —

"When may I tell Melissa Blake about the Knitting School?"

"I see no reason," he answered, "why she shouldn't know at once. We shall be ready to begin operations in a month at most, and ought to know her decision."

"Isn't it capital?" Edith explained, turning toward Helen. "The Knitting School is really to be started. Mrs. Bodewin Ranger guarantees the funds for a year, and we have contracts for work to be delivered in the fall that will keep from a dozen to twenty girls busy all summer; while the matron's salary will put Melissa Blake on her feet very nicely. It's such a relief to have some of those girls provided for."

"That's the Melissa Blake, isn't it," Helen asked, "that Mr. Hubbard spoke of at dinner?"

"Yes," answered Edith, "but it is impossible that he should be right."

Helen replied only by that look of general sympathy which does duty as an answer when one has no possible interest in the subject under discussion, but Mr. Candish, who knew Melissa, shook his head with an air of conviction.

"No," he observed, "Miss Blake has too much principle to be guilty of a breach of confidence. I am sure Mr. Hubbard must be mistaken."

"And yet," commented Helen, "there is such a general feeling that if one keeps the letter of his word he may do as he pleases about the spirit, that she may have contrived to give her lover a hint without actually breaking her promise as she would understand it."

"I don't know," Edith returned earnestly, "that we have any right to judge other people more harshly than we should ourselves. If one of our friends had betrayed Mr. Hubbard's plans we should say he was a rascal because we should assume that he knew what he was doing; and we wouldn't believe such a charge unless we knew he was really bad."

"But," persisted Helen, with an unconscious irony which Fenton would have keenly appreciated had he but been there to hear, "in our class of course it's different. A nice sense of honor is after all very much a social matter nowadays. That may sound a bit snobbish, but don't you think it is true?"

"It is and it isn't," was Mr. Candish's reply. "It would undoubtedly be true if religious principle did not come into the matter; but religious principle is stronger in what we call the middle classes than among their social superiors."

Mrs. Greyson was not sufficiently interested to continue the discussion, and she let the matter drop, while Edith contented herself with reiterating her conviction in Melissa's perfect trustworthiness.

They chatted upon indifferent subjects for a little while, and then Mr. Candish went to keep an appointment at the bedside of a sick parishioner; so that Helen and Edith were left alone.

They sat together a little longer, and then Helen asked casually, —

"By the way, Edith, how long has Arthur been painting Ninitta?"

"Painting Ninitta?" echoed Edith.

She remembered the wrap she had seen in the studio, with the wavering evasion of her husband's eyes when her glance had sought his in question, and painful forebodings against which she had striven, lest they should become suspicions, were awakened by Helen's words.

"Yes," the other went on. "Fred Rangely told me at dinner to-night that he couldn't get into the studio this morning because Arthur was painting Mrs. Herman."

"What did you say to him?" asked Edith.

"I said," her companion returned, looking up in surprise at her tone, "that I fancied the picture must be intended as a surprise for Mr. Herman and he'd better not speak of it."

"But," Edith objected, "if Arthur told him she was there" —

"He didn't," interrupted Helen; "a man outside the door said he had seen her go in."

Edith grew pale as ashes. She evidently made a strong effort at self-control; and then, burying her face in her hands, she burst into violent weeping. Helen bent forward and put her arms about her. She drew the quivering form close, resting Edith's beautiful head upon her bosom. She did not speak, but with soft, caressing touch she smoothed the other's hair. She remembered vividly the time, six years before, when Edith, who had left her at night in indignation and disapproval, had come to her on the morning after her husband's death. She could almost have said to this weeping woman, the words with which she remembered the other had then greeted her, —

"You must feel so lonely."

She dared not speak now. She feared to ask the cause of this outburst, both lest Edith might be led to say what she would afterward wish unspoken, and because she dreaded to hear unpleasant truths in regard to Arthur.

"Oh, Helen," Edith sobbed. "Life is too hard! Life is too hard!"

Still Helen did not answer, save by the caress of her fingers. The tears were in her own eyes. One woman instinctively appreciates the tragedy of another's life, and her unspoken sympathy was balm to Edith's soul.

"Come," she said, patting Edith's shoulder as one might soothe a weeping child, "you're all tired out. I can't take the responsibility of letting you have hysterics; Arthur would never leave you alone with me again."

She spoke with as much lightness of tone as she could command, while her embrace and her caresses conveyed the sympathy she would not put into words.

Presently Mrs. Fenton disengaged herself from her companion's arms and sat up, wiping away her tears.

"I must be tired," she said, "or I shouldn't be so foolish."

"You do too much," Helen returned. Then, with the design of giving her friend a chance to retreat from their dangerous nearness to confidences, she added,—

"Now tell me what you've done to-day."

"I have done a good deal," the other replied, smiling faintly and showing the recovery of her self-possession by sundry little touches to the crushed roses in her gown. "At nine o'clock I went to the Saturday Morning Club, to hear Mr. Jefferson's paper on 'The Over-Soul in Buddhism'; then, at eleven, I went to Mrs. Gore's to see an example of the way they teach deaf and dumb children to read lip language; then Arthur and I went to luncheon at Christopher Plant's, and at half past three was the meeting of the committee on the Knitting School; then there was the reception at Uncle Peter's, and the tea at Mrs. West's, before I came home to dress for dinner."

Helen leaned back in her chair and laughed musically. She felt, with mingled relief and a faint sense of disappointment, that her effort to avoid a confidence had been successful.

"I should think," she said, "that you Boston women would be worn to shreds, and I don't wonder that you have a leaning toward hysterics. Did you carry a clear idea of the Buddhistic over-soul through all the things that came after it in the day?"

She rose as she spoke, with the desire to hasten away. She had little mind to know more than she must of the causes of Edith's unhappiness. She was glad to help her friend, but she felt that she could do so no better from knowing anything Edith could tell her; and she was, moreover, sure that Mrs. Fenton's loyal soul would bitterly regret it if she were by the emotion of the minute betrayed into revelations that involved her husband.

"No," Edith answered, rising in her turn; "I am not even sure whether the Buddhists believe themselves to have an over-soul. But why must you go? Wait, and let Arthur walk home with you."

"Oh, I shall take a car," Helen said. "I don't in the least mind going alone; and it's time both of us were in bed. Good-night, dear; do try and get rested."

XXVIII

BEDECKING ORNAMENTS OF PRAISE.

Love's Labor's Lost; ii. — I.

EDITH FENTON did not, however, follow Helen's advice and go to bed. She went to her room and exchanged her dinner gown for a wrapper, and then sat down before the wood fire in her chamber to wait for Arthur's return.

It is a dismal vigil when a wife watches for her husband and questions herself of the love between them. It was Edith's conviction that it is a wife's duty to love her husband till death; not alone to fulfil her wifely obligations, to preserve an outward semblance of affection, but to love him in her heart according to the vows she has taken at the altar. Had one told her that the limit of human power lay at self-deception, and that, while it was possible to cheat one's self into the belief of loving, affection could not be constrained, she would with perfect honesty have replied as she had answered Helen in her allusion to St. Theresa. She said to herself to-night, with unshaken conviction and the concentration of all her will, that she would not cease to love Arthur;

but she could not wholly ignore the difference between the unquestioning affection she had once given him and this love whose force lay in her will.

A picture of Caldwell, painted a year ago just before his long hair had been sacrificed at his boyish entreaties, hung over her mantel. She looked up at it while her lip quivered and her eyes filled with tears. The keenly sensitive soul instead of becoming hardened to suffering feels it more and more sharply. The powers of endurance become worn out, and to the pain is added a sense of injustice. Since it suffered yesterday the heart claims the right to be happy to-day, and feels wronged that this is denied it. With all her endurance, and with all her faith, Edith could scarcely repress the feeling of passionate protest which rose in her bosom. She said to herself that she had done all, and been all, that lay in her power; that there was no sacrifice in life she was not ready to make to preserve her husband's love; and the most cruel pang of all she felt in thinking of her boy. For herself, it seemed to her, she could have borne anything; but that the atmosphere of the home in which her son was reared should fall short in anything of the utmost ideal possibilities caused her intolerable anguish. It seemed to her a cruel wrong to Caldwell that the love and confidence between his parents should not be perfect. It is probable that more of her personal pain was covered by this pity for her son than she was aware ; but as she looked up at his picture she felt almost as if he were half-orphaned by this estrangement between herself and Arthur, which it were vain for her to attempt to ignore.

It was after midnight when she heard the street door open and close ; and a moment later came her husband's tap.

"I saw the light in your room, as I came down street," he said. "What on earth kept you up so late?"

"I was waiting," Edith replied, "to talk with you."

He came across the chamber, and regarded her a moment curiously; then he turned away with a slight shrug of the shoulders.

"You will perhaps excuse me," he said, "if I make myself comfortable. I am pretty tired."

He went to his dressing-room, coming back a moment later in smoking jacket and slippers, cutting a cigar as he walked. The reaction from the excitement of the evening already showed itself in the darkened circles beneath his eyes, and the pallor of his lips.

"Do you mind my smoking?" he asked, carelessly. "We've been having the deuce of a time at the club, and my nerves have all gone to pieces. I tell you, Edith," he went on, a sudden spark of excitement showing in his eyes, "I've had a tremendous row, but I've beaten. I made them pass a vote of censure on the Executive Committee, and then Herman got them to instruct the Secretary to send out a printed notice taking back that vote of theirs ; and then I offered my resignation, and they voted unanimously not to accept it."

"I am so glad!" Edith responded warmly. "That censure was so outrageous. Tell me all about it."

She was so pleased to find herself talking cordially and intimately with her husband that she forgot for the moment what she had meant to say to him. She listened with eager interest while he gave her a picturesque version of the exciting scene at the club. Edith hardly realized how little of the old familiarity there was now between herself and Arthur. It was his nature to be communicative. He enjoyed talking, partly from his pleasure in words and the delight he found in effective and picturesque phrasing, and partly because it pleased his vanity to excite attention and to produce striking effects. He had an inveterate habit of telling his most intimate and inner experiences in some sort of fantastic disguise. The very vain man is apt to be either extremely reticent or very communicative. The only secrets which Fenton kept well were those which his vanity guarded. As desire for admiration and attention provoked him to continual revelations, so the fear that the disclosure of a secret would react to his disadvantage could cause him to be silent.

From the feeling that his wife disapproved of much that he told her had grown up in Fenton's mind, at first, an irritated desire to shock and startle her as much as possible. As there came into his life, however, things which he knew she would view not only with disapproval but with abhorrence, and especially since his entanglement with Ninitta, he had grown constantly more guarded in his speech. Edith felt keenly the loss of the old familiar talks, though, womanlike, she invented a thousand excuses to prevent herself from believing in the growing estrangement of her husband. To-night she yielded herself to the pleasure of the moment, and she had almost forgotten both the sad thoughts of her vigil and the fear that troubled her, as she listened to Arthur's animated words. It was not until he rose as if to say good-night, that her mind came back suddenly to the matter of which she wished to speak.

It was in a very different mood, however, from that in which she would have spoken half an hour before, that she now brought up the thing that had been troubling her. She hesitated a little how to question her husband without seeming to jar upon the friendly tone in which they had been talking. He was watching her keenly, wondering why she had waited for his coming, and speculating whether it were possible that she might altogether have forgotten what she meant to say. He thought she was about to speak, and anticipated her by saying, —

"Really, Edith, it would be hard to find, even in Boston, a more incongruous company than we gathered together at dinner to-night."

"There was a good deal of variety," she returned; adding defensively, "but then they fitted together pretty well."

"What a funny old party Miss Penwick is," Arthur went on, inwardly gathering himself up for a rapid retreat. "Almost as soon as she had said, 'how do you do' she asked me what I thought the object of life was."

"How very like her; what did you tell her?"

"Oh, I said I supposed the object of life is to transform the crude animal and vegetable substances of our food into passions and petty sentiments."

Edith laughed absently, her thoughts elsewhere.

"And she looked dreadfully puzzled," Fenton continued, "as to whether she ought to be shocked or not. But bless me, how late it is! Good-night, my dear."

He stretched up his arms in a yawn. Edith turned quickly toward him.

"Arthur," she said abruptly, but with the kindness of her softened mood, "are you painting Ninitta?"

He gave her a startled glance and sat down

again in his chair. There ran through his mind a sudden pang of fear, but he said to himself instantly that Edith was not one to suspect evil, and she could not possibly know the truth.

"Painting Ninitta?" he returned. "Why do you ask that?"

"Because Fred Rangely told Helen at dinner to-night that you were."

"Where did he get his information?" asked Fenton, with a feeling of tightness in his throat as he remembered how Rangely had knocked at his door that morning.

"He said," was Edith's answer, "that a carpenter told him Mrs. Herman was in the studio to-day; and I remembered seeing her wrap there last week."

Fenton felt the insecurity of a man about whom all things totter in the shock of an earthquake, but he refused to yield to fear. He wondered how much was to be inferred from the fact that an unknown mechanic was aware of Mrs. Herman's visits. He had an overwhelming sense of being trapped, and he inwardly gnashed his teeth with rage against Ninitta and against fate.

But he felt the supreme importance of self-control, and he was outwardly collected as he asked, —

"What did Helen say to him?"

"She said," answered Edith, with an exquisite note of sadness in her voice, "that you must be making a portrait for a surprise to her husband."

The artist's heart gave a bound and he caught eagerly at this suggestion, which afforded him a means of escape.

"Helen is too shrewd by half," he said, with a smile. "It is for Grant's birthday and nobody was to know. As a matter of fact," he added, his invention quickly leaping to the refinements of details in his falsehood, "I fancy Ninitta really wants it for the *bambino*, as she calls him."

He smiled with relief as he went on, and rose again to his feet.

"Deception," he observed, with his natural lightness of manner, "is the bane of married life, but marital felicity is impossible without discreet reserves. It wasn't my secret, you see, so I didn't feel at liberty to tell you."

"You were perfectly right," she answered. "The truth is," she continued, hesitatingly, "I was afraid you had persuaded Ninitta to sit for the *Fatima*, you know you said once that she was the only model in Boston who was what you wanted."

"Did I say that? What a dreadful memory you have. I should expect Grant to make a burnt sacrifice of me if I had beguiled her into such an indiscretion. He won't even have her sit to himself since she was married."

"Of course not," rejoined Edith, emphatically. "Poor Grant! He can't be very happy with

Ninitta. She never can get the taint of Bohemia out of her blood."

.Arthur laughed and flung his cigar end into the fire.

"You speak," he said, "as if that were a hopeless poison."

He stood smiling to himself an instant. He had pushed off one slipper and was endeavoring to pick it up, using his foot like a hand. He was in that state of high excitement when he would have found relief in the wildest and most boisterous actions; and it pleased him to be able still to retain the appearance of his ordinary calm.

"Modern civilization," he observed, "consists largely in learning to live without the use of either truth or the toes. Good-night, my dear. I want to get a nap before the church bells begin to ring."

He stooped and kissed her, and went to his chamber. He closed the door and began to recite with exaggerated gestures a fragment from *Macbeth.* The varied emotions of the evening had set every nerve quivering. He was so excited that he was not even despondent over the collapse of Princeton Platinum stock, although this meant to him desperate financial straits. He knew that he was in no condition to consider anything calmly; but half the remainder of the night he tossed upon a sleepless bed, reacting the scene at the club, reflecting upon his narrow escape from the discovery of his relations with Ninitta, resolving to begin her portrait at once, and thinking a thousand confused things which made his brain seem to him filled with whirling masses of fiery thought-clouds.

It was really only just before the church bells began to ring that he fell asleep at last, to dreams hardly less vivid than his waking reflections.

XXIX

CRUEL PROOF OF THIS MAN'S STRENGTH.

As You Like It; i. — 2.

ORIN STANTON had been tolerably sure of getting the commission for the *America*, and had been busily at work preparing his model for the figure. By the time the decision of the committee was reached, his study was practically complete, and only a day or two after he had been officially notified that the choice had fallen upon him the public were invited to his studio to view the statue.

Whatever else Orin might or might not be, he was undeniably energetic. He missed no opportunities through neglect, and he never left undone anything which was likely to tell for his own advantage. He had once before called upon the world to admire his work on the completion of his masterpiece, a figure called *Hop Scotch*, representing according to Bently "a tenement-house girl having a fit on the sidewalk." He therefore understood well enough the usual methods of managing these affairs, and as the ladies who had taken him up felt bound to make a point of patronizing the exhibition, the affair succeeded capitally.

Stanton had no regular studio in Boston, and had for this work secured a room on the ground floor of a business building. The light, to be sure, was not all that might have been desired, but it was abundant, window screens were cheap and the sculptor not over sensitive to subtile gradations of values. He made no attempt to decorate the room for his exhibition, partly from a certain indifference to its bareness, and partly from a native shrewdness which enabled him to feel both the difficulty of doing this adequately, and the fact that the statue appeared better as things were. There were a few benches, scantily cushioned, two or three chairs, not all in perfect repair, with the paraphernalia essential to his work. A few sketches in crayon and pencil were pinned to the wall, and among them the artist had had the fatuity to pin up a photograph of that most beautiful figure, the *Winged Victory* of Paionios.

The study for *America*, which was of colossal size, represented a woman seated, leaning her left hand upon a rock. The right hand held slightly uplifted a bunch of maize and tobacco plant ; her head wore a crown in which the architectural embattlements not uncommon in classic headdresses had been curiously and wonderfully transformed into the likeness of the domed capitol at Washington. The figure was completely draped, only the head, the left hand and the right arm to the elbow emerging from the voluminous folds in which it was wrapped, save that the tip of one sandalled foot was visible, resting upon a ballot box. Half covered by the hem of the robe were seen a tomahawk, an axe, a printer's stick, a calumet, and various other emblems of American life, civilized and barbarous.

A secret which Stanton did not impart to the public and which, with a boldness allied to impudence, he trusted to their never discovering, was the fact that his figure had been stolen bodily from an antique. There exists in the museum of the Vatican a statuette representing a work by Eutychides of Sikyon. Bas-reliefs of the same figure exist also on certain coins of Antioch still extant. The figure represented the city goddess *Tyche* resting her foot upon the shoulder of the river god *Orontes*, who seems to swim from beneath the rock upon which she is seated. Stanton had a sketch of the statuette which he had made in Rome, and from this he had modelled his *America*, replacing the god *Orontes* by a ballot-box, changing the accessories and adding as many symbolical articles as he could crowd around the feet. He was not wholly untroubled by an inward dread lest the source of his inspiration should be discovered; but when he had been complimented by Peter Calvin upon the marked originality of the design, he threw his fear to the winds and delivered himself up to the enjoyment of receiving the praises of his visitors.

There was a strange mixture of people present. Stanton had invited the artists, members of the press, and all the people that he knew, whether they knew him or not. Mrs. Frostwinch was there, Mrs. Staggchase, Elsie Dimmont, and Ethel Mott; and although Mrs. Bodewin Ranger was not actually present, she in a manner lent her countenance by sending her carriage to the door to call for one of her friends. Fred Rangely was present, talking in a satirical undertone to Miss Merrivale and viewing the statue with a wicked look in his eye which boded little good to the sculptor. Melissa Blake was there, rather overpowered by the crowd and clinging tightly to the arm of her companion, a girl whose acquaintance she had made in her boarding-house, and who was much given to an affectation of profound culture as represented by attendance upon stereopticon lectures and the exhibitions of the local art clubs.

"Oh, I should think," this young lady said to Melissa, in a simpering rapture, "you'd be just too proud for anything, to know Mr. Stanton. It must be too lovely to know a real sculptor."

"I don't know him so very well," returned the conscientious Melissa.

"But you really know him," persisted the other, "and he's been to call on you. Isn't it funny how some men can make things just out of their heads without anything to go by?"

Rangely, who was standing close by, caught the

remark and secretly made a grimace for the benefit of Miss Merrivale.

"That," said he in her ear, "is genuine Boston culture."

She laughed softly, not in the least knowing what to say. The statue meant nothing whatever to her, and had the original of Eutychides been placed by its side she would have been unable to understand that in copying it Stanton had transformed its dignity into clumsiness, its grace into vulgarity. Had she been at home in New York, she would have said frankly that she neither knew nor cared anything about the *America;* being in Boston, she had a superstitious feeling that such frankness would be ill-judged, and she therefore contented herself with non-committal laughter.

"How do you do, Miss Merrivale?" at this moment said a cheery voice close by her.

She looked up to see the merry eyes and corn-colored beard of Chauncy Wilson.

"I say, Fred," went on the doctor, confidentially, "don't you think this thing is beastly rubbish? It looks like an old grandmother wrapped up in her bedclothes. And what has she got that toy village on her head for?"

"Oh, Doctor Wilson!" exclaimed Miss Merrivale, in a manner that might mean reproval or amusement.

Miss Frances was having a very good time. Although Mrs. Staggchase had been throwing her guest and Rangely together for motives of her own, the result to Miss Merrivale had been as pleasing as if her hostess had been purely disinterested. It is true, the time for her return to New York drew near, but visions of the pleasure of imparting to her family and friends the news of her engagement to the brilliant young novelist did much to alleviate her regret at departing from Boston. She had a pleasant consciousness that afternoon, of sharing in the attention which Rangely received in public nowadays, especially since his novel had been violently attacked in the *London Spectator* and defended in the *Saturday Review.* She noted the glances that were cast at him, receiving their homage with a certain secret feeling of having a share in it.

But bliss in this world is always transient, and at her happiest moment Miss Merrivale looked up to perceive Mrs. Amanda Welsh Sampson bearing down upon her. Mrs. Sampson was accompanied by the Hon. Tom Greenfield, who both felt and looked utterly out of place; and who was dragged along in the wake of his companion quite as much by his unwillingness to be left to his own devices in a crowd of strangers, as by any particular desire to follow her.

"My dear Frances," the widow said effusively, kissing Miss Merrivale on both cheeks. "I am *so* glad to see you. Really it is perfectly cruel that you haven't been to see me. But then, I know," she ran on without giving the other time to speak, "how busy you've been. I've seen your name in the *Gossip*, and you've been everywhere."

"Yes, I have," returned Miss Merrivale, catching rather awkwardly at the excuse supplied to her.

Chauncy Wilson laughed significantly. He never felt it necessary to treat the widow with any especial respect.

"Mrs. Sampson passes the whole of Sunday forenoon committing the society columns of the *Gossip* to memory, and wishing her name was there," he chuckled, with a jocoseness which seemed to that lady extremely ill-timed.

But she kept her temper beautifully, long years of social struggle having taught her at least this art of self-restraint.

"Dr. Wilson is nothing if not satirical," she returned, with a conventional smile.

It would not have been displeasing to Miss Merrivale had the floor at that particular instant opened and engulfed her former hostess. It needs unusual breadth of mind to forgive those toward whom we have been discourteous. On the other side of the statue, Frances saw Mrs. Staggchase watching the encounter with a sort of quiet amusement. It flashed across her mind that if she were to become Mrs. Rangely, and live in Boston, it would be necessary to drop Mrs. Sampson from her calling list, and the reflection instantly followed that the sooner the process of breaking the acquaintance were begun the better. Her face insensibly. hardened a little.

"Of course," she said, "one can't help being put into the *Gossip*, but I should never think of reading it."

Mrs. Sampson understood that this was a snub, and her cheek flushed. Wilson laughed maliciously.

"Oh, everybody reads the *Gossip*," Rangely interposed, good-naturedly coming to the rescue; "although it's to the credit of humanity that everybody has the grace to be ashamed of it."

There was a bustle and stir in the crowd as Tom Bently pushed his way up to the group.

"By Jove, Rangely," he said, "have you got on to that statue? Do you know what it's cribbed from?"

"No," returned Fred; "is it from anything in particular? I supposed it was just a general steal from the antique, and Stanton appropriates only to destroy."

"I don't know what it is," was Bently's reply, "but I know there's a cut of it in a book I've got at the studio."

Rangely's eyes flashed.

"Good," said he, "I'll come round to-night and we'll look it up. I'm going to do a notice of the *America* for the *Observer*."

The two exchanged significant glances, laughing

inwardly at the discomfiture of the unfortunate sculptor.

"But don't you admire the figure?" asked Mrs. Sampson, eagerly seizing an opportunity to get into the conversation.

"It's the kind of thing I should have liked when I was young," Bently returned. "I was taught to like that sort of thing; but all the preliminary rubbish that was plastered on to me when I was a youngster, I have shed as a snake sheds its skin."

The movement in the crowd gave Miss Merrivale an excuse for changing her position; and she improved the opportunity to turn away from the widow until the latter could see little except her back. Mrs. Sampson flushed angrily, but she covered her discomfiture, as well as she was able, by turning her attention to the statue, and descanting upon its beauties to Greenfield.

"How exquisitely dignified the drapery is," she remarked, "and so beautifully modest."

"Big thing, ain't it," said the strident voice of Irons, close to her ear. "I think we've hit something good this time. I'm really obliged to you, Greenfield, for putting me up to vote for Stanton. I like a statue with some meaning to it. Now just look at the significance of all those emblems of American progress."

"Yes, it is very fine," admitted Greenfield, with a helpless air. "I'll work it into a speech, sometime," he added, his face brightening with the relief of having an idea; "there's the ballot-box at the bottom as a foundation, and you work up through all the industries till you get to the capitol, the centre of government, at the top."

"Hear! hear!" exclaimed the widow, clapping her hands very softly and prettily; "really you must speak at the unveiling of the statue."

"Capital idea," exclaimed Irons, to whose gratitude for Greenfield's aid in the railroad matter was added the politic forecast that he might some time need his help again; "there's Hubbard over there now; I'll go and ask him whether our committee chooses the orator."

He started to make his way through the crowd, followed by the admiring looks of various young women who had been frankly listening to the conversation, although they were strangers.

"Oh, isn't the statue just too lovely for anything," gushingly remarked one of them, with startling originality; "it's so noble and —. And, oh," she broke off suddenly, the light of a new discovery shining in her face, "just see, girls, that's corn in her hand."

"Oh, yes, and cotton," responded her companion. "See, it really is cotton, and something else."

"Yes, that must be maize," returned the other, oracularly; "it's all so beautifully American."

The crowd moved and swayed and changed, until Ethel Mott stood close to the *America*, with her back turned squarely upon the figure. She evidently found more pleasure in looking at her companion than in studying the work of the sculptor, which she had nominally come to see.

"I think it will be too cold, Thayer, to go out in the dog-cart," she said, with one of those glances whose meaning not even a poet could put into words.

"Oh, no," Kent answered. "I have a tremendously heavy rug, and you can wrap up."

"Well," was her answer, "if it's pleasant, and the sun shines, and I don't change my mind, and I feel like it, perhaps I'll go. At any rate you may come round about ten o'clock."

Rangely was too far away to catch, amid the babble of the crowd, a single word of this conversation, but he noted the looks which the pair exchanged.

"Oh, do come along," a corpulent lady in the crowd observed to her companion. "We've seen everybody here that we know, and I want to go down to Winter Street and get some buttons for my grey dress. Miranda wanted me to have them covered with the cloth, but I think steel ones would be prettier."

"Yes, they say steel's going to be awfully fashionable this spring. Are they going to put that statue up just as it is?"

"Oh, they bake it or paint it or something," was the lucid answer, as the corpulent lady threw herself against Mr. Hubbard, nearly annihilating him in her effort to clear a path through the crowd.

"I think, my dear," Hubbard observed to his wife, "unless you've designs on my life insurance, you'd better take me out of this crowd."

"But we haven't seen the statue," she returned.

"I have," he retorted grimly, "and I assure you you haven't lost anything. You'll see it enough when it's set up, and you'll go about perjuring your soul by denying that I was ever on the committee."

"Hush," she said, "do be quiet; people will think you're cross because you were overruled."

On the other side of the statue the sculptor had been receiving congratulations all the afternoon, and now Mr. Calvin and Mrs. Frostwinch chanced to approach him at the same time to take their leave.

"I am so glad to have seen the statue," was the latter's form of adieu, "it is distinctly inspiring. Thank you so much."

He bowed awkwardly enough, stammering some unintelligible reply, and the lady moved away with Mr. Calvin, who observed as the pair emerged into the open air:

"It is such a relief to me that this statue has turned out so well. There has really been a good deal of feeling and wire-pulling, and some New

York friends of mine will never forgive me that the commission was not given to one of their men. I really feel as if the thing had been made almost a personal matter."

"It must be a great satisfaction to you," his companion returned, "that he has succeeded."

"It is," was Calvin's reply. "I meant to see Mr. Rangley and ask him to say a good word in the *Observer*, but everybody is so much pleased that I think he may be trusted to be."

"Oh, he must be," she answered.

And as she spoke Tom Bently passed by, quietly smiling to himself.

XXX

THE WORLD IS STILL DECEIVED.

Merchant of Venice ; iii. — 2.

ON the evening following his reception, Orin Stanton presented himself at the rooms of Melissa. He was fairly beaming with self-complacency and gratification. He had been awarded the commission, the exhibition of his model had been attended, as he assured Melissa, "by no end of swells," and five thousand dollars had been paid over to him as an advance upon which to begin his work. He felt as if the world were under his feet and he spoke to Melissa with an air of lofty condescension which should have amused her, but which she received with the utmost humility.

"Well," he said, "what do you think of that for a crowd ? Wasn't that a swell mob ? Didn't you notice what a lot of bang-up people there were at the studio this afternoon ?"

"Of course I didn't know many of them," Melissa returned humbly ; "but I could see that there were a lot of people that everybody seemed to know. I'm glad that you were pleased."

Orin pulled out a big cigar and bit the end off it excitedly.

"Pleased!" he echoed. "I was more than pleased — I was delighted. All the committee were there, of course, and half the fashionable women of Boston."

"I heard a lady telling another who the artists were," Milly observed, glad to find a subject upon which she could talk to Orin easily.

"O yes, there were a lot of artists there, but they don't count for much in getting a fellow commissions."

Stanton had evidently no intention of being satirical, but spoke with straightforward plainness what he would have regarded, had he given the matter any thought at all, as being a truth too obvious to need any disguises. His Philistinism was of the perfectly ingrained, inborn sort, which never having appreciated that it is naked has never felt the need of being ashamed; and he let it be seen on any occasion with a frankness which arose from the fact that it had never occurred to him that there was any reason why he should conceal it. He was one of those artists who never would be able wholly to separate his idea of the muse from that of a serving-maid; and he viewed art from the strictly utilitarian standpoint which considers it a means toward the payment of butcher and baker and candlestick maker. He was not indifferent to the opinion of his fellow sculptors; but the criticism of Alfred Irons, which he knew to be backed by a substantial bank account, would have outweighed in his mind the judgment of Michael Angelo or Phidias.

Milly, of course, had no ideas about art beyond a faint sentimental tendency to regard it as a mysterious and glorious thing which one could not wholly escape in Boston; while her thrifty New England nurture enabled her to appreciate perfectly the force of the considerations Orin brought forward.

"I am glad you are getting commissions," she said, "but it must be nice to have the artists like your work, for after all, don't you think rich people depend a good deal upon what the artists say?"

"Oh yes, they do, some," admitted the sculptor.

He puffed his cigar, and with the aid of a penknife performed upon his nails certain operations of the toilet which are more usually attended to in private. Milly sat nervously trying to think of something to say, and wondering what had brought the sculptor to visit her. She was too kindly to suspect that possibly he had come because in her company he could enjoy the pleasure of giving free rein to his self-conceit. The words of her companion of the afternoon had given her a new sense of the honor of a visit from her prospective brother-in-law, although this increased her diffidence rather than her pleasure.

"Was Mr. Fenton there this afternoon?" she asked, at length, simply for the sake of saying something.

The face of her companion darkened.

"Damn Fenton!" he returned, with coarse brutality. "He's a cad and a snob; he says Herman ought to have made the *America*, and he abuses my model without ever having seen it."

The remark of Fenton's which had given offence to Stanton had been made at the club in comment upon a photograph of the model which somebody was showing.

"The only capitol thing about it," Fenton had said, "is the headgear."

The remark was severe rather than witty, and it was its severity which had given it wings to bear it to the sculptor's ears.

"I don't like Mr. Fenton very well," Milly admitted, "but Mrs. Fenton is perfectly lovely; she's been awfully good to me."

By way of reply the sculptor, with a somewhat ponderous air, unbuttoned his coat and produced a red leather pocket-book. This he opened, took out a handful of bills, and procceded to count them with great deliberation. Melissa watched while he counted out a sum which seemed to have been fixed in his mind. He smoothed the package of bills in his hand, then he glanced up at her furtively as if to ascertain whether she knew how much he had laid out. She involuntarily averted her glance. Instantly Orin gathered up several of the bills quickly, conveying them out of sight with a guilty air as if he were purloining them.

Then he held the remainder toward his companion.

"There," he said, "I should have kept my promise if you hadn't hinted by speaking of Fenton. Of course you understand that I can't give you anything very tremendous, but there's a hundred and fifty dollars."

Melissa flushed and drew back.

"I had no idea of hinting," was her reply. "Of course I thank you very much, but you ought to give the money to John, not to me."

"No," Orin insisted, "you helped me with Mrs. Fenton, and John might as well know that I wouldn't put this money into a hole just to please him. I know John. He'll set more by you if the money comes through you."

"But I don't believe," protested she, "that what I said to Mrs. Fenton really made any difference."

But in Orin's abounding good nature her disclaimer passed unheeded. He pressed the money upon her, and went away full of the consciousness of having exercised a noble philanthropy.

It is possible that had he waited to read Fred Rangely's criticism upon his *America* which appeared in the *Daily Observer* next morning he might never have made this contribution toward paying his father's debts. With Bently's help Rangely had discovered the original of the statue, and had then written a careful comparison between the work of Eutychides and that of Stanton. It hardly need be added that the result was not at all flattering to the latter. Rangely possessed a very pretty gift of sarcasm, and it was his humor to consider that in attacking the sculptor he was to a certain degree settling scores with Mrs. Staggchase for her change in attitude toward him after Miss Merrivale came. He served up the unlucky statue and its more unlucky maker with a piquancy and a zest which made his article town talk for a month. The sculptor sheltered himself, so far as he could, by keeping out of sight, while Peter Calvin, unable to endure the jibes and laughter which everywhere met him, abandoned the cause of his *protegé* and the town together, by starting two months earlier than he had intended on a trip to Europe.

Rangely was angry with himself for having been persuaded by Mrs. Staggchase to write an article sustaining Stanton's claims in the first place, and not having signed it, he endeavored to give to this criticism a tone which should indicate, without its being specifically stated, that he had not written the former paper. He understood perfectly well that Mrs. Staggchase would regard his position as a declaration of independence, and indeed when the lady read the *Observer* that morning she smiled with an air of comprehension.

"That's an end to that," she said to herself. "When you've known a man as long as I have

Fred Rangely, he's like a book that's been read; you've got all the good there is in him. There are other men in the world."

When Orin had gone, Milly stood turning over and over in her hand the roll of bills he had given her. Then she spread them out upon the table, counting them and gloating over them, with a delight which arose quite as largely from her foretaste of John's pleasure and the joy of having helped to cause it, as it did from mere love of money. She had just taken the precious roll to put it away, when her lover himself appeared.

John Stanton was really of more kindly disposition than might have been inferred from his misunderstanding with his betrothed. He had been half a dozen weeks coming to his right mind, but whatever he did he did thoroughly, and in the end he had reached a point where he was willing to acknowledge himself wrong, and to make whatever amends lay in his power. He came in to-night with the determined air of one who has made up his mind to get through a disagreeable duty as speedily as possible.

Milly opened the door for him, and stood back to let him pass; she had learned in these weeks of their estrangement to restrain the manifestation of her joy at his coming. It was with so great a rush of blissful surprise that she now found herself suddenly caught up into his arms, that she clung closely to his neck for one joyful instant, and then burst into a passion of weeping.

"There, there," her lover said, caressing her; "don't cry, Milly. I've been a brute, and I know it; but if you'll forgive me this time I'll see that you never need to again."

He moved toward a chair as he spoke, half carrying her in his arms. In her excitement she loosened her hold upon the roll of money, which was still in her hand, and the bills were scattered on the floor behind him as he walked. He sat down and took her in his lap, stroking her hair and soothing her as well as he was able. By a strong effort she controlled herself, dried her tears, and sat up, half laughing.

"I'm getting to be dreadful teary," she said. "I" —

"What in the world," he interrupted her in amazement, "is that on the floor?"

She turned and saw the money, and burst into a peal of laughter. Springing down from his knee, she ran and gathered up the bills in her two hands; then, dancing up to him, half wild with delight, her cheeks flushed, her eyes shining, she scattered the precious bits of green paper fantastically over his head and shoulders.

"'Take, oh take, the rosy, rosy crown!'"

she sang, in the very abandonment of gayety.

"Are you gone crazy?" he demanded, clutching the floating bills, and then catching her about the waist. "You act like a witch! Where did all this money come from? The savings-bank?"

"No," she returned, becoming quiet, and nestling close to him. "The Lord sent it by the hand of your brother Orin."

It was some time before John could be made to understand the whole story; and when it had been told, he instantly leaped to the conclusion that the whole credit of Orin's getting the commission belonged of right to Milly, a conviction in which he remained steadfast despite all her disclaimers.

At last she gave up protesting, and shut his mouth with a kiss. Since John, as well as Orin, thought so, she felt that her part must have been more important than she had realized; but she was too modest to bear so much praise.

"John," she said at length, "I have something awful to confess. I've been keeping a secret from you."

"I'm afraid I've been too much of a bear for it to have been safe to tell me," returned her lover, smiling.

His own heart was filled with the double joy of reconciliation, and of having brought it about himself by a manly confession of his fault.

"It wasn't that at all," she protested. "It was because I wasn't sure about it; and then I wanted to surprise you if I got it."

"Got what? You speak as if it was the smallpox. Is it anything catching?"

"Oh, no," answered Milly, laughing gleefully at his sally, which to her present mood seemed the most exquisite wit. "You needn't be afraid; it's only the matronship of the new Knitting School, thank you, with a salary of five hundred dollars a year."

"Really, Milly?"

"Really, John; and don't you think" —

"Think what?"

She had made up her mind to say it even before this blessed agreement had come about, but now that the moment came, the habits and trammels of generations held her back.

"Why," she stammered, blushing and hesitating, "don't you think, — wouldn't it seem more appropriate if a matron was" — Her voice failed utterly. She flung her arms convulsively about her lover's neck, and drew his ear close to her lips. "Surely, now, John, dear," she whispered, "we could afford to" —

She finished with a kiss.

"If you can put up with me, darling," he answered her, with a mighty hug; "we'll be married in a week, or, better still, in a day."

"I think in a month will do," responded Mistress Milly, demurely, sitting up to blush with decorum.

XXXI

PARTED OUR FELLOWSHIP.

Othello ; ii. — i.

THE news of the collapse of Princeton Platinum stock, which Dr. Wilson had given Arthur on Saturday night, proved to be somewhat premature. On Sunday it was decided at the club, where the matter was discussed in a cold-blooded and leisurely fashion, that the whole scheme had gone to pieces ; and of course this decision was accompanied by the statement, in various forms, that everybody knew that there was nothing substantial behind the certificates. On Monday, however, the stock took an unexpected rise, and for two or three days held its own with a firmness which greatly encouraged its holders.

Fenton had bought the bulk of his shares at two and seven-eights, and still held them, notwithstanding the rumors of disaster in the air. With a folly that would be incredible were it not one of the most common things in amateur stock transactions, the artist had by this time put the bulk of his little fortune into this wild-cat stock, which he now held with a desperate determination not to sell below the figure at which he had purchased. He could so little afford the least loss, that, with the genuine instinct of the gambler, he trusted to luck, and ran the risk of utter ruin for the sake of the chance of making a brilliant stroke, or at least of coming out even. Having made up his mind to hold on, he clung to the position with his customary obstinacy, even dismissing the matter, as far as was possible, from his thoughts.

He was very busy preparing an exhibition of pictures at the St. Filipe club. The matter had been left in his hands by the other members of the Art Committee, of which he was chairman; but his attitude toward the club had prevented his taking any steps until after the meeting on Saturday night. Now, he was particularly anxious to make the exhibition a brilliant success, to give a signal instance of the value of his services.

He had gone to his studio on Sunday afternoon and sketched in a head of Ninitta, and upon this he worked, now and then, with a desperate energy born of the feeling that it substantiated his story to Edith. He had been seized with grave doubts as to the advisability of exhibiting the *Fatima* just now; but he did not see his way clear to spare so large and important a picture from the collection, and he comforted himself with the thought that the face was different, and that if the model were recognized he would be supposed to have worked up old sketches taken when Ninitta had posed for him before her marriage.

He worked with all his marvellous energy, collecting pictures, directing their hanging, soothing artists whose canvases were not placed to their liking, making out the catalogue, and arranging all the details which in such a connection are fatiguing and well-nigh innumerable.

The exhibition was opened on Wednesday evening with a reception to ladies, and by nine o'clock the gallery began to fill. Fenton had decorated the rooms a little, chiefly with live pampas grass and palms and India-rubber trees. It is difficult to see how mankind in the nineteenth century could exist without the India-rubber tree. If that plant were destroyed, civilization would be left gasping, helpless and crippled ; and of late years, not content with making it serviceable in every department of practical life, men have brought the shrub into the domain of æsthetics by using it for decorative purposes.

The collection of paintings was an interesting one, made up of the work of the best artists in town. Fenton had spared no pains either in procuring what he wanted, or in arranging the gallery. The *Fatima* hung in a position of honor opposite the main entrance. The selection of so prominent a place for his own work offended Fenton's taste, and annoyed him with an uncomfortable sense of how strongly the picture was in evidence. The exigencies of hanging, and the fact that the canvas was the most important one in the room forced him to place it as he did; and Bently, whom he called to his assistance, laughed at his scruples. None of the artists had seen the picture, and Bently was quite carried away by his admiration of it.

"By Jove! Fenton," he said, "I didn't know you had it in you. It's perfectly stunning. But it's beastly wicked," he added. "Perhaps that's the reason it's so good."

"Come," Fenton said with a laugh, "that sounds quite like the old Pagan days."

"But how in the dickens," Tom went on, "did you get Mrs. Herman to pose for you?"

"Great Heavens!" ejaculated Fenton, "don't say that to anybody else. I had no end of studies of her, made long ago; but I didn't suppose I had followed them closely enough for it to be recognized."

"You don't mean," Tom returned, "that that side and arm are done from old studies!"

Fenton had a delicate dislike to literal falsehood. It was not a question of morality directly, but one of taste. Albeit, since taste is simply morality remote from the springs of action, it perhaps came to much the same thing in the end. He felt now, however, that the time for the selfish indulgence of his individual whims was past, and that he owed to Ninitta the grace of a downright and hearty falsehood.

"Why, of course," he said, "I had one or two

models to help me out ; but the inspiration came from the old studies."

"And she didn't pose for you ?" Tom persisted increduously.

"Pose for me ?" echoed Fenton, impatiently. "Why, man alive, think what you're saying ! Of course, she didn't pose for me. She never has posed for anybody since she was married."

"And a devilish shame it is, too," responded Tom.

This conversation, which took place Wednesday afternoon, made Fenton extremely uneasy. Fate seemed to have worked against him. He had painted the picture to go to the New York Exhibition, where he hoped it would be sold without ever coming under the eye of Herman at all. He reflected now that Ninitta had posed for Helen and for several of his brother painters, while it was scarcely credible that the likeness which Bently had perceived at a glance should escape the trained artist's eye of her husband ; and it seemed to him now, little less than madness to have brought the picture here at all.

Upon second thought, however, he reflected that even were the picture recognized, no great harm would probably come of it. No one would be likely to speak on the subject to Herman, and, least of all, was there a probability that the latter would confess that he was aware of what his wife had done. Herman's condemnation, Fenton said to himself with a shrug, he must, if worst came to worst, endure; this was to be set down with other unpleasantnesses which belong to the unpleasant conditions of life as they exist in these days. As long as there was no open scandal, he could ignore whatever lay beneath the surface, and he assured himself that in any event it were wisest, as he had long ago learned, to carry things off with a high hand.

It was about half past nine when Fenton brought Edith into the gallery. The crowd had by this time become pretty dense, and just inside the door they halted, exchanging greeting with the acquaintances who appeared on every side. The St. Filipe was an old club, and for more than a quarter of a century had maintained the reputation of leading in matters of art and literature. Its influence had, on the whole, been remarkably even and intelligent; but of late it began to be felt, among those who were radical in their views, that the club was coming under Philistine influence. Half a dozen years before, when Fenton had proposed Peter Calvin for membership, even the social influence of the candidate did not save him from a rejection so marked that Arthur had threatened to resign his own membership. Now, however, Peter Calvin was not only a member of the St. Filipe, but he was on the Election Committee. The club was held in favor in the circles over which his influence extended, and although workers in all branches of art were still included among the members, they were pretty closely pushed by the more fashionable element of the town. Fenton was not far from right in asserting, as he did one day to Mrs. Greyson, after her return from Europe, that the change in his own attitude toward art was pretty exactly paralleled by the alteration which had taken place in that of Boston.

The character of the membership of the club was indicated to-night by the brilliancy of the company present. It was one of those occasions when everybody is there, and the scene, as the new comers looked over the gallery, was most bright and animated. Although the ladies had evidently labored under the usual uncertainty in regard to the proper dress which seems inseparable from an art exhibition in Boston, and were in all varieties of costume from street attire to full evening toilette, there were enough handsome gowns to supply the necessary color. There was also abundance of pretty and of striking faces, and the crowd had that pleasant look of familiarity which one gets from recognizing acquaintances all through it.

One of the first persons the Fentons saw was Ethel Mott, who, under the chaperonage of Mrs. Frostwinch, was making the tour of the gallery with Kent, and paying far more attention to her companion than to the pictures.

"Oh, Arthur," Edith whispered, "I saw Mrs.

Staggchase in the dressing-room, and she told me that Ethel's engagement is out to-day."

Arthur smiled, remembering his perspicacity when Ethel had driven away from his dinner with Kent in her carriage.

"Isn't the crowd dreadful?" the voice of Mrs. Bodewin Ranger said, at Edith's elbow. "I'm really getting too old to trust myself in such a crush."

While Edith chatted with her, the steward called Fenton away, in connection with some question about the catalogues, and when Mrs. Ranger moved on, Edith found herself for an instant alone. The mention of her husband's name behind her caught her ear and her attention.

"Fenton's cheeky enough for anything!" said an unknown voice. "But he makes a point of his good taste, and I think it's beastly poor form for him to show that picture here."

"Bently says," returned another voice, also strange to Edith, "that Fenton says she didn't pose for him, but that he worked it up from old studies."

"I don't care if he did," was the response. "All the fellows know it, and Herman must feel like the deuce."

"But you can't suppress every picture that has a study of her in it."

"Hush," said the other voice, "there comes Herman himself."

It seemed to Edith that this brief dialogue had been shouted out so that it could not be inaudible to any one in the room. She looked about for her husband. Her ears rang with the meaningless babble of voices, the jargon of human sounds conveying far less impression of intelligence than the noise of water on the shore, or the sound of the wind in the tree-tops. All about her were faces wreathed in conventional smiles, the inevitable laughter, the usual absence of earnestness, and in the midst of all, with a shock hardly less painful than that of the discovery she had just made, she heard the voice of Herman bidding her good evening.

She held out her hand to him with a hasty, excited gesture. She was painfully conscious that he had but to lift his eyes to see the *Fatima* hanging on the opposite wall of the gallery, and she instinctively felt that she must draw his attention away.

"How do you do, Mr. Herman," she said, with eager warmth. "Is Mrs. Herman with you?

She moved half around him as she spoke, as if compelled by the shifting of the crowd to change her position; and while she shook hands managed to bring herself almost face to the picture, so that his back was toward it.

"No," he answered, "she never comes to these things if she can possibly help it. I hear your husband has outdone himself on this exhibition."

Edith looked about despairingly for Arthur. She felt herself unequal to the emergency, and longed for his clever wits to contrive some means of escape from the cruel dilemma in which his act had placed her and his friend. Indignation, shame, and sorrow filled her heart. She recognized that Arthur had not told her the truth in regard to Ninitta. The dread and the suspicion which she had felt on the night of the dinner returned to her with tenfold force. But the greatest triumph of modern civilization is the power it has bestowed upon women of concealing their feelings. The pressing need of the moment was to show to Herman a smiling and untroubled face, and to avoid arousing his suspicion that anything was wrong.

"The truth is," she returned, "that I haven't seen the exhibition. It's impossible to see pictures in such a crowd, don't you think? I know Arthur has worked very hard. I've hardly seen him this week."

"He has a most tremendous power of accomplishing what he undertakes," Herman said heartily. "But tell me about yourself. You're looking tired."

"It is the time of year to look tired. I believe I am feeling a little anxious that spring should arrive."

She was struggling in her thoughts for a means of preventing the discovery, which it seemed to her must be inevitable the moment she ceased to engage Herman in conversation and he turned away. Over his shoulder she could see the beautiful, sensuous *Fatima* lying with long sleek limbs amid bright-hued cushions. Now that she knew the truth, she could see Ninitta in every line, and her whole soul rose in indignant protest. It was her friend, the wife of this man she honored, who was delivered up on the wall yonder to the curious eyes of all these people. The stinging blush of shame burned in Edith's cheeks, and, as at this instant she turned to find her husband beside her, the glance which darted from her eyes to his was one of righteous scorn and indignation.

His wife's burning look showed Arthur that she knew; and, reflecting quickly, he decided that Herman did not. It was characteristic of him that he instantly chose the boldest policy.

"Come," he said to Herman as soon as they had greeted each other, "I know you haven't seen my *Fatima.* The boys say its the best thing I've done, but I couldn't get a decent model, and had to depend so much on old studies, that, for the life of me, I can't tell whether it's good or not."

Like two blows at once came to Edith a sense of shame that she could even involuntarily have wished for her husband's aid, and an overwhelming consciousness of the readiness and boldness of his falsity. She saw the face of Grant Herman, nobly instinct with truth in every line, and, as he turned at her husband's word, everything blurred before her vision. She believed she was going to faint, and she rallied all her self-command to hold herself steady. The lights danced, and the sound of voices faded as into the distance. Then, with a supreme effort of will, she rallied, and the voices rolled back upon her ear with a noise like the roar of an incoming wave.

A sphere of silence seemed to envelop Herman and Arthur and herself in the very midst of the crowd, as for an instant which seemed to her cruelly long she stood waiting for what the sculptor should say.

"Your friends are right, Fenton," Herman said, at length, in a voice so changed from its previous cordiality that it was idle to suppose the likeness had escaped him. "You have never painted anything better."

"Thank you," Fenton responded, brightly. "I am awfully glad you like it. I fancy," he added, with a laugh, "that the tabby-cats will be shocked."

His companion made no reply, and the approach of Rangely afforded Arthur a chance to change the conversation.

"I say, Fred," he demanded, "have you congratulated Thayer Kent yet?"

"Congratulated him?" echoed Rangely.

"Yes. Didn't you know his engagement is out?"

Rangely might have been said to take a page out of Fenton's own book, as he answered, —

"But what's the etiquette of precedence?"

"Of precedence?" echoed Arthur, in his turn.

"Yes," Rangely returned. "Which of us should congratulate the other first? Only," he added, hitting to his own delight upon a position which might save him from some awkwardness in the future, "of course my engagement can't be announced until Miss Merrivale gets home to her mother."

"Well," Arthur said, "marriage is that ceremony by which man lays aside the pleasures of life and takes up its duties. I congratulate you on your determination to do anything so virtuous."

"Sardonic, as usual," retorted Fred, laughing; and then he went to find Miss Merrivale, convinced that under the circumstances the sooner he proposed to her the better.

XXXII

HEART-BURNING HEAT OF DUTY.

Love's Labor's Lost; i.—I.

ALL the world feels the pathos of helplessness hurt and wounded; but only some recognize how this applies to a great and noble nature attacked by unscrupulousness. In an encounter with dishonesty, nobility of soul may be, in its effect for the moment, utter weakness. Assailed by deceit or treachery the great heart has often no resource but endurance; and while endurance may save, it cannot defend.

The moment Grant Herman's eyes fell upon the *Fatima*, he understood fully why Fenton had so volubly remarked that he had painted the picture from old studies. He tried to fight with his conviction that what the artist said was false, although even as he did so he could not crush down the feeling of having been wounded by the hand of a friend. It seemed to him incredible that Fenton, even though the painter's defection from the Pagans had caused something of a breach between them, could have been guilty of this outrage. He choked with an intolerable sense of shame for himself, for the artist, and for Ninitta. A terrible anguish wrung his heart as he looked across the crowded gallery gay with lights, with the rich dresses, with laughter, and with the beauty of women, to where hung the picture of the mother of his boy, an image of sensuous enticement. The fact that Fenton had substituted another face for that of Ninitta did not, for the moment, console him. To his sculptor's eye, form was the important thing, and the fact that he recognized the model bore down all else. He remembered how marked had been Ninitta's unwillingness to accompany him to the exhibition, and the possible connection between this and the picture forced itself upon his mind.

With all the instinctive generosity of his soul, however, Herman strove to believe that the *Fatima* had been painted, as Fenton said, from old studies, and that his wife had not been guilty of the painful indecorum of posing. He compelled himself to answer the artist calmly, although he could not make his manner cordial. And as he spoke, his eye, searching the picture for confirmation of his hope or of his fear, recognized among the draperies a Turkish shawl he had himself given his wife after their marriage.

He made his way out of the gallery and out of the club house. He felt that he must get away from the innumerable eyes by which he was surrounded. He started toward home, but before he had gone a block, he stopped, hesitated a moment, and struck off into a side street. He was not ready to go home. He had said to himself too often, reiterating it in his mind constantly for six years, that in dealing with his wife his must be the wisdom, the patience, and the forbearance of both. He remembered a night long ago, when he had gone to Ninitta's room, in a mood of contrition, to renew the troth of his youth, and had fallen instead into a fit of bitter anger. With no evident reason, came back to him to-night the beautiful weeping figure of the Italian as she had cast herself at his feet and implored his forgiveness. He would not go to her now until he was calmer, and until he had considered carefully all the points of the situation.

In that whirl which comes in desperate circumstances before the startled and bewildered thoughts can be reduced to order, Herman wandered on, not thinking where he was going, until he found himself leaning against a railing and looking over the waters of the Charles River. It was a beautiful starlight night with a wavering wind that came in uncertain gusts only to die away again. The water was like a flood of ink, across which streamed thin tremulous lines of brightness, and over which were strewn the flickering reflections of the stars. The gas jets of the city across the flood, the rows of lamps which marked the bridges, the distant horse cars which rumbled between Cambridge and Boston with their colored lights, the green and red lanterns that glowed from the railroad tracks farther down the river, all suggested the busy life of men with its passions, its greed, and its heartlessness; but the darkness held all remote, as if the world of men were a dream. And overhead the immovable stars, like the unpitying gods, hung above the city and were reflected in the water, and wounded the soul of the lonely man with the terrible sense of power illimitably removed, of passionless strength which served to humanity but as a measure of its own weakness and triviality. The misfortunes of life might be endured; its disappointments, its anguish, even its inviolable loneliness might be supported, but a sense of the awful futility of existence crushes man to the depths of impotent despair.

A review of the past is usually a protest against fate, and manly as Herman was it was inevitable that into his reverie should come a sense that the wrong and suffering of his life had been thrust upon him undeserved. He could not be blind to the fact that it had been through his virtues that he had been wounded. A sense of injustice comes with the consciousness of having suffered through merit. Many a man is too noble basely to avoid the consequences of his acts, but few can wholly rid themselves of the feeling that the uncomplaining acceptance of painful results should serve as expiation for the deeds which caused them. The nobility of his nature, the purity of his intentions had made of a boyish folly the curse of a lifetime. With whatever tenderness the sculptor regarded Ninitta as the mother of his son, it was vain for him to attempt to deceive himself in regard to his love for her. A man with whom cordiality was instinctive, who was born for the most frank and intimate domestic relations, he found in his wife small sympathy and less comprehension. He had married her, believing that she had a right to claim happiness at his hands because he had taught her to love him. He had long since been obliged to own to himself that he had done this at the expense of his own peace, and he now questioned whether the experiment had succeeded better in her case than in his. If she had not been able to comprehend his aims and to enter into his scheme of life, it was equally true that she must have found in him little response to the calls of her own nature. The bitterness of the sigh which wrung his bosom, as he stood with his hand upon the railing and looked over the water with the lights reflected on its blackness, was as much for her as for himself.

Yet he would not have been human had he not felt thrills of anger when he thought of the *Fatima*. No faintest suspicion crossed his mind of any darker shame which might lie behind the fact that his wife had posed for Fenton. This he could not doubt that she had done. This explained her frequent absences from home in the morning, to which he had before given no thought. He remembered, too, that for weeks a furtive restlessness, poorly concealed, had been evident in Ninitta's manner. He had attributed it to her intense opposition to Nino's being sent to school; but now he read it differently. He could not but be angry, yet his pity was greater than his wrath; and he resolved not only to be forbearing with his wife, but hereafter to use greater endeavors to enrich her colorless life. He was too thoroughly an artist himself not to feel and appreciate how much the old love of posing, the longing for the air of a studio, and the art instinct might have had to do with Ninitta's fault.

But in regard to Fenton his heart burned with that rage which is largely grief. It was like the anger, which is half astonishment, of a child who is unexpectedly struck by its playmate. The fact that he was incapable of comprehending how it was possible to betray a friend made him confused in thinking of the artist's share in the transaction; and the fact that he could vent upon Fenton his righteous indignation enabled him to free his feelings toward Ninitta of almost all animosity. When at last he turned to go home, it was with a profound pity that he thought of his wife.

It was a little after eleven when he reached his house. The gas was burning in his chamber and Ninitta lay apparently sleeping. The wretched woman feigned a slumber which she had in vain courted. She was convinced that her husband could not see the *Fatima* without discovering her secret, and the guilty knowledge in her heart filled her with growing fears as the moments went on.

When at last she heard Herman's step, she had started up in bed like a wild creature, her heart fluttering, her ears strained as if to catch from the sound some clue to his mood. But instantly she had lain down again, and, with an instinct like that of the timorous animals whose nature it is to feign death when they cannot flee, had composed herself into the appearance of slumber.

Herman paused a moment, just inside the chamber door, and looked at his wife. Something in her pose suggested to him so vividly the *Fatima* that, despite his self-conquest on the bridge, a flood of anger swelled within him. The masculine instinct, nourished through a thousand generations, that no palliation gives the wife a right to claim forgiveness from her husband for the shame she has put upon him by a violation of modesty, surged up within him. He drew in a deep inspiration and started forward with an inarticulate sound as if he could throw himself upon this woman and tighten his fingers on her throat.

Ninitta raised herself in bed with an exclamation of fear. Her black hair streamed loose, and her dark eyes shone. Her swarthy passionate face was an image of terror. She was not far enough away from her peasant ancestors not to be moved by the size and strength of her husband's large and vigorous frame. Many generations and much subtlety of refinement must lie between herself and savagery before a woman can learn instinctively to fear the soul of a man rather than his muscles in a crisis like this. Husband and wife confronted each other as he walked quickly across the chamber. Her cowering attitude, the fear which was written in every line of her face, fed his anger, until, in his blind rage, all pity and self-restraint seemed to be swept away.

But just as he neared the bed, when in his burning look Ninitta seemed already to feel his hands clutching her with cruel force, his foot struck against something which lay on the floor. It was one of Nino's wooden soldiers. The father stopped, and his look changed. He remembered how Nino had come in from the nursery while he was dressing that night, bringing his arms full of more or less shattered figures which he had appealed to his father to put to rights for a grand battle which was to be fought in the morning. Herman looked down at the toy and forgot his anger. He looked up at his wife and she saw with wonder the change in his face. It had been full of indignation against the wife who had deceived him ; on it now was written reproachful anguish, and pity for the mother of his son.

"Ninitta," he said. "How could you do it ?"

She cowered down in the bed, burying her face

in her hands. She could not answer, and there came over him a painful sense of the uselessness of words.

"Everybody must recognize Fenton's picture," he said. "If you did not remember me, Ninitta, how could you forget Nino? How will he feel when he is old enough to realize what you have done?"

The frightened woman burst into convulsive sobs mixed with moans like those of a hurt animal. In the last hours she had been thinking no less than her husband; but where he had considered her, she had thought chiefly of her boy. Mingled with the fear of her husband's anger had been the nobler feeling, that she was no longer worthy to be with her son. The very passion of the love she bore him moved her now with the determination to leave him. It was always Ninitta's instinct to run away in trouble, and now, added to the impulse to escape from her husband was the determination forming itself with awful stress of anguish in her soul, to go away from Nino; to take away from her son whom she loved better than life itself, this woman who had no right in his pure presence. She did not look upon it as an expiation of her fault; it was only that maternal love gathered up whatever was noble in her nature, in this supreme sacrifice for her son.

To Herman, looking down upon the cowering figure of his wife, with a heartbreaking sense of the impossibility of effecting anything by words, she was simply a cowardly woman who took refuge in tears from the reproaches which her conduct deserved. Could he have known what was passing in her heart, it would have moved him to a deeper respect and a keener pity than he had ever felt for her. No more than a dumb animal had she any language in which she could have made him understand her feelings had she tried ; and at last he turned away with a choking in his throat.

XXXIII

A BOND OF AIR.

Troilus and Cressida; i. — 3.

THE stock of the Princeton Platinum Company was issued in ten-dollar shares, it being the conviction of Erastus Snaffle, deduced from a more or less extensive experience, that the gullible portion of the public is more likely to buy stock of a low par value. On the morning after the exhibition at the St. Filipe Club, the shares were quoted at two dollars and an eighth.

Arthur Fenton read the stock reports at breakfast. He laid the paper down calmly, drank his coffee in silence, and absently played with his fork, while his wife attended to Caldwell's breakfast and her own. He said nothing until the boy, whose mind was intent upon some new toy or other, having hastily finished his meal, asked to be excused.

"Don't be in a hurry, Caldwell," his mother said, gently. "I want you to learn to wait for older people."

"Let him go, Edith," his father interposed. "I want to talk to you."

The boy jumped down quickly and ran to give his father a hasty kiss. He had learned to look to Fenton to help him in evading his mother's attempts at discipline, and Edith noted with pain, as she had too often noticed before, the knowing smile which came into the child's face at her husband's words. Caldwell evidently regarded his father's remark merely as a convenient excuse, and it hurt Edith to see how in subtile ways her son was learning to distrust the honesty of his father.

On this occasion, however, Arthur had meant what he said. When the door had closed behind the little fellow, he looked up to observe in the most matter-of-fact tone, —

"I suppose it is only fair, Edith, that I should tell you that we are ruined."

She looked at him with a puzzled face.

"What do you mean?" she said.

"I mean," he returned, "that I have been getting into no end of a mess, and that some stock I bought to help myself out of it, has gone down and made things ten times worse."

She folded her hands in her lap and regarded him wistfully. She had been so often repressed when she had tried to gain his confidence in regard to business matters that she hesitated to speak now.

"Should I understand if you told me about it?" she asked.

"Oh, very likely not," he returned, coolly; "but I don't in the least mind telling you, if it's any satisfaction to you. It isn't any great matter, only that I live so near the ragged edge that a dollar or two either way makes all the difference between poverty and independence."

Edith breathed more freely. Her husband's self-possessed manner, and the fact that she knew him to be so given to exaggeration, made her feel that things were not so hopeless as his words had at first implied.

"I have three thousand shares of Princeton Platinum stock," Fenton went on, with the condescending air of one who elaborately explains details which he knows will not be understood. "I bought at two and seven-eighths, with money that should go to pay notes due on Saturday. The stock was worth two and an eighth last night and very likely by to-night won't be worth anything."

"Then why didn't you sell yesterday?" Edith asked.

Arthur smiled at the feminine turn of her words.

"Because, my shrewd financier, I don't want to sell at a loss, and Mr. Irons assures me that there will be a rise before the final collapse."

He did not add, as he might have done, the substance of the talk between himself and Irons. That wily financier had said to him one day,—

"Fenton, you were almighty toploftical about those railroad shares, and I'll give you another chance. I've had four thousand shares of Princeton Platinum turned over to me on an assignment.

It cost me two, and you may have it at that figure, though it's worth two and a half in the market to-day."

"You are too generous, by half," Fenton had answered.

"Well, the fact is," Irons had responded, "I hate infernally to be under obligations. Princeton Platinum is wild-cat fast enough, but it will touch four before they let the bottom drop out. That I happen to know. This will give you a chance to make a neat thing out of it, and it will square off the obligation our syndicate's under to you."

"Thank you," was Fenton's answer; "but the obligation, such as it is, I prefer to have stand, and I haven't any money to put into stock of any kind now."

"Well, think it over. Don't let your sentiments interfere too much with business. I'll hold the stock for you for three days. If you're fool enough to miss your opportunity after that I'm not responsible."

Naturally, this portion of the conversation Fenton did not impart to his wife.

Edith's look became more perplexed as her talk with her husband continued; and the matter-of-fact way in which he spoke of approaching disaster was to her unintelligible.

"What is going to collapse?" she asked at length. "The stock?"

"Certainly, my dear. There isn't anything

behind it. I doubt if there ever was any Princeton Platinum mine, but I did think the men who were managing it were clever enough to get it to four or four and a half before they let go."

"But how could they get it to four or four and a half, if there isn't any mine?"

"By gulling fools like me, my dear; that's the way these things are always done."

A troubled look came over Mrs. Fenton's face, and her lips closed a little more tightly.

"Well," demanded her husband impatiently, "what is it? Moral scruples?"

"It doesn't seem to me to be very honest stock to be dealing in," Edith replied, timidly.

"To discuss the morality of stock speculation," he replied, with coolly elaborate courtesy, "is much like eating a fig. You may be biting the seeds all day without being sure you've finished them."

She was silenced, and cast down her eyes waiting for what he might choose to say next.

"The situation," he continued, after a pause, "is merely this. I haven't the cleverness properly to manage being in debt. I don't know how those notes are to be paid Saturday, and have been given to understand that there are reasons, doubtless judicious, but extremely inconvenient, why they will not be renewed."

His manner was as calm as ever, but there was a growing hardness in his tone and a cruel tightening of his lips. His restraint had much of the calmness of despair. His was a nature which always outran actualities with imagined possibilities, and thus found in even the fullest joy a sense of loss and failure; while in misfortune, it magnified all evils until it was overwhelmed with the burden of their weight. He suffered the more acutely because he endured not only the sting of the present evil, but of all those which he foresaw might follow in its wake. He felt at this moment a growing necessity to find some one against whom he might logically turn his anger; and while he was firmly determined not to vent his displeasure upon his wife, his attitude toward her became constantly more stern.

"If Uncle Peter were at home," Edith began, after a pause, "he might"—

"He might not," interrupted Arthur, roughly. "In any case he has taken the light of his countenance abroad, so he's out of the question."

"But some of your friends, Arthur, might lend you the money you want."

"My dear Edith, do you fancy that within the past month I have failed to go over the list of my friends, backward and forward? Don't say those tiresome, obvious things. I'll fail and have an auction, and give up the house, and lose caste, and have a pleasant tea-party generally. That's the only thing there is to do."

Edith rose from her seat, and went around to

where he was sitting. Standing behind his chair she laid her hands on his shoulders, and, bending forward, kissed his cheek.

"I dare say, Arthur," she said, "that we should be quite as happy if we gave up trying to live in a way that we can't afford; but meanwhile there is godmamma."

"Mrs. Glendower?"

"Yes. You know she has left me five thousand dollars in her will; and she told me once that if the time came that I needed the money desperately I should have it for the asking."

"That is kind of her," was her husband's comment, "but it would be kinder to let you get it at once in the natural way. The comfort about a bequest is that you don't have to feel grateful to any live man for it."

His words were brutal enough, but there was a new lightness in his tone. He caught instantly at this hope of relief, and he showed his appreciation of his wife's cleverness in devising this scheme by caressing the hand which lay upon his shoulder.

"You can go to New York to-night," remarked Edith thoughtfully, ignoring his words, "and be back by Saturday morning. If you didn't so much dislike going to New York in the day time, you might get there in time to see godmamma to-night."

"To-morrow will be time enough," he answered. "You are a brick, Edith, to help me out of this scrape, and the magnitude of the moral reforms I'll institute in honor of my deliverance will astonish you."

He sprang up as light-heartedly as a boy. The means of escaping the annoyance of the present moment had been found, and his buoyant spirits lifted him above the doubts and troubles of the future.

They discussed together the details of his coming interview with Mrs. Glendower, and the terms of the letter which Edith should write to her. There was something most touching in the tender eagerness with which Edith prolonged the talk and clung to the occasion which had brought her and her husband, for the moment, together. She even forgot to deplore the misfortune which had given rise to this confidence, and, in her desire to be helpful to Arthur, she did not even remember that once her pride would have risen in rebellion at the bare suggestion of taking advantage of Mrs. Glendower's offer. All day long she went about with a happier smile on her lips than had been there for many a long day. The danger of impending ruin seemed to have brought her consolation instead of grief; and in the prayers which she murmured in her heart as she stood with her arms clasped about Caldwell, when Fenton drove away that night, there was not a little thanksgiving mingled with her supplications.

XXXIV

WHAT TIME SHE CHANTED.

Hamlet; iv. — 7.

THE stock report which caused Fenton such unpleasant sensations was read that same morning by Mrs. Amanda Welsh Sampson with keen satisfaction of a sort seldom known to the truly virtuous. Mrs. Sampson was engaged in financial transactions of which the very magnitude caused her naïve satisfaction, while the possible results made her bosom glow with unwonted emotion. Mrs. Sampson's affection for Alfred Irons was neither deep nor tender in its nature, and in settling the bill for services rendered in the railroad case there was no sentiment likely to restrain her from making the best possible bargain. The bargain she made was of a nature to send her about her flat singing songs of triumph such as Deborah sang over the slaughter of the unfortunate Sisera.

The wily but impressible Erastus Snaffle, cheered by the widow's wine, warmed by her smile, and smitten by her amiable conversation, had bestowed upon her, merely as a tribute which mammon might pay to the ever-womanly, three thousand shares of Princeton Platinum stock. He had done this at a time when it seemed doubtful whether even his adroitness could make the scheme a success; and it somewhat mars the lustre of his generosity to record that he afterward regretted his impulsive open-handedness. He had been able to prevent Mrs. Sampson from realizing on her stock, very reasonably feeling that he was making philanthropic endeavors to benefit an ungrateful world rather against its will, and he did not mean that she should make a stumbling-block for him of his own generosity by putting this gift on the market when he wished to supply all buyers himself.

When it was quoted at three, the high-water mark so far, he had beguiled the widow with a cock-and-bull story about the formalities of transferrence on the books of the company of stocks which had been given away; and by the time Mrs. Sampson had cleared her mind from the entanglements of this ingenious fiction the bottom had dropped out of the market.

In the midst of her disappointment in seeing what to her would have been almost a fortune melting into thin air, the fertile brain of Mrs. Sampson had given birth to what was nothing less than an inspiration, She had gone to see Alfred Irons, and delicately but firmly insinuated that it was high time she received substantial tokens of the gratitude of the Wachusett Syndicate, for her efforts in their behalf with the Hon. Thomas Greenfield. Mr. Irons had answered, as she had expected him to, that she had presented no bill. To this her reply was ready. She was prepared to state what would satisfy her. She explained that she felt the delicacy of her position, since, if any consideration passed to her directly from the corporation, it was sure to be known, and unpleasant comment made. She had in her possession, she continued, certain stock, of which the market value was somewhere between two and two and a half, which, it struck her, might serve admirably to veil the generosity which had been promised her. Her proposition, in brief, was that Irons should take her three thousand shares of stock at four dollars, the difference between this and the market value, of course, being refunded to him by the company.

"By Gad! you're a cheeky one!" had been Iron's comment, more expressive than elegant, when the widow had laid her scheme wholly before him.

The railroad matter had, however, been settled to the satisfaction of the syndicate. Mr. Greenfield's support of the Wachusett scheme at the hearing had been of the utmost importance, especially as Mrs. Sampson had been able to persuade "Honest Tom" that a perfectly fair proposition made to him by Mr. Staggchase was in the nature of a high-handed bribe. This proposition had been presented in a somewhat scandalous light, and in the face of it Hubbard had induced his associates to throw up the whole Feltonville scheme. The Railroad Commissioners had issued the coveted certificate for the Wachusett route, and the rest was easy. Irons was therefore grateful to the widow, and he at length agreed to consult his associates, and he did not deny Mrs. Sampson's observation that it was as much for the benefit of the corporation as of herself that money passing between them should be covered by some such disguise as that of this stock operation.

The widow had returned home not over sanguine, and her astonishment was scarcely less than her pleasure when, on Wednesday afternoon, she received a note from Irons, assenting to her proposition with the modification that the purchasing figure should be three dollars instead of four. It was a fact as far beyond the limits of the widow's knowledge as it was beyond that of his colleagues, that Irons meant to make this transaction the means of increasing a revenge which he already had in train. That gentleman had never forgiven Fenton for burning the order for railroad bonds, and when accident threw the Princeton Platinum stock into his hands he determined to make it the means of the artist's discomfiture. It was only the day after he had offered Fenton his four thousand shares that Mrs. Sampson appeared with her offer of three thousand more, He had no doubt of his ability to entrap Fenton into buying, the one weak spot in his plan being the fact, of which he was in complete ignorance, that Fenton already held stock and had nothing whatever with which to buy more. He was willing to let the widow's bribe pass to her under so plausible a disguise, and he said to himself with a chuckle that he had far rather sell Fenton the seven thousand shares than four.

If he were unable to sell to Fenton it appeared to Irons as on the whole highly probable that he could dispose of the stock for the corporation at a price which would materially lessen the amount of their bonus to the widow; or if the market should chance to look promising, he might find it worth while to buy it from his colleagues with a view to realizing something on it himself.

Perhaps it was because he was doing business with a woman, perhaps it was the consciousness of the bribe which the bargain covered and a desire to leave as little record of it as possible, perhaps it was only the carelessness of extreme haste, that caused Irons to send to the widow so ambiguous and dangerous a note as the following, —

"DEAR MRS. SAMPSON, — I am suddenly called to New York, and leave to-night. I will take all your Princeton Platinum stock at three dollars. Please deliver it at my office to-morrow with this note as a voucher. Yours truly,

"ALFRED IRONS."

It was the misfortune of Alfred Irons that Mrs. Sampson took an extra cup of coffee that evening and could not sleep; and in the watches of the night, either the devil or her own soul — the inspirations of the two being too similar for one rashly to venture to discriminate between them — said to her, "Amanda! Now is your chance." Thereafter, no fumes of coffee were necessary to keep the widow awake for the remainder of the night; and on Thursday morning before she presented herself at Irons's office she had an interesting interview with no less a personage than Mr. Erastus Snaffle himself.

Mrs. Sampson began by declaring that she wished to purchase a certain amount of Princeton Platinum stock, but before long the need she felt of having her feminine guile supported by masculine intelligence had led her to make a clean breast of the situation. She showed Mr. Snaffle Mr. Irons's note, calling his attention particularly to the ill-chosen word "all" which seemed to her to afford the means of unloading indefinitely at the expense of the absent financier. Her enthusiasm received a cruel shock when Snaffle retorted with a burst of ill-bred laughter, —

"Oh Lord! You must think Irons is a dog-goned fool!"

"But," the widow persisted, "it says 'all' the stock, doesn't it?"

"Do you think you could make his firm buy up

all the Princeton on that flimsy dodge?" retorted Snaffle contemptuously.

"We'll see," Amanda declared, nodding her head determinedly. "The question is how much do you think they will stand? A man ought to know that better than a woman."

A new look of cunning came into the fat face of the speculator, and his numerous superfluous chins began to be agitated as if with excitement.

"Well," he said, "if you can stick them for any I don't see why you can't for a lot. I've just four thousand shares left, and you might as well run them all in on the old man."

The widow laughed with malicious glee.

"I don't know," she replied, "how this will turn out, but if I wasn't going to get a cent from it, I'd try it just for the sake of getting even with Al Irons."

"Oh, its your opportunity," he said, with agile change of base, "and as for getting ahead of him, I'm blessed if I wouldn't bet on you every time. Seven thousand shares isn't much for a house like theirs. We put the stock at ten dollars on purpose so folks could handle a lot of it and talk big without having much money in. Come, you just clear out the whole thing for me, and I'll let you have it at two and a half, just for your good looks."

"Thank you for nothing," was the reply of the redoubtable widow. "I took the trouble to find out the market price on my way down here and anybody can buy plenty of it for two and an eighth, without being good looking at all."

Erastus chuckled, rubbing his fat hands together in delighted appreciation of his companion's wit.

"Come," he pleaded, "when you get to making eyes at that clerk, he'll buy anything you offer, no matter what Irons told him. I wouldn't give much for the man that would let a little memorandum stand in the way of obliging a lady."

Amanda did not have good blood in her veins without appreciating the coarse vulgarity of Snaffle; but neither had she associated for years with his kind without having the edge of her distaste worn away. She was, besides, a woman and a vain one, and the undisguised admiration with which he regarded her put her in excellent humor. It confirmed the verdict of her mirror that the care with which she had arrayed herself for this expedition had not been wasted. She smiled as she answered him, tapping her chin with her well-gloved forefinger.

"But, of course," she observed, dispassionately, "if I bought of you at all I should buy conditionally. I'll give you two for the stock, and take it if I can sell it to Irons."

"Oh, don't rob yourself," Snaffle returned, with good-natured sarcasm. "What's to hinder my selling it for two and an eighth myself?"

"Two and an eighth asked and no buyers is what they told me!" retorted the widow imperturbably. "I don't know much about stocks, but I know that if you could have sold for almost any price you'd have done it long ago."

"Right you are," admitted Snaffle, good-naturedly, "if I'd nobody to consider but myself; but just the same, I sha'n't kick the bottom out of the market before it falls out of itself."

"Then I understand," said the widow, with an air, gathering herself together as if to depart, "that you won't take my offer."

"Oh, come now," protested Snaffle, "why don't you ask me to give it to you as I did the other?"

"So delicate of him," murmured the widow, confidentially to the universe at large, "to fling that at me."

"I ain't flinging it at you," Snaffle returned, unabashed. "But, come now, let's talk business. If I give you an option on this, so long as you are going to sell it at three dollars, of course you ought to pay me more than the market price. I'll be d'ed if I let you have it less than two and a half."

"One doesn't know which to admire most, Mr. Snaffle, your politeness to ladies or your generosity."

"Oh, don't mention it," was the speculator's grinning reply. "Come, now, don't be a pig. Twenty per cent profit ought to satisfy anybody."

"I'll give you two," said Mrs. Sampson, with feminine persistency.

Snaffle turned on his heel with a word seldom spoken in the presence of ladies.

"Well, you might as well get out of this, then," he remarked, brusquely. "You're a beauty, but you don't know anything about business."

Amanda regarded him with an inscrutable glance for an instant, evidently making up her mind that he meant what he said.

"Well," she observed; "if you want to rob me, I'm only a woman with nobody to take my part, and I shall have to give you what you ask."

"Gad!" he ejaculated. "If one man in ten was as well able to take his own part as you are, things 'd be some different from what they are now."

And the smile of Mrs. Amanda Welsh Sampson indicated that even so high-flavored a compliment as this was not wholly displeasing to her.

The certificates of stock were produced and duly endorsed, and, tucking them into her hand-bag, the widow went on her way attended by wishes for her success which were probably the more genuine because the transaction was only conditional.

"Well," Snaffle communed with himself after she had departed; "there ain't no flies on the widow, and I guess she'll manage that clerk. She's a clever one, but if she'd been a little cleverer, so as to appreciate that I couldn't put that amount of stock on the market without sending the price down to bed rock, she might have had the lot at her own figure. I'd have been glad to take one fifty for it."

Meanwhile the widow had pursued her scheming way toward State Street. The moral support of Snaffle's testimony to her ability and his admiration for her personal appearance probably upheld her during her interview with Mr. Iron's clerk. That young man, an exquisite creature, who had the appearance of giving his mind largely to his collars, was overwhelmed by the amount of stock which Mrs. Sampson produced. He explained with some confusion that in the hurry incident upon Mr. Iron's unexpected departure, he had neglected to make a memorandum, but that he understood that he was to receive three thousand shares of Princeton Platinum with Mr. Iron's letter as a voucher.

"I may have been mistaken," he observed, apologetically. "Mr. Irons was called away in a great hurry, and I did get some of his directions confused. It's singular that he didn't name the amount in the letter."

"I'm very sorry he didn't," returned the widow, with an engaging air of appealing to the other's generosity. "It puts me in a very awkward position, just as if I were trying to impose on you. Mr. Irons knew just what I had and said he'd take it all."

"Oh, I didn't mean for an instant," the clerk protested, blushing with confusion, "that you were trying to impose on us."

The clerk was young and susceptible, the widow was mature and adroit ; he was confused and uncertain, she was definite and determined. Mr. Irons had, moreover, given the young man to understand that the transaction was a confidential and personal one, which involved more than appeared on the surface. Confronted by the phraseology of Mr. Iron's note, backed by Mrs. Sampson's insinuating manner and unblushing statements, the clerk laid aside his discretion, and in the end allowed himself to fall a victim to the wiles of the astute widow, who walked away considerably richer than she came, besides being able to bring joy to the heart of Erastus Snaffle by a neat sum of ready cash, which she delivered after another prolonged discussion over the price she should pay him for the stock.

And on the following morning when she read in the stock reports that Princeton Platinum had fallen to one and a half, she remembered her stroke of yesterday with a conscience which if not wholly clear was thoroughly satisfied.

XXXV

HEARTSICK WITH THOUGHT.

Two Gentlemen of Verona; i. — 1.

FENTON'S forenoon at his studio was broken by a visit from Ninitta. His mind full of his trip to New York, and of speculations concerning his interview with Mrs. Glendower, he had let the whole question of the *Fatima* and his entanglement with its model slip from his mind, and when he opened the door to find Mrs. Herman standing there, the shock of his surprise was a most painful one. Ninitta's eyes were swollen with weeping, and the sleepless night had made her plain face haggard and ugly. With a quick, irritated gesture, the artist put his hand upon her arm and drew her impatiently into the studio. Closing the door, he stood confronting her a moment, studying her expression, as if to discover the cause of her disturbance.

"Well," at length he said, harshly, "have you betrayed me?"

Ninitta answered his look with one of helpless and confused despair. The anguish of the long hours during which she had been making up her mind what to do in the emergency that had arisen, had stupefied her so that she could not think clearly. She still suffered, and Fenton's brutal manner brought tears to her eyes, but she was benumbed and dazed, and could neither think nor feel clearly.

"Grant found out himself," she said, "that I posed."

"Well?" Fenton demanded, with an intensity that made his smooth voice hoarse.

"That's all," Ninitta responded dully. "I'm going away."

"Going away?" echoed Fenton, the words arousing again his fears that the worst might have been discovered. "Then Herman does know?"

"He only knows that I posed," repeated Ninitta; "but he says Nino would be ashamed, and I am going away."

"But where are you going?"

"Home; to Capri."

The artist looked at her with an impatient feeling that it was idle to reason with her, and that she had somehow passed beyond his control. He moved away a few steps, and sat down in an old carved monkish chair, while his visitor leaned, as if for support, against the casing of the door. He looked at her curiously, wondering what her mental processes were like, and saying to himself, with mingled chagrin and philosophy, that it was impossible to deal with a creature so irrational, but that fortunately he was not responsible for her movements His glance wandered about the studio, noting with artistic appreciation the pleasant coloring of a heap of cushions thrown carelessly on the divan. He wondered if it would have been better had he arranged that blue one in a fuller light, as a background for the beautiful shoulder of his *Fatima*, yet reflected that on the whole the value he had chosen better brought out the quality of the flesh-tones. What a splendid picture the *Fatima* was. It was worth some inconvenience to have achieved such a success, and, after all, he would not be so foolish as to begrudge the price he must pay for his triumph.

And yet, and yet — He turned back with a movement of impatience toward that sad, silent figure standing just inside his door. A wave of anger rose within him. He felt that he had a right to consider himself aggrieved by her persistent presence. Why must his will, his happiness, his artistic powers be hampered and thwarted by this woman who was only fit to serve his art and be laid aside, like his mahl-stick and palette.

"It seems to me," he burst out, more harshly than ever, "that you might have had the sense to keep away from here, at least until Herman gets over his anger."

"But I am going away," she said, "and I came to you for some money."

He stared at her in fresh amazement an instant; then he burst into derisive laughter.

"Well," he said, "I like that. Why, I'm going to New York myself to-night, to try to beg enough to keep me out of the poor-house."

"But I can't ask Mr. Herman," Ninitta said, beseechingly.

"In Heaven's name, Ninitta," exclaimed Fenton, "don't be an idiot. There's no sense in running away. Besides, what are you afraid of?"

"But it might hurt Nino if I stayed," returned poor Ninitta.

Through the bitter watches of the night, she had been saying that over and over to herself. With all her weakness and her sin, her mother-love stood the supreme test. As she had been able to give up her Italian friends when the boy was born, because, as she said, Nino was born a gentleman and must not associate with them; now, when she was convinced that he would be better without her, she was able to give him up, although with a breaking heart. Many times she had been forced to confess to herself that Nino's mother was not a lady like Mrs. Fenton or Helen Greyson, or others of her husband's friends; and although she had always comforted herself with the reflection that at least no boy had a mother who loved him more than she did her son, the thought that her child might be better without her had more than once forced itself upon her mind. It was idle for Fenton to argue; Ninitta's decision had passed beyond argument, and perhaps her understanding was, for the time being, too benumbed by suffering clearly to follow her companion's reasoning.

"At least," she said at last, utterly ignoring his earnest endeavor to shake her resolution, "if you cannot let me have any money, you will write a note for me to tell Mr. Herman that I am gone, and to say good-by to the *bambino.*"

"Good God, Ninitta! Are you mad?" Fenton cried, jumping up and coming to confront her. "Why should you mix me up in this business? He knows my writing, and think what he might suspect if I wrote such a note."

His voice insensibly softened as he spoke. He could not but be touched by the utter helplessness, the anguish, the baffled weakness so evident in her face and manner. He was cruel only from selfishness and the instinct of self-defence, and his pity was sharply aroused by Ninitta's suffering and her miserable condition.

"Come," he said gently, laying his hand on her arm, "you are tired and frightened. There is no need for you to go away and, besides, you could not live without the *bambino.* Think, you would have no letters; you would never even hear from him."

A spasm of pain contracted Ninitta's features. She pressed her hands upon her bosom with interlaced fingers working convulsively.

"Oh, Mother of God!" she moaned, in a voice

of intensest agony, which thrilled Fenton with a keen pang that yet did not prevent his remembering how like was the cry to that of a great tragic actress as he had heard it in *Phédre.*

"Don't, Ninitta," he pleaded, unlocking her hands and taking them in his. "I" —

"You will write me?" she interrupted eagerly. "You will tell me about Nino? I shall find somebody to read it to me. Oh, you are good. That is the best kindness you could do me."

She pressed his hands eagerly, a divine yearning, a gleam of passionate hope shone in her dark eyes. Fenton tried to smile, but despite himself his lip trembled. He had hard work to control himself, but he reflected that with him lay the responsibility of dissuading Ninitta from her mad project.

"But it will be better still," he urged, "to be with him. What can a boy do without his mother?"

She bent her head forward, gazing into his eyes as if she were trying to read his very soul; then she threw it backward with a sharp moan, shaking his hands from hers with a tragic gesture."

"He would be ashamed," she said. "Now he is too young to know that he is better without his mother."

She looked around the familiar studio with a sweeping, panting glance; then she turned again to Fenton, clasping both his hands with one of hers.

"Think of what I have done for you," she said; "and write me about him. I shall die if you do not."

And there shot through Fenton's mind a sense of the terrible tragedy which lay in such an appeal for such an end.

When she was gone, Fenton consoled himself with the reflection that the lack of money would prevent Ninitta from carrying out her wild whim. He, of course, could not know that soon after Nino's birth Herman had started a fund for him in a savings bank, and to the mother's intense gratification had the deposits made in her name as trustee. He had taught Ninitta to sign her name; and great had been her pleasure in watching the little fund grow. It indicated the desperateness of her resolve, that now she broke into this cherished fund, drawing barely enough money to take her back to Capri. She was going away for Nino's sake she argued with herself, and that justified even this.

All through the day she busied herself with preparations for departure. She would take nothing but the barest necessities; only that the hand-satchel into which she compressed her few belongings held Nino's first baby socks, a lock of his hair, his picture, a broken toy, and other dear trifles, each of which she packed wet with tears and covered with kisses.

Late in the afternoon she took Nino into her

chamber alone to bid him good-by. Her limbs failed her as the door closed and he stood looking at her in innocent wonder. She sank into a chair, faint and trembling, soul and body rent with an intolerable anguish so great that for a moment she wondered if she were not dying.

"What is the matter, mamma?" Nino cried out in his musical Italian, running across the room to stand by her knee.

He took one of her hands in his, stroking it softly and looking up into her face with pity and wonder.

"I am going away, Nino," she said, speaking with a mighty effort. "You must be a good boy and always mind and love papa. And, oh!" she cried, her self-control breaking down, "love me too, Nino; love me, love me."

She clasped her arms convulsively about his neck, but she choked the first sob that rose in her throat. She did not dare give way. She instinctively knew that she needed all her strength to carry her through what she had undertaken. She kissed the startled child with burning fervor. She drew him into her lap and held him close to her. Her very lips were white.

"Nino," she said, "can you remember something to say to papa?"

"Oh, yes," he answered. "I am quite old enough for that. Don't you remember how I repeated, —

"'*Questo domanda del pan ;*
Questo dise, no ghe n'è ;
Questo dise come faremo ;
Quell' altro dise ; rubaremo ;
Il mignolo dise ; chi ruba 'mpicca, 'mpicca !'"

It was a folk rhyme she had taught him to say, telling off his chubby fingers one by one ; and she remembered how proud the boy had been when he had repeated it to his father. Her mouth twitched convulsively, but she went on steadily.

"You remembered it beautifully, Nino," she said, "and you are to say to papa, 'Mamma has gone away to Italy for my sake, and she leaves you her love.' Say it over, Nino."

"'Mamma has gone away to Italy for my sake,'" repeated the child. "But, mamma," he broke in, "I don't want you to go."

She embraced him as if in her death struggle the waters of the sea were closing over her.

"Say it, Nino," she repeated. "Say it all."

The child did as she bade him. She knew she could not prolong this interview, and still have strength to carry out her resolution. She embraced and kissed her child so frantically that he became frightened and began to cry. Then she soothed him and led him to the chamber door. She put her hand on the latch. She looked at him, her Nino, her baby. She tottered as she stood. But the force of character which had given her strength to fight her way for ten years and across half the world to seek Nino's father gave her power now. She opened the door and put the boy out gently. She could not trust herself to kiss him again, or even again to say good-by.

But when the door was closed, she rolled upon the floor in agony, stifling her moans lest they should be heard outside, beating her breast and biting her arms like a mad creature.

When Herman came home to dinner that night his wife was gone, and Nino gave him her message.

XXXVI

FAREWELL AT ONCE, FOR ONCE, FOR ALL AND EVER.

Richard II.; ii. — 2.

FENTON'S reflections as he sat in the train that evening, bound for New York, were varied rather than pleasing. There are crises in a man's life when it is perhaps quite as wise that he should not attempt to reason; he cannot do better than to keep his attention occupied with indifferent subjects, trusting to that instinct or higher self, or whatever it may be within us which works independently of our outer consciousness, to settle all perplexities. Some idea of this sort was in Arthur's mind as he sped along towards the Sound steamer. He could not prevent himself from thinking more or less of the situation of his affairs, but he made no attempt to consider them reasonably or in order.

"It would have saved me an awkward interview," he reflected, "if Mrs. Glendower could have taken herself opportunely out of the world. If we may trust the usual form of mortuary resolutions, Divine Providence is habitually pleased with the removal of mortals from this sublunary sphere; and in this case I should share the sentiment."

His musings took on a darker tone as time went on. He thought with bitterness of the failure of his past, and he loathed himself for what he was. The hateful mystery of life tormented him with its poisonous uncertainty. He groaned inwardly at the curse that one day should still follow another. Then the phrasing of his thought pleased him, and with veering fancy he went on stringing epigrams in his brain.

"After all," he thought, "what we call a fool in this world is a man who has his own way at the expense of the wise. There's Candish, now; I call him a fool and he goes ahead and is damned virtuous and stupid and exasperating, and gets through life beautifully; while I, who wouldn't be such an idiot for any money, am always in some confounded scrape or other. I wonder, by the way, what's the connection between sanctity and a waistcoat put on hind side before. Candish and Edith wouldn't make a bad pair. She wouldn't mind his ugly mug in the least, and his idiocies of temperament would be rather pleasing to her. Heaven knows it was an ill day for her when she fell into my clutches. I can't say that it seems to have been any great advantage to any woman to be fond of me. Helen was awfully cut up when I went back on the Pagans, and as for

Ninitta, I've played the very dickens with her. Upon my word I have my doubts if I could be really respectable without cutting my own acquaintance."

Fenton retired to his stateroom almost as soon as he went on board the steamer. He was tired with the strain of the last weeks, he hated the vulgar crowd one met in travelling, so that to sleep and avoid his companions seemed the only course desirable under the circumstances.

He was dimly conscious of the progress of the boat, the bustle in the saloon, which gradually subsided as the evening wore on; and then his slumber grew deeper. Even the frequent whistling which the ever-increasing fog made necessary only caused him, now and then, to turn uneasily in his berth. His stateroom was well aft, and in his drowsy, half-waking moments, he was conscious that the sea was running heavily. He remembered that the wind had been east all day, and that he had seen the danger-signal floating that afternoon.

Toward morning he grew more wakeful. The whistling of the fog-signal, which had now become almost constant, vanquished at length his inclination toward slumber. He found his watch, but it was too dark to tell the time. He raised himself up in his berth, and, pulling open the window blind, was able with difficulty to make out that it was almost four o'clock. Outside, he saw a bank of fog, as impenetrable to the eye as a wall. He pulled the blind to, with an impatient sigh.

"This confounded fog," he thought, "will make us late, and I sha'n't have time to see those pictures at the Academy."

He lay back in his berth, broad awake, with an objurgation at the whistle, which was shrieking furiously, and which, he suddenly became aware, was being answered by the dull bellow of a fog horn blown near at hand. At that moment the engines of the boat stopped, with that cessation of the quivering jar which is so terrifying. Fenton could feel the steamer losing its headway, and being more heavily tossed about by the waves as it did so. He sat up in his berth with a startled consciousness of danger, and at the same instant something struck the steamer with a terrific crash which seemed powerful enough to rend every timber apart. A tumult of sound broke forth, amid which a piercing human shriek rang out with awful sharpness. Fenton was thrown from his berth by the shock, and landed on the floor, bruised and half-stunned, but otherwise unhurt. His valise was dashed against him, but after the first concussion there was no further violent movement, and, as soon as he was able to recover himself, he had no difficulty in getting to his feet. The terrible cries which continued, reinforced by a babel of screams and confused noises, seemed to him to come from some stateroom near at hand.

It was evident that some one had been seriously hurt in the collision which must have occurred. The trampling of feet, the voices of men and women and children, the sound of the wind and of the water, and those formless noises which are the more terrifying because it is impossible to tell whence they arise, filled the air on every side, and told Fenton that some serious calamity had befallen the steamer.

He felt about in the darkness for his clothing, then pulled open the shutter hastily, and dressed himself in the dim light as well as he was able. He was excited but not panic-stricken, yet the time seemed long, although in reality it was but a few moments before he was ready to open his door into the saloon. As he came out he had a startled impression of finding himself in an unexpected place, and then he realized that the side of the boat had been broken in clean through the range of staterooms, and that he was looking out into the heavy wall of fog through a hole made by the collision. He could see dimly the shape of a ship's prow, and the broken end of a bowsprit was not yet wholly disentangled from the rent in the side of the steamer. The two vessels, locked together like a pair of sea-monsters that had perished in the death grapple of a desperate encounter, tossed up and down on the long swell, swayed by the wind which seemed to be increasing in fury every moment.

On the floor of the saloon just before him, Fenton saw a wounded man, ghastly with blood, and moaning terribly. Half-dressed people hovered about him in utter bewilderment, while others continually hurried up simply to hasten away again in frantic confusion. The wounded man was in his night clothes, and a half-dressed old woman, her gray hair straggling about her face, seemed to be attempting to stanch the blood which was flowing freely. She was evidently a stranger, since from time to time she appealed to those around to take her place, and let her go and look after her own folk, but the kindly old creature plainly could not bring herself, even in that hour of peril, to desert one hurt and helpless.

On every side were the evidences of panic. Stateroom doors were open, people in all stages of disarray were hurrying wildly along, or clinging frantically to each other. The hysterical sobs of women, piercing cries from the thin voices of children, deep-toned curses and wild ejaculations from men sounded on every hand. People were donning life-preservers, some putting on two or three in their eagerness and fear; and here and there fighting for the possession of an extra one in a mad fury. The whole saloon was filled with a wild and terrifying tumult. It was a frenzied scene of fear and awful bewilderment.

However great his mental pluck, Fenton was physically a coward, and he knew it. The New

England climate and life have given to most of her children, of any degree of cultivation, a nervous organization too acutely sensitive to pain for them to be physically brave ; but to this disposition the New England training, the inherited manliness of sturdy ancestors, has added a splendid moral energy to overcome this weakness.

In the first terrible shock of fear which followed his discovery that the steamer had been run down, Fenton's body trembled with terror. He felt a wild and dizzy impulse to rush somewhere madly ; but in a moment his will reasserted itself. He was intensely frightened, but he beat down his fear with the lash of self-scorn, as he would have whipped a hound that refused to do his bidding. He steadied himself for a moment against the doorway with tense muscles, setting his teeth together. He drew a deep breath, turned back into his stateroom, and put on a cork jacket. He was cool enough. Before he buckled it he transferred his wallet and papers from the pocket of his coat to that on the inside of his waistcoat. Then he hurried out through the saloon on to the afterdeck. The place was crowded, and the confusion was indescribable. Fenton's first impulse was to put his hands over his ears, to shut out the horrible din. The officers were shouting orders and getting the boats manned, for even in this short time the steamer was settling. The hissing swash of the waves beating into the breach, the prayers, the imprecations, the hysterical sobs, the agonized cries of the struggling passengers, the darkness, the terror, the yawning abyss of death beneath them, — combined to sweep away all human feelings save the instinct of self-preservation. The brute side of human nature revealed itself with a hideousness more horrible than the terror of the night and the sea. Unprotected women were crushed and trampled, and as the boats were lowered a fierce hand-to-hand conflict ensued, men fighting like wild cats to force their way into them. The officers beat them back, and made way for the women as well as they could, struggling at the same time with the difficult task of maintaining discipline among the crew.

Shrill amid the uproar, a child's cry smote Fenton's ear as he came out upon the deck. Directly before him a man was trying to pull a life-preserver off from a boy, while a woman fought with him in a desperate endeavor to shield her child. The lad was about the size of Caldwell and in the confused light not wholly unlike him. With a sob and a curse, Fenton struck the man full in the face with all his force, sending the brute reeling backward into the crowd which was too dense to allow of his falling. The mother hurriedly pulled the child into the dense stream of people crowding toward the boats, and Fenton saw the pair disappear over the side of the steamer, helped by one of the officers.

There ran through his mind a momentary speculation of their chances of escape, and the thought brought him back to the consideration of his own situation. A sudden unreasonable disgust of the conditions which made his salvation so improbable seized upon him. He reflected that he might still baffle fate by taking his own life, and for an instant the idea of thus escaping from all the vexations which surrounded him presented itself to his mind in alluring colors. The idea of self-destruction was one with which he had played so often that he entertained it without a shock; and he realized now, almost with a conviction that the fact forced him to suicide for the sake of consistency, that his death under these circumstances would surely be attributed to accident. He even began to fumble with the buckles of his life-preserver; then with a smile of bitter scorn he looked down at his hands, of which the fingers were trembling with nervous fear.

"Bah," he said to himself, "why should I pose to myself? Fate is too much for me; if a gentle and beneficent Providence intends to make away with me, so be it. I haven't the nerve to anticipate it."

He started toward the boats, and at that instant he caught sight of the face of Ninitta. She was standing perfectly quiet, with her arm around one of the small pillars supporting the covering to the deck. She was fully dressed, though her head was uncovered and the rings of hair clung about her face. Fenton forgot everything else at sight of her. In a moment of supreme egotism there flashed through his mind the consequences of Ninitta's being here. The consciousness of all that lay between them made him keenly alive to the evil construction which might be placed upon her having fled from home on the same boat which carried him. He realized, with a profound feeling of impotence, that if they were lost together he should be forever unable to explain or to dispel the suspicion to which her presence might give rise; he felt with keen bitterness how useless would be all his cleverness, and his heart swelled with rage at the thought that his adroitness would be wasted for lack of opportunity.

He forgot the danger, the terror of the wreck, the shrieking of the women, the brutality of the men, and, for the moment, felt with the keen desperation of enormous vanity the danger to his reputation. He forced his way madly across the deck and confronted her in the ghastly light of the swinging lantern and the gray foregleams of the coming dawn.

"You followed me!" he cried with bitter harshness.

She looked at him in a calm, stunned way, as if she were past suffering and almost past feeling. The recognition in her eyes came slowly, as if she were dazed or as if some powerful mental stress held her attention.

"Now," he began, "your boy" — He was going to add, "will grow up to believe you ran away with me;" but his manliness asserted itself and he could not continue. It was like striking a woman, and the brutal words died on his lip.

At the mention of her boy a sudden passion flamed in her eyes. She loosed her hold upon the pillar and a sudden lurch of the sinking ship threw her into Fenton's arms. She clung to him frantically.

"My boy!" she moaned. "My boy!"

Like quickly shifting pictures, there ran through Fenton's mind the images of Nino, of the boy whose life-preserver he had saved, and of his own son, asleep in safety in his nursery at home. With a quick revulsion of feeling came the desire to save Ninitta, and with instinctive quickness he hit upon a possible means of escape. As he came through the saloon he had seen a man, a dim shape in the fog, clambering through the shattered staterooms to climb over the broken bowsprit into the vessel that had run them down. Hastily drawing Ninitta along, he forced his way back into the saloon. The body of the man who had been hurt in the collision lay dead and deserted on the floor. He lifted his companion over it and made his way to the side of the steamer. Others had discovered this road to safety and he had to fight for his foothold amid the waves that now washed over his feet. The men on the stranger vessel were sawing off the broken spar which was entangled under the steamer's upper deck, lest their craft should be dragged down by the sinking boat. He urged Ninitta forward, swinging her by main force up into the tangled rigging.

"No, no," she cried, endeavoring to throw herself back. "I do not want to go. It will be better for Nino."

The sublimity of her self-sacrifice smote him like a lash. He could not stop to argue, but he forced her forward, and one of the men above, feeling himself in safety, caught her by the arm to drag her up. But at that instant the spar, cut nearly through, broke with a sharp crack like the sound of a gun. The end fell, and with it the wretched woman was carried down. She shrieked as she went, the water cutting short her cry of mortal anguish. Fenton saw her face an instant, and then in the fog and the darkness the lapping water closed over her.

An awful sickening shudder ran through him, a fear too great to be resisted. There rose from his heart a despairing prayer; and the unbeliever has sounded the depth of agony when he calls upon God.

At that instant a beam loosened from the upper deck, dragged downward by the ropes of the falling bowsprit, fell with a crash, dashing him downward into the gulf below. He felt the awful stinging pain of the blow, like the thrust of a spear; a mighty wave seemed to mount upward to meet and to engulf him. Then he lost all perception of what he was doing or of what happened to him; and it might to his consciousness have been either moments or hours before he found himself struggling in the icy water. He swam instinctively, and he even remembered to try to increase his distance from the steamer, that he might not be caught in the eddy when it went down. He heard still the cries and shrieks, but the noise of the sea at his ears was like a mighty uproar confusing all. He could not tell in which direction lay the vessel; a mighty pressure crushed his chest, and innumerable lights twinkling against a background of intensest black seemed to shine before his eyes. He was past thinking clearly. His memory was like a broken mirror whose shattered fragments reflected a thousand bits from his past life, confused, detached, and meaningless.

Then with a last supreme effort his strong will asserted itself in a command upon his consciousness. For one intense instant, briefer than the flash of the tiniest spark, he realized everything, save that the blow or the nearness of death seemed to have dulled all sense of fear. The most vivid thought of all was the reflection that he might have been saved but for his efforts to help Ninitta. The grim humor of the situation tickled his fancy, and in the very flood of death he faintly smiled at the irony of fate which thus balanced accounts. And this flash of cynical amusement was the last gleam of his earthly consciousness.

XXXVII

A SYMPATHY OF WOE.

Titus Andronicus; iii. — 1.

FORTUNATELY Ninitta had made no secret of her departure except to conceal it from her husband. She had been to see some Italian friends of former days to ask about people she had known in Italy, and from them her husband learned pretty nearly what her plans had been, Fenton might have spared himself his fears lest she be suspected of going with him. Such a thought did not for an instant enter into Herman's mind. The sculptor found himself appreciating better than ever before the strength of his wife's character. The knowledge of Ninitta's faults died with her, and her memory was transmitted to her son enriched with the halo of a martyr who has died in the path of supreme self-sacrifice. Nino's father understood fairly well the train of reasoning which had led his wife to the tragic resolve to leave their boy. Ignorant of her fault, he blamed himself for the reproach by which he feared he had forced her to believe that it were better for her son to be freed from her presence.

His generous nature forgot, too, all anger

against Fenton. To the noble soul, death, by a reasoning which is above logic, seems to settle all accounts. He remembered the artist's brightness, his quick sympathy, his keen imagination, and his ready adaptability. The flippancy that had often shocked him, the treachery to principles which he held sacred that had wounded him, his kind memory put out of sight, as one wipes the stains from a crystal; and in the mind of the man he had wronged, the remembrance of Arthur Fenton remained fair and gracious, and nobler than the nature whose monument it was.

He went to see Mrs. Fenton, but when he met her he at first could say nothing. He stammered brokenly, tears choking his voice, holding her hand in his, and vainly striving to put into words the sympathy he felt. Then he stooped suddenly and kissed her hand.

"Our boys," — he said, with awkward phrasing, but with an instinct which reached to the ground of their deepest sympathy. "It might comfort them a little to play together."

The widow clung with both her small hands to the large strong one which had clasped hers; and bending down over it she burst into convulsive sobs. He stood silent a moment, his lip trembling then with grave kindness, he said,—

"I know how hard it is; but you have the comfort of being able to tell the boy that his father was a genius and a noble man. Do you know that a woman who was rescued says that your husband saved her boy, a little lad like Caldwell. Arthur knocked down the man that was trying to rob him of his life-preserver. The Captain told her afterward who it was."

He was perfectly sincere in what he said. It was difficult for him to think evil of the living; of the dead it was impossible.

After he had gone, Edith took Caldwell on her knee and told him the story. It was the brightest ray of comfort in all that sad time to be able thus to glorify his father in the eyes of her son. The incident dwelt in her mind, and her loving fancy added to it a hundred details and drew from it numberless deductions with which to enrich the memory of her dead. It came in time to be the most prominent thing in her remembrance of her husband. It was the fact which she could recall with the most unmixed satisfaction, which needed no evasions, no mental reservations, no warpings of belief, to appear wholly noble. In the light of this deed, the impulse of a moment, Fenton stood in her memory as a hero; and in viewing him thus, she was able to lose sight of everything which she must forgive, of everything which she wished to forget.

Edith was happily spared the harassing complications of financial difficulty which it had seemed must inevitably result from the condition in which her husband's affairs were left.

On Mr. Irons's return from New York, he had been astounded and enraged to find that he had been outwitted by the combined cleverness of Mrs. Sampson and the stupidity of his clerk, and that he was in possession of eleven thousand shares of Princeton Platinum stock. For seven thousand shares he had paid at the rate of three dollars, and the stock was now quoted at one and three eighths asked, with no particular reason for supposing that the putting of even half his shares on the market would not reduce it to zero. Irons blasphemed prodigiously and emphatically, discharged his clerk, and went to call on Mrs. Sampson, whom he threatened with all sorts of condign punishments if she did not disgorge her ill-gotten gains. The widow received him affably, and laughed in his face at this proposal, a course of action which won his respect more fully than any other which she could have chosen. There was evidently nothing left but to do what he could with the market, and by methods best known to himself he succeeded in bulling the stock so that he was able to unload at three dollars and a half.

The brokers in whose hands Fenton had left his stock had been watching their opportunity, and closed it out at the top of the market, a consummation for which Fenton had so devoutly longed that it seemed cruel he could not have lived to see it. The returns from this and from her husband's life insurance secured to Edith and her son a small income, which was considerably increased by the sale of Fenton's pictures which was soon after organized by the artists of the St. Filipe Club.

It was about a month after Ninitta's death that Grant Herman went to visit Helen. He had chosen to see her at her studio rather than at her home. Poignant memories of the past were less likely to be aroused by the unfamiliar appearance of this room which he had never before entered. It was late in the afternoon, and Helen was standing by the figure of a child upon which she had been working. She gave him her hand impulsively, forgetting that the fingers were stained with clay.

"I beg your pardon," she said.

"It is no matter," he returned, and the commonplace phrases bridged the awkwardness which belongs to the meeting of two people whose minds are full of intense feeling which they are not prepared to speak. Helen led him toward another modelling stand.

"I want you to see this bust," she remarked. "It's quite in the manner which you used to say was my best."

He stood watching her with a swelling heart as she removed the damp wrappings which kept the clay moist. Keen in the minds of both was the knowledge that now there were no barriers between them; that the time had come at last when they were free to love each other and to unite their lives. The closeness of Ninitta's death kept this wholly from their words, but it could not banish the exultation, so sharp as to be almost pain, which would arise from the mere fact of their being together. Both understood that however great the sorrow at her death which he was too noble-hearted not to feel, he must rejoice in the right to follow the dictates of his love at last.

He forced himself to examine the bust critically, and to speak of it calmly; but he soon turned away from it, and stood looking at her a moment, as if trying to find speech in which to phrase what he had come to say. She waited for him to speak, meeting his glance frankly. Her head was thrown backward a little, and he noted with pitying eagerness that she was paler than of old, and that there were dark circles beneath her eyes. He thought of the years in which their lives had been separated, and sorrow for her suffering made his heart swell.

"Helen," he said, "I have come to ask a favor. I want you to look after Nino a little. He has been given up to servants too much, and I am perfectly helpless when it comes to managing his nurse. Is there any way in which you can do anything for him?"

"Of course there is," she answered. "I will come in and see him every day and find out how things go with him ; then, if anything is wrong, I can let you know."

"Thank you," he returned simply. "I was sure you would help me. But do you think," he added, hesitating, "that it will be in any way awkward for you?"

She smiled on him and she could not keep out of her eyes the joy she felt at being able to serve him.

"Do you think," was her reply, "that I am likely to let that consideration stand in my way? It is rather late in life for me to begin to let conventionality interfere with what I think it right to do Besides," she continued, dropping her eyes, though without a shade of self-consciousness, "I shall go when you are at the studio."

"And it will not be too much trouble?"

"I shall love to do what I can for Nino."

"I thank you," he said again.

Then without more words he held out his hand.

"Good-night," he said.

"Good-night," she repeated.